When Lust Has Conceived

Raimund Auerbach

ISBN: 9798872371342
Imprint: Independently published

Raimund Auerbach
raimund.auerbach@gmail.com
www.raimundauerbach.com

For H.

"Then when lust hath conceived, it bringeth forth sin: and sin, when it is finished, bringeth forth death" (James 1:15 KJV)

In the year 2011, 433 murders were committed in the
City of Chicago.
Of those, only 128 were cleared by the Police.

Friday, February 11

3:45 a.m.

A few inches… just a few more inches and he would be able to reach it. Tom Maddock stretched out his arm as much as he could–which, considering the rather delicate position he currently found himself in, was not an easy task. Yet however much he contorted and bent his body, he could not reach the object of his desire. The restraints around his ankles and wrists, which not too long ago he so willingly had permitted to be applied, made sure of that.

Turning his head, he only now realized that she was standing directly over him again. He gazed at her beautiful, slim legs, which seemed to reach to the sky. The high heels and black stay-ups made them look almost endless. Ever since he was a boy, he had been aroused by women's legs in silk stockings. The desire to gently stroke her calf, fondle her knee, caress her thigh–this longing was almost unbearable now.

Tom could feel his blood pulsating stronger again and wondered how she might respond to his oncoming erection. No, he had to focus and think about something else, or he would never succeed! But he was simply unable to take his eyes off her.

The lace border of her stockings framing her immaculate, soft skin… oh how he wanted to touch both with his hands and lips. All he had to do was sit up, and his head would be in her lap. He would grasp her firm, round buttocks, and pull her toward him just far enough so that he could stick his tongue into her. He wanted to taste her and feel her moist warmth. If she'd only untie him…

1

But she just stood there, smirking. She had no intention of letting him go. She savored the moment. She had him exactly where she wanted him. At this point, she wasn't changing the rules of her game anymore.

Before today, Tom had always been used to calling the shots in the bedroom. He was convinced that he had a special gift–the gift to stimulate any woman to the extent that she would let him do anything he wanted or please him as instructed. He had never felt the desire to degrade a woman or even use force. Rather, he knew how to touch and caress his companion and to arouse her lust to the point that she would give herself freely to him. Most of the time, a tender push with his hand or just a single finger sufficed to make her spread her legs, lift her pelvis, or kneel before him. Sometimes he would whisper in her ear–typically when he asked her to submit to less conventional practices. Occasionally, a lady would be coy and find it difficult to release her corset of moralistic prudery–a sad result of her upbringing. Usually, all he had to do in such a case was to simply arouse her even more, and she would eventually set aside her concerns and surrender to her physical longing.

But this time everything was different. This time he had lost control and had become someone else's toy.

He had met the beauty only a couple of hours earlier in the cocktail lounge of his hotel. All he had wanted to do was to have a few drinks at the bar and relax from a long and exhausting day full of meetings. Since eight o'clock in the morning, he had battled arrogant bank managers and financial advisers to secure additional funding for his almost bankrupt company. Fortunately, the negotiations had been successful, and his initial exhaustion had soon given way to complacent excitement. He simply wanted to treat himself to a little fun before flying home tomorrow. Back in the hotel, he had quickly showered and changed before he had taken the elevator down to the lobby...

The moment he stepped into the bar he knew exactly how he would reward himself. Facing the entrance, she was sitting alone with crossed legs on a red leather sofa and studied the menu. She did not notice him, giving him plenty of time to thoroughly check her out. She was wearing a tight black skirt, which was tucked up just enough so that he could see the top of her stay-ups. When she changed position, she even opened her legs for a brief moment, allowing him a peek at her black lace panties. Almost provocatively, the fitting bra showed through her white blouse, whose top three buttons were undone. A pearl necklace adorned her beautiful bust. Since she was looking downwards, he could not really see her face. But her dark ruby-red hair, which waved around her shoulders, convinced him that she was a true "10."

He approached her without hesitation and casually asked if he could join her.

She did not seem to be the least bit surprised but slowly raised her head and looked him in the eye.

Tom started to feel a bit uncomfortable when she–without a word–took her time to scrutinize him from head to toe.

After what seemed to be an eternity, she put away the menu, sat back on the sofa, and responded with a simple "Why not?"

Immediately, it was clear to him that this woman was different than all the others he had hooked up with during his frequent business trips. Her classic beauty, combined with her blatant self-confidence, had an almost magical appeal for him. However, it also awakened a strange and unusual feeling–a sense of insecurity.

He sat down across from her and ordered Champagne. When he asked her if she approved of his choice, she only nodded slightly.

"I'm sorry, I haven't even introduced myself yet–Tom Maddock. What is a beautiful woman like you doing alone in a hotel bar at this time of day? Do you happen to suffer from insomnia?" He checked his watch and saw that it was already past midnight. That would be a short night if he could indeed pick her up.

3

"I am here for the same reason you are, Tom," she said so softly that he could hardly hear her. Yet when she spread her legs and unmistakably invited him to look up her skirt, he knew for sure that he had heard right. Without taking her eyes off him, she scooted a bit forward on the couch, put her hands on her knees, just to slide them sensuously farther up her inner thighs–all the way up to her panties. Almost imperceptibly, she licked her upper lip with the tip of her tongue. Tom could not remember having met a more self-confident human being in his life.

When the waiter returned with a bottle of Champagne and two glasses, it was he who found the whole situation a bit embarrassing, not her. The woman did not appear to mind the server at all or find it necessary to close her spread legs. On the contrary, her hands, which by now had pushed up her skirt even higher, rested on her thighs, and her fingers almost incidentally caressed her nylons, leaving all subtlety behind.

The waiter, whose behavior gave no clue he had even noticed the rather unusual behavior of his patrons, handed both a glass of Champagne, placed the bottle in a cooler, and disappeared.

They raised their glasses in silence.

Tom was relieved that for a brief moment he did not need to withstand her piercing stare. Even though he still believed himself to be the hunter, he instinctively felt that this time he had met his match. When he put down his glass and their eyes met again, he realized that she had watched him all along. Like a predator stalking its prey.

Just when he was about to feel uncomfortable again, she kicked off her high-heeled shoes and began to stroke his leg. As her toes slipped under his cuff, he could feel the warmth of her skin through her sheer stockings. A gentle push and his legs were spread. Slowly, very slowly, she moved upwards–first to his knee and then to his crotch.

When she felt his hard penis, it looked as if she was smiling. But it was not a kind smile but a supercilious, disparaging sneer.

4

Tom was so excited he could barely breathe. His inner voice told him to run as fast as he could, yet he pushed his groin only harder against her foot, which by now targeted his shaft. Her hands glided higher as the pinky of her left hand pulled her panties to the side. He could see now that she was sporting a Brazilian, which raised his libido even further. Fervently, he moved his loin back and forth while she spread her labia with her right hand and entered herself with two fingers.

"You like that, don't you?" she breathed.

But before he could even respond, her foot pushed so hard against his phallus that it almost took his breath away. It was a feeling beyond pain, and still it raised his lust to a new, unimagined level. He was no stranger to the game of pain and pleasure. However, usually he decided to whom, where, when, and how pain would be inflicted in order to achieve sexual gratification. This time, without warning, he had been cruelly kicked in the balls.

She did not pay any attention to his bewilderment but simply pinched him again with her toes, rhythmically massaging his hard-on.

Pruriently, he watched her play with her clit. At first, the tip of her finger merely circled the delicate, pink bud gently, even cautiously. But soon she closed in on her target, squeezed and pushed her center of lust before fiercely pulling on it with her red varnished fingernails. Tom was close to having an orgasm. Moving his pelvis faster and faster, he thrust himself vehemently against her, shoving her couch a bit backwards.

All of a sudden, she put her foot down on the floor and flaunted her bare vulva. Rubbing herself feverishly, she started to sigh.

He was so horny now that he could hardly contain his desire to unzip his fly and either fuck her right here or at least jerk off. However, he could not risk a scandal. Tom was certain that, so far, no one else had noticed anything–neither the waiters nor any of the few other patrons absorbed in conversations on the other side of the dim lounge. And he did not want that to change. Therefore, he had to content himself with just watching her as she brought herself to culmination.

Usually, he greatly enjoyed observing a masturbating woman. Pleasure, though, was not the only thing he felt now. He also felt apprehension. At first, he did not know why. Was it because they were not alone? No, he got turned on by that. It was something else: she had never stopped looking at him. Each and every woman he had ever been with had either closed her eyes or at least had let her gaze wander while having sex. With her, on the other hand, he had not seen her blink, much less see her eyes wander. Even now, as her lap juddered spasmodically, her steel blue eyes seemed to pierce right through him.

It was simply impossible for him to read her. And so–while she was straightening up on the sofa, taking a sip as if nothing had happened–he asked himself if, maybe, he was out of his league this time.

Before he had time to make the decision to leave, her lascivious voice pulled him out of his thoughts. "Would you like more?"

And like a mouse hypnotized by a snake, he just answered: "Of course!"

She said that she had a loft nearby, and he was surprised that she was not a hotel guest. Thinking about it, it wasn't such a bad idea to leave his usual territory in order to commit adultery. After all, he always stayed here when he was in Chicago, even when his wife accompanied him from time to time. There was a real possibility that next time one of the employees might remember having seen him with this woman. He hoped to avoid the kind of trouble this might cause, especially since he cheated on Lauren practically every time he was on a business trip.

They took a cab and within five minutes reached their destination: a former factory west of the Loop. The red brick building had only recently been converted into a hip apartment complex with cast-iron balconies. Apparently, the renovation had not been

6

completed as there was a lot of construction waste lying around everywhere. There was no light in any of the windows. It did not seem as if anyone had moved in yet.

He paid the driver, and they took some kind of freight elevator to a loft on the top floor.

The entire floor had been transformed into one huge apartment. The hall-like room had been divided into different areas using partition walls, which, despite being at least ten feet high, did not even reach halfway up to the ceiling. Since the building bordered the Chicago River, the enormous picture windows provided a spectacular view of the water and the downtown skyline.

The apartment furniture was contemporary and elegant. In the center of the room, there were two humongous semi-circular black leather sofas, which together formed a ring almost twenty feet in diameter. Interestingly, because of the sheer size of the loft, this unusual seating accommodation looked neither out of place nor too bulky. The sofas were framed by eight evenly-spaced, shoulder-high wrought iron candle holders. The white-lacquered kitchen was open to the great room and contained a bar.

Tom was told to take a seat on one of the leather counter stools while the beauty took a bottle of bourbon and two glasses out of a cabinet and got some ice cubes from the high-gloss black fridge.

Not only her choice of drink astonished Tom but also how generously she filled the tumblers. Instead of handing him one of them, she just put his glass on the polished granite countertop and took a large gulp from the other.

She was standing directly before him now, forcing herself between his legs. Still holding her glass in her left hand, she grabbed the back of his neck with her right, pulled him toward her, and kissed him without any passion.

As Tom was about to reciprocate her kiss, an almost stifling flush of cold yet burning alcohol filled his mouth. Since she did not loosen her grip and he was in fear of falling off the backless stool, he had no other option than to swallow the bourbon as fast as he could.

When she briefly turned to the side to take another gulp, he had just enough time to utter "Hey!" before she pressed her lips to his again and infused more alcohol into his mouth.

Pushing her body against his, she started to undo his belt and, after putting down her glass and taking a step back, pulled his pants down to his ankles. She kneeled down in front of him, untied his shoelaces, and stripped off his trousers, socks, and shoes in one single motion.

Tom, who was still wearing shirt and jacket, suddenly felt oddly naked and vulnerable.

When she got up again, she matter-of-factly grabbed his stiff penis and began to massage it dexterously.

Tom leaned against the counter, tilted his head back, and closed his eyes. He had looked forward to being caressed by this extraordinary woman all night long. Despite the fact that he had been jerked off numerous times before, he was pleasantly surprised how expertly she fondled him. Most women simply did not know what to do with this thing in their hand and just kneaded it awkwardly until he had enough and finally banged them.

She, on the other hand, encircled the root of his penis with her long fingers and pressed rhythmically onto it as if she wanted to inflate it more. And indeed, he got even harder. She let her hand run up and down his shaft a few times before suddenly forming a crown around the tip of his penis with her soft fingertips. When she started to squeeze him gently, Tom responded with loud sighs. He would never have thought it possible that a woman could ever give him a better hand job than he himself.

Forgotten were his previous concerns as he imagined how he would do it to her later. Since he felt that it should be him winning the day, he planned to take her harder than any of her predecessors– much harder. Perhaps he would even chastise her with his belt. He

8

envisioned her kneeling in front of him, pushing her butt out, screaming with pain and pleasure every time he whipped her.

As his arousal increased, he felt that it was not long before he would come–but that was alright. He didn't have any plans to sleep tonight. A short break and he would be fit again and ready for more action.

Suddenly, he was harshly pulled out of his fantasy when her razor-sharp fingernails clawed into the tip of his dick, and an ice-cold flush of alcohol gushed all over his penis. Once again, she had shown him who was in charge here.

And just as before, she did not give him any time to complain but lowered her head into his lap and started to passionately lick the whiskey off his cock. When he felt her tongue and full lips, he relaxed a bit and leaned back again. He did not even care when he heard her taking something out of one of the drawers directly behind him. Indeed, he enjoyed her fondling almost too much. Much to his disappointment, though, she ceased just before he was ready to ejaculate as she got up and grabbed his left wrist.

He opened his eyes and realized that she was about to put leather cuffs on him. When he tried to pull back his hand, she simply breathed "Don't be scared, you'll like it!"

Eager to eventually get sexual satisfaction at one point tonight, he gave up his resistance and willingly let her shackle his hands and, a moment later, his feet.

She told him to get up, nimbly took him by his stiff dick, and instructed him to spread his legs, bend over, and lie prone onto the stool.

Tom, firmly pulled by his genitals, had no choice but to obey. With his legs widespread on the floor, his stretched arms did not reach to the ground on the other side of the stool.

Again, she took something out of the drawer, and when she knelt down next to him, he realized that she was about to fasten the metal eyelets of his shackles to the cross brace of the stool using carabiners.

Everything happened so quickly that he was strapped to the stool before he could react.

Tom knew that he was at her mercy now, which made him a bit anxious. This feeling became even more intense when she blindfolded him.

As if to make him forget his worries, she grabbed his stiff penis and began to stroke it.

Tom sighed and yelled: "Do it to me, you little cunt!" As soon as he had said these words, not only did he regret having lost his cool, but he also knew that he had made a mistake.

And indeed, to his dismay, he realized a moment later that she was about to gag him.

Frantically, he threw his head back and forth and clenched his teeth, but all she had to do was pinch his nostrils. Afraid he might choke, he opened his mouth.

Tom remembered having seen this kind of gag in the S&M-section of sex shops–an egg-shaped rubber ball which could be secured with straps–but he had never used one himself. Since the ball completely filled his mouth and only allowed him to breathe through his nose, for a moment he feared that he might asphyxiate. But as soon as he felt her gentle fingers on his cock again, he talked himself into believing that all this was just an exciting game, and he started to relax. Once he could breathe more easily, all that mattered was her sweet caress. Now that he was totally helpless, he even began to enjoy his role as her sub, curious what might happen next.

As she continued to fondle him, he heard her rummaging with her other hand through this goddamn drawer again.

She must have sensed his tension because she coolly said: "You better relax!" And at the same moment, an oily finger started to massage his anus.

The simultaneous stimulation of his dick and butt aroused Tom in an unexpectedly intense way. And, thus, he did relax and moved his pelvis as much as he could, anxious to culminate. While one of

10

her hands rhythmically slid up and down his cock, the other fiddled around his backside. A finger entered him briefly, but then it was gone again. For a moment, he could just feel her hand on his penis, but suddenly he wheezed a muffled cry of pain into his gag when, with brute force, she rammed a hard object into his ass. He tried to resist and reared up on the stool, but she nipped his opposition in the bud by ruthlessly squeezing his balls and forcing the object even farther up his butt.

Tears in his eyes, not daring to move, Tom asked himself how he could have ended up in such a situation–he was being abused.

At the exact same moment, she started to gently stroke his penis again and pushed the object, which Tom was convinced now was a glass-dildo, more gingerly into him.

As the pain slowly subsided, it gave way to an unfamiliar, brutish fleshly desire–and he knew exactly what had brought him here.

Soon, she worked more intensely on his dick again and also shoved the dildo harder, more brutally up his behind.

Yet, by now, Tom was in such ecstasy that the hard object in his ass did not hurt anymore but only caused pleasure.

Her hands moved in sync: the left slid down his shaft while her right pushed the dildo up farther; then the hand on his dick reversed its direction, as she pulled the glass-toy a little bit out. The motion reminded him of someone inflating a tire with a bicycle pump.

For the umpteenth time, he was close to having an orgasm and wondered if she would suspend the fondling again. Much to his surprise, however, she pumped even harder when she noticed how far along he was. No, this time she did not intend to deny him the relief of his sexual tension. Faster and faster she stroked his cock while she forced the dildo violently up his ass.

But the pain that Tom experienced at this point only intensified his lust. Finally, he felt the long-desired tension build up deep in his

11

lower abdomen, which at any moment would be alleviated in pulsating eruptions.

His breathing and sighing was heavier now. Like a rabid animal, he moved his pelvis up and down the few inches that he could lift and lower it on the stool by laboriously flexing and stretching his naked legs. Forgotten was any angst or shame–he only wanted to come.

When she grabbed his dick especially hard with her long fingers and shoved the dildo more brutally than ever into his anus, Tom squirted his semen with such force in several pulses toward the floor that he feared to lose consciousness. Never before in his life had he experienced a more intense orgasm. Like in a trance, he collapsed onto the stool, too exhausted to move an inch.

Thus, he did not resist when she opened the carabiners, with which his fetters had been attached to the stool and connected the shackles through a short chain. A moment later, she did the same with his handcuffs.

"Get up!" she commanded in a tone which made clear that she would not tolerate any defiance.

When Tom did not immediately comply–simply because he was still too tired–she pinched his nose again.

Filled with panic, he reared up and rose arduously from the seat.

She rewarded him by loosening her grip, which allowed him to frantically fill his lungs with air.

Before he could think straight, he noticed through a small gap between the blindfold and his nose that she connected the two shorter chains with a longer one. He now felt like a prisoner.

Step by step, she led him in the direction of where he believed the sofas were. Since he could not see anything and could only totter because of his foot chain, he tripped a few times and almost fell down. Still, he somehow managed to stay on his feet–despite the fact that she did not help him but mercilessly dragged him on his chain behind her.

Suddenly, she stopped and ordered him to lie down.

He did as he was told and descended down onto his aching butt. Since his shackles did not allow him to use his hands for support, he rolled over his right side to lower himself to the ground. The floor was hard and cold, especially on his bare butt and naked legs. He believed that she had led him into the circle between the two sofas where, earlier, he had noticed an almost black hardwood floor.

She fumbled with his shackles, opened the long chain, and steered his arms above his head. Then she attached his right wrist with a carabiner onto something in the floor. After loosening the short chain that linked his arms, she repeated the procedure on the left side.

Tom yanked on his manacles but could not free himself.

A moment later, his legs were also attached to the ground.

His position reminded him of Leonardo da Vinci's Vitruvian Man, which he had once seen in a museum in Venice on a trip to Italy. Tom was not really interested in art, but his wife always made sure that they would also get their share of culture when on vacation.

He was pulled out of his thoughts by a metallic noise that came from some distance. It sounded as if she was foraging different parts of the apartment, searching for something.

Then he could hear the unique sound that matches make when they are ignited. The slight smell of sulfur, which a moment later entered his nose, seemed to confirm his suspicion that she had lit the candles around the sofas.

Through the gap under the blindfold, he could also recognize that she must have turned off the other lights. It was much darker around him now.

Suddenly, she kneeled beside him and took off his mask.

He was indeed lying between the sofas, and his hands and feet were attached to massive eye bolts anchored in the floor.

When she rose again and stood over him, he could see in the candlelight that she had taken off almost all of her clothing. Besides her stockings and her high-heels, the pearl necklace was the only thing she was still wearing. And even if Tom had known from the

13

first moment that she was an exceptionally good-looking woman, he was still deeply impressed with how incredibly beautiful she really was.

Full of self-confidence, with her hands on her hips and her legs spread wide, she stood directly in front of him. Fully aware of her beauty, she did not even think of covering her bosom or her private parts. On the contrary, she enjoyed exhibiting her impeccable body. Her dark-red hair, hanging down her long neck onto her shoulders, seemed to blaze in the dim flickering candlelight. Just below her pearl necklace, her grapefruit-sized, round and firm breasts pointed toward him. Her slim waist merged into curvaceous hips, which formed the perfect frame for her clean-shaved pubic region. Her long, spread legs were slender and fit. In fact, her whole body emanated a natural physical vigor, which in no way vitiated her femininity but rather emphasized it.

Never before had Tom desired a woman more than her. And despite the fact that she had already mortified and humiliated him today, he felt lucky that she had deemed him worthy to spend the night with her. If this was the way she liked it, he didn't care–at least as long as he also got his money worth.

All of a sudden, she bent down and started to search his jacket. He was surprised when she took out his wallet and rummaged through it. As she crouched, her legs spread wide over his belly, giving him an unobstructed view of her pussy. He got hard again and hoped she would move a bit back and graze him.

But she had obviously found what she had been looking for and gracefully got up without touching him. She was holding something in her hand that looked like a credit card.

Tom wondered if it was possible that she had brought him here simply to rob him. But then he recognized that it was his hotel keycard that she reflectively was rotating between her fingers now. He had no idea what she needed that for.

14

Once more, she bent down toward him, but this time she reached behind his head and loosened the gag.

Tom was relieved to finally be able to breathe through his mouth and relax his jaw again.

"What's your room-number, Tom?" she asked with an unusually friendly, almost sweet tone.

"Twenty-one seventeen," he answered hoarsely. "Why?"

"Just so that I know were to drop you off later, in case you are too drunk to get back to the hotel by yourself."

The very moment Tom was about to relax, he realized that she wanted to gag him again. Forcefully, he turned his head to the side and yelled: "What's your name? Please, I wanna know your name!"

But only after she had rudely pushed the gag back in his mouth and had fastened it behind his head, she leaned down to him to give him an answer. Her face was right next to his now. She hissed only one word into his ear: "Tisiphone!"

Tom could not remember ever having heard this name but guessed that it might be of Greek origin. An unusual name for an unusual woman, he thought, as she suddenly tightened the leather band around his right wrist. Even before that he had not been able to move, but now the manacle cut off the blood supply to his hand.

Tisiphone ignored his desperate attempts at protest and fetched a heavy, stick-like object from behind one of the sofas.

Tom's first thought was that she hopefully was not planning on clubbing him. But when he comprehended what the thing in her hand really was, panic took hold of him. It was an ax.

As she strode toward him in her high heels, dragging the heavy tool behind her, Tom rampageously yanked on his shackles, which cut deeply into his skin now. He was a fighter; he did not want to get slaughtered like an animal. But the leather bands around his arms were too sturdy and the metal bolts they were fastened to too deeply anchored in the floor. He screamed and begged her to let him go. He promised to forget about the whole thing and not to go to the police.

15

He also could give her money, a lot of money, if that was what she was after. He screamed and screamed. He screamed like he had never screamed before in his life.

And yet, all he could hear was a guttural rattle that was almost completely deadened by the gag.

She took no heed. Instead, she calmly stood above him, looking at him with her lifeless cold eyes.

All of a sudden, in a single swift motion, she effortlessly lifted the heavy ax above her head, and Tom could just see the shiny-sharpened blade flash down on him before he fainted.

He regained consciousness only when a bucket of cold water was dumped over his head. At first, he did not know where he was. But when he saw the naked woman standing over him, he remembered that he had met her in the hotel. A good choice!

He felt oddly weak and dizzy. Had he really had so much to drink that he could not remember anything else? Whatever, all that mattered now was this shapely beauty standing above him, fondling herself.

While her one hand started to gently knead her right breast, the other glided slowly downwards over her flat, naked belly and farther into her crotch. At first, she only cupped the mound between her legs with the palm of her hand, pushing softly onto it. Then, however, she pulled back her hand a bit, stretched her middle finger a little, and began to masturbate.

At that moment, Tom felt an incredible flash of pain, which pulled him back to reality with brute force. He suddenly remembered that this woman had tied him up and had abused him. And he realized with fear that even though she stood over him now, naked, rubbing herself, she represented danger. He could not trust her.

Again, Tom felt an incredible, almost unbearable pang running through his body, and he turned his head to find the source of his suffering.

16

When he saw what she had done to him, he was overwhelmed with unprecedented, primordial horror. He wanted to get out of here. No, he absolutely had to get out of here!

But not without getting it back first–his right hand, which lay on the black hardwood floor, about four inches away from the bloody stump that once had been his wrist.

7:53 a.m.

The darn pager was beeping again! Why hadn't he just put it on silent mode last night? Why had he given in to Bob Miller's request to be available at all times? Too late now–he had made a promise.

They had successfully ignored his continuously ringing phone so far, and the cute blonde under the blanket was still emphatically working on him, getting ready to treat herself to a pre-breakfast protein shake. However, now that Richard was close to culmination, he was a bit concerned that the hottie might get distracted at the last moment.

Yet he knew that there was no reason to be worried when she friskily continued to suck him off. By the time the pager beeped for the fourth time, he ejaculated into her mouth.

The cutie crawled out from under the blanket and, with a radiant smile on her face, wiped off the corner of her mouth with the back of her hand.

There couldn't have been a better start to the day.

"When do you have to be at McCormick Place?" Richard asked. He had met Stephanie only last night at the Chicago Auto Show where she jobbed as a hostess at the Chrysler-booth.

"Doors open at ten, but I should be there about half an hour early–so, at around nine thirty."

17

Since it wasn't even eight o'clock yet, and McCormick was less than ten minutes away from his apartment, they had plenty of time to enjoy some coffee and a breakfast.

Richard had already sent Maria, his Mexican housekeeper, a text message letting her know to come later today.

"Excellent! Then I would suggest that you get ready while I make us some eggs. You should find everything you need in the tall cabinet to the right of the mirror."

Richard had a broad cache of beauty products for his female guests including four different brands of toothbrushes, shampoos and conditioners, body lotions, make up kits, expensive perfumes, and even eye creams. When he invited a woman to spend the night with him, he wanted to indulge her in every way possible–not only sexually.

Naked as she was, Stephanie climbed out of bed and walked toward the bathroom, swinging her hips. After a few steps, she suddenly turned around, smiled as she saw Richard gaze at her full of admiration, and threw him a kiss.

Richard could not help but grin. Not only had he tremendously enjoyed having sex with her, he also felt incredibly good just being around her. Even though intelligence and a pleasant character always played as important a role for Richard as a woman's looks, Stephanie's natural and kind personality was awakening a long-forgotten feeling–he might be falling in love.

When he heard her turn the shower on, he got up and went to the kitchen.

Maria always made sure that for occasions like these there was enough food in the fridge.

He found eggs, fresh tomatoes on the vine, Italian prosciutto, and Dutch cheese for an omelet. Richard was a passionate foody and only needed a few minutes to put all the ingredients into a hot pan.

He got himself a double espresso from his Italian espresso machine and, finally, picked up his phone.

"Chief Miller's office, this is Jennifer Walker speaking! How may I help you?" a friendly yet business-like voice answered.

"Hello, Jenny, this is Richard Stanton. Bob has been trying to reach me. Do you know what this is about?"

"Good morning, Dr. Stanton, how are you? Just a moment, please. I'll put you through."

The excitement in her voice reminded Richard that Bob was convinced that Jenny had a crush on him.

He liked Jenny a lot. She was an attractive, loveable, and intelligent woman. Actually, she was just his type. Nevertheless, Richard had pledged never to mix his love-life and his job even when, nowadays, the latter was more like a hobby. But he wasn't the type who would make the same mistake twice.

It took just a moment, and he heard the deep voice of Bob Miller, the head of the Homicide Section of the Chicago Police Department.

"Finally! Rick, you have promised to always be available, remember? Let me guess: a hot-blooded Latina!" he said in a somewhat reproachful tone.

"Not quite, more like a Nordic goddess! What's up?" Richard had left the police force five years ago but was called in as a consultant on particularly difficult cases whenever the homicide section was baffled and didn't have a clue where to start.

He had originally quit the job when he unexpectedly had inherited more than one hundred and fifty million dollars from his uncle in England. After circumnavigating the globe in his new yacht for almost two years, he had gotten a bit bored and had actually started to miss the thrill of hunting crazy serial killers. Therefore, he had not been too upset when, back in Chicago, he learned that Bob had never forwarded his resignation but rather had put him on "indefinite administrative leave." By now, he was something of a freelancer, who wasn't on the payroll but could use all of the

19

division's resources and carry a gun. He could afford to only take on a case when it caught his imagination.

"Rick, we need you! I'm sure that there is another serial killer in town, but I've got nothing to go on except my gut. I have no idea how to approach this."

It wasn't so much the desperation in Bob's voice as it was the presumed hopelessness of the case that raised Richard's interest. He liked challenges. "Have you informed the FBI?"

"No, the case falls in our jurisdiction, and I do not intend to change that," the Chief answered.

The Federal Bureau of Investigation only needed to be called in when a perpetrator crossed the border to another state.

"If you help us, we don't need the Feds."

Richard thought about it for a brief moment before he asked Bob for the address of the crime scene.

He went to the stove to turn the omelet and picked up the phone again to make a few more calls.

Just as he hung up, Stephanie came out of the bathroom. It was obvious that she had found the make-up kits in the cabinet. The unobtrusively applied turquoise blue eye shadow accentuated the sheen of her jade green eyes perfectly. And even though she had worn the little black dress already last night, she looked as if she had just stepped out of a fashion magazine. With her long legs in ivory-colored stockings, she looked like a model on a catwalk as she strode elegantly toward Richard. Just looking at her gave him butterflies in his stomach, making him feel like a love-struck teenager.

Even though she was wearing high-heeled peep-toe shoes, which permitted a view of her French pedicure, she had to stretch a bit to reach his lips. At six foot two, he wasn't a giant, but he was still significantly taller than she.

As Richard felt her soft lips, he knew that he was enamored with her.

After a while, she peeled back and, with a pixyish smile, said: "Based on the beauty shop in your bathroom, I'm not the first woman you've taken home–am I right?"

The mere fact that Stephanie had agreed to a one-night stand was proof enough that she herself enjoyed life. And yet Richard was strangely relieved by her easy-going reaction. "How can you say that? All these things belong to my granny, who occasionally pays me a visit!"

She laughed cordially, kissed him again, and put a solemn face on. "Alright then. I'll forgive you for now!"

"Thank you. You have no idea how happy this makes me… really!"

Stephanie seemed a bit surprised by his response. For a while, she just looked at him– measuring his gaze. But when she finally gave him an answer, it was full of sincerity: "Well, maybe, one day, I'll get the chance to meet your grandmother."

They looked at each other and Richard knew that this wouldn't remain only a one-nighter.

"Now, let's have breakfast!" He took Stephanie by the hand and led her to the dining table, which Maria last night had already set for two. The housekeeper knew exactly that whenever Richard was entertaining a "guest," she was supposed to come in later the next day.

The table was located by the huge windows, which afforded them a wonderful view of Lake Michigan. The lake was so wide that, even from the eighty-sixth floor, one could not see the eastern shore, giving the impression of looking at the sea. Moments like these made Richard pleased that he had bought this condo with its incredible unrestricted view.

It was one of these typical Midwestern clear blue winter days. For this time of day, the sun was already surprisingly high in the sky, lighting up the east side of the apartment, almost making them forget how bitterly cold it was outside. Clearly, February wasn't the most comfortable time of the year in Chicago.

While Stephanie enjoyed the view, Richard fetched a big tray from the kitchen. On it were the omelet, fresh baked rolls, orange juice, and two cappuccinos.

"I'm impressed," she said as he asked her to take a seat and started to serve her.

They took a sip from their coffees and silently looked at each other for a while. Finally, Richard mustered all his courage and made the next move. "Stephanie, I have a confession to make: I like you. I like you a lot, and I would love to see you again."

Stephanie put down her cup. "Do you think your granny would approve?"

When Richard nodded, she smiled and said: "Yes, I also want to see you again." She took his hand and stroked it gently.

"Well, since I had hoped you would say yes, I took the liberty of making a dinner reservation for tonight. I know that you have to stay at the Auto Show until ten, so it may get a bit late, but I am sure that you will like it. I just hope that you don't feel pressured now. I don't want to rush you–I can easily cancel the reservation. No problem."

Stephanie lightly squeezed his hand. "Hush! I'm very much looking forward to having dinner with you. Where are we going? "

Again, Richard felt relieved and told her that he wanted to surprise her. They agreed on Richard picking her up at McCormick Place around ten.

It was almost nine o'clock now, and they hurried to finish breakfast.

After putting on his usual T-shirt and suit, Richard helped Stephanie into her coat, and they took the elevator to the parking garage.

When he unlocked his car with his remote, she was quite impressed. "Ooh, sweet wheels! But now I really have to ask you: you've got money, don't you?"

Richard had almost forgotten that they had taken a cab to his place last night. He was always a bit uneasy when people could tell that he was well-off. He was no showoff. He just enjoyed the amenities that came with his new measure of wealth–like the black Porsche convertible that he had bought because he simply liked the car, and not to impress others. He had a lot of fun being pinned back into his seat when he stepped on the gas of his more than five hundred horse power 911 Turbo S. "Yeah. I hope you don't mind."

Stephanie, realizing that he was serious and wasn't just boasting, stopped, pulled him back by his hand, and answered: "Listen! I liked you the moment I saw you at the Auto Show, not knowing that you have a fabulous apartment and drive a fancy car. She pulled him closer and kissed him. "No, I don't mind! But to be perfectly honest–it's not so bad either. Now we better be going, or I'll be late for work!"

9:38 a.m.

At last, she could relax. The warm water that had been running over her naked body for more than half an hour not only flushed away the last traces of Tom Maddock but also relieved the physical and mental tension that had built up over the last few days.

To make sure that not a single cell, a hair, or even blood of the victim clung to her, she repeatedly pulled the fine-tooth comb through her hair and soaped herself several times from head to toe. Finally, she scrubbed her hands and feet with a nail brush until she felt clean again.

She turned off the water, got out of the shower, took the thick, warmed bath towel from the rack, and dried herself.

She felt renewed and was ready to slip into a new role.

Already a few days ago, she had selected a new hair color, which would play an important part in her transformation. Carefully, she applied Vaseline along the hair line of her face and neck, put on her gloves, and mixed dye and developer into a homogeneous paste. Starting at her forehead, she parted her hair with a comb and started to apply the dark dye strand by strand with a brush.

When no red hair was visible anymore, she washed her hands and took the jar with the body butter out of the mirrored cabinet. Since she had to leave the dye on for twenty minutes, she could take her time putting on the moisturizer.

Maria Callas' voice came out of the bedroom. Puccini's "O mio babbino caro" from "Gianni Schicchi" was one of her favorite arias, and she started to hum along softly.

Even in her youth, the melancholy of Italian operas had deeply touched her and had awakened an almost suicidal sentimentality in her.

Nowadays, the music helped her to clear her mind and forget the world around her.

She put her right foot on the rim of the bathtub, dispersed an approximately grape-sized amount of the fragrant, white cream in her palms, and gently massaged it with circular motions into her silky skin.

Starting at her toes, she slowly worked her way up. As her hands glided along her inner thigh, she became aware of how much her own touch aroused her.

She distributed the rest of the body butter in her hand onto her bottom, then reached into the jar again, and repeated the procedure on her left leg. Deliberately slow, she moved her fingers up bit by bit. As she closed in on her vulva, inch by inch, the desire to touch and gratify herself increased. Yet, since it was precisely this sexual

24

excitement that she craved and wished to protract for as long as possible, she quickly pulled her right middle finger through the slit between her legs, raised her hand to her face, closed her eyes, and drew in the smell of her vagina. Her eyes still closed, she took some more body butter out of the jar and applied it to her upper body, making sure not to touch her breasts.

Suddenly, the alarm clock she had set went off, and she was surprised how quickly the time had passed.

Leaning over the sink, she thoroughly rinsed her scalp with cool water, flushing away any excess dye, and then washed her hair with a mild revitalizing shampoo.

After blow-drying her hair, she scrutinized herself in the mirror.

Something was not quite right, yet.

She knew from experience how important clothes, body language, and accent were when creating another persona, and she was planning on giving these things her full attention eventually.

However, it was something else that bothered her right now: the face staring at her did not yet correspond with the idea of her new "Me." She was still looking like an elegant, successful businesswoman. That wasn't what she had in mind. Her eyebrows needed shaping.

Quickly, she took a pair of tweezers out of the cabinet and plucked away until her brows were narrow lines, rising to a slight arch that peaked above her eyes only to descend again toward her temple. Much better! Later, she would create the perfect cat eye look with eye liner and shadow.

Satisfied and still naked, she grabbed the jar of cream and went to the bedroom.

To the sound of Bellini's "Casta diva" from "Norma," she took the silicone dildo out of the

nightstand and positioned herself, legs spread wide, in front of the mirror, which took up almost the entire wall across from her bed.

She put down the plastic dick on the foot end of the mattress, reached into the jar, and closed her eyes again. The greasy substance, which felt weirdly obscene, played havoc with her natural senses. She couldn't make up her mind if it reminded her of cold cum, the sweet-sourly juice of a pussy, spit, or a congealed blend of all these bodily fluids. Perhaps, all these associations were just the result of her knowledge that soon the body butter would serve as an ideal lubricant for her masturbation. She got wet again and could hardly resist the urge to grease the dildo and ram it into herself. But before she would devote her attention to her vagina, she wanted to cream her bosom to intensify her lust.

Only when both of her hands were evenly slithered and greased, she grabbed her breasts, pressing her thumbs down onto her nipples, cupping and slightly pushing her round breasts upwards with her other fingers.

Instantly, an almost overwhelming flood of electrical pulses that originated from her upper body was firing toward her lap.

She succumbed to her longing and started to fervently squeeze her breasts, sighing loudly. To increase the level of stimulation even further, she took her nipples between her fingers and pushed and pulled on them as if trying to milk herself.

She was so ecstatic now that every time she exhaled, she released a throaty pant. Shortly before climaxing, she let go of her breasts, sat down on the mattress, legs bent and spread wide, and pulled apart her labia.

When she opened her eyes, she a saw a naked, strange woman in the mirror, and her sexual desire was enhanced even more by the desire to possess her. She wanted to penetrate and dominate this raven-haired beauty sitting on the bed across from her. She wanted to gain possession of and become one with her. It pleased her to see the other woman move her pelvis back and forth as she began to caress her clit.

Still, she wasn't ready yet to grant herself gratification but felt the urge to tease herself a bit longer. Therefore, she pinched the sensitive bud a few times with her long nails, which was answered by her vis-à-vis with loud screams.

When she had enough of the foreplay, she hastily put cream on the dildo, pulled the beauty's labia apart again, and pushed the plastic dick so far into her vagina that it almost completely disappeared. She waited a moment to give her time to stretch a little and adjust to the object between her legs before she pulled it out again. The next thrust was already much harder than the first and elicited a blaring squeal. Madly, she jabbed the dildo faster and fiercer into herself until she collapsed onto the bed, convulsing wildly.

A few minutes passed until Tisiphone emerged from the bed and watched herself, self-satisfied, in the mirror. The metamorphosis was complete.

10:14 a.m.

The former factory had been cordoned off by the police with yellow tape. Clouds of smoke billowed out of the burst windows on the upper floor, rising ghostly along the facade and toward the sky.

Besides three huge fire engines, Richard also saw Chicago's only fire boat on the river, which made him believe that this must have been a much more intense blaze than what it appeared now.

Since the outer brick walls of such old buildings were mostly steel-reinforced, they usually withstood even ravaging fires surprisingly well. That, however, did not change the fact that all too often within the building itself not much was left.

Richard parked his car directly in front of the yellow tape and showed his badge and ID card to one of the many uniformed police officers securing the area.

Just as he stepped over the tape, Liz Chen and Steven Kowalski, the two detectives Bob Miller had assigned to this case, came toward him. They were both experienced investigators and formed a good team, and yet, they were clearly relieved to see Richard.

"Richard, am I glad to see you! Your timing is perfect. What did Bob tell you?" Liz asked, shaking his hand.

"Not much. Just that a charred body was found in a burning loft and that it might be the work of a serial killer."

Steven cleared his throat. "Well, we can't really say that for sure at this point. However, this looks a lot like a case we worked about five weeks ago. Not far from here, a badly charred body was found in another former factory."

Richard looked at them and raised his eyebrows. "That's all?"

Now it was Liz' turn to answer: "Not quite. Both bodies were tied to the floor, arms and legs were spread, and both were missing a hand. The first one the left, this one the right."

"And the fire made it difficult to find any DNA or even fingerprints," Richard concluded. "Exactly!" answered Steven.

Richard looked up to the smoking windows, thinking that he was indeed intrigued by this case.

While they were lifted to one of the less smoking windows by a hydraulic platform, Liz and Steven gave him a quick account of what they knew so far: The other body had been found early January three blocks from here; the victim had been a middle-aged male, who had not been identified yet; his left hand had been severed at the wrist; he had been tied to steel hooks in the floor with leather bands; his position resembled the letter X; and they had not been able to find fingerprints or even DNA of any other persons. That was all.

When they reached the window, a fire fighter assisted them in entering the apartment via a set of portable metal stairs.

Richard's first view of the building's interior reminded him of a gigantic chimney. The walls were blackened with soot, and the furniture and everything else was either incinerated to ash heaps or

28

charred beyond recognition. Because of the risk of collapse, the fire fighter cautiously led them to the body.

The moment Richard saw the horribly disfigured corpse, he was convinced that they were indeed dealing with a repeat offender. Clearly, the circumstances leading to the deaths of the two victims were too similar to be coincidental. But there was another indication of a serial killer that was even more compelling: there was no sign of the severed hand. They were dealing with a trophy collector.

Richard took another look at the burnt loft before he and the two investigators stepped onto the hydraulic platform again to exit the charred building.

"Do you already know whose apartment this is? Maybe the victim is the owner?" Richard speculated.

Skeptically, Liz shook her head. "Possible, but I doubt it. It's true that we haven't located the owner of the apartment yet nor has the body been identified. But last time the owner contacted us after a couple of days when he returned from a vacation, and his home was gone."

Richard waited until they had solid ground under their feet again before he gave his instructions: "Alright. Liz, try to locate the owner, and tell Ron that I need a DNA analysis of the victim as soon as possible! It's unlikely that we can retrieve any useful prints from the left hand so he should also take a good look at the victim's teeth. Like it or not, if we can't find his DNA in any of the databanks, we will have to contact all dentists in the area and go through their records."

Ron Howard was the Medical Examiner, or ME, the department usually worked with, and he happened to be a good friend of Richard's. Since they were both medical doctors and single, they had more in common than just their love of jazz.

"Steven, I don't think that there are many traffic or security cameras in this area. But perhaps you can find something that gives us a clue who was hanging out in this neighborhood last night. Try also to dig up similar cases in the data bank! Search for severed body parts, charred corpses, unidentified victims, maybe even warehouses, and anything you can think of! Contact me as soon as you've got some news, okay? And send everything you have on the first case home to me: autopsy report, crime scene photos, forensics report, and your own notes."

Richard said goodbye and was almost at his car when he thought of something else: "Steven, also check the missing persons listing!"

****

Richard knew that there wasn't much he could do at the moment. It wasn't his job to do the painstaking and often boring day-to-day work of a common police officer. The department had enough people that, competently led by Liz and Steven, could collect and document evidence or perform databank searches. No, Bob wanted something else from him–his intuition.

The head of the homicide section was profoundly aware that Richard had a rare gift for analyzing situations and facts, and for recognizing connections and motives where other investigators were typically in the dark.

With that thought, Richard decided to go home and relax a bit. It would take at least two hours until the documents would be delivered, which gave him enough time to swim a few laps around the pool and have lunch.

As he entered his apartment, Maria was putting fresh sheets on his bed. Even though he could have taken advantage of the building's housekeeping service that was available to condominium owners, he had insisted that she continue taking care of his household when he had moved here.

"Hello, Maria, how are you doing?"

"Hola, Dr. Stanton. I am fine, thank you. As I could see, you had a pleasant night."

Without question, Maria was hinting at the rumpled pillows and soiled sheets. She loved Richard like a son but did not approve of his sex life, which she considered to be a bit too promiscuous.

30

Richard went around the bed, gently took her face in his hands, and kissed her on the forehead. "Maria, I had a wonderful night. I am feeling great!"

The gray-haired Mexican looked mildly up at him. "I can see something in your eyes that I haven't seen in a long time. This sparkle... you're in love!"

Richard knew that she couldn't be fooled. "I think you're right. Is it that obvious?" he nervously asked.

"To me it is!" Maria answered in her maternal manner.

Richard took the elevator down to the spa located on the fourteenth floor, which also housed the health club. The 23,000 square foot facility contained numerous treatment rooms, steam rooms, saunas, top-of-the-line fitness equipment, and a 75-foot indoor pool. When Richard wasn't away on a trip, he exercised here every day for at least an hour, alternating between strength and endurance training, and swimming. Today was pool day.

After taking a shower and putting on his swimming trunks in one of the private changing rooms, he entered the pool area, whose ten-foot floor-to-ceiling windows offered a great view of the city.

There were only two elderly ladies in the water, doing some aqua exercises at the edge of the pool. At this time of day, it was much less crowded than early in the morning or in the evening as most of the residents or hotel guests were at work or sightseeing.

Richard said a friendly hello, took the wide, tiled steps into the pool, put his goggles on, and glided into the water while the two followed every move he made with admiring looks.

Today, it took him a little longer than usual to find his rhythm, but after a few laps his movements and breathing were regular. After a mile and a quarter, he had enough, showered, and went up to his apartment.

Maria was already waiting with lunch–a beef carpaccio with arugula and balsamic vinegar, garnished with toasted pine nuts. Since

31

Richard dined out most of the time and often enjoyed multicourse meals, he had asked Maria to keep lunches light.

He sat down at the affectionately set table and poured himself a glass of water.

Just as he was taking the first sip, Maria came in with a sealed cardboard file box.

"Dr. Stanton, this was just delivered for you. Have they talked you into taking on another murder case again?" She looked at him, disapproving and troubled at the same time. "Richard, you should enjoy life! Get married, make babies! Why do you always let them drag you into this muck?"

The mere fact that she had called him by his first name told Richard that she was really concerned about him.

"Maria, I'll be careful. Don't worry! I will only assist the department in an advisory capacity. What's the worst that could happen? And, by the way, I have a date tonight. Who knows, perhaps I have already found the girl to make babies with."

Maria just looked at him with disbelief, shook her head, and took the box to his office. Richard was in no hurry to sift through the documents. He was certain that Liz and Steven had shared with him the most essential information before, and he had doubts that he would find any groundbreaking new evidence in the files. Therefore, he decided to enjoy his lunch first.

He looked out of the window, but instead of the gray-blue lake, which stretched to the horizon, he saw a burnt-out loft and a charred body.

"Dr. Stanton, would you like some coffee?"

Richard almost startled when he suddenly heard Maria's voice right next to him. "What's that?" he muttered.

Maria, looking even more concerned than before, repeated her question: "Would you like some coffee?"

Richard had been so absorbed in his thoughts that he had forgotten everything around him.

32

"Yes, please. That would be great!" He watched Maria as she fetched him an espresso, and he knew all too well why she was so worried about him.

Richard took the coffee with him to his office, opened the seal, and spread out the contents of the box on his spacious desk.

He first looked at the crime scene photos before he studied the reports of the fire department and the forensics team. Finally, he examined the autopsy report. The fire had destroyed almost all evidence; neither fingerprints nor any other clues as to the identity of the murderer had been found. The gas chromatographic analysis had revealed that gasoline had been used as an accelerant, but no fuel cans or similar containers had been found.

The perpetrator certainly didn't make it easy for them.

In general, fire made it more difficult to recover useful fingermarks, but that didn't mean that invariably all prints were destroyed. A number of factors influenced the survival of prints such as the temperature of the fire, how far away an object touched by someone was from its origin, or what material the article was made of. For example, it was often possible to find marks on metal fuel cans.

The fact that, this time, nothing useful had been discovered made Richard believe that the murderer had destroyed most of the evidence even before starting the fire. Focusing on the photos, he couldn't help but wonder what the severed hands was all about.

10:05 p.m.

Richard was sitting impatiently in the black limousine which was parked right in front of the main entrance to the McCormick Place Convention Center. By now it had become quite cold so he decided to wait for Stephanie in the car.

It was already five past ten and Richard was surprised how many visitors had stayed until the end of the Auto Show, just now leaving the building. After a while, the first exhibitors, recognizable by their name tags, came through the tall glass doors, some visibly startled by the temperature change.

When he saw Stephanie, he turned up his coat collar, took the single red rose lying on the seat next to him, and got out of the car.

She looked fabulous. Under her three-quarter length coat, she was wearing a chic, gray pantsuit and black high-heeled pumps. Her blond hair was tied in a chignon, which emphasized her classic elegance.

When she saw Richard walking up to her with the red rose in his hand, she cocked her head slightly to one side, smiling.

"You look absolutely stunning!" he said full of admiration as he handed her the flower.

"And you are a true gentleman, Richard."

The two looked at each other for a moment, then embraced and kissed passionately.

"So, what's your surprise for me? The whole day, I've been looking forward to seeing you again," Stephanie said once they were sitting in the car as it moved toward his chosen destination.

"You'll see! We are going to visit friends of mine, who live not far from here."

In fact, it did not even take them five minutes to reach the destination.

As soon as Stephanie realized where they were, she couldn't hide her amazement. "The aquarium? What are we going to do here?"

Richard was happy that he had been able to surprise her. "Just be patient for a little longer!"

They entered the octagonally shaped Shedd Aquarium via an unlocked side door.

Richard, who seemed to know the way, led Stephanie through a number of dim corridors until they reached a small, blue shimmering chamber. In the center of this area, there was a table set for two, complete with candlesticks and a large bouquet of red roses.

Only now did Stephanie notice that the faint light that scantily illuminated everything around them was coming through big glass panels, which separated them from a vast pool on the other side.

She let go of Richard's hand and walked right toward the gleaming blue. Eagerly, she looked through the glass, but, besides water and a kind of stone column in the center of the pool, she could not make out anything. Suddenly, two large shadows quickly shot up to her, making her cringe and instinctively step backwards. However, when she saw out of the corner of her eye what curiously watched her through the window, she enthusiastically flung her arms around Richard's neck. "Belugas! Oh, Richard, what a wonderful surprise!"

"Stephanie, may I acquaint you with Nunavik and his mother, Puiji. Nunavik is a little over a year now and already weighs more than four hundred pounds!"

Stephanie gave Richard a kiss on the cheek. "I suppose that you come here on a regular basis. These two seem to know you."

Indeed, the two small whales were swimming up and down in front of the window, bumping their round snouts against the glass again and again.

"Yes, I do. I love the Shedd Aquarium. Especially when there aren't too many visitors around, it is the perfect place to unwind. Did you know that there are more than thirty-two thousand animals here?"

Just at this moment the waiter came by carrying a tray with two glasses of Champagne.

"I took the liberty of ordering for us in advance. Since I knew that it would get late, I asked them to put together just a small menu. I hope that's alright with you." Richard handed Stephanie one of the glasses, led her to the table, and pushed in her chair as she sat down.

35

She turned around, took his hand and, misty-eyed, said: "Richard, this is by far the most romantic date I've ever had. It's marvelous! And the Champagne is amazing!"

Richard took the seat across from her. "That's a 1966 Dom Pérignon Brut. I thought you might like it."

They enjoyed the appetizer, smoked salmon-rillettes with asparagus, and watched the belugas as they swam calmly around the pool.

"Richard, I think it's about time that you let me get to know you a bit better. The only thing I know so far is that I like you, that you have excellent taste, and that you are a true romantic. Yes, and that you have money, as we have already established." Expectantly, Stephanie looked at Richard and took a sip from her glass.

"Well, where shall I begin? I grew up in a small town about an hour away from Chicago. My father was a police officer and my mother a stay-at-home mom. No siblings. Already in high school, I was on the swim team, which helped me to get a scholarship at the university. First, I got my bachelor's degree in biochemistry here in Chicago, and then, I went to med school in Madison. After I graduated, I also did my residency there. Actually, I was specializing in internal medicine. But then, everything turned out quite differently." For a moment, Richard silently watched the beluga whales. "Yes, then everything turned out differently."

Stephanie sensed that it was hard for him to continue. "Richard, what happened? I am so sorry if I conjured up painful memories."

"Don't worry, it's alright! I am very happy that you want to get to know me, and this happens to be a part of me. I was assisting at an appendectomy when I was called out of the OR. An appendix–isn't it weird what we sometimes remember? I was told that my parents had passed away, but at that point nobody could give me any details. Only later, I was told by the police that my parents had been killed by bank robbers while Christmas shopping in Chicago. They were getting some cash at an ATM when the bank was robbed. My father must have noticed something and used his cell phone to call the police. Although he wasn't armed, he managed to overpower the driver of the getaway car. Until today, I have no idea what he was thinking or if he had any plan at all. However, it doesn't matter now, does it? Anyway, he was still at the car when the rest of the gang left the bank. They didn't hesitate–not for a moment–and just shot him. They also killed my mother cold-bloodedly when she rushed to his aid."

Stephanie got up, went over to him, and hugged him. "Oh Richard, that's terrible! I am so sorry!"

Richard embraced her, and they kissed tenderly. "I am so glad that I could tell you. Twelve years have passed since this happened, but it sometimes feels like yesterday."

Stephanie looked at him sadly. "Would you rather change the topic?"

Richard kissed her gently on the cheek. "No, I want to tell you the whole story first, and then we can enjoy the rest of the evening!"

Stephanie returned to her seat and Richard continued. He told her that the police hadn't made any real progress looking for his parents' murderers; that he himself had gotten more and more involved in the investigation, following clues and exchanging information with the detectives in charge; and that, eventually, he had led them to the perps.

"Well, then they just offered me a job. I think that, in a way, I had already become addicted to chasing criminals so that, from one day to the next, I just quit medicine and started working for the homicide department. It was a somewhat unusual career-start, but due to my medical training, I was ranked quite highly and only had to go through some basic law enforcement training."

Stephanie looked surprised. "That means that you are a cop and an M.D.–that's quite unusual, I suppose! But how did you come about your money? Policemen don't earn that much, right?"

Richard shook his head. "No, not at all! Five years ago, a notary informed me that my uncle in England had passed on and that I was his sole heir. I knew that my uncle had never been married and didn't have any children, but I was a bit surprised that he'd left everything to me. As a teenager, I had spent a few summers with him at his country estate in the Lake District. I have fond memories of us going fishing, playing pool, or watching soccer–real men stuff. We always had a lot of fun, but besides these few months, we'd never had much contact, especially later. So I was dumbstruck when I learned how much he had left me."

Stephanie looked at him expectantly.

"A lot! Enough that I could afford to quit my job and sail around the world. My uncle was an electrical engineer and owned a patent, which, in the seventies, made him rich–very rich."

In that moment, the waiter brought the next course, lamb tenderloins with wild garlic pasta and spring greens. Richard had picked a 2004 Dominio de Pingus as a wine pairing. He took a bite of the medium-rare prepared meat and continued: "After two years, I got a bit bored, and I've been working on cases that I find interesting ever since. But enough of me–now it's your turn! I want to know everything about you!"

Stephanie put down her silverware and took a deep breath. "Alright then. I grew up in California. My parents are both lawyers and have their own firm. I have two older brothers, which explains why I know a little bit about cars. After high school, I studied art history at UCLA, which I really enjoyed a lot. About five years ago, I came to Chicago to get my MBA. That wasn't too bad either, but in reality, I did it to get my father off my back. He always said that art alone isn't enough to earn a living. So now I work at the Art Institute."

Richard looked at her with amazement. "And I thought you were a mechanic."

Stephanie laughed. "The Auto Show thing was a coincidence. When I was still at the university, a friend of mine earned a little money on the side doing this job. She looks pretty good and had been asked on the street if she would be interested in representing one of the big American automobile manufacturers for ten days at the Auto Show. So, she worked there with some other hostesses, and one of them one day got sick, and they needed a replacement. You really don't have to do too much besides look good and be able to answer the occasional question. Most of the time you talk about all kinds of things with all kinds of people, and occasionally you may even meet an interesting bachelor."

Richard raised his glass for a toast. "I am most certainly glad that we've met. And by the way... I wouldn't mind meeting this friend of yours. Especially, if she is really as good-looking as you say."

Stephanie slightly kicked his shin under the table but then said: "That's certainly possible. I think you would like her."

Since Richard was starting to feel a bit warm in his suit, he asked Stephanie if it wouldn't be more comfortable if they took off their jackets.

For a moment, she seemed to contemplate what to do but then smiled at him and started to slowly open the buttons of her jacket with two fingers. "You know, this was supposed to be a surprise for later, but if you insist..."

With these words, she opened her jacket, and Richard saw that underneath she was wearing only a black, skintight camisole. The material was so delicate and transparent that her round breasts were clearly shining through.

Immediately, Richard felt his penis filling with blood. "Wow, that's quite a surprise!"

Stephanie looked at him invitingly and began to caress her nipples through the thin fabric. "I just wanted to thank you appropriately for the invitation."

When suddenly the waiter came with the next course, a rhubarb mousse with strawberry coulis and pistachios, she quickly closed her jacket and whispered: "You'll see more later, I promise!"

39

Richard looked at her with lustful eyes and, with a hint of a smile, said: "I can hardly wait!"

The way home turned out to be a cat-and mouse game. Already in the corridors of the Shedd Aquarium, Richard constantly tried to touch Stephanie. As soon as they were out of the waiters' sight, he pulled her toward him and kissed her tempestuously. But when he tried to slide his hand under her jacket, she managed to featly break away from his embrace and ran toward the exit. When she reached the door, she turned around, opened her jacket again, and called to him: "Catch me if you can!"

Richard chased after her but caught up with her only at the limo, which was waiting for them in front of the building. The driver was already getting out of the car preparing to open the door for them when Richard called: "Thank you, Edgar, I'll do it myself!"

As he opened the door with his right hand, he pushed himself against Stephanie and forced his other hand between her legs. "Gotcha!"

Surprised by the touch, she jumped a little. But when she leaned forward to get into the car, she pressed her groin against his hand and clinched her thighs. Since he was unable to get away quickly enough, he could only let her drag him into the car.

Just when he thought he would fall headfirst onto the backseat, she released her grip and said: "Who got whom now?"

Richard shut the door and asked the driver to take them back to his apartment. He scooted closer to Stephanie and whispered in her ear: "Just wait until we are at my place!"

Both in the car and in the elevator, she obviously enjoyed teasing him. Again and again, she opened her jacket to show him her breasts, threw him kisses while seductively batting her eyelids, or reached between her legs.

Although it wasn't easy for Richard to resist the temptation, he pretended to be unimpressed and didn't make any further advances until, at last, they were in his apartment.

40

After closing the door, he stepped behind her, acting as if he wanted to help her out of her coat. Instead, he pulled it down to her elbows, thereby catching her arms behind her back.

He quickly hugged her and kissed her emphatically on the neck, lasciviously squeezing her breasts.

Although Stephanie responded with a lustful sigh, she tried to fend Richard off. Yet her mock resistance aroused him only more. As he pushed her against the wall and unbuttoned her pants, she started kicking and tried to get her arms free. She wasn't planning on surrendering that easily. "Do you want me? Then you have to show a bit more! Is that all you've got?"

Richard was certainly in the mood for this kind of game. "Are you sure you're up for more? Is that what you want?"

Stephanie, gasping for breath by now, simply panted: "You can do with me whatever you like, silly!"

When Richard loosened his grip just a little to pull down her pants, she managed to get away from him and out of her coat and jacket. Giggling, she tried to run away on her high heels, but after only a few steps he caught up with her, grabbed her by the hips, and dragged her to the floor.

Stephanie tried to crawl away from him on all fours, but Richard got a hold of her waistband and pulled her pants down to her knees.

Only now, he realized that she wasn't wearing a camisole under her suit at all, but a crotchless bodystocking.

Richard pulled her back and leaned over her from behind. While he grabbed her pelvis with his left arm, he used his right hand to unzip.

Stephanie was still trying to free herself, but his grip was too tight.

Determined, he reached between her thighs, spread her legs, and entered her. It was obvious that her game had not only aroused him as her vagina was moist and hot and more than ready to welcome him.

"Fuck me! I want you to fuck me real hard!"

41

Richard moved within her with swift, long strokes while, at the same time, he reached around her body and started to caress her clit.

Stephanie's sighing got louder as Richard's movements became fiercer and he intensified the rubbing. When he loosened his grip, she lowered her upper body onto the floor, spread her legs even more, and pushed her butt up as much as she could toward him. She dug her fingernails into the carpet, moving her pelvis up and down faster and faster, until Richard felt her getting tight, snugly enclosing his hard penis in rhythmic contractions. He fondled her a bit longer before he pulled his dick out and lay her on her back.

After taking off her shoes and pants, he kneeled between her thighs, grabbed her ankles, and placed her spread legs on his shoulders. While pulling apart her labia with his thumb and index finger, he took his penis and rubbed it against her blood-filled, bulging button.

Stephanie turned her head to the side and closed her eyes. While with one hand she alternated caressing her breasts through the sheer fabric of her bodystocking, she ecstatically sucked and chewed on the middle finger of the other hand.

Richard rhythmically moved his loins back and forth until he felt that Stephanie was close to culminating again. With the next forward motion, he pushed his penis a bit down and entered her again.

Since Stephanie's legs were still on his shoulders, he automatically lifted her pelvis a bit as he leaned over her. Wildly, he rammed his dick again and again into the moist warmth of her lap until they both climaxed, and he ejected his semen into her.

Exhausted, Richard sank down next to Stephanie's motionless body.

After they had lain like that for a few minutes, he noticed that she had fallen asleep. Gently, he lifted her up and carried her to the bedroom where he put her down on the bed. Stephanie was still wearing the bodystocking, which enclosed her like a second skin. Richard admired her flawless body and started to softly run his fingers over the delicate fabric. Slowly, his hands slid from Stephanie's shoulders downwards, tracing the curvature of her breasts, and continued along her hips, toward her thighs and her knees.

With a soft sigh, Stephanie turned to the side.

For a moment, Richard petted her buttocks, then he pulled his hand up to her back. It was soothing and exciting at the same time to touch and explore her sleeping body. Carefully, he pushed against her hips to turn her around on her back again.

She mumbled something unintelligible, seemingly unwilling to change her position, but at last gave up her resistance and turned over.

Richard opened her legs a little and put his hand on her mound of Venus. When he briefly hesitated, she opened her eyes for just a moment and said: "Don't stop now!"

As he caressed her, she started to sigh peacefully. Just as he considered to roll on top of her and sleep with her again, he caught sight of his hand gently massaging her crotch. He put his middle finger on her clit and rubbed her gently until she had an orgasm.

He waited until she fell asleep and breathed regularly again before he got up and went to the living room. For a while, he looked out of the window, watching the lake glistening in the moonlight. Then he took his cell phone to send Bob a text message.

All he typed was "Woman!"

Saturday, February 12

9:46 a.m.

After having breakfast in bed, Richard dropped Stephanie off at McCormick Place and drove to the Chicago Police Department to find out if there were any new developments.

As soon as he entered the anteroom to Chief Miller's office, he was greeted enthusiastically by Jenny. "Good morning, Dr. Stanton, how wonderful to see you! I thought that you might be coming in today. Bob already told me that you will be working on the new case."

It seemed like she had been waiting for him the whole morning, and now, she came around her desk to collect her usual kiss from Richard. She always looked good and was very spiffy, but Richard couldn't help but think that today she was particularly prettied up. She was wearing a bright red business suit, whose tight-fitting skirt ended about a handbreadth above her knee, and high heels, which made her appear quite a bit taller than she actually was.

When Richard bent down to her, he noticed that she was wearing Chanel No. 5.

"Jenny, how am I supposed to resist you?"

Although he hoped that his question didn't sound serious, he himself wasn't sure if one day he wouldn't just forsake his principles and ask Jenny out on a date.

"But Dr. Stanton, you aren't… Not at all!"

Richard was somewhat baffled by this unusual candor, and he was glad when suddenly Bob came out of his office with a big folder and put it on Jenny's desk.

"Jenny, would you please return this to Human Resources right away! Thanks!" Only now, he turned to Richard, gave him an inconspicuous wink, and said casually: "Oh, Richard, you are here, too? Come in, we have to talk!"

Chief Miller closed the door, and they sat down at the big conference table. "How long will it be until you finally take that girl out? I can virtually smell the pheromones coming through the closed door as soon as you enter the building. Whenever she knows that you are coming, she behaves like a cat in heat. I hope that you have at least noticed how dolled up she got for you! For heaven's sake, how am I supposed to focus on my work here?"

Richard sat down across from Bob and took a deep breath. "You bet I've noticed! But I certainly can't risk that your better half leaves you because of a little hanky-panky with me. What would you do without Jenny?" Richard referred to the fact that Jenny was far more than just an ordinary office manager. Bob trusted her completely and gladly let her make decisions on stuff he didn't want to be bothered with. He hated the bureaucratic minutiae with which the administration seemingly tried to overwhelm his office every day. He preferred to devote his time to more important things. In all those years, Jenny had never disappointed him and had always been an exemplary and very loyal coworker. During Christmas parties, in particular, Bob sometimes joked that Jenny probably knew him better than his wife of twenty-eight years.

"Yes, yes, I know. But it hurts to see how she worships you, just to be turned down all the time. She is a gorgeous woman and deserves better, don't you agree?"

"Bob, you know very well that I like her at least as much as you do and that I have my reasons for not getting involved with her. And, by the way, I met someone."

Bob looked at him with surprise. "Don't tell me it's the Nordic goddess – that would be fast! But, after all, it's none of my business. Well, let's talk about the case then! I hope that your mysterious text message didn't refer to your love life but meant that you may already be on to something."

45

Richard shook his head. "No, I wouldn't say that. It's more like a hunch. I was just wondering what might make someone cut off a victim's hand."

Bob was anxious to hear more. "So, what does your hunch tell you?"

"Well, imagine a woman that was sexually assaulted or perhaps still is! The hands could represent unwanted touching, and their severing is some act of revenge or liberation. In principle, the perpetrator could also be a man, but I doubt it."

"Do you want to imply that all victims were rapists?"

"No, not at all. Although, we can't rule this out at this time. We really need to identify them to find out if they knew each other or if there is any other link between them. Have you heard back from Liz or Steven?"

Bob shook his head. "No, I don't think they are back yet. I am sure they'll give us an update as soon as there are any new developments."

"Of course. In the meantime, I'll pay Ron a visit to see if he has made any progress."

Jenny was on the phone when Richard left, and so he just waived to her before he took the elevator to the parking garage.

The office of the County Medical Examiner was only about fifteen minutes away from the headquarters of the Chicago Police Department–at least, when there was no traffic jam. Richard was lucky, and it took him less than ten minutes to cover the six miles in his Porsche. After checking in at the reception desk, he went directly to Forensic Pathology where Ron Howard worked.

Ron was one of twelve assistant medical examiners who worked under the Chief Medical Examiner and did the typical day-to-day practical work of a pathologist. Medical examiners were called in when foul play was suspected or when the cause of death was unclear. In such cases, the ME took charge of the body and performed a

46

preliminary on-site examination after which he or she decided if further investigation was needed.

Ron was sitting at his desk, studying an autopsy report.

"Hi, Ron. I hope I'm not disturbing you. How are you doing?"

When Ron looked up, Richard immediately noticed the dark rings under his eyes.

"What do you think? I didn't get much sleep lately. After Liz, in her inimitable way, made it clear to me that your new case is of greatest importance, I worked around the clock to get something for you."

Richard was thrilled. "That's fantastic, Ron! What have you found out?"

Ron handed him the papers. "If you are interested in details, I would suggest that you go over the report yourself. After all, you're a colleague. The short version is that the victim is male, around forty, and was still alive when the fire was started. That wasn't obvious at first as there wasn't the usual soot in the respiratory tract, and the amount of carboxyhemoglobin in his blood wasn't very high either. However, we found gasoline in his blood, with the concentration being higher in his left ventricle than in the right. The fire was extinguished quickly enough so that the extremities were largely preserved–with the exception of the severed hand, of course, which is missing. I have consulted with a forensic anthropologist, and we agree that the stump looks as if the hand was amputated antemortem. If you ask my opinion, the guy was tied to the floor, then someone chopped off his hand, doused him in gasoline, and set him on fire. Looks like a cult killing to me."

Richard flipped through the report. "I see that you already have the results of the DNA-analysis. Do you have any idea yet who the victim might be?"

Ron took a sip from his oversized coffee mug. "No, sorry! The databank search didn't give us any names. We have also performed a thorough examination of his teeth, but as long as we don't have

47

anything to compare the results with, it doesn't lead anywhere. And the fingers of the left hand were too destroyed to give any useful prints. So, you have to find another way to figure out who the deceased may have been. Then, all we can do is confirm or refute that."

12:39 p.m.

Just as Richard left the County Medical Examiner building, his phone rang. It was Steven calling from his car.

Repeatedly, the conversation was interrupted by loud cracks and buzzes. The only words he could hear loud and clear were "Richard" and "news."

When the connection was dropped, he decided to send Steven a text message asking him to get together as soon as possible. Since it was lunchtime, he suggested meeting at a tapas bar where they could have a bite.

The restaurant was on the way to the police department and, at this time of day, was a popular spot for businesspeople so they wouldn't attract any attention there.

The tapas bar was located on the second floor of the venerable Blackstone Hotel, which was built between 1908 and 1910 directly on Michigan Avenue, the main shopping promenade in downtown Chicago. The luxury hotel, which was sometimes referred to as "The Hotel of Presidents," had served as accommodation for at least twelve different U.S.-presidents in the last century. Among them was John F. Kennedy, who, on October 20, 1962, at the height of the Cuban Missile Crisis, had received a phone call here from his brother Robert, informing him that the Executive Committee of the National Security Council had recommended a blockade of the Caribbean island. JFK, who was on a campaign trip in Illinois at the time, immediately returned to Washington and ordered the blockade as the American response to the Soviets' placing of nuclear missiles the next day.

Over the years, the hotel had pretty much gone to hell and had even been empty for some time before, in 2008, after a 130-million-dollar renovation, it had been reopened in its former splendor.

As soon as Richard entered the restaurant, he was joyfully greeted by Angelina, the

chocolate-brown hostess, who led him to one of the tables by the big windows. From here, one had a nice view of Michigan Avenue, which was right at your feet, and Grant Park, the most prominent park in Chicago.

Richard ordered some of his favorite dishes and a glass of Rioja.

Just as Richard wanted to take another quick look at the autopsy report, Steven entered the restaurant. He seemed to be out of breath and came right toward Richard, without so much as looking at Angelina.

"Richard, I may have got something!" he said full of excitement before he even sat down. "Sorry about the poor connection before. I must have been so lost in my thoughts that I didn't realize that the reception in Lower Wacker Drive is so bad."

Wacker Drive was one of the major traffic routes through the so-called Chicago Loop, the area south and east of the Chicago River. The street had two and, on a short section, even three levels. Lower Wacker Drive, which ran underground, was mostly used by locals and cabbies who wanted to get across town quickly.

"You asked me to check the missing persons listing. To be perfectly honest, at first, I thought that this would be a waste of time; especially, since most people still firmly believe that forty-eight hours have to pass before you can file a missing person report. But I have to admit that I was wrong. This could be our lucky day! Since Thursday night, not too many persons were reported missing, and most of them are either elderlies suffering from senile dementia, who probably got lost, or teenagers who, hopefully, just ran away from home. However, this morning, a report came in that was filed by a woman in Massachusetts, who is concerned for her husband's whereabouts. She hasn't heard from him since Thursday evening, and he missed his flight from Chicago to Boston yesterday morning."

Anxiously, Richard cut him off: "How old is the man?"

Steven took the copy of a photograph out of his pocket and laid it on the table. "Forty-six. He is the CFO of a midsize pharmaceutical company on the East Coast that is doing something with antibodies. His wife thinks that he was in Chicago to secure funding for the next round of an important project."

In the Greater Chicago area, there were several big pharma and biotech companies that either developed or bought antibodies from subcontractors for diagnostic and therapeutic applications.

"Seems like his wife was told that he checked out of the hotel Friday morning," Steven said.

Richard thought this over for a moment. "I think we should pay the hotel a visit. Let's have a quick bite, and then we can drive there together. Have you found out if there are any cameras in the vicinity of the crime scene?"

"Unfortunately, the next ones are at least three blocks away, and traffic there is so busy that you need to know who to look for if you want to have a chance of finding someone. On the other hand, it may be worthwhile looking for this gentleman." Steven tapped the photo, which showed a tanned, handsome man with a chiseled face smiling for the camera.

****

When they arrived at the hotel, Richard immediately asked the receptionist to fetch the manager.

It didn't take very long, and an elegant, gray-haired gentleman in a perfectly fitting, navy blue suit approached them.

"Good afternoon, my name is Luigi Castelloni. How can I be of assistance?"

The manager's dignified demeanor aptly embodied the luxurious flair of the hotel where, even at this time of year, room prices started around four hundred dollars per night.

"Mister Castelloni, we have a few questions concerning a man who stayed here Wednesday through Friday. If you have no objections, I would suggest that we continue our conversation in your office." Richard was friendly but made clear who was in charge.

The manager seemed to understand at once that the two police officers in plainclothes weren't conducting a routine investigation and that it would be best if the hotel guests didn't find out what this was really about. "Of course. Gentlemen, please follow me! May I offer you an espresso or a cappuccino? Like everything else our house offers, the coffee is first class! "

Since Richard and Steven had not had coffee after their rushed lunch, they gladly accepted the invitation.

Luigi Castelloni had a quick word with his assistant, who–arms crossed behind her back–had been standing at attention, before leading them to his office.

In the generously spaced room, there was a contemporary glass desk and a designer-sectional, which apparently took the place of a conference table.

They took a seat, and Richard got right to the point. "Mister Castelloni, the man we are looking for may have become the victim of a violent crime. We need to find out when he was last seen at the hotel."

Someone knocked at the door and Castelloni's assistant came in, followed by a waiter with coffee and cold beverages, a bowl of fresh fruit, and a selection of tartlets on a serving cart.

"Thank you very much, Ronda. If the gentlemen have no objections, I would ask you to stay."

Richard simply nodded briefly.

After the waiter left, Castelloni introduced the young woman. "Gentlemen, may I introduce my assistant, Ronda Green. Miss Green

51

has been working at my side for several years and is most familiar with all aspects of our house. I have no doubt that she will be able to help you."

With these words, the manager turned to his assistant, who, as before in the lobby, waited at attention like a soldier, ready to get her orders from Castelloni.

Richard wasn't misled by Ronda's behavior. Her alert eyes revealed that she was an intelligent, dynamic young woman, who, in a hotel with hundreds of employees, was second in command for a reason.

"Ronda, if you would please assist these officers! I have promised them our unrestricted cooperation. The gentlemen have a few questions regarding one of our guests. By the way, what is his name?"

Steven looked at his notepad. "Thomas D. Maddock from Boston, Massachusetts."

****

"It appears that Mister Maddock checked in at the reception desk on Wednesday, February 9, at 6:49 p.m. He got a room on the twenty-first floor, number 2117. About an hour later, he ordered a steak and a bottle of wine from room service. It doesn't look like he left the hotel that night. Rather, I can see here that he watched two on-demand movies." Ronda briefly looked up from her computer. "Adult movies."

With a click of the mouse, she opened another file. "Naturally, we have a state-of-the-art, computer-controlled key system in our house. Therefore, I am able to tell you exactly when the guest entered his room. According to the event log, he used his key card again only at 7:35 a.m. This implies that he went back to his room after having breakfast. Based on his folio, he had a ham and cheese omelet and orange juice in our restaurant. Coffee, of course, is included in our breakfast so it is not listed here. I don't know when the guest left again, but Juanita Gonzalez from the cleaning services crew entered

52

the room at 9:13 a.m., which suggests that Mister Maddock wasn't there at that point of time anymore."

Steven's stunned face indicated that he was quite surprised at the surveillance potential of electronic hotel locking systems.

"The guest used his key again at 11:38 p.m. and then one more time at 6:08 a.m. Friday morning." Ronda opened another window and stared spellbound at the computer screen. "I see here that Mister Maddock ordered a bottle of Champagne at the hotel bar at 12:12 a.m. Friday morning. The last entrance says that he checked out by phone at 6:24 a.m."

Steven was disappointed. "That's it then. At that time, the fire department was already busy extinguishing the fire. It was worth a try…"

For a moment, Richard contemplated the information they had been given. "Miss Green, do you have any sort of proof that it was indeed Mister Maddock himself who checked out of the room?"

"No. This is a fully automated service the guest can call. He or she just needs to type in their room number–that's all! Of course, it is possible that someone else checked out for Mister Maddock."

Steven's face lightened up again. "Where in the building do you have security cameras? Are there perhaps any in the bar?"

Ronda quickly typed something into her computer. "This site map shows all installed cameras. In the bar, there are just two above the counter. We have cameras in all elevators, at all entrances, and a few more in the lobby. In addition, there are several in the parking garage. In order to respect our guests' privacy, we consciously decided against installing any in the hallways… We have a well-trained security service."

"Can you tell us if, in the meantime, room 2117 has been occupied by any other guests?" Richard wanted to know.

Again, it took Ronda only a second to find out the answer to his question. "No. At the moment, our occupancy rate is at about 75%. Most of the business people, who stayed with us for the work week, already left, and we will be fully booked again only on Valentine's Day. Right now, 2117 is vacant."

"Great! I would ask you not to rent out that room again until we have searched it! I would also appreciate if you could give Detective Kowalski access to the recordings of your surveillance cameras. Steven, you know what to do!" Richard thanked Ronda for her help and said goodbye. He was glad that they had at least some kind of lead to follow up now.

Unknowingly, Ronda had reminded him that he urgently needed to take care of something else.

On the way to his car, he hurried to call Stephanie's number and left a message: "Hi, Stephanie, this is Richard. I wanted to ask you if you already have any plans for Monday night. I really want to see you again. So, if you like and you are available, it would be wonderful if we could spend the evening together. Maybe you can find somebody who could sub for you at the booth. Just give me a call when you get a chance! I am looking forward to hearing from you."

Richard and Stephanie had agreed on not seeing each other today. For the last two days, she had just been at her home briefly at lunchtime to change clothes. Furthermore, she hadn't gotten much sleep, and all the sex had caused some vaginal chafing. Therefore, Richard had been very understanding when she had suggested a one-day break.

He had been very happy, however, when she had invited him to have dinner at her house on Sunday.

Richard made two more calls before he got into his car and drove to Michigan Avenue. He wanted to run a few errands.

10:07 p.m.

Tisiphone had spent the whole morning with preparations. She had driven along all routes she was planning on taking tonight, had strolled around the neighborhood of the singles bar she wanted to go to, and had rehearsed poses and accents for hours.

Everything should go smoothly. She still had a long way to go, and she couldn't afford to make a mistake if she wanted her mission to be completed successfully. Therefore, it was of the utmost importance to carefully plan every single step and, as far as possible, leave nothing to chance. However, she knew exactly that there was always room for unforeseen circumstances. But little surprises didn't worry her the least; on the contrary, they intensified the excitement.

She felt well-prepared and could hardly wait to finally leave the house. The nagging restlessness, which briefly had given way to a feeling of inner satisfaction, had soon returned and was getting stronger every hour. Now, so close to the next strike, the compulsion to stalk the next prey, to play with it, and finally bag it was almost unbearable. The thrill of the hunt had taken a hold of her again–much sooner than last time.

But before she could leave, she needed to get dressed.

She had already put on her make-up and was now standing naked in her bedroom. Satisfied, she looked at her wardrobe, which was neatly laid out on her bed.

Carefully, she stroked the leather of the strapless corset with the oblong metal front-buckles. The idea alone of feeling the cool, smooth material on her breasts was enough to get her aroused.

Nevertheless, for the time being, she resisted the temptation and took one of the black thigh highs, bunched it up, and carefully slid her right foot in. Gingerly, she rolled the stocking up, pulling at it until it was smooth and the wide border ended about six inches under her butt. She looked in the mirror to make sure that the back seam, which ran the full length of the leg, was straight.

She repeated the procedure with the other stocking before she finally reached for the corset again.

Careful not to break her long, black-lacquered fingernails, she slowly opened one buckle at a time.

Laid out on the bed, the unusual piece of clothing looked just like a leather scarf, decorated with stitched seams and metal clips. Yet its simple appearance was deceiving. She knew exactly what effect it would have on all the hopeful, horny men in the bar.

Eager to savor the moment, she looked at the corset a little longer. Finally, she took it, put it around her waist, and began to close it, starting at the bottom. When she pulled the leather up over her breast to close the last buckle, her nipples got hard.

For a moment, she thought about giving herself a little pleasure; but she did not want to jeopardize her timeline and, instead, suppressed her desire and put on the miniskirt with the shimmering silver-gray sequins.

She sat down at the edge of the bed and, looking at her mirror-image, checked out once more how far she had to pull up her skirt for her bare pussy to show. Without panties it might get a bit chilly on such a cold winter's night. Yet the effect that her uncovered pubes would later have on the chosen one was worth this small sacrifice.

The thought that the increased blood flow to her crotch, which she already started to feel now, would also help to keep her warm, amused her.

After putting on the almost plain silver jewelry, she slipped into high-heeled leather boots, which reached almost up to her knees, and slid into her black, tailor-made mink coat.

The hunt could begin.

10:34 p.m.

Richard was reading an article about cult killings on the internet when the phone rang.

It was Stephanie. "Hello, Richard, I hope it's alright that I call you this late. I was very happy about your invitation for Monday. However, I wasn't sure if you knew that the day after tomorrow will be Valentine's Day.

For a moment, Richard considered teasing her a little by pretending that he had forgotten. But since he understood what her phone call meant, he decided to be sincere about it. If nothing else, spending the evening of February 14 together meant as much as avowing to a steady relationship.

"Hello, Stephanie. Of course, I know that! The happier it would make me if you accepted."

Richard thought he heard a little sigh on the other end. "Stephanie, you still there?"

He was sure that she was crying.

It took a moment until she answered, and although she was still sobbing, she sounded cheerful. "Oh, Richard, I am so happy! I would love to accept your invitation, I do, I do, I do! Joanne has already agreed on subbing for me."

Richard beamed. "I'm also happy. I'll pick you up at half past seven. But I am not telling you what we are going to do then–that's a surprise!"

"No Problem, you should know by now that I love surprises, especially yours. But Richard, please don't forget that we are having dinner tomorrow at my place. We are going to have something special–Latin American. I hope you'll like it!"

****

After the pleasant phone conversation with Stephanie, Richard wasn't feeling like racking his brain anymore about the possibility of the murders having been committed by someone with a religious motivation or even a sect.

In his opinion, nothing indicated that there had been more than one perp. However, since no useful evidence had been found, it would have been premature to rule out anything at this point. But Richard was convinced that a sect would have left something behind–maybe even intentionally. The more people at a crime scene the greater the chances that something could be found. Ron's comment that they might be dealing with cultural killings, though, wasn't unfounded. The positioning of the victims, especially in combination with their mutilation and their burning, certainly could hint at some kind of ritual. But this didn't necessarily mean that it was of a religious-ceremonial nature; also, retaliatory acts often had a ritual character.

Richard topped off his wine glass and went to the living room to take another look at the present he had bought for Stephanie. He was glad that the sales lady had given him such good advice. It hadn't been easy for him to make a decision, but with her help he had finally picked something that was precious and lofty but not extravagant. Richard hoped that Stephanie would see it the same way and would like his Valentine's Day present.

He could hardly wait to give it to her but, unfortunately, it wasn't Monday yet.

Tomorrow, he would just bring a bottle of red wine for dinner; that was all Stephanie had agreed to.

Thoughtfully, he looked at the lake, asking himself if, maybe, he was rushing into things with Stephanie. After all, they had met just two days ago.

Two days.

It seemed much longer.

Richard had slept with many women, but he had been in only two steady relationships in his life. One, when he was in high school. And then there had been Monica; they had been together for two years. Since that time, he had enjoyed his life as a bachelor and had seldom spent more than one night with the same woman.

He simply hadn't seen himself waking up next to one of them for the rest of his life.

This time it was different. Both his heart and his mind told him that she was Ms. Right.

When the phone rang again, he was sure that it was Stephanie who wanted to say goodnight again.

"Do you have trouble falling asleep, darling?" he said with a sweet voice.

"Ahem, no. Not really, because I'm still at work. But perhaps you can later sing me a lullaby... darling," Steven mocked him.

"Steven! I hope you have good news, or else...," Richard said, trying to sound stern.

"You can say that! I had a chat with the waiter who served Thomas Maddock Thursday night. Maddock was in the hotel lobby with a woman. The waiter said that she was a real knockout, and that there was a lot going on between the two."

"What do you mean? Did they have an altercation?"

"On the contrary! It sounded like the lady gave him a foot job. Unfortunately, they were sitting outside the viewing angle of the camera–I would have loved to see that!"

"And we would have had a picture of her, you pervert!" Richard remarked with reproach.

"Don't worry, we've got one anyway. Not a very good one, but still... The two later left the hotel together, and there the camera got them. You can only briefly see the woman from the side and then once more from the back, but even that is a treat!"

Richard had the feeling that they were on the right track. "Send the picture to my cell! Have you found anything else? What about Maddock's room?"

"We've found a ton of fingerprints, but that is to be expected in a hotel room. Nothing else caught our attention. Maddock doesn't seem to have left anything behind when he moved out. At least, the cleaning crew couldn't remember finding anything. It looks like he just checked out and left the hotel–period."

Richard didn't agree. "Steven, tell Liz to get something from Maddock's wife that we can use for a DNA-analysis! As long as we aren't 100% sure that the victim isn't Maddock, we need to keep following this lead. I want you to go back to the hotel again tomorrow; try to find out where they went after leaving the hotel! Maybe they took a cab. If we can prove that they went to the former factory–then, Bingo! You should also take another look at the surveillance videos! Focus on the time frame shortly after Maddock checked out! If he really left the hotel, one of the cameras should have caught him, for instance in one of the elevators or in the lobby. Who knows, perhaps we won't just find him but also the beautiful stranger. In any case, make sure that we get a facial composite!"

"You're right, Richard. Maybe it's really Maddock who we've found. I will call Liz right away, and we'll get back to you as soon as we know more. Thanks and goodnight… darling."

11:11 p.m.

The moment Tisiphone set foot into the dim singles bar, she attracted admiring looks from all the men. Moreover, not even the female patrons, who certainly weren't a minority here, could keep their eyes off her.

In their faces, however, Tisiphone recognized not so much kindness as envy and hostility.

Despite the fact that she understood why these women considered her unwelcome competition, she wanted to make it clear right here and now who the alpha animal was in this territory. Chin up, her coat wide open, and her breasts, which seemed to almost burst

60

the tight corset, provocatively stuck out, she swaggered to the counter and sat down on one of the white swivel stools.

She let her mink slide from her shoulders and ordered a Bloody Cesar–not because she liked the drink, but because she enjoyed the irony.

When the bartender put the drink in front of her, she could almost feel the curious looks of the other patrons.

She pulled her skirt up a bit more, grabbed her glass, and pushed with her foot just enough against the bar that her stool spun around 180 degrees. While the women immediately averted their eyes, the men instinctively looked down to her legs and her lap. Tisiphone sipped on her glass with relish and gazed at them one by one. It was exactly as she had imagined.

There were numerous clubs in Chicago that were all hot spots for singles. But Tisiphone had no interest in hopping around for hours on an overcrowded dance floor with half-naked teenagers or being hit on by pubescent college boys.

She was looking for real men–and to find those wasn't quite that easy. Fortunately, there were a couple of places in town that aimed at a much more distinguished clientele. This bar was one of them. The patrons here were successful business people, doctors, or lawyers, and anywhere between thirty and fifty years old.

Both men and women were well-dressed, trim, and exceptionally good-looking.

The austere bouncer, who, without mercy, denied entrance to everybody who didn't meet these criteria, made sure of that. For Tisiphone, who matter-of-factly had skipped the line of people waiting to get in, the hulk had opened the door with an approving smile.

The atmosphere in the bar was vibrant yet civilized. The rules of the game were clear. Nobody expected to find a partner for life. You came here to hook up with a suitable companion for the night.

There was such a selection of men that Tisiphone almost had trouble deciding on one. She felt like a lioness watching a herd of gazelles, able to pick her prey at will.

In contrast to a feline predator in the wild, however, she did not intend to hunt the weakest animal.

Quite the opposite: she wanted to bring down the dominant stag.

When she searched the room for the second time, she mainly focused on two potential victims. Both men were good-looking, wore expensive suits, and radiated the kind of self-confidence typical for arrogant highflyers.

While the guy to her left was sitting at a window table, the other one was slouching on one of the sofas across from her at the back wall. The fact that both of them were in the company of young women, who, by all means, were quite alluring, did not stop them from casting furtive glances in her direction.

She was checking out the man at the window when she suddenly heard unpleasantly loud, bumptious laughter reverberating through the room. It was coming from candidate number two. The decision was made. Tisiphone turned her stool a little so that she was sitting directly vis-à-vis from him now.

Looking past his companion, the man stared right at her, and Tisiphone got the feeling that he had hoped to get her attention with his laughter.

That clearly had worked.

She reciprocated the look, took another sip from her drink, and leaned back on her stool.

When she opened her legs a bit more, his eyes automatically drifted downward.

It was as if she had flipped a switch. The man briefly turned to his companion, then he took his glass, got up, and walked toward her.

She didn't know what he had told the young lady, but the fact that she was gawking at Tisiphone with hateful eyes indicated that she didn't like it.

The man was standing right in front of her now. "May I buy you a drink?"

Tisiphone took a blasé look at her half-full glass but then shrugged her shoulders and asked the bartender to bring her another one.

"What did you tell the cutie-pie that she is so pissed now?"

The man briefly turned around, and the woman, who seemed to be fuming, showed him the finger.

"Do you really wanna know?"

Tisiphone just nodded silently.

"I just told her that you are an old friend of mine."

Tisiphone raised her eyebrows in disbelief.

"Well… and that I didn't want to waste any more time with her." Again, there was this bumptious laughter.

"But now, you have to allow me a question," he said with a fat grin on his face.

Tisiphone looked at him expectantly.

The man leaned forward, reaching out as if he wanted to embrace her but, instead, reached for her armrests. His face was only a few inches away from hers. "Hasn't your mama told you that it isn't proper for a lady not to wear panties?"

Tisiphone looked him directly in the eyes. "I'm a dirty girl!"

"I like dirty," he answered, and his right hand grabbed her thigh.

Before he could reach under her skirt, though, Tisiphone snatched the back of his hand and pressed with her middle finger onto the crest between thumb and index finger.

At once, the man groaned in pain and slumped downward.

"Jeez! What was that?" he asked indignantly.

"Don't be such a pussy! That was just a little acupuncture. I prefer a slower pace. Take a seat!"

The man glanced back over his shoulder to find out if anyone in the bar had been witness to his embarrassment. When he saw that the other patrons weren't paying any attention to them anymore, he calmed down and sat down next to her.

"That's much better! What's your name?" Tisiphone asked friendly.

"Conrad, Conrad Donnahan. I'm a broker at the CME."

The Chicago Mercantile Exchange was one of the world's largest derivatives and futures exchanges where such diverse commodities as copper and corn were traded. Even weather derivatives, which were intended to transfer climate-based risks, like poor harvests, from companies to banks or insurance companies, were traded here.

"And, are you good?" Tisiphone asked innocently.

"Believe me, baby, I am! If you like, I can show you what I am particularly good at…"

It was going smoother than she had hoped. "Oh, yes, I'd like to see that. But not here! My car is parked outside. How do you feel about taking a drive? I know a quiet spot where we could gaze at the stars and get to know each other a little better."

He frowned. "You mean… in the car? Isn't it too cold for that?"

She had anticipated that it might require some arm twisting to persuade a man to have sex in a car in a cold February night. So, she gently grabbed the index and middle finger of his right hand, dipped them into her drink, and then started to obscenely suck on them.

The effect was quite obvious, and still, he wasn't totally convinced. This wasn't good. She had to make him think with his dick, not his brain.

Slowly, she pulled his fingers out of her mouth, placed them on her full lips, and stuck her tongue through them a few times.

The unambiguity of this gesture made him forget his objections.

"Why not? I hope you have heating."

She looked at him enticingly with her cat eyes. "Oh, sweetie, I have all kinds of things in my car!"

Sunday, February 13

9:52 a.m.

Should he really increase the speed of his treadmill again? Already, beads of sweat were pouring off Richard's forehead, and he was about to run out of breath. He hadn't slept too well last night and had been in the health club since half past seven. After a little chitchat with Christina, the spa's joyful receptionist, Richard had first warmed up on the elliptical trainer and then lifted weights for over an hour. His plan had been to finish with some cardio training and jog casually for fifteen minutes or so on the treadmill.

Now, a glance at the red-glowing display revealed that he had already run close to four miles.

He would have had enough for today, but the good-looking young woman next to him was relentless.

Light-footed and seemingly without any effort, she jogged by his side, smiling teasingly. He even imagined reading a silent "Come on!" from her lips.

She had been sprinting next to him for almost twenty minutes but still looked ridiculously fresh and rested. Richard knew from experience that the reason for that wasn't just her tender age–he guessed she was in her early twenties. No, the girl was as fit as a fiddle.

He had been a bit surprised when, of all the vacant treadmills that were lined up along the windows, she had picked the one right next to him.

She smelled like peach blossoms and wore a pale blue sports bra and short, dark-gray hotpants. The clothes were made out of spandex and had undoubtedly been chosen with the intent to accentuate her tight butt and her shapely breasts.

As she was jogging next to him, her long, brown hair, which was tied into a ponytail with a rubber band, wasn't the only thing moving up and down synchronously with her steps.

Richard, who watched her reflection in the window, could clearly see her smile at him, waiting for him to catch up with her.

Even before she had started to run, she had checked his speed, just to set her own treadmill a notch higher.

With his competitive spirit challenged, Richard had accelerated until he was as fast as her. But every time he reached her speed, she smiled and picked up the pace.

By now, his display showed eleven miles per hour, hers the maximal twelve and a half.

Richard watched her for a moment, but then he couldn't resist the temptation and set his speed higher again. The machine made a suspiciously loud, groaning sound under his steps, and he doubted that it had ever before been put to such a test.

It became more and more difficult for him to adjust his pace to the increasing velocity of the belt, which seemed to fly along under his feet. It would take only one misstep and he would fall.

Richard focused on the grinding noise, which became louder and appeared to originate somewhere under his soles, and set one foot in front of the other with his last ounce of strength.

When eventually he was as fast as his opponent, he continued running alongside her for a mere moment before he slowed down and let the treadmill come to a stop. He certainly wasn't in the mood for an endurance sprinting contest, which he couldn't win anyway.

When his treadmill stopped, he applauded the young woman and went to one of the exercise rooms to relax his muscles with some stretching. The way he felt right now, he'd probably overdone it today. After all, he wasn't twenty anymore.

The left leg extended, the right bent backwards, he was sitting on the floor when the door opened, and the young woman came in.

Without a word, she took a yoga mat from the shelf, flounced in Richard's direction, and rolled out the pink pad no more than six feet from him.

Her legs spread wide, her back toward him, she stepped onto the mat and started to stretch out her arms one at a time above her head like a dancer. While she elegantly pointed her slender hands toward the ceiling, she sinuously moved her behind from left to right in synchronicity with her upper body.

Richard was reminded of tall grass swaying in the wind.

Her fit body was unusually tan for the season–just like she had recently been sunbathing. As he was contemplating if one could get such a natural color in a tanning studio, she suddenly bent over, grabbed her ankles, and cheekily looked at him through her spread legs.

Richard, who was convinced that she brazenly tried to turn him on, returned the smile in a friendly but, as he hoped, noncommittal way.

While he changed his position to stretch the right leg now, she slowly sank forward to the floor, briefly sat on her heels, and then arched her back, stretching her butt right in his face. She stayed like that for an instant before she quickly turned around to him in one smooth motion.

Bolstered up on her hands, she first just sat across from Richard, relaxed, watching him with her large, hazel eyes. It looked as if she had to make up her mind about something.

After a while, she stretched her legs, lifted them about a foot above the ground, and spread them wide. The outline of her labia showed clearly through her tight fitting pants.

"You come here often to work out?" she asked jauntily.

"Basically, every day. I am a club member. Are you staying at the hotel?"

She slowly closed her legs in front of her body, held them there for a moment, and spread them again. "Yes. My parents are here in Chicago on a business trip and invited me to come along. You're in pretty good shape–considering your age."

He decided to ignore the dig. "Thank you, but so are you! Are you a competitive athlete?"

"Florida Gators. Until recently, I've run 5Ks."

Richard was impressed. The University of Florida in Gainesville had one of the strongest track and field programs in the U.S.

"Then I don't have to feel too bad about not being able to keep up with you, I guess."

"Not at all. As I said, you are in good shape. Do you know what's really super relaxing after a workout?"

Richard wasn't quite sure what she was getting at, so he just shrugged his shoulders.

"Giving each other a massage in a hot shower! You wanna try?"

Only three days ago, Richard for sure hadn't turned down this kind of invitation. However, since then his situation had changed considerably.

"I'm sorry, I have a girlfriend."

Again, she spread her thighs, grabbed her toes, and pulled her legs out to a side split. "Don't you worry, I don't want to marry you! And I can keep a secret…"

Richard was too much of a man not to be tempted.

Nevertheless, he stayed steadfast. "I'm in love."

The young woman looked at him clemently. "I understand! But just in case you change your mind–we'll be in town for two weeks. My room is on the twentieth floor, number 2040. My parents are on another floor and hardly ever here anyway."

She pulled her legs apart a bit more. "You two been together long?"

Richard smiled at her. "By my standards–yes!"

Back in his apartment, Richard saw that Liz had left a message for him, and he called her back on her cell right away. "Liz, what's up? Do you have any news?"

"Not about the last case."

Richard was puzzled. "What are you saying?"

She audibly blew into her phone. "Richard, I believe the killer has struck again."

"That would be rather unusual, after only two days…" Richard answered with surprise.

One characteristic of serial murders was that, typically, there was a longer period of time between the individual killings. Sometimes, months or even years passed until the murderer became active again. Occasionally, the intervals between successive murders became shorter, but this was usually a gradual process that was often attributed to the killer's increasing difficulty to suppress the homicidal urge.

The idea that the murderer might have struck again so soon made Richard somewhat uncomfortable. "You're sure it's the same killer?"

Again, Liz blew into the phone. "Not at all! The modus operandi is completely different. Who knows, maybe I'm barking up the wrong tree, but I thought I better let you know about it."

Richard had always encouraged his colleagues to follow their instincts. In his opinion, it was better to follow one lead too many than to miss something. In their job, the stakes were simply too high.

"Shoot!"

"When I came to the office this morning to get everything going for Maddock's DNA-analysis, I saw a report from the night shift saying that a man had been burned in a minivan. This immediately raised a red flag and…"

Richard didn't give her time to finish the sentence, interrupting her impatiently: "Was the victim missing a hand?"

"No, but he was tied with leather bands to one of the back seats; you know–one of those captain's seats. The car was found in a parking lot at Lincoln Park Zoo. Our colleagues are convinced that it's gang-related."

Richard's curiosity had been aroused. "Obviously you don't agree with them. Why? "

"Okay. The car was reported stolen two days ago. What is interesting is that it disappeared from the valet lot of a pretty fancy restaurant. I don't see that some stoned gangstas did that. They would have attracted way too much attention in this kind of neighborhood. And, furthermore, they wouldn't have gone through the trouble of removing the license plates from a car of exactly the same make and putting 'em on the stolen car. The family whose plates were removed only learned about it when our colleagues came to their house last night. You can't blame them: their car still had plates–just different ones!"

Richard agreed with her. This didn't sound like the typical gang-related homicide; it was way too sophisticated. "Has there been an autopsy yet?"

"No, but I went ahead and rousted Ron out of his bed. He didn't appreciate it much but agreed to perform it as soon as possible."

Richard was proud of Liz. "Well done, girl! I'll get in touch with Ron. Have the report of the night shift and everything else you find sent to me! But don't forget to also contact Mrs. Maddock! We urgently need a brush or something like that from her husband. If we can prove that he and the previous victim are one and the same, we have made a huge step forward. At the moment, this is our only lead."

After he had hung up, he got himself an espresso and took a shower. In his mind he reflected on the conversation he'd had with Liz.

If she was right and the perp had struck again, they were in trouble. Not just because the killer didn't give them any time to catch a breath but because his or her behavior was even more erratic than he had thought.

Contrary to some of his colleagues, he had been much more cautious attempting to predict what a serial killer might be up to next.

Even though criminal psychologists had always tried to understand and categorize the motives, actions, and psyche of such people, it was generally accepted nowadays that this was difficult, if not impossible. Yes, many serial killers showed the symptoms of a psychopathy–like a lack of empathy or remorse; but their acts usually couldn't be explained only with this kind of personality disorder. Often, there were no recognizable clear-cut motives, which could range from power thrills or sexual gratification to hatred of certain ethnic groups. Simple greed, which happened to be the most common motive of robbery-related homicides, seemed almost banal in comparison. Also with regard to their general characteristics, no reliable predictions were possible. While Hollywood-productions often depicted serial killers as white males and societal outcasts, there had been a number of murderers not fitting this profile at all.

Richard was fully aware of all that.

But as much as he wanted to remain faithful to his principles and not jump to any conclusions, he couldn't get the picture of the woman in the hotel lobby that Steven had sent him out of his mind.

He stayed a little longer in the shower before he finally turned off the water, slid–wet as he still was–into his robe, and grabbed his phone. "Steven, have you got anything?"

"Good morning to you, too, Richard. Did you get up on the wrong side of the bed this morning?" Steven answered irritated.

Richard bit his lower lip. "I'm sorry, Steven. Good morning! I was so wrapped up in my thoughts... Liz thinks that the murderer may have struck again last night. We urgently need to find out if this woman from the hotel bar played any role in Maddock's disappearance."

71

When Steven didn't answer immediately, Richard added an inquisitory "And?"

"Well, I've been here in the hotel for more than two hours, watching surveillance videos. So far, I have seen neither Maddock nor our beautiful stranger again. The waiter is at the station right now, helping with the facial composite. I have also assigned a couple of officers to inquire with all taxi companies whether one of their employees drove Maddock from the hotel to the old factory Friday morning. Do you have any idea how many cabs there are in Chicago? Close to seven thousand!"

Richard knew that there were a number of different companies, which had formed almost two dozen affiliations, but this number surprised even him. "Don't the dispatchers have logs or something like that? If I am not mistaken, in the last couple of years, all cabs had to get GPS."

"In theory, yes. That doesn't mean that these systems can automatically be used to locate vehicles or track their routes. So far, the drivers have successfully resisted such uses and many have never installed an instrument. However, the companies have to keep records of all the calls they receive and the dispatches they make. But since there are always cabs waiting outside of hotels day and night, I don't think that they had to call one–so we can forget about that."

"Then the companies simply have to contact each and every one of their drivers. Perhaps, one of them remembers the fare."

Steven cleared his throat. "Richard, we don't even know if the two took a cab or not. They could have walked or driven with a private car."

"Nonsense! Would you, in the middle of the night, at minus four degrees, walk in a mini skirt and high heels around Chicago? And I guarantee that they didn't drive themselves after having a bottle of Champagne. Furthermore, they left through the main entrance, and there is no parking. A private car would have been in the parking garage, which you reach by elevator. No, they took a cab, I'm sure!"

11:02 a.m.

"Today is Sunday, February 13, 2011; it's exactly 11:02 a.m. My name is Dr. Ron Howard; I am assistant medical examiner in the Cook County Medical Examiner Office. I am beginning with the autopsy of a non-identified body, listed as John Doe, number 2011-17. Present are my assistant, Gregory Barton, and my colleague, Dr. Arnold Settler, who performed the preliminary examination at the crime scene.

The deceased was brought here in a blue body bag, which also contained charred material of a car seat. The victim's clothes have largely been incinerated, especially ventrally. Dorsally, the remnants of a suit are discernable.

Attached to the extremities, there are leather straps with metal buckles and rings.

The body is that of a completely charred male of medium age, weighing one hundred and forty-three pounds at a height of seventy inches.

Based on the bone structure of the skull, the victim is Caucasian. There are no remains of head hair, and the skullcap is externally charred. The soft tissue of the face including nose, ears, and eyeballs is charred. The mouth is charred. The neck is stiff and the muscles in this area have largely been destroyed. The skin of the torso is completely charred, but the ribs are intact. Both upper and lower extremities show extensive thermal injuries with skin and muscle tissue being completely charred. The abdominal wall is charred and open, with loops of the small bowel extending outward. The genitals are largely destroyed.

I am now opening the mouth to examine oral cavity and pharynx…

Oh, that is a surprise! Gregory, would you please contact Dr. Stanton right away! I am sure that he would like to see this. Arnie, look at that! What do you think? Pretty clean cut, isn't it? Any idea what might have been used to do that?"

"Good question! I'd say that it was certainly a sharp instrument. But this also requires some counterpressure. Maybe pruning shears?"

"Yes, something like that. Could you please take a couple more pictures! For the record: I am now continuing with the description of the body. The teeth are intact and show signs of excellent dental work. There are soot deposits in the oral cavity. Particularly noteworthy is a subtotal glossectomy."

****

When Richard was leaving the parking garage, he didn't immediately notice the old Chevy Monte Carlo that was following him at a distance. The driver of the red car had almost missed him since he wasn't using the Porsche today but instead was relying on his Range Rover Supercharged.

Although no precipitation was forecast for Chicago, temperatures were finally rising after the bitter cold of the last few days, causing the snow that was piled up along the streets since the blizzard earlier this month to melt during the day. After sunset, however, the water froze again and turned the roads into a skating rink in no time.

With weather conditions like that, Richard particularly appreciated the four-wheel-drive of the SUV, which he didn't usually use in the city. He had purchased the Rover last year with the goal to occasionally get out of town on a hiking trip. So far, he hadn't done that very often.

Only once, in fall, when the leaves were starting to change color, he had actually thrown a few things in the back of the car and driven north...

After a stop in Madison, where he had lunch with a few old friends, he continued on to Pictured Rocks National Lakeshore, which, since 1966, was part of the National Park System. The park, located on the

74

shore of Lake Superior, offered breath-taking views of up to 200-foot-high sandstone cliffs that had been sculptured over thousands of years into caves and magnificent formations. Furthermore, there were waterfalls, gigantic dunes, beaches, and over one hundred miles of trails.

Richard stayed on the more than forty-mile-long part of the North Country Trail that led along the lake and afforded spectacular outlooks over the unique landscape.

The timing couldn't have been better. The forests were gleaming in the warm autumn sun in colors ranging from yellow-gold to blood-red; the sky was cloudless and dark-blue; and, besides the sound of the waves and the occasional birdcall, it was quiet.

Since it was midweek and school was in session, there were hardly any other people, which greatly increased the chance of seeing some of the animals that lived in the park.

Richard had been very lucky as he had not only been able to observe countless deer and some coyotes but also two black bears and even a wolf.

Even though there weren't any confirmed packs permanently living in the park, it wasn't unusual to come across tracks or even catch sight of a wolf, especially close to the shore and particularly when there was no snow on the ground.

Two days into his backpacking trip, Richard was just sitting down on the beach for a little snack when, not even ten yards away, an imposing black wolf sneaked out of the boscage, prowled curiously sniffing through the sand, and guzzled from the lake. Since Richard was upwind, the wolf had not yet picked up his scent, which gave him enough time to get his camera out and take some pictures. He had always been interested in photography and was the proud owner of Nikon D3X. The 24.5-megapixel resolution of the DSLR allowed him to print his favorite shot on a large canvas. The black and white photo, in which the dark animal formed an accentuated but picturesque contrast to the light sandy beach and the breaking waves in the background, was now hanging in his office.

Only when he turned onto the Eisenhower Expressway, the freeway leading from downtown to the western suburbs of Chicago, Richard noticed that he had seen the rust bucket that was now two cars behind him earlier, on Wacker Drive.

Was he being followed?

He slowed down a tad to let the car come closer, but the driver changed lanes and disappeared behind a truck.

Richard took the next exit, South Damen Avenue, and, after three hundred yards, turned right onto West Harrison Street.

When he had reached his destination, he stayed in the car for a while, waiting. Five minutes passed, but there was no sign of the red Chevy. Everything seemed normal, and he came to the conclusion that the driver had gone in the same direction as he by coincidence.

Little did Richard know that his pursuer, who was hiding behind a jeep on the other side of the street, was watching him through a telephoto lens and pressed the shutter button the moment he stepped into the Medical Examiner's Office.

****

"You owe me big time! I hope you'll remember that!" Since Ron was wearing scrubs including a cap and a surgical mask, Richard couldn't see much of his face. And still, the dark rings under his eyes, which seemed to be even bigger than yesterday, implied that he hadn't gotten much sleep again last night.

"I'll invite you to dinner, promise!" Richard knew exactly that Ron, just as he did himself, enjoyed good food, and that the prospect of an evening of culinary prodigality would propitiate him.

"My favorite restaurant! And I'll have the large tasting menu– with wine pairing, of course!"

Richard was happy that his offer was so well received, and he decided to make a reservation as soon as they were done here.

76

There were a number of excellent restaurants in Chicago, but Ron's favorite was considered one of the best in the country, if not in the world.

Since it had been awarded three stars by the Michelin Guide, ordinary mortals often had to wait months to get a table. Richard, however, was a regular and always welcome so that he usually got in even on short notice.

"Sure, but now show me why you wanted me to come here so urgently! Gregory wouldn't or couldn't give me any details."

"If I may…" Ron handed Richard a surgical mask and led him to the autopsy table with the grossly burnt and disfigured body. The skull had been opened and the brain removed for further examination. The thorax and abdomen were, except for thermal injuries, still intact.

"May I introduce you to John Doe number 2011-17, or should I say 'Quirinus of Chicago'?"

The name didn't ring a bell for Richard. "I don't understand."

Ron seemed to be in the best of moods now and gladly seized the opportunity to make fun of his friend. "And once again, it has become apparent that you are a tragic victim of the public educational system and–unlike me–didn't have the privilege to attend a private catholic school. Saint Quirinus was a Roman tribune, who lived and– what is of greater interest to us–died around 100 A.D. After converting to Christianity, the poor man was prosecuted and tortured. The latter isn't without a certain irony considering that he himself had been a turnkey prior to his martyrdom. Be it as it may… before he lost his hands, his feet, and, last but not least, his head, he lost something else…"

With these words, Ron, who was leaning over the body's head, signaled Richard to join him. "See for yourself," he said, opening the victim's mouth.

As soon as Richard realized the tongue was missing, he was convinced that Liz had had the right instinct. He knew the answer to his next question, but he needed assurance. "Are you certain that the tongue was cut off and didn't just burn?"

Ron looked at him disapprovingly. "You can't be serious! You should know better, that's a clean cut! And, by the way, a tongue doesn't just burn and disappear into thin air. Your reaction lets me assume that this doesn't square with your theory. Am I right?"

Worried, Richard shook his head. "On the contrary!"

****

As soon as Richard was back in his car, he called the star-rated restaurant, whose number he had on speed-dial. "Hello Sonya, this is Richard Stanton. I was wondering if you had a table for me this week. My friend Ron, for a change, needs to return to the living, and I have promised him dinner at your place. Can you help me to cheer him up a bit?"

"Of course, Dr. Stanton. We're fully booked for the next few weeks, but I am sure that I can arrange something for you. Which day did you have in mind?"

Richard could hear in the background that Sonya was working on the computer. "Let me think. Tomorrow doesn't work for me, but you are closed anyway; and, if I remember correctly, you'll be closed also the day after tomorrow. So, how about Wednesday or Thursday?" Again, he could hear her typing on the keyboard.

"That should work, Dr. Stanton. But, please, allow me to double-check with the kitchen first."

Richard understood why Sonya wanted to get her boss's approval. A restaurant of this caliber was a complex, well-organized enterprise and adding tables on short notice wasn't a trivial task.

"No problem, I'll hold." Richard closed his eyes and listened to the music coming through the speakers of his handsfree system until someone was at the other end of the line again. Much to his surprise, it wasn't Sonya but the celebrity chef himself.

"Richard, I heard that you'll grace us with your presence this week, that's wonderful! We have a number of new creations on the menu–real revelations! You'll love them! I can give you a table on Thursday at seven o'clock. Party of two?"

"That sounds fantastic! But most likely it'll be three if that's not a problem."

"Not at all! I'll let you talk with Sonya again to discuss the details. I am looking forward to seeing you on Thursday. Take care!"

Richard was about to start his car when suddenly a man with a black woolen hat, scarf, and sun glasses knocked on the passenger side window.

Despite the disguise, Richard immediately recognized who it was. So, he hadn't been hallucinating–he had been followed!

When the man knocked again, Richard reluctantly opened the window. "What do you want?"

"I was hoping you'd have time for a little chat. I would really like to talk with you," the man said.

"We have nothing to talk about, get lost!"

"My, oh my, where are your manners? We both know that your being here is no accident and that you've visited your pathology buddy for a reason. So, what can you tell me?"

"Nothing! If you want information, contact CPD's public relations department." Richard started the car and was about to take off when the man stuck a photo in his face.

"If you prefer, I can continue following you to get the information. But sooner or later, you'll have to talk with me–you know that!"

Richard took a look at the photo, weighing the options. "You repugnant rat! I knew you played dirty, but even for you this is too low! Alright then! But I am only willing to share information with you under the following conditions." Richard was feeling like beating the shit out of this guy. But he was right: sooner or later they would have to talk to the press.

"What conditions?"

"You stop spying on me, and you don't publish anything without my approval."

"You must be crazy!"

When Richard started to close the window, the man quickly shouted: "Good, good! But you have to promise me that the information is exclusive. I want at least a twenty-four-hour head start."

"You do understand that I can only speak for myself! I have no control over what the department does. But I can give you twenty-four hours if you keep your end of the bargain."

"Then, we've got a deal! I knew all along that we would come to an agreement. Here, you can keep the picture! I have a copy above my bed."

Richard quickly reached over the passenger seat, grabbed the reporter by his scarf, and roughly pulled his head through the window. At the same time, he pushed the power switch until his head was jammed between the window and the door frame.

"Are you out of your mind? Let me loose, that hurts!"

Richard closed the window a bit more. "I want this to be clear: that's the only warning you're going to get. You comply, or you'll wish you never had met me!"

"Okay, okay! No reason to go mental, I was only joking!"

"You better believe me. I don't like this kind of joke! Now, get in!"

Richard picked up the photo from the passenger seat and put it in his coat pocket. It showed Stephanie and himself in the lobby of his apartment building. They had just stepped into the elevator and were waiting for the doors to close. While Richard was seen in profile, the picture showed Stephanie from the front–her jacket wide open and her breasts clearly visible.

2:06 p.m.

"How did this scoundrel know that you're working on the case in the first place?" Chief Miller took off his glasses and scratched his bald head.

"Pure chance. He must have seen me as I arrived at the burnt-out factory and just put two and two together. Then he just followed me to make sure. You have to give it to him: he's no fool!" Richard said.

"That's for sure. We only have to make certain that not too much leaks out. The longer you can stall him the better. I have already talked with the Mayor's Office. He is truly concerned that the rest of the pack also gets wind of this. If we start seeing headlines like 'Serial Killer in Chicago' on the tabloids' front pages, heads are gonna roll. Maybe even mine."

Richard had never envied Bob his job. Pushing papers day in and day out was boring enough. But what he really couldn't stand was the fact that constantly some power-hungry politicians, whose only goal it was to become re-elected, meddled in police investigations.

"I only told him that you asked my advice because two people died under similar circumstances in apartment fires within a few weeks. I haven't mentioned leather restraints or severed extremities and certainly not the last victim," Richard said.

Bob gave him a skeptical look. "And you believe that he bought that?"

Richard shrugged. "I thought I was pretty convincing. Besides, I told him that the fires were most likely caused by faulty wiring. But one thing is clear: sooner or later I'll have to tell him more. We know that McLean doesn't give up this easily."

Forrester McLean had been causing the department major headaches for a long time. More than once, the freelance journalist

81

had used unscrupulous, wrongful methods to obtain confidential information and gain access to classified documents, whose untimely publication had jeopardized a number of investigations. One time, he had–masked with a beard and turban–passed himself off as a janitor and had made copies of files that hadn't been locked up. Another time, he had managed to smuggle a bug hidden in a pizza box into a conference room. Never ever had there been sufficient substantive evidence for his prosecution.

"You decide what you wanna tell him! If the plan goes awry, I can still blame you. Unlike me, you can afford to lose this job."

****

"Here you can see how, at 6:27 a.m., the woman gets into the elevator on the twenty-first floor. Unfortunately, it was pretty crowded, and the other people partially block the view so we can't be sure that it is the woman from the bar. The sun glasses and the hat don't make it any easier. A little later, she was video-taped in the lobby, but only from behind."

Richard stared at the computer monitor. "Did any other unaccompanied women use the elevator around that time?"

Steven shook his head. "None that would have looked even half as good as our Queen of the Night."

"And you haven't found any videos of Thomas Maddock?"

"No. He hasn't surfaced again."

"I believe we are on the right track. We just have to prove somehow that the deceased is indeed Maddock."

Richard looked out the window and tried to figure out how they could amp up the investigation. The way he saw it, it could very well be that they wouldn't have to wait long for more victims to turn up.

"I may have an idea." Liz took the mouse out of Steven's hand and went back to the picture in which the woman stepped into the elevator. "You see what I'm seeing?"

Richard and Steven moved even closer to the screen.

82

"Sorry, but I can't say for sure that it's the same woman. I have looked at the picture a dozen times–I still can't say for sure that it's her." Steven sounded quite annoyed.

"Just look!" Liz scrolled down a bit and activated the zoom function.

"Liz, you're a genius! Do you have Mrs. Maddock's phone number?" Richard got his cell out of his pocket.

"Here, use mine, the number is programmed in!" Liz pushed a few buttons on her phone and handed it to Richard.

It rang twice and a concerned sounding woman answered: "Hello?"

Richard bit his lower lip. "Mrs. Maddock? This is Richard Stanton from the Chicago Police. You already talked with my colleague, Detective Chen, earlier today. Sorry for bothering you again."

"Do you need anything else? I already gave Tom's toothbrush to someone from the Boston Police. You know, when he is on a business trip, he always has one of these little travel toothbrushes with him." She had a warm, pleasant voice.

"No, that's not why I'm calling."

"Have you found him?" There was both hope and fear in her tone.

"Not yet. I was hoping you might give us some additional information." Richard could hear the woman panting.

"What do you want to know?"

"Mrs. Maddock, I was wondering if you'd be able to describe your husband's luggage."

"Yes, of course. I am the one who packs his suitcase. It's a mid-sized carry-on that he doesn't have to check. In addition, he always has his matching attaché case with him, which is made from the same material, brown leather. I gave him the set two years ago for Christmas."

Again, Richard bit his lower lip. He liked the woman. And she had excellent taste–the matching set looked very nice.

8:10 p.m.

Richard couldn't help being a little surprised when he saw where Stephanie lived. He was somewhat familiar with the real estate prices in Chicago and had a pretty good idea what a single-family home here in Lincoln Park was worth–despite the real estate crash.

As was common in this neighborhood, a wrought iron fence with a gate separated the property from the street. There was a boxwood-framed bench in the front yard, which didn't measure more than three hundred square feet. The entrance to the residence, whose stone facade contained neoclassical elements, was not at ground level; one had to climb a few steps to reach the front door.

There were three door bells at the gate, but none of them had a name plate.

Richard had no idea where in the house Stephanie lived and chose to ring the one at the top. Somewhere in the house Big Ben's bells sounded.

After a short while, the door opened and a stunningly beautiful young woman with long, mahogany hair appeared. She was wearing a strapless red chiffon cocktail dress, whose slightly shirred bodice– from the waist down–transitioned into several layers of delicate fabric embellished with dainty chiffon flowers in the same color. The stiletto pumps, which perfectly matched the shade of the short dress, emphasized her already long legs.

For a moment, Richard, mesmerized by what he saw, didn't know where to look or what to say until he finally regained his composure.

"Oh, I'm sorry, I must have rung the wrong bell after all. My name is Richard Stanton, and I have an appointment with Stephanie. She lives here, doesn't she?"

The beauty smiled at him. "Richard, how nice to meet you, come in! I am Consuela. Stephanie is still getting dressed so she asked me to open the door."

The gate opened with a loud buzz.

When Richard reached out to shake her hand, Consuela unexpectedly took a step toward him and kissed him on the cheek. "Why so formal? Stephanie's friends are my friends, too. Come inside, it's getting cold out here!"

A door across from the entrance indicated that there was an apartment on this level, but Consuela led the way up a stylish acrylic glass staircase. On the second floor, a door was propped open, but she continued on all the way up where Stephanie was already waiting for them.

She, too, looked absolutely ravishing. It seemed as if the girls had dressed up deliberately just for the fun of it.

Stephanie was wearing a black sequin mini dress and, like her friend, she was bare-legged. The heels of her black patent leather shoes, however, were even a tad higher than Consuela's.

"Hello, Richard, I'm so glad you're here! I'm sure the two of you already got acquainted. I hope you don't mind that I invited Consuela to join us. I really wanted you guys to get to know each other."

Richard gave her a kiss, took a rose bouquet out of the bag he had brought with him, and handed it to them. "That's a wonderful idea, but it means that you'll have to share this. At least, I brought enough wine."

Stephanie beamed at him. "That's alright, we don't mind sharing. Consuela, if you look after the food, I'll give Richard a quick tour."

Yet again, Consuela gave Richard a kiss–this time on the other cheek. "Thank you for the flowers. Have fun!"

After her friend had disappeared into the apartment, Stephanie pulled Richard toward her and kissed him passionately. "And? What do you think about her? I bet you wouldn't throw her out of your bed, am I right?"

Richard nodded commendatorily. "She is really great! But you could have warned me! If I had known that you are dressed up like that, I'd put on my tux."

Stephanie laughed. "Richard, as usual, you look very handsome; and you are even wearing a shirt and tie with your suit!" She took a step back and–her arms crossed in front of her chest–examined him from head to toe with an approving look. "You may enter!"

****

"My parents bought the house right after they visited me in Chicago for the first time. When they realized how much rent you have to pay just for a run-down studio apartment, they immediately went to a realtor. They rebuffed my objection that I wanted to become independent by simply saying that they wouldn't allow their daughter to live in–and I cite, 'such a pigsty'–and that I could pay them rent as soon as I had a job."

"And, do you do that now?" Richard asked.

"Of course!" Stephanie answered, playing to be offended. After a brief pause, however, she added with an innocent blink: "But not very much."

Richard looked around. He liked the spacious floor plan, the high ceilings, and especially the white wood paneling, which in most rooms was about four feet high but in some covered the whole wall.

"The house is magnificent! I suppose that your parents' firm must be going well."

"You bet! They are very successful and bought this house also as an investment. They have a good nose for this kind of thing; after all, Lincoln Park is pretty hip, and despite the financial crisis, this is

86

one of the few neighborhoods where real estate prices actually went up."

"So, who else lives in the house?"

"My parents have kept the apartment on the first floor for themselves so that they don't have to go to a hotel when they come for a visit. Well, and last year, Consuela moved into the other one."

When Richard saw the impish smile on her face, he had no trouble imagining that she'd got her parents wrapped around her little finger, and that it hadn't been very difficult for her to persuade them to let her friend move in.

"Am I right in assuming that the 'conditions' for Consuela are just as good?"

"Of course!"

They looked at each other and started to laugh heartily.

"Well, you two certainly seem to be in a good mood! Here, let's have a toast!" Consuela was holding a tray with three cocktail glasses, which were filled almost to the brim with a foam-covered, greenish-yellowish liquid.

"Hmm, that looks… interesting. What is it?" Richard asked cautiously.

"Don't worry, that's a Pisco Sour, a Peruvian cocktail. It's made from Pisco, a Peruvian brandy, lime juice, a little sugar, and egg white. I also add a few drops of bitters. ¡Salud!"

They clinked their glasses, and Richard took a sip. "Wow, this is not for the faint of heart!"

Consuela grinned. "I have to admit that I always use a bit more Pisco than what the recipe says. On the other hand, Stephanie suggested that you are a real man so I thought you could take it. But maybe we misjudged you…"

When Consuela looked at Richard with her dark eyes, her gaze was not just tantalizing–it was also seductive.

Richard noticed that Stephanie was curious to see how he would respond.

87

For a moment, he didn't say anything but just looked at them. Finally, he raised his glass: "¡Salud!"

****

Slowly but surely it was getting cold. To avoid alerting the neighbors, Forrester McLean had turned off his car soon after arriving. Without through traffic, a car with the engine running would have attracted too much attention in this cul-de-sac.

The journalist turned up his coat collar and lit a cigarette.

Except for the windows on the top floor, the house was dark. Even the exterior lights only turned on automatically when someone approached the fence. This he had found out earlier when he had tried to sidle up to the house, hoping to get a better glimpse of what was going on in there. But the lit windows were too high up, and in most rooms the curtains were drawn anyway.

He'd wait another fifteen minutes. If nothing happened during that time, he'd leave and have a drink somewhere. Fifteen minutes– that much he owed himself.

How stupid did this arrogant prick think he was? Faulty wiring– he couldn't be fobbed off that easily! Stanton would never waste his time on such chickenshit. Actually, the wannabe playboy didn't have to get his hands dirty at all!

Since he had inherited a fortune, he lived like a bee in clover: he wore tailor-made suits, banged the hottest chicks, and flew to New York to have dinner whenever he wanted.

He didn't have to freeze his butt off in a frigging cold car at minus four degrees. No, the case had to be really interesting! And, Forrester McLean couldn't be intimidated… he wasn't afraid of anything or anyone!

He stubbed out his cigarette in the overflowing ashtray and turned on the police radio. Bored, he flipped through the channels but couldn't find anything that would have intrigued him. Mostly, it was about the typical 10-50s, common accidents. He wouldn't be distracted with this stuff even if there were casualties. He was the man for the biggies!

Impatiently, he grabbed the binoculars and looked up to the windows again.

Nothing! Probably, Stanton was doing it with the blonde cutie at this very moment.

He delved into his glove compartment and got out one of the pictures that showed the girl's boobs particularly well. Shit! Nothing would happen here anyway!

Sullenly, he started his car. Just as he turned onto the main street, a 10-32 was reported. A "Man with gun" could be worth his time. For a moment, he considered driving there.

Fuck it! Tonight, he would get drunk!

****

Consuela took the shrimp out of the pan, drained them briefly on a paper towel, and dished them up on a white porcelain platter garnished with parsley and some slices of lime.

The sweet potato and plantain chips were already on the table.

"Now, take a seat! Starters taste best when they are warm."

Stephanie and Richard, who were looking at family pictures on the fireplace mantel, obeyed and sat down on the leather designer chairs.

Earlier, Consuela had banished them from the kitchen under the pretext of wanting to keep her "family recipes" a secret; in reality, she had just intended to give them some time for themselves.

"So, this is pretty ordinary avocado-salsa. Just as this citrus salsa, it's quite harmless. However, you should be careful with the habañero salsa, it's rather insidious!"

Richard dipped a plantain chip into the red-green paste and took a hearty bite. "But it's not very hot… wait a moment!" Not two seconds later, he gaped and gasped for air.

Hastily, he grabbed his glass and gulped some water.

89

Amused, Consuela shook her head and got a bowel of yogurt from the fridge. "Here, eat a spoonful of this; that should help! Water just makes it worse."

This time, Richard followed her advice and sheepishly answered: "I guess I should listen to you."

At first, Consuela gazed at him with sham commiseration, but then she gave him an enchanting smile.

She raised her wineglass for a toast: "At least, he's a quick learner!"

When the laughter had died down, Richard also raised his glass: "Stephanie, that was a wonderful idea you had. Consuela, I'm really glad that we got a chance to meet... and I'm not just saying this because you probably just saved my life."

Consuela beamed at him. "The pleasure is all mine. You know, over the last few days, Stephanie couldn't stop talking about you. That is, when I actually saw her–which wasn't very often. However, I have to admit that, now that I've met you, I truly understand why she has been raving about you..."

Again, Richard had the impression that Stephanie was curiously waiting to see how he'd react.

Consuela's self-confident and overt nature wasn't just refreshing and disarming–it was also incredibly sexy. And even though he himself didn't yet know what to make of her behavior, Stephanie didn't seem to mind her explicit looks and comments at all. The two had to get along real well... or, perhaps, the whole thing was merely some kind of test.

Richard didn't want to make a mistake and preferred to ignore the comment. Instead, he only smiled. "How long have you known each other?"

The girls thought about it for a moment, then it was Stephanie who answered: "About five years, right?"

Consuela nodded affirmatively and took another coconut-shrimp. "Yep, you'd just moved to Chicago and wanted to take a samba class with me."

"Samba? Don't tell me you're a dance instructor!"

Again, Stephanie responded: "That's not all! At that time Consuela was still dancing professionally herself, and she only taught to earn a little extra on the side. But now she owns her own studio!"

Richard remembered admiring Consuela's legs when she was leading the way up the stairs earlier, and yes, she had the legs of a dancer!

"It wouldn't surprise me if people beat a path to your door. I would have loved to have an instructor like you! I still remember good old Ms. Jackson, my dance teacher." Richard pursed his lips and raised his eyebrows.

The girls laughed.

"I have no reason to complain. Most classes are full, and I am thinking about expanding."

Consuela was obviously proud of her accomplishments. "But I could never have done it without Stephanie's parents. They gave me a loan and made the whole thing possible."

Richard nodded appreciatively. "Stephanie has already indicated that her parents have a good nose for business. Maybe I can also take a class with you one of these days."

Once again, Consuela gazed at him with her seductive eyes. "I also give private lessons–if you are interested!"

"Why don't we start right now?" Stephanie suggested enthusiastically. "I thought we might dance later anyway, but since the roast needs another fifteen minutes or so, there is no reason why we shouldn't shake a leg now!"

She got up, went to the stereo cabinet, and tapped on an iPod, which was connected to a hi-fi system. Loud sounds of drums, rattles, and bells in the samba-typical 2/4 time signature came through the speakers.

At once, Stephanie started to swing her hips and move her abdomen lissomly back and forth.

Then, Consuela also got out of her chair, reaching for Richard. "Come on, show us what you've got!"

Richard liked to dance, but he wasn't particularly good at samba. Nevertheless, he took off his jacket and tie and tried awkwardly to adjust his movements to the rhythm of the music.

The girls jovially danced around him and giggled.

"Of course, I'm no match for you professionals. Maybe we should dance something else," Richard suggested.

"Don't throw in the sponge so easily! Look!" Consuela took Richard by the hand and positioned herself next to him.

"The easiest way to get into it is to first lift only your heels. Twice right, twice left–don't set down your heel in between; it's kind of a double-bounce. However, don't jump; you compensate the movement largely with your hip! Like this, see?"

She was now facing Richard, demonstrating the supposedly easy exercise once more. Her motions were supple and seemingly effortless, and in spite of the dynamic swinging of her hips, her upper body was practically steady.

He tried it again.

"That looks pretty good, you're a natural! Now pay attention, I'm going to show the complete sequence!" She lifted and set down her feet very slowly until she was sure that he had got it. "Excellent, now we do the whole thing in the rhythm of the music!"

Richard tried hard to set his steps right despite the much faster tempo, but Consuela wasn't quite satisfied. "As I said before, you're a quick learner… but your hip swing needs to improve. Stephanie, why don't you show him how it's done!"

Standing close to him, Stephanie took his hands and placed them on her hips. But just when Richard thought that he finally might get a hang of the movements, the kitchen timer went off.

"Okay, guys, dinner is ready! Let's continue later!" Consuela called them and turned down the music.

9:17 p.m.

"And, is he positive?"

"Lady, how should I know? You should be happy that I even called you!"

"Sure, sure. Thanks a lot. So, let's start from the beginning again: he thinks that he remembers them, but he doesn't want to speak with us directly?"

"Yes, you could say that."

"Did he give any reasons?"

"You really that dense or just inexperienced?"

"Now, cut it out! I am a detective with the Chicago Police Department and I can do without your offensive comments. If you prefer, you can come to the station to make a statement."

"Alright, alright, I'm sorry. He probably has his reasons…"

"Doesn't he have a visa?"

"What gives you this idea all of a sudden?"

"Stop fucking around with me! Is he in the country illegally?"

"I don't know, maybe! I don't hire these guys. You should ask my boss!"

"Whatever, tell the man that we are not with Immigration Services and that it might be to his advantage to cooperate with us!"

"Okay, I'll tell him."

"Do that! And if I don't hear back from him by ten o'clock tomorrow morning at the latest, I will have you arrested for obstruction of justice. Understood? Are we clear?"

"Yeah, yeah, cool it! I want to help. Why do you think I called you in the first place?"

"Ten o'clock, or I'll send two officers to pick you up!"

As soon as Liz had hung up the receiver of her office phone, she got her cell out of her bag and called Richard's number.

It rang four times before the mailbox picked up.

"Richard, it's Liz. I just talked with a taxi-dispatcher, who said that one of their drivers may have taken a man and a woman to the former factory Thursday night. I believe that the cabby didn't come himself because he's an illegal alien. But that shouldn't be a problem. I put a bit of pressure on the dispatcher, and I am sure that he'll convince the driver to come forward. Otherwise, no news! See you tomorrow. Good night!"

****

"The food is excellent! Is it a Cuban recipe?" With great relish, Richard put another piece of the succulent meat in his mouth.

"Not quite. That's Pernil de Cerdo al Horno, prepared according to my Puerto Rican grandmother's recipe. The Cuban version is similar. I'm glad you like it!" Consuela carved another slice from the roast pork that emitted a delicious smell of herbs and put it on Richard's plate.

"That means that your family is from Borinquen?"

With big eyes, Consuela first looked at Richard and then at Stephanie. "Me has dejado pasmado... ¿Hablas español?"

Richard shook his head. "Unfortunately, I don't. My Spanish is pretty rusty–what did you say?"

"That I'm speechless. After all, I haven't met many people here that know the Taíno-name for my homeland."

Stephanie gave Richard a kiss on the cheek and beamed at Consuela. "Haven't I told you that he's irresistible?"

Consuela nodded almost imperceptibly at Richard and took a sip of the red wine. Once again, there was this look; but this time it was even more ardent, more amorous than before. "Irresistible... Sí, lo es. To answer your question: I was born in Puerto Rico. My family moved to Chicago when I was two years old, but we still have

94

relatives there, who we visit sometimes. Have you ever been to Puerto Rico?"

"Yes, I have sailed around the island once and went on a few excursions: San Juan, of course; Ponce; San Germán. What's the name of the rain forest again? El…?"

"El Yunque," Stephanie said triumphant. "Two years ago, we went there when we visited Consuela's grandparents. Consuela, wasn't there something about a god? I can't recall the name, sorry!"

"You probably mean the god of the rainforest, Yuquiyu. The Taíno believed that he ruled the forest from the top of the mountain and watched over them. By the way, my abuela, I mean my granny, still believes this to be true."

"If that's the case, let's have a toast in honor of your grandmother, her culinary skills, and the god of the rainforest!"

10:51 p.m.

"I don't think I can move anymore. The Dulce de Leche Crêpes were incredible but a bit too much." Richard leaned back in his chair and stretched his legs.

"No way, you'll get a little digestif and then we dance!" Stephanie sat down on his lap and held a glass with a brandy-colored liquid right under his nose. "Here, this will do you good!"

Richard took a sip. He was surprised how smooth and well-balanced the high-proof drink was, which was reminiscent of chocolate and coffee. "That's yummy! What is it?"

"It's a twenty-five year old rum from Guatemala." Stephanie took the glass and put it on the table. "That's enough for now, or you really won't be able to dance anymore. Consuela, put on some good music!"

When samba music came through the speakers, Richard exclaimed with despair: "Samba? Again?"

"Come on, don't be a spoilsport! You were doing such a good job before! I promise that we'll put on something else later." Stephanie gave him a kiss, then she whispered into his ear: "Now, we're going to show you how to really dance the Samba!"

Still sitting on his lap, she pulled her short dress all the way up over her hips, and began to naughtily rub herself against Richard's groin, swinging her pelvis in a circular motion.

He was perplexed by how unbridled she behaved in Consuela's presence but blamed the alcohol for it. "If you continue doing what you're doing, I won't be able to dance anyway …"

She got up and lit a few candles while Consuela moved the chairs out of the way.

Richard preferred not to get up quite yet and took another sip from the rum. After the intense lap-dance, any kind of excuse that allowed him to remain seated for a little longer was good enough for him.

Stephanie turned the volume up and looked at him auspiciously.

As if they had agreed in advance on what to do next, both girls now came toward him and pulled him up from his chair.

Despite the fact that the combined living and dining room would have been large enough to accommodate twenty people, the two snuggled closely to him over and over again as they brushed their slim bodies against him.

Richard felt magically intoxicated. Not only the alcohol but also the samba rhythm and the beautiful girls frolicking around him in the candlelight had a dis-inhibiting, exhilarating effect. He surrendered to the music and the seductive atmosphere and didn't find it strange at all when, suddenly, Consuela started to unbutton his shirt.

Meanwhile, Stephanie, who gave him a passionate French kiss, lustfully pushing herself against his left thigh, was gently stroking her girlfriend's neck.

Together, they stripped his dress shirt off his shoulders before also taking off his undershirt.

Richard felt Consuela's hot lips caressing his neck as her fingernails slid down his bare chest.

Without much success, he fumbled with her zipper until Stephanie unexpectedly came to his aid and opened Consuela's dress.

When Richard looked at his girlfriend, she only smiled lovingly.

She took a step back and, standing behind Consuela now, pulled down her dress over her waist. While she passionately ran the tip of her tongue up and down between her shoulder blades, she reached around Consuela, grabbed her breasts, and pulled her red bra just far enough down for her nipples to stick out above the lace-embellished rim.

Stephanie squeezed the stiffening nipples for a moment, then reached for Richard's neck and pulled his head gently onto Consuela's left breast.

He took both the sweet tasting nipple and Stephanie's finger in his mouth and started to suck and nibble on both of them.

Consuela was moaning fervently now and adroitly opened Richard's belt and pants. Her warm hands slid into his boxers, grasped his stiff penis, and massaged it tenderly.

At the same time, Stephanie pulled down her girlfriend's panties and took off her own sequin dress. Then she opened her strapless bandeau bra and huddled against Consuela's naked back.

As she reached with one hand between her girlfriend's legs and slid her middle finger into her, the other hand clasped Richard's manhood.

Meanwhile, Consuela stripped down his pants and boxers, clawed her fingers into his buttocks, and pulled him toward her.

They were all panting hard when Stephanie spread Consuela's labia and gently guided Richard's penis into her vagina.

Richard heaved a sigh when he felt Consuela's warm and moist embrace.

Monday, February 14

8:48 a.m.

"Mr. Akoto, thank you very much for coming forward and making a statement." Liz Chen was convinced that friendliness would be the best course of action with this extremely intimidated man sitting across from her in her office.

"I… no choice!" The man spoke quietly and with an almost incomprehensible accent. He nervously scooted around on his chair, constantly biting his fingernails. From the moment he had taken his seat, he had not looked at her once but had only stared at the floor.

"Mr. Akoto, let me cut to the chase: we have learned from your dispatcher that Thursday night you may have given a man and a woman a ride to one of the new loft buildings in the West Loop. Is that correct?"

Still averting her gaze, the cabby silently nodded.

"Could you please answer my question! Did you make the fare, yes or no?" Liz' tone was much firmer now.

Without taking his fingers out of his mouth, he responded with a drawn-out, guttural "Aah."

"Good, I am going to show you a few pictures, and I would like to know if these are the people." Liz opened the folder that was lying in front of her, took out a photo of Tom Maddock, and handed it to him.

The cabby looked up briefly and nodded.

"Mr. Akoto, are you sure? Is this the man?"

"Aaaaah! Is… man!" he grunted like a tormented animal.

Liz didn't know how to interpret his almost contumacious reaction. Was his anxiety turning into anger, or was there another explanation for this bizarre behavior? Critically, she looked at the picture of misery across from her, huddled up on the chair, gnawing at his hands until they bled. No, the poor guy wasn't unfriendly… he was afraid. Not to agitate him even more, so far, she had refrained from asking to see his ID. But sooner or later she would have to take down his personal data, such were the rules. If it turned out that he was in the country illegally or just didn't have a work permit, he was facing deportation. Of course, he was afraid!

"Mr. Akoto, don't worry! If you help us, I can put in a good word for you with Immigration Services."

For the first time, Joseph Akoto raised his head and looked at her, puzzled.

"Mr. Akoto, don't you understand? I can help you!"

"Nooooo, you not understand! Shaking his head, he rummaged through his jacket and got out an American passport. "Me US-citizen, here legal!"

Liz struggled to hide her astonishment. "Of course, I am sorry! I must have received some false information. Even better, let's come back to the pictures! If you would please take a look at these here: is this the woman who accompanied him?" Liz held up the composite that had been made based on the surveillance videos and the waiter's statement.

Again, he just stared at the floor.

"Mr. Akoto, please look at the picture, it is important!"

Slowly, almost hesitantly, Joseph Akoto raised his head. When he saw the woman in the photo, his expression changed. Where Liz had just seen fear before, she now recognized sheer panic.

Finally, she knew what he was afraid of.

9:13 a.m.

The first thing he saw when he opened his eyes, was naked, golden brown skin. The diffuse light that fell through the drawn curtains immersed the room in shades of soft yellow and ocher. The warm body by his side peacefully expanded and contracted at regular intervals with each breath.

It took Richard a moment to remember where he was.

What a night that had been!

Cautiously, he groped around the sheet behind him, but Stephanie must have gotten up already. Then, he gingerly reached over and gently caressed Consuela's belly.

She appeared to be completely content and relaxed. Richard watched her naval for a while before he started to circle it leisurely with the tips of his fingers.

Irresistible–wasn't that the word she had used?

After what had happened with Monica, he had never thought it possible to find somebody he could feel at home with again.

And now, within only a few days, he had met not just one such person but two.

Richard was suddenly getting hot, and his heart was pounding. Had he made a mistake? What if he had frivolously risked his relationship with Stephanie for just one night of excitement?

He tried to collect his thoughts.

Yes, what a night it had been…

Never in his life would he forget what it felt like when he entered her for the first time. Hot and full of desire, she had taken him in, and nothing in this world seemed to matter but their fondling genitals.

At first, overwhelmed by pure lust, he drove his penis wildly into her lap. But then, her pelvis exacted a gentler pace.

Slowly and with utmost tenderness, her slippery lap pulled away from him until her labia enclosed only his glans.

Just when he thought she would release him, she moved a few inches forward and started to massage the tip of his cock so exquisitely that he soon came.

Consuela, still being caressed by Stephanie, who was standing behind her, happily beamed at Richard and kissed him lovingly. Then, they all sank to the floor.

For a while, they just lay there, embracing each other. But soon, the girls began to cuddle and fondle each other. Richard wasn't prudish at all, and yet, at first, he was a bit surprised to see how candidly they made love to each other. However, it wasn't an unpleasant surprise at all. Rather, he interpreted their forthright demonstration of sexual desire as a significant sign of confidence in him.

Furthermore, it was incredibly sexy to watch their amorous act. It was pure. For Richard, watching these two flawless creatures giving themselves to each other tenderly and passionately was like witnessing a celestial, elysian demonstration of divine eroticism.

By the time Stephanie leaned over her girlfriend and slowly ran her tongue over her neck and breasts down to her lap, Richard was hard again.

"Hello there! It looks like somebody is already wide awake! Good morning to both of you…" Consuela lifted her head a little, gave Richard a kiss, and gently stroked with the back of her hand over his erect penis.

Before he had time to respond, she swung her leg over his pelvis and swiftly sat on top of him. "Happy Valentine's Day!"

****

Somewhere, something was buzzing. Richard opened his eyes and listened. Was he just imagining things? No, there it was again: his phone!

101

Carefully, he pulled out his arm from under Consuela's head and got up.

Again, he heard his phone, but where was it?

Richard followed the sound into the living room. The buzzing came out of his jacket, which was still hanging over one of the chairs. Of course, he had silenced his cell and put it on vibration mode before dinner!

He looked at the display and saw that he had three new messages–and all of them were from Liz, the first one from last night.

He probably hadn't heard the phone because of the loud music. That shouldn't have happened.

Maybe it was better this way. Who knows how the evening would have gone had he answered.

Before even listening to the messages, he immediately called Liz. "Liz, sorry that I didn't get back to you sooner. I just saw that you tried to reach me. What's happened?"

"Don't worry, everything is under control here! I just wanted to let you know that we've had a breakthrough in our investigations," she said proudly.

"Let me guess: Ron sent you the results of the DNA-analysis."

"No, not yet. But I know what they'll say."

When Liz didn't say anything else, Richard knew that she wanted to keep him on tenterhooks, a payback for not being reachable. "Okay then, tell me!"

"You were right, Maddock and the woman really took a cab. I've already talked with the driver."

"And, did he take them to the crime scene?"

"Sure! I told you that you were right, didn't I?"

"Did you get any other useful information from the cabby? Did he notice anything unusual?"

"Regarding her appearance, he merely confirmed what we already knew. The waiter's description and the composite seem to be spot-on. But there's something else: the driver was scared shitless.

102

When I showed him the picture of the woman, I thought he might have a nervous breakdown!"

"Any idea why? Did she threaten him? Or did he perhaps even witness the crime?"

"No, that's what makes it so weird: when I asked him why he was so afraid, he just spouted twaddle, most of it in a foreign language. He's originally from somewhere in sub-Saharan Africa. But one word he repeated over and over: 'Demon'."

****

Demon! If that wasn't the stupidest thing he had heard in a long time. Probably, the crazy coon had just smoked too much weed.

Whatever, one thing was clear: he had to find out who the woman was! First of all, he needed to get a copy of her picture. He was sure that he would come up with something then. Maybe he could tail her and even persuade her to be interviewed–anonymously, of course!

That would be a real smash! The thing might even develop into a series of articles, even before the stupid police knew what was going on.

Forrester McLean could already see the headlines in his mind. The story had unlimited potential. Publishing houses would court him… radio interviews, TV appearances. Finally, he would be where he belonged!

Tonight he'd go to the police headquarters, copy a few files, and plant some additional bugs in the right spots.

He couldn't have asked for a better day. Nobody would work longer than necessary today.

Pleased with himself, he leaned back and listened to the crackling and rustling that was coming through the speakers.

That must have been the fourth piece of chocolate Liz Chen was treating herself to since she had found the box of candy on her desk.

"From a secret admirer," he had signed the heart-shaped card.

10:59 a.m.

Spellbound, Richard looked at the huge LED flat-screen monitor in the conference room. Something in the larger-than-life Identikit picture that silently looked down at him bothered him.

For the last five minutes, he'd been trying to figure out what it was–to no avail. As much as he labored, he couldn't find the answer.

The woman looked even better than the blurry videos had implied. She had a perfectly proportioned, symmetrical face with high cheekbones and full lips. Her forehead was…

"What do you think? Should we inform Mrs. Maddock at this time or not?"

Liz' question suddenly interrupted his thoughts. "Beg your pardon, what did you just say?"

"I just wanted to know if we should inform Mrs. Maddock."

Richard, who needed a moment to get back into reality, took a deep breath before he answered: "Certainly not! As long as we can't unambiguously prove that the victim is her husband, we won't do anything like that. We have to wait for the result of the DNA-analysis!"

Again, he looked back at the picture and, line by line, started to study the contours of the face. The long hair was swept to the side and was flowing over her shoulders in waves ….

When Steven cleared his throat and saved him from blanking out again, Richard resolutely reached for the remote control and turned off the monitor. "Do you have any idea when we might get the results?" He was convinced that the findings would just confirm what they already knew. For him, it had been clear that Tom Maddock was dead the moment he had seen the video of the woman in the elevator. Without a doubt, the suitcases by her side had been his.

Liz shook her head. "The lab merely promised to give our case the highest priority. But nobody can say what that really means. They are up to their eyeballs in work. Have you ever seen how many dead bodies Ron alone has in his coolers? There must be a few hundred bodies in the institute at any given time. I've even seen bagged bodies stacked up outside a cooler…"

"That's none of our business! We are just interested in getting the lab results ASAP. Put some pressure on them and nag them with phone calls! After all, we've been instructed by the higher ups to solve the case quickly." Richard grabbed the Styrofoam cup and took a sip of the brownish-black, lukewarm swill he had gotten from the vending machine before the meeting. That wasn't coffee at all! Peevishly, he threw the cup into the trash.

"Alright, then let's recapitulate what we know: Maddock and the beautiful stranger drink Champagne in the hotel bar. Things are getting steamy and they leave the hotel together. We know all that from the waiter and the surveillance videos." Richard prompted Liz to continue with the summary.

"The two take a cab to go to the loft building in the West Loop. Since there aren't any surveillance cameras in the taxi and they don't use a credit card to pay for the ride, we don't have any hard proof that it was really Maddock and the woman, but we don't have any reason to doubt that either. Akoto is a credible witness. Maybe a bit confused but credible nonetheless."

"Okay. The most important question is: what happened next?" Richard cast Steven an enjoining look.

The detective cleared his throat once again and deliberated for a moment as to how he should respond. "I think I know where you're going with this. Even if the victim is Maddock, it doesn't automatically mean that the woman killed him."

Richard nodded encouragingly.

"I'm sure we all agree that the very same woman was in the bar and in the cab with him, checked out for him the next morning, and left the hotel with his luggage. But… would that be enough for her to get convicted for murder? That's all circumstantial evidence! No prosecutor in the world can convince a jury to find a good-looking, young woman guilty of such an unspeakable crime based only on that!" Expectantly, Steven looked at the others.

"I couldn't agree more," Liz said full of confidence. "Furthermore, we have no idea what motive she might have had to kill him. If you want my opinion, no district attorney will touch this– it's too risky. The woman doesn't need a celebrity defense attorney to be acquitted, any half-decent court-appointed counsel will do."

Richard rubbed his stubbly chin. He hadn't had time to shave this morning. "That's exactly what I think, too. Even if we caught the woman, we couldn't make anything stick at this point. Still, we have to do whatever it takes to find her. Did the database search result in any hits?"

"No, not yet. But I have a few ideas how we could extend the search. The facial recognition software can easily go through data bases of private clubs or social media pages. But we would need a warrant for that…" Liz gave Richard an innocent look.

"I'll talk with Bob. Maybe he can pull some strings. Just promise to wait until we get a go-ahead! Otherwise, we risk that the evidence may not be admissible later at trial. Now, let's come back to the question about a possible motive: any ideas?" Richard leaned back in his chair and looked again at the dark screen, which seemed to hover over Steven's head.

The large, smooth surface possessed an almost irresistible attraction. It felt as if the monitor was just waiting to be turned on again, only to pull Richard inside. Like a black hole that swallowed anything within its gravitational force field, never ever releasing it again.

This time, Liz saved him from reaching for the remote. "Perhaps the woman and Maddock weren't strangers. What if they had had an affair, and he wanted to end it? After all, he was in town quite regularly. We could show Mrs. Maddock a picture of her. Maybe they even know each other." Liz sounded almost euphoric.

Richard raised his hand to mollify his colleagues and redirect the conversation. "Now, slow down! Let's take one step at a time! As long as we don't have the result of the DNA-analysis, we leave the woman alone! That'll be hard enough on her. Just imagine: not only has her husband fallen victim to an unimaginable crime; no, before that he also cheated on her! If, later, he turns out to be alive, we are facing a lawsuit of biblical proportions. And if she doesn't file it, he will for sure! And by the way: aren't we forgetting about the other victims? Did she also have an affair with them? And every single one of them wanted to leave her?" Richard shook his head. "Sorry, but that's a bit absurd!"

"Maybe you're both right," Steven tried to mediate. "If we assume that all murders were committed by the same perpetrator–and I don't think that we have any reason to doubt that–then it's reasonable to assume that the motive is the same in all cases. Yes, perhaps she knew the victims. Does that mean that she had an affair with all of them? No! Maybe there's another link between them!"

Again, Richard rubbed his chin. "Okay. That's certainly a possibility, and it would be foolish not to consider it. As soon as we know for sure that the victim is Maddock, you may contact his wife and start digging up dirt from his past. Nevertheless, I want to remind you that no one in the hotel could remember ever having seen Maddock and the woman together before."

"That's certainly true. If I'm not mistaken, the waiter even said that he didn't have the impression that the two had known each other for long." Steven went through his files, pulled out a copy of the interrogation records, and started reading: "They didn't waste any time. Less than ten minutes after they met, she had her feet in his lap…" Steven showed them the copy. "Tell me! How do you interpret that?"

Without addressing his question, Richard grabbed the remote again and turned the monitor on.

Liz and Steven were puzzled when he leaned back, interlocked his hands behind his head, and stared at the screen for several minutes without uttering a single word.

At last, he calmly said: "I can't help it, but this is one thankless case!"

Even though Richard's comment may not have sounded very optimistic, he didn't mean to be fatalistic. It was true: the perp hadn't left much evidence and convicting him or her wouldn't be easy. But this was what made the case interesting in the first place.

Yet, there was another reason why Richard felt some satisfaction right now: finally, he knew what had bothered him before.

Unflinchingly, he looked at the monitor on the wall. He had seen countless composites in his career. What they all had had in common was that the faces were lifeless and the eyes inanimate.

However, this time it was different: he felt like he was being watched.

****

"I'll get the warrant, don't worry! My first stop will be Judge Kuebler. He is up for re-election and could use some good press. If we catch the perp with his help, he'll gladly exploit it in his campaign. Are you sure that the woman is also responsible for the other murders?" Chief Miller stroked his bald head and put the copy of the composite on the desk.

"You wanna know if we're sure? No, of course not! The only thing the murders have in common is the modus operandi: all the victims are males; they were all mutilated; and the killer made sure to destroy all evidence he or she may have left by torching the crime scene." Richard looked directly in Bob's eyes and said: "But let's be honest here: if this were a straightforward case, you wouldn't have brought me in."

Chief Miller took off his heavy horn-rimmed glasses and nodded with resignation. "Okay, if you think it's the woman, I'll get

108

you the warrant. But in the meantime, do you have any clues yet regarding the latest victim?"

Richard shook his head. "Bob, you have to give us time! We haven't received any DNA-analyses. The victims are all disfigured beyond recognition. This is a real tricky case! To tell you the truth, I'm surprised that we already have a lead."

"This doesn't sound very optimistic to me. What the heck shall I tell the Mayor's Office? They are getting a bit nervous over there."

Richard looked at Bob with disbelief. "You can't be serious! You know exactly how I feel about this office. If you like, you can give them this message from me!" Richard showed him the finger.

Bob raised his hands apologetically. "I didn't mean it that way. I just want to know how you assess the situation."

"You want my earnest opinion? I think we are going to find many more mutilated and burnt bodies before we catch the killer."

4:36 p.m.

Gently, with the back of her hand, she stroked over the gauzy straps which–zigzagging in a trellis-like pattern–linked the lace-trimmed half-cup bra with the mini thong.

The luxurious French teddy wasn't cheap. On the other hand, the precious and delicate fabric had been skillfully crafted into a true masterpiece of erotic lingerie. Not only the fact that the top merely served to push up the bare breasts and put them on display but also the absence of any fabric that may have connected the two ribbons, located on either side of the pubic mound, made clear that this black piece of clothing was not at all intended to cover anything; on the contrary, its sole purpose was to raise the wearer's sexual appeal to the level of absolute irresistibility.

Perfect! This was exactly what she was looking for. After all, it was Valentine's Day, and she was planning on being especially alluring today.

She would never have expected to find a sumptuous piece like this in such a backstreet store.

Just as she was about to take another look at the little white price tag, she heard a voice behind her: "Beautiful, isn't it?"

Startled, she turned around, realizing only now that the handsome young salesman, who had greeted her so friendly when she had entered the store, was standing so close.

"Oh, I'm sorry! I didn't mean to scare you," he said in a concerned voice. "I just wanted to ask if you need any help. Would you like to try this on? It's really sexy! This should be the right size, but if the front part is too long, it doesn't look quite right, if you know what I mean. I always recommend trying on the merchandise before purchasing it. Underwear can't be returned, you know."

When he saw her checking out the price tag, he quickly added: "We can certainly talk about the price. Our typical customers aren't willing to pay that kind of money. They don't come here to acquire Parisian couture lingerie. In fact, let me tell you a secret: our bestseller is the chambermaid-costume for twenty-four ninety-nine. What can I say? My lady boss wanted to test whether we can also sell higher-quality products, which have a much higher profit margin. I guess that didn't work out…"

She returned his smile and simply asked: "Which means?"

"Well, if you don't tell anybody, I can give you a sixty percent discount."

He quickly looked around the store crammed with merchandise. "Lady Boss wants to get rid of these things, but if she finds out that I didn't even try to negotiate a better deal, she's going to fire me."

"I understand. Don't worry, I won't tell anyone. For this price, I am at least willing to try it on. Maybe it doesn't even suit me." She took the hanger from the clothes rack and held the teddy up in front of her body.

"Oh, I'm sure it does! But as I said before, the length has to be right. The fitting room is over there in the back. Make yourself at home! If you need anything, just holler! And by the way, feel free to take your clothes off. You're the first customer that has actually tried this thing on, and if you leave your underwear on, you'll never be able to tell if it fits or not! I'll be in the front, stocking shelves."

She placed the teddy over her arm and squeezed past rows of garment racks toward the back of the store.

While in the front less "objectionable" items like stockings, lingerie, and dildos were on display, the products back here were obviously aimed at a particularly licentious clientele.

Suspended from the ceiling were leather masks, whips, and various metallic tools like spreaders, hooks, and pliers, which bore an undeniable resemblance to surgical instruments.

And sure enough, in a glass cabinet along the wall next to some old-fashioned straight razors, there was a selection of differently shaped scalpels made from cold, shiny stainless steel.

Yet, by far, the most distinctive "product" here was a cubic metal cage that had an edge length of about eight feet and was sitting right in the middle of the room. Both on the in- and the outside, manacles and collars were dangling from O-rings, attached at various heights.

The secret pleasures people engaged in…

With a chuckle, she pulled back the red velvet curtains and stepped into the surprisingly roomy fitting room, whose entire back wall was covered with a mirror. Carefully, she put the feather-light teddy on the chair, which was upholstered with the same velvet fabric, and drew the curtains behind her.

****

As soon as the woman was out of sight, Kenneth Collins hurried on fleet feet to the store entrance door, quietly locked it, and turned around the sign that was attached to the glass panel; instead of the capitalized "OPEN," it now showed a friendly-noncommittal "Sorry, we're closed."

Since the store didn't have regular opening hours anyway, no one would wonder why the business was closed at this time of day.

Back behind the counter, he slithered through the colorful PVC stripped curtain and entered the dark hallway, which on one side led to the storeroom and the office but on the other side led to a small chamber. The back wall of this room was covered with the same kind of heavy velvet curtain that had also been used in the fitting room.

Kenneth turned on the camera, which was mounted on a tripod, slowly opened the curtain, and looked with wide eyes through the window behind it.

The blonde was unbuttoning her knitted dark-gray dress. Her coat was hanging over the

armrest of the chair and her boots were standing side by side at the wall.

He could hardly believe his luck. All his previous videos had been reasonably successful and had earned him good money. For a movie with such a leading actress, however, he could easily raise the price many times over. His customers would pay almost anything to get a copy.

Lecherously, he licked his lips with his pierced tongue. With each button she opened and with every little bit of naked skin she revealed in the process, his arousal increased.

She was standing right in front of him–less than a yard away.

He watched as her dress split apart and slid to the floor. She was just wearing an intricately embroidered white bra with matching panties and gray stockings.

Kenneth was surprised that she wasn't wearing tights–he didn't see wool hold-ups very often. The delicately ribbed material accentuated her surprisingly long slim legs, and the black floral lace top made the unusual stockings extremely sexy. With a critical look,

112

the woman examined her image in the mirror, then reached behind her back, and opened her bra.

Kenneth didn't dare to breathe when he saw her naked breasts. She was something very special, maybe even a model. He would never get such an opportunity again and had to be particularly careful not to screw up the shots. This woman could make him rich.

When the blonde gracefully got out of her panties and he saw her clean-shaved pubic region, he grabbed his stiff cock and started to rub it fiercely. If he jerked off now, he'd last much longer later in front of the camera.

What a woman… Wearing only her stockings, she turned a bit to the left and then to the right, always scrutinizing herself in the mirror.

Or maybe not? Somehow, he got the feeling that she was looking right through the mirror and into his eyes. And, although he knew that this wasn't possible, the mere idea made him very uncomfortable.

Just as his penis was about to get limp, the woman turned away, took the teddy from the chair, spread the ribbons of the bottom part, and stepped into it. Skillfully, she tugged the thong in position, then pulled the top over her flat belly, and hooked the closure of the bra. Only then did she make sure that her breasts were positioned comfortably and precisely in the half-cups.

It was obvious from her smooth movements that she had a lot of experience with this type of clothing.

He'd been right: these "designer duds" looked extraordinarily good on her.

But, clearly, even in rags this woman would have looked fabulous.

He quickly pulled a Kleenex out of the box next to him and ejaculated into it.

It was time. He had to rush now to get to her before she got dressed again.

113

With difficulty, he put his semi-erect penis back in his pants, pulled the mask over his head, and took the Taser from the shelf.

****

The attack came without a warning, giving her no chance to defend herself. She was about to open the top of the teddy when a gun-like instrument shot through the curtains, right toward her. Before she had time to react, she felt such tremendous pain in her back she thought she had been struck by lightning. Then she passed out.

5:01 p.m.

Slowly but surely, Richard was getting worried. This was the fourth time he was trying to call Stephanie's cell but, once again, just got her mailbox. That wasn't like her at all! Usually, she answered her phone after no more than three rings. Something was wrong.

He considered giving Consuela a call. Maybe she knew where Stephanie was.

For whatever reason, though, he hesitated to dial her number.

It occurred to him that he probably had a guilty conscience. After all, he was planning on spending a romantic evening with Stephanie although he had slept with Consuela as recently as this morning.

Regardless of his concern, he called Consuela anyway. The phone rang twice before Consuela answered with a brief "¿Sí?"

"Hello Consuela, its Richard."

"Richard, how nice of you to call! How are you? I hope you had time to rest a little today! At any rate, none of us got a lot of sleep last night." She sounded so cheerful and congenial that Richard didn't know whether to feel better or worse.

After a short pause, all he could get out was: "No, not really."

"I was so sorry that you had to leave so soon this morning–it was sooo nice…"

When he responded with a monosyllabic "Yeah, for me, too," she seemed to sense that something was bothering him.

"Richard, what's the matter? Did something happen?" She sounded concerned.

"No. I just don't know what's going to happen with the three of us, and that troubles me a little." He didn't want to play games with her. He felt he needed to be honest.

"Richard, you're sweet! Don't worry! I know that you and Stephanie are an item and that it's not just a short-lived fling. I don't want to get between you–well, except in situations like last night… But seriously, we both like you a lot, and we all get along so well that we don't need to be jealous of each other. We'll figure this out! For now, I'd suggest that the two of you spend a wonderful evening together, and next time the three of us meet, we talk it over–openly and honestly.

He shook his head in disbelief. "That sounds too good to be true. Are you certain?"

"Absolutely! But you must promise me one thing: if this is supposed to work out, we have to be truthful with each other. Alright?"

"I promise!" Richard, relieved, was glad that they had been able to discuss the situation so candidly. "Listen, why don't you just join us tonight?"

"Hmm, that's surely a tempting offer, but I think you guys should have the evening for yourselves. After all, it's Valentine's Day! And besides…"

"You have other plans?" Richard felt a sinking feeling and hoped she'd say no.

"Well, since you asked: one of my students invited me to have dinner with him."

115

"And?" Richard asked with more concern in his voice than he had intended.

Consuela laughed. "What 'and'? Are you jealous?" The way she said it implied that she might even like the idea.

"To be honest–I think I am. Maybe this sounds crazy: I don't mind sharing you with Stephanie, but with another man…? Sorry, but I'd have a real problem with that! Does this make any sense?"

When Consuela finally answered, her voice was tender and empathetic. "I'd be sad if it wasn't like this. It's so romantic and old-fashioned. I like that. But you can relax, I already cancelled this afternoon. Instead of having dinner in a fancy restaurant and being seduced by a gorgeous man, I'll spend a quiet evening at home watching a movie, maybe a real tearjerker like 'Out of Africa,' and go to bed early. Maybe I'll see you when you pick up Stephanie. By the way, what time are you meeting her? She's still out shopping."

****

When she regained consciousness, the first thing she felt was an unpleasant burning sensation in her back. She turned to the side and decided to go back to sleep again. She'd surely feel much better in the morning.

It took a while until she realized that she was feeling cold.

No way she'd be able to fall asleep like this. Where the heck was her blanket?

Searching, she groped around her surroundings. The surface she was lying on was hard and cold. Where was she? This didn't feel like her bed! She tried to open her eyes.

The massive surge of adrenaline, which suddenly flooded her body, brutally pulled her out of her dizziness, making her wide awake and alert at once.

How had she come here? How long had she been lying on the floor already?

She forced herself to remain calm and resisted the urge to get up. It was of utmost importance to keep a cool head!

116

First, she had to assess her situation: her arms and legs were stiff from the cold but functional. Carefully, she stretched and bent, one by one, her fingers and toes before she moved her hands and feet back and forth a little to check if she might be cuffed. No, it didn't appear as if her mobility was restricted–barring the fact that she was in a cage.

****

"You mean she's not home?" Richard felt the onset of a panic attack creeping through his body. "We'd agreed that I would pick her up at seven thirty and I can't reach her!" he said with a little anxiety in his voice.

Consuela tried to calm him down. "Don't worry! My guess is that she's still somewhere in a department store where she doesn't have reception. And by the way: Stephanie's a big girl–she can take care of herself."

****

After he had positioned the camera in front of the cage, he fetched the aluminum case with his tools from the office and closed the curtains to the front part of the store. He didn't want to be disturbed.

He could hardly wait to make delicate, small incisions in her skin and to pull it off her flawless body stripe by stripe.

Maybe he'd start with her thighs this time… or better yet, with her breasts?

His customers wouldn't care one way or the other; they didn't appreciate his ingenuity anyway. They just wanted to get turned on by and jerk off to the torment of a beautiful woman.

Kenneth Collins, however, wanted to create something for eternity.

Surely, he was way ahead of his time, and the bigoted society he, unfortunately, had been born into, didn't get his art.

It didn't matter. His motherfucker-customers paid a whole lot of money for his movies.

117

When he looked in the cage to make sure that he hadn't forgotten something, he realized that he hadn't covered the floor with a drop cloth.

Damn, how could that have happened? The sheeting was supposed to catch her blood and pee. He couldn't risk leaving dubious stains in the middle of the store!

Slightly annoyed, he ran back to the office to get the box with the heavy-duty painter's plastic. After all, he already had knives and scissors in his tool case that he could use to cut it to length.

However, when he returned and saw her lying on the floor, he comprehended that his original idea, namely, to work on her in the cage, would create unforeseen difficulties: it was virtually impossible to spread out the sheeting as long as she was in there. There was simply not enough room in the cage! On the other hand, he really didn't want to drag her out of there, put the cloth in place, and carry her back in. That would be much too exhausting and time-consuming.

Therefore, he decided to spread out the sheeting in front of the cage, bring her out, and tie her to the rings that were attached to the outside. If he pointed the two spotlights directly at her but left the rest of the room dark, the visual effect would be rather appealing. In addition, the whole setting wouldn't be quite as claustrophobic as in the cage. Besides, he had already gotten some good shots of her behind bars.

With a thrill of anticipation, he smoothed down the drop cloth and got the spotlights and the camera into position. Everything was perfect! Gratified, he lowered his head and closed his eyes. Just for a moment, he wanted to take in the peaceful silence, which soon would yield to her fearful pleading and her agonized mourning.

The sweet scent of roses emanating from her body was slowly giving way to the overpowering smell of the plastic sheeting. He took two deep breaths before he kneeled down, solemnly opened his tool case, and lovingly stroked the handles of his stainless-steel instruments. Now, the show would begin.

118

Consuela's words had given Richard some comfort. He couldn't afford to lose his head and automatically expect the worst to happen just because someone he was close to couldn't be reached for a few hours... However, it wasn't that simple.

It had all started with his parents' deaths and had become unbearable after Monica's accident. At the time, his shrink had told him that it was a common posttraumatic reaction to fear the loss of a loved-one. He just needed to consciously "rationalize" his anxiety. What a wonderful term! For all those years, he had been at peace. But at what cost? Why had he never allowed himself to fall in love again? Was it really true that he just hadn't met the right woman? Richard could hardly remember their names–there had been so many. But their faces he could still see in his mind's eye. Admittedly, he had never given them a chance to get close to him. He had always fought off any temptation to fall in love... until now. This time, he was sensing that the battle was over–and the fear had returned.

Lost in his thoughts, he stared at his cell. A push of a button, and his phone would call Stephanie's number yet again. But he simply couldn't get Consuela's voice out of his head: "Stephanie is a big girl." That was certainly true.

With a heavy heart he put his cell away and started the car.

****

Kenneth grabbed the remote control and turned the CD-player on. Through the ceiling speakers, the first guitar-riffs of David Bowies' version of "Wild is the wind" penetrated the silence.

He switched on the camera and went around the cage.

Slowly, he put the key into the padlock and pulled back the heavy locking bolt.

The moment Bowie began to sing, he opened the door and entered the cage.

His hands on his hips, he looked through the cage bars–right into the camera.

In a moment, the guitar would change back from E7 to A minor. The timing was perfect.

At the end of the verse, he would lean down, grab her underneath her shoulders, and pull her out of the cage.

Just as Bowie started to sing again and Kenneth was about to grab the woman, she brought up her arm with lightning speed and delivered a powerful knifehand strike to his Adam's apple. If the leather mask hadn't blocked the punch a bit, the well-aimed blow would have crushed his windpipe, and he would have been dead by now.

Paralyzed with surprise, he watched as she leaped like a cat into a squat and threw a straight right toward his groin.

Instinctively, Kenneth blocked the punch with his leg, snatched her long blond hair, and yanked it with brutal force to the side. If this didn't break her neck, it would at least incapacitate her long enough for him to knock her out with a fist-blow.

The power of his motion made him lose his balance and he tumbled sideways into the cage wall. Incredulously, he looked at the blond shock of hair in his hand while the woman gracefully dove away from him and jumped up.

He had just enough time to realize that he had pulled a wig off her head before her elbow hit the side of his throat.

****

Richard hadn't driven two blocks when his phone rang. The display showed Consuela's number.

He didn't turn on his handsfree system but turned right into an alley and grabbed his cell. "Have you heard from Stephanie?"

After a short moment of silence, it wasn't Consuela but Stephanie herself who answered: "Richard, it's me! Consuela told me that you're worried. I'm so sorry! I wanted to call you, but I must have left my phone at McCormick Place. I was shopping, and I completely forgot the time."

120

Richard could physically feel the relief spreading throughout his body and his muscles relax. "It doesn't matter, I'm just glad you're alright! Do you think you have enough time to get ready, or would it be better if I picked you up a little later?"

"No, I've got more than enough time, thank you. However, I wanted to ask you something: listen, what would you say if Consuela accompanied us tonight?"

Richard smiled to himself. "Do you think that's a good idea?"

"Don't you?" she answered baffled. Her response made it unmistakably clear how important it was to her to include Consuela in their relationship.

He certainly didn't have a problem with that. "I think that's an excellent idea! To be honest, I've already asked her, but she declined. Do you think you can persuade her to come?"

"I've already done that! Just now, she's in the bathroom, getting ready. And, by the way: you better dress up if you wanna keep up with us!"

7:41 p.m.

Seeing Consuela and Stephanie descending the stairs side by side took Richard's breath away– they looked incredible!

Under their capes, they were both wearing long evening gowns, whose bottoms they had to lift a bit to prevent the hems from trailing along the ground. Their smiling faces radiated so much happiness and joie de vivre that Richard abandoned his doubts about the veracity of the developing ménage à trois. For the moment, he was just feeling very happy that he had had the good fortune to meet the two.

He handed each of them a long-stemmed red rose and was awarded by both with a kiss on the cheek–one left, the other right.

"You're looking fabulous! Consuela, I'm so glad that you changed your mind and decided to join us."

Consuela sized him up from head to toe and gently stroked over the silk lapels of his tux. "Who could say no to this?" When she saw Edgar waiting at the limousine with Champagne glasses on a tray, she shook her head amused. "And besides–I must have seen 'Out of Africa' at least ten times already."

****

It took them less than ten minutes to arrive at Navy Pier.

Since its opening in 1916, the over three-thousand-foot-long wharf had not only been used as a working and pleasure pier but at times had also served as an entertainment center, naval base, or even university campus.

With the construction of a Ferris wheel, a convention center, and a shopping mall with theaters in the 1990s, it finally had become Chicago's most important tourist attraction.

Stephanie was still surprised to see so many cabs and limos lined up to drop off their passengers at the pier. "What's going on here? I don't think there are enough restaurants here to accommodate all those people, and the theater is closed on Mondays, isn't it?"

"Maybe they are offering special tours through the Children's Museum," Consuela joked, well aware that the Chicago's Children Museum attracted more than half a million visitors to Navy Pier every year.

"No, I don't think so. The people are here for another reason. You'll see!" Richard had no intention to reveal his surprise yet. When they had finally advanced to the drop-off bay, Edgar opened the door for them and wished them a pleasant evening.

Hundreds of elegantly dressed people moved toward the landing on the south side of the quay, where a number of brightly illuminated cruising ships were moored.

"A dinner cruise? I thought they run only during the summer… I always wanted to do this kind of thing, great!" Stephanie excitedly pulled Richard's hand.

"Do you think we'll get a window table? I've heard that from the lake you have a beautiful view of the skyline." Consuela turned around for a moment and looked in the direction of the city. Even from the pier, one had a magnificent view of the skyscrapers looming in the night sky.

"I wouldn't worry about that!" Richard answered mysteriously.

The farther he led the girls out onto the pier the lonelier it got around them. All other people had found their ships by now and had gone aboard. Richard, however, hadn't shown any interest in taking any of the gangplanks so far.

Just as Stephanie was wondering if she had celebrated too soon, she saw someone waving at them from the last landing place.

A captain was standing with two crew members in front of a sleek white motor yacht and waited with a wide grin on his face to welcome them aboard.

The amicable way in which Richard greeted the crew left no doubt that they were all old friends here.

"Stephanie, Consuela, may I introduce Andrew Kendrick, the captain of this splendid ship and a good friend of mine. Andrew will show us a different side of the city tonight."

"It's a pleasure to meet you! Usually, we don't make this kind of trip in the winter, but Richard was so persistent. Now I know why…" Andrew looked at Consuela and Stephanie with admiration and gave Richard a cheeky wink. "Fortunately, the weather has been on our side so that we don't have to be afraid of colliding with ice floes."

Andrew himself led the three to the main salon on the upper deck, where three waiters were waiting for them with cocktails and canapés. In the center of the room, directly under an enormous moon roof, there was a beautifully set single table.

123

A jazz combo was playing "My one and only love." The quartet was comprised of a trumpet player, a percussionist, a pianist, and a bassist.

"Don't tell me we're the only guests!" Consuela remarked with surprise.

Stephanie, who stood next to her with tears in her eyes, laid her arm around her shoulders and pulled her toward her. "Didn't I tell you that you should join us?"

As one of the waiters helped the girls out of their capes, Richard enjoyed the opportunity to admire their elegant evening gowns.

Stephanie was wearing a strapless black chiffon dress with a slightly ruffled top, which smoothly hugged her body. Between the left thigh and the right knee there was a diagonal inset of full-length tulle, which extended to the floor, giving the dress a wonderful lightness.

Consuela's golden, pearl-embroidered bodice culminated in a frilled skirt, which wrapped around her legs several times and ended in a train.

From a window on the port side, they watched as the moorings were released and they slowly cruised away from the quay.

Soon after, they gained speed, leaving Navy Pier behind. Silently, they marveled at the breathtaking view of the skyline.

On the southern edge of downtown, Sears Tower, which had only recently been rechristened Willis Tower, topped every other building. With its one hundred and eight floors and a pinnacle height of more than seventeen hundred feet, the skyscraper had held the title of the "tallest building in the world" for almost twenty-five years following its construction in 1973. In the North, the most distinct structure was the John Hancock Center; it was easily recognizable by its crisscrossed trusses and the two antennas.

Stephanie's personal favorite, however, was placed exactly between those two structures both in location and height. "Look, there's the Trump Tower! If we had binoculars, we might be able to look into your living room! Consuela, you have no idea what the view is like from up there."

Richard gave Stephanie a kiss and took Consuela's hand. "Well, I thought we could show Consuela my apartment later tonight–if you don't have any other plans, of course."

9:06 p.m.

It took a while before the analgesic effect of the painkiller finally kicked in.

Tisiphone was standing in the bathroom and, using a hand mirror, looked at the mark the Taser had left on her back. While the skin was severely reddened, it was otherwise unscathed. She squeezed a strip of burn ointment out of the tube and gently applied the whitish paste onto the area, which was still sensitive.

Originally, she had had very different plans for tonight. But that didn't matter now. She was just glad that all had turned out well after all–for her, at least.

Once again, the many years of self-defense and martial arts training had paid off and had saved her life. And although she had every reason to enjoy the costly triumph, she was racked with self-doubt: she should never have been so unassuming, leaving her guard down for even one minute. A lesson learned for sure.

With her hands resting on the rim of the sink, she looked into the tired face in the mirror...

After she had knocked down the young man and locked him in the cage, she explored the rest of the store to make sure that they were alone. At that point she found the other camera as well as a whole bunch of DVDs with footage from the fitting room. She deleted the current video cassette of the regular surveillance system, which she turned off. While she removed all recordings of herself, she left everything else just where she had found it—with the exception of the Taser, which she thought might come in handy sometime later.

It didn't take her long to weigh her options: to spare his life was out of the question. But how would she kill him? Quickly and painlessly, and then get the hell out of here? Or should she treat herself to a little fun?

When she felt the pain in her back, she knew that she wanted him to suffer.

In a cleaning cupboard she found two bottles of turpentine, and in the office she discovered an unopened bottle of high-proof vodka. This would be more than enough to start a fire, especially because the store was so crammed with flammable textiles that it would completely burn down in no time.

As she was looking for some clothing to wear during the devised payback, she found a nurse costume, which included knee-highs, a hat, and an apron. Fittingly, a red cross was sewn onto the front.

Since the boy was still unconscious, it was easy enough to undress him and tie him to the cage. Tisiphone merely had to lift his upper body, wedging him carefully so that his arms and legs were splayed in front of the iron-barred wall of his prison. She fetched the instrument case holding his torture devices and, for a brief moment, considered gagging him but dismissed the thought.

She wanted to hear his cries.

After she slapped him three times, he moved a little but wasn't fully responsive yet. Her elbow must have hit him harder than she had thought.

Before he could doze off again, she took a scalpel out of the case and rammed it with brutal force into his left thigh.

His earsplitting howl was music in her ears. "Hello, my darling. Welcome to hell…"

****

126

"So, I suppose that you know Andrew and the crew quite well." Stephanie didn't think that the yacht had been taken out of winter storage just as a favor to Richard. "Am I right?"

"You could say that! These guys sailed around the globe with me for two years!" Richard smiled at her. "But that isn't what you really wanted to know, is it?"

"How can it be that you know me so well after just a few days?" Stephanie looked at him in anticipation. "Admit it: this is your ship!"

"Is that true?" Consuela asked surprised.

Richard shook his head. "No, it's not true... at least not completely. I only own a part of it."

"And who owns the rest?" Stephanie wanted to know.

"The guys, of course!"

"Does this mean that they are all loaded playboys like you?" Consuela tutted.

Richard knew that she just wanted to tease him a little, and so he wasn't miffed at her comment. "No, I am the only 'playboy' here. The others are all shareholders and earn their living with the boat. Business is good, especially in the summer of course, where we are fully booked for at least six months. You'd be surprised how many companies and clubs, but also private individuals, are willing to pay a lot of money to charter such a yacht–sometimes only for a few hours or a day but occasionally for a couple of weeks at a time."

"I'd like that: leave your everyday worries behind for a while, sunbathe the whole day, read, and go for a swim once in a while. Doesn't that sound fantastic?" Consuela leaned back in her chair with a dreamy expression on her face and took a sip from her wine glass.

"Then we should do exactly that! We could sail to Puerto Rico together. How would you like that?"

The girls looked at Richard with wide eyes.

"Are you serious?" Consuela asked perplexed.

"Sure! Why not? My sailboat is somewhere in the Caribbean anyway. We just have to find a time it's not booked up."

127

"Does this mean that you still own your sailing yacht, too?" Stephanie wanted to know.

"Of course, I love that boat and it makes a lot of money! I have a permanent crew under contract that takes care of everything. And every now and then, when my sailing fever flares up, I spend a few days on board myself."

"One could almost get envious," Consuela joked.

Richard tried not to show how he felt about this comment. After all, Consuela couldn't possibly know what a sensitive issue she had touched upon. He responded with a little hesitancy: "Yes, I guess one could. But money can't buy happiness, to use this time-honored expression. And let me tell you: from my experience it's true…"

Stephanie took Richard's hand and kissed it gently. "But now you're happy, aren't you?"

And all at once, just like that, he was in the best of moods again. "You bet!"

10:28 p.m.

When she woke up, she was lying on her bed, naked. The combination of wine and painkillers must have been too much and had simply knocked her out.

She got her bathrobe out of the closet and went to the kitchen. A little snack would help her get back on her feet. She hadn't had any food since lunchtime.

Everywhere in the apartment the lights were on, and her clothes were scattered all over the floor. She hadn't even been able to tidy up.

She got an apple from the fridge and sat down at the kitchen table, directly in front of the canning jar. Her latest acquisition floated lifelessly in a seventy-percent solution of alcohol, which by now had turned reddish from the remnants of the blood…

128

In contrast to all her other victims, he never pleaded for his life and never gave up fighting–until the end. Rather, he reviled and insulted her with such vulgarity that she finally changed her mind and decided to muzzle him after all. This, at least, stopped him from spitting at her.

When he realized what she was planning to do, despite being tied up, he put up such a fight that she had to stun him with the Taser. Since she had already found all necessary instruments and materials in his case before, she had no trouble to sew his mouth shut.

After she was done, she moved one of the garment racks with an attached mirror on its short side to the front of the cage.

Since he obviously had a special, though sick, interest in medical technology, she wanted to give him the opportunity to admire her perfect Donati suture.

"I'm sure you'll appreciate this, don't you?"

Beside himself with pain and rage, he furiously threw himself from side to side.

It took a few hours until she had tried out each and every tool in his case.

Some were so unusual that she almost reached the limits of her imagination–almost. Not only her ingenuity but also her sadism turned out to be inexhaustible that evening.

More than once, he passed out, but she always immediately revived him, never granting him any rest.

Only when it became clear that he wouldn't last any longer, her thirst for revenge was satisfied.

It took only two cuts with the big amputation knife to castrate him. Then, she doused him with turpentine and set him on fire.

****

For dessert, they had caramelized figs with goat-cheese ice cream and almond tuiles, and a 1967 Château d'Yquem.

On shore, the white-shimmering dome of the Baha'i Temple appeared. After Andrew had first taken a southern course, he changed directions and they now reached Wilmette, which was north of the city.

Upon Richard's signal, one of the waiters brought a silver tray decorated with rose petals, on which two little gift boxes lay.

"Stephanie, Consuela, even though we haven't known each other for very long, I consider our relationship something very special and precious. I have to admit that I've never spent Valentine's Day with two girls before, but I feel so close to you–both of you–that I can't imagine anymore how life was before I got to know you. Please, allow me to give you these presents as a token of my appreciation." First, Richard gave Stephanie a kiss and handed her the bigger of the two boxes, which were gift-wrapped in robin's-egg-blue paper tied with white satin ribbons. Then, he kissed Consuela and gave her the smaller box.

"Richard, we can't possibly accept such valuable gifts. We've just met!" Consuela was deeply moved, but at the same time she was torn between accepting and declining the present.

"But you don't even know what's in the box," Richard said trying to encourage her.

"No, but we recognize the wrapping," Stephanie remarked with empathy.

"It would really mean a lot to me..." Richard certainly understood why they might have concerns, yet he would have been deeply hurt had they rejected his gifts.

The girls seemed to sense that.

"Alright then! But we have one condition: if we should ever fall out, you take everything back, no questions asked!" Consuela said.

Richard had not expected this. For a moment, he contemplated how he should respond. He would have never tied a gift, regardless how valuable it was, to any conditions. On the other hand, the girls wanted him to understand that they weren't dating him for his money. And although he was well aware of that, their reaction filled him with pride and admiration. "Agreed, now will you please unwrap your gifts!"

"Not so fast, we've also got something for you!" Stephanie got a flat parcel out of her clutch bag and put it on the table. "It's really just a little something."

The girls were thrilled when they opened their boxes.

"Richard, you gotta be crazy, the necklace must be worth a fortune!" Stephanie flung her arms around his neck and gave him a big hug. "It's gorgeous!"

"Just look at my earrings, they are fantastic–¡estupendo! I love diamonds… thank you so much!" Consuela pushed Stephanie aside and gave Richard a passionate kiss.

"I'm glad that you like it. But now let's see what you got for me!" Carefully, Richard opened his parcel, which contained a book-like object enfolded in tissue paper. When he removed the wrapping, he saw that his present wasn't a book at all but a framed photo.

"Stephanie told me that you don't have any family pictures in your apartment. That has to change!" Consuela said with determination.

Full of emotion, Richard looked at the black and white print, which showed the two girls happily smiling at the camera. "You couldn't have chosen a better present for me."

11:04 p.m.

Forrester McLean was livid. Despite the fact that the guy had agreed to a price when they had talked on the phone that very afternoon, he now refused to let him enter the building.

He had a family to take care of, he told him insolently.

Nervously, the reporter bit his fingernails, trying to decide whether to just give him the two hundred dollars more or to attempt intimidating him with threats.

If it were uncovered that he, as foreman of a cleaning crew, had given unauthorized persons access to the police department, he wouldn't just lose his job–he would go to jail. "Make up your mind! You wanna come in or not? I don't have all night!"

The guy even got brazen-faced! He just stood there, calm and relaxed, nonchalantly leaning his arm against the frame of the steel door–a bull-necked, frowsy hulk, who would probably have been proud of being called a "redneck."

No, he couldn't be intimidated.

And besides, it wasn't easy to establish this kind of contact.

Forrester McLean gave the foreman the envelope containing the five hundred dollars they had originally agreed on, and then he took, with a heavy heart, another four fifties out of his wallet.

The giant put the money away and lowered his arm. "There's a cart for you! You've got one hour, then you have to be out of here again. I haven't seen anyone on that floor before but be careful anyway–I don't want any trouble!"

The reporter knew the building well as he was here quite often, either to attend press conferences or to investigate.

Most of the time, his visits were official and he used his press card and the main entrance. Sometimes, however, he sneaked in through a side door in the basement. Like today.

He pushed the cart with the cleaning supplies into the service elevator and pressed the button that would bring him to Homicide.

Before the door closed, he hit another one… the one for two levels up. If someone else happened to get on, he would simply pretend to have pushed a wrong button and would get off on the higher floor. In that case, he would leave the cart behind and take the stairs down.

The air in the elevator was stale and had a fetid smell of sweat.

132

Forrester McLean covered his nose with his hand, impatiently watching the control panel. It seemed to take an eternity until one light went out and the next number was lit.

When he couldn't stomach the foul odor any longer, he desperately rummaged through the bags and baskets attached to the side of the cart and found a household deodorizer: lavender.

He squeezed the handle of the pump dispenser a couple of times, and soon the cabin was filled with clouds of synthetic fragrances.

At first, he was glad to have drowned the unpleasant smell of sweat, but it didn't take very long before he felt a strong tickle in his throat, and his eyes started to burn and water. He had replaced one evil with another.

Just as he thought he'd faint, he heard a metallic chime, and the elevator door opened. Gasping for air, he pushed the cart into the vinyl-floored hallway.

The fluorescent ceiling fixtures flooded everything with a harsh, unnatural light.

After two yards, he stopped and listened. Somewhere an air vent rattled, but otherwise it was quiet.

He had brought a whole selection of surveillance cameras, which he was planning on installing tonight. But first, he'd hijack the secretary's computer and equip it with a receiver that would allow him to control and access all audio and video recordings from the comfort of his home.

He didn't have any trouble finding her desk. An engraved brass name plate read "Jennifer Walker."

Before he sat down on her chair, he stroked the seat cushion a few times with his hand and sniffed at the back rest. Oh, he would have done anything to fuck this cookie!

But he was sure that he would get his money worth one way or the other.

Less than three minutes later, he had cracked her password and had uploaded his software. It didn't take much longer to install the receiver.

Everything went according to plan.

Originally, he had intended to put in the really essential units first. However, as he envisioned how, not long ago, she had been sitting on this very chair, he decided to change his plans and crawled under the desk.

****

After they had danced for a while, Richard asked the girls to take a seat again and excuse him for a moment. "Don't worry; I'll be back in an instant. I have another surprise for you."

He kissed them and walked over to the band, which greeted him enthusiastically and slapped him on the back.

Only when he took a tenor saxophone out of a case that was lying next to the drum set, they started to realize what was about to happen.

While Stephanie just shook her head in disbelief, Consuela muttered a "Now, this is going to be interesting!"

When he was ready, Richard signaled the pianist to begin. After a few beats, the drums joined in, and a moment later Richard started to play the melody of "My Funny Valentine."

The piece, which had originally been composed in 1937 by Richard Rodgers and Lorenz Hart for the musical "Babes in Arms" had since evolved into a genre-transcending classic. Especially the legendary recording by the Gerry Mulligan Quartet featuring Chet Baker on the trumpet from the year 1952, as well as interpretations by Miles Davis and Ella Fitzgerald, had been largely responsible for establishing the song as a jazz standard.

Richard had always preferred the slower versions of "My Funny Valentine" and, therefore, also played the piece as a melancholic ballad.

134

As the band let the final chord linger, the girls applauded fervently and demanded an encore.

Richard briefly consulted with the other musicians, then they followed with Charlie Parker's "Scrapple from the Apple" and Telonius Monk's "Round Midnight."

By now, the crew members had joined Stephanie, Consuela, and the waiters, and they all listened in awe to the musical performance.

At the end of the performance, they thanked the band with enthusiastic applause and let Richard take a seat again only after playing "When I Fall in Love" as the finale.

"Richard, that was lovely!" Consuela raved when he came back to the table.

The girls hugged and kissed him and bombarded him with questions: "How long have you been playing the sax? Have you ever played professionally? Have you performed in public? Do you play any other instruments?"

"Calm down, it's not such a big deal!" he tried to downplay the issue.

"Don't make me laugh! You could have told me that, incidentally, you play the sax like John Coltrane! Do you have any other unusual talents we should know about?" Stephanie asked with feigned indignation. "Maybe you're a chess grandmaster or you can run the 100 meters in less than ten seconds..."

Richard laughed and shook his head. "No. Although I know how to play chess, I am certainly no grandmaster, and I have never won any running races–I've always preferred swimming."

"But your saxophone playing isn't just a hobby, right? You're simply too good for that." Consuela knew enough to recognize that Richard didn't just have talent but had also enjoyed excellent musical training.

"As a matter of fact, there was a time where I was thinking about becoming a professional musician. But I chose medicine instead and just settled on a "minor" in music. While I was at med school, I made

135

a little money on the side performing–that is, as long as I had enough time to do that. Nowadays, I hardly play anymore. We occasionally perform in lesser-known jazz clubs, but just for fun."

"I would love to know how to play an instrument," Stephanie said wistfully.

"Now, wait a minute! At least, you are an excellent painter," Consuela countered.

"See, you haven't told me that yet either!" Richard complained.

"We haven't known each other that long and, after all, we don't spend a lot of time talking when we're together…" Stephanie blew him a kiss.

"By the way, when do we go ashore again?" Consuela asked. "I'd really like to see your apartment now…"

Tuesday, February 15

2:40 a.m.

Richard was about to get out of bed when suddenly his cell started to vibrate on the nightstand.

The girls were sound asleep by now and weren't the least bothered by the sound that was reminiscent of a swarm of metallic bees.

Richard grabbed the phone, hurried out of the bedroom, and managed to push the "talk" button before the ring tone had a chance to possibly awaken the girls. "Morning, Liz, what's up?"

"Hello, Richard. Sorry for rousing you out of slumber in the middle of the night! The Fire Marshal called about an hour ago–they've found another burnt body, this time in a sex shop in Cicero. I think you should get here as quickly as possible. We're still waiting to get permission to enter the building, but I've already seen pictures of the victim."

"And, any body parts missing?"

"You could say that!"

****

Since Richard didn't want to trouble the drivers of his building's limo-service, he asked the concierge to call a cab. It was out of the question for him to drive himself–he had had way too much wine and sex to do that.

Already from a distance one could make out the colorful warning lights of the emergency vehicles, which illuminated the houses along the street with frantic flashes of red, white, and blue.

Access to the one-story building, which was still giving off smoke, was closed, and some curious onlookers, obviously

137

undeterred by the bitter cold, were standing in the middle of the street, pryingly watching the police and fire department do their job.

The cabby, not overly eager to get any closer to the crowd, stopped the car two blocks before they reached their destination.

Richard handed him two twenties, turned up his coat collar, and got out without even trying to argue with him. He would just walk the rest of the way.

The air smelled of smoke and burnt plastic, and the ice-cold wind blew inch-sized soot particles, which in the yellow light of the street lantern looked like charcoaled snowflakes, into his face.

Ghostly billows of gray steam rose from the drain covers and dispersed above the dark asphalt.

Richard showed his badge, and a young policewoman led him to Liz, who, wrapped in a thick blue down coat, was impatiently hopping up and down, trying to stay warm.

"Richard, you're finally here! The Fire Marshal has cleared the building a minute ago. The Medical Examiner hasn't arrived yet, but we are allowed to go in anyway. We don't need respirators, but we should put these on." Liz gave Richard a dust mask and gestured to him to follow her.

"According to the fire department, it's a clear case of arson. They found cans of turpentine and the water line to the sprinkler system had been shut off."

"I am assuming that the victim is male," Richard said as they were entering the building.

"This couldn't be confirmed yet."

A number of portable halogen work lights, connected to a noisy row of emergency generators in front of the store, filled the shop with a cold, unnatural light.

The same cheap wire hangers that had previously served to present colorful chemises, bustiers, or other types of lingerie, were still dangling from the garment racks. The fire, however, had transformed the merchandise into black, shapeless scraps, from which draped dark, solidified strings of synthetic polymers.

The farther back in the store they went the stuffier the air became.

Richard regretted now that he hadn't insisted on a respirator. The dust masks were completely unsuited to protect them from the acrid smoke.

"That must be it!" Panting heavily between two coughing fits, Liz pointed at the oversized metal grid cube, which was standing amidst ashes and rubble in the center of the back room.

The charred corpse was sitting on the floor with its back against the wall.

Richard immediately noticed that the body wasn't quite as badly burnt as the other victims.

Since there weren't any windows back here, he assumed that the lack of oxygen had prevented the fire from getting more intense and, thus, from causing even greater damage.

Being a medical doctor, he didn't need an autopsy to see that this was the corpse of a man–even though his penis and testicles were missing. He immediately concluded that the culprit had taken the sex organs as souvenirs.

Anyhow, Richard had the feeling that the murderer had had a hard time deciding what trophies to collect this time… Why else had the victims' hands and feet been severed but left behind?

7:32 a.m.

"Dammit!"

The loud beeping noise had startled him so much that he had spilled the milk, which should have gone over his cornflakes. Not minding the old breadcrumbs and other moldy residues on the countertop, Forrester McLean bent over and lapped up the puddle.

Angrily, he kicked an empty beer can to the side and pushed his way through the piles of old newspapers and dirty clothes that were scattered all over the floor of his apartment. The time would come where he'd buy some garbage bags and throw out everything–everything!

For more than eight years, he had been living in this dump, and it was almost that long since the place had been cleaned the last time.

Back then, shortly after their divorce, Cheryl had paid him one last visit. One fine day she had called him, asking for a reconciliatory talk. "I wish we could stay friends," she had said. Friends–what was she thinking? That they would meet once in a while for coffee and a little chitchat? Maybe babble about her new house in Winnetka? Or her two brats, who she had born to Mr. Nice Guy at the advanced age of forty, just before her biological clock stopped ticking?

No, he didn't care about all this, and he certainly didn't need anyone to tell him that he was drinking too much and not showering often enough. He knew that himself–and he didn't give a shit.

Nevertheless, he had agreed to the meeting at last.

Why? He couldn't remember anymore. Perhaps, because she had been willing to pick him up at his place. After all, it was at the time he didn't have a license because he had totaled his car at a lamp post in a DUI.

She looked good, standing there at the door in a dark-blue designer costume–almost distinguished. She had lost some weight and looked much younger and healthier.

Nothing reminded him of the woman he had been married to for almost twenty years. No stringy hair, no puffy eyes, no shiners.

When she saw all the dirt and clutter in his apartment, she just looked at him with pity, put her Gucci bag down next to the entrance, and sent him off to the bar next door.

He must have forgotten the time as it was already way past midnight when he returned.

The apartment was nice and clean now, but she was gone. She probably got tired of waiting–who would have blamed her?

At least, she had left a note, which he found on the living room table the next morning.

"Take care!" it said, written in blue ink on a piece of paper which, ironically, was displaying her husband's company logo.

He had never heard from her again.

He sank into the dilapidated recliner that had been serving as an office chair for many years and pushed the "Enter" key to quiet the shrill sound that told him that one of the hidden cameras in the police department had been activated.

The high-definition picture he saw a moment later on his computer-screen made him smack his lips. "That's what I've been waiting for!"

Jennifer Walker was standing in the breakfast room of the homicide department and was making coffee. She was wearing a tight black turtleneck and an anthracite-colored, knee length pencil skirt. He could even see the delicate vertical stripes of her stockings. Well, maybe it was pantyhose–which he would find out soon enough. Her shoes were hidden by a chair's backrest; yet the way she moved around led him to the conclusion that she was probably wearing pumps.

The reporter quickly switched to the main menu to make sure that the recording function was working properly. When he returned to the breakfast room, the secretary was just bending over to get a bottle out of the refrigerator.

What an ass! He would enjoy looking at these videos for a long time to come.

Finally, when the coffee was ready, she poured herself a big cup and added a little milk. As she put the bottle back in the fridge, he got the chance to admire her derriere once again. Then, she left the room.

The next shot showed her walking down the hallway toward her office. Now he knew she was wearing pumps!

Forrester McLean impatiently waited for her to finally sit down at her desk. Installing the camera at her place had been especially challenging. Naturally, he had substituted the original smoke detector with a spy cam version. But the ceiling-mounted instrument wasn't suited to provide him with the kind of shots he was particularly interested in.

A pen on the floor would probably have been spotted and picked up, and a clock radio, a Kleenex-box, or even a stuffed animal would have been way too obvious.

But he had been lucky.

There had been an electrical outlet mounted knee-high on the back wall of her desk. Within two minutes, he had replaced it.

He could already hear the clicking of her heels. Any moment now, the secret–stockings or pantyhose–would be revealed.

As if moved by a ghost, the chair was pushed backwards, and first one and then another leg appeared. She was standing at her desk, and it sounded as if she was turning the pages of a newspaper.

What the heck was she doing? Why didn't she sit down?

Fretfully, he switched to the bird's view provided by the smoke detector.

Indeed, she was reading the Tribune! Why couldn't she do this sitting down?

After five minutes, she finally put the paper away, pulled the chair a bit back, and was just about to take a seat when he suddenly heard a male voice: "Good morning, Jenny. Could you, please, go down to the vice squad and pick up some files for me! Thanks."

It was porky Chief Miller. Why did he have to show up just now?

Whatever, he just had to be patient. It would certainly be worth it!

He wasn't in a hurry. If necessary, he could spend the whole day at his computer–doing research, of course.

9:03 a.m.

Richard was jolted out of his sleep by bright sunlight. It hadn't been three hours yet since he had returned home and sneaked back into bed with the girls.

"Buenos días, Dr. Stanton. I think it's time for you to get up now!" Maria was standing by the window, draping the curtains that she, just a moment ago, had pulled open with a jerk without any compassion for the sleeping Richard.

"Maria, what's the matter with you?" Usually, she left him alone when he wanted to sleep in.

"Dr. Stanton, don't you think that you should attend to your guests?" Maria gave him a reproachful look.

So, that was the problem: the girls!

Obviously, Richard had forgotten to ask Maria to come in later today. And it seemed as if she had already met Stephanie and Consuela.

He looked at her with an innocent face and tried to calm her down. "Please, forgive me! I should have notified you. Where are they?"

"In the kitchen! I did offer to make breakfast, but the señoritas insisted on helping. Dr. Stanton–you better come before they mess up everything!"

Richard slipped into his dressing gown and went to the kitchen.

Wearing T-shirts and boxer shorts, the girls were standing at the stove, frizzling something in a pan.

143

"Good morning, you two. That smells good, are you making scrambled eggs?"

"Scrambled eggs? You can't be serious! These are Revoltillos de jamón!" Consuela poured a little vinegar into the pan and added a pinch of salt. "I guess you could call them scrambled eggs–but special ones! Maria, what do you think, anything missing?" Consuela smiled at the housekeeper and handed her a fork.

Richard and the girls looked curiously at her as she skeptically poked around in the pan.

When she finally tasted a bite, her face brightened up. "¡Esto sabe bien! Señorita, if you don't mind, can I have the recipe?"

Consuela beamed at her. "Usually, I don't share my family recipes with anyone, but in your case, I will make an exception. And, please, call me Consuela!"

Maria couldn't suppress a quick grin, but then she turned to Stephanie with a stern face: "And you, Señorita, can you also cook?"

Richard had never seen his girlfriend embarrassed, but now she was blushing.

"Uh, to tell the truth: not as well as Consuela."

When Maria saw how intimidated Stephanie was, she went over to her and affectionately patted her on the cheek. "Doesn't matter, honey, we'll teach you! What's your name?"

"Stephanie, estimada Señora Maria."

"Chiquita, just call me Maria! And now, sit down and let me do my job!"

11:15 a.m.

"Good morning, Dr. Stanton. Chief Miller is expecting you in the conference room. Everyone else has already arrived." Jennifer Walker came around the desk and leaned forward to collect a kiss on

144

the cheek. "And by the way, thank you very much for the flowers and the wonderful gift basket."

As he was giving her a little peck, she unexpectedly grabbed the sleeve of his jacket and whispered something into his ear–unfortunately, he couldn't decipher what she said.

Why, for crying out loud, were women drawn to this guy like moths to a flame?

Didn't they see what a smug boaster he really was?

Now he was standing there like a fool, stammering "Jenny, Jenny, Jenny. What am I supposed to do with you?"

How dumb was that? Even she should have realized how shallow that was!

But instead of giving him a kick in the butt, she was fluttering her eyelashes at him and said: "Oh, I've got a few ideas what you could do!"

Unbelievable!

The money, it had to be the money! Women were all whores and threw themselves at any man as long as he was loaded.

Like his Cheryl. Why else would she have left him?

Disgusted by these ridiculous mating rituals, Forrester McLean switched back to the other channel.

In the conference room, Chief Miller, Liz Chen, Steven Kowalski, and Ron Howard, the Medical Examiner, were already waiting. They all had arrived a few minutes ago but, so far, had only exchanged pleasantries.

They obviously didn't want to begin without Richard Stanton, who only a moment later entered the room.

"Let's get started then!" the Chief remarked succinctly.

****

Four murders already–four! And even with severed body parts... Once again, he'd had the right instinct: this was a big story!

All he had to do now was to find the beautiful stranger.

But how?

Not even the police, with all their resources, had any idea who the suspect might be.

Anyhow, he was known to be the most famous investigative reporter in the Midwest for a reason.

He had an impressive track-record of locating tax dodgers, child snatchers, and even Nazi war criminals long before the authorities with all their useless bureaucracy had had the chance to just issue warrants for their arrest.

Yet, how should he proceed this time?

It was clear that he wouldn't run into the beauty by pure chance.

With more than two and a half million people living in the city and almost ten million in the metropolitan area, it was virtually impossible to find somebody in Chicago without knowing their present whereabouts.

So far, the woman didn't seem to follow any discernible pattern.

Yes, she had targeted one victim in a luxury hotel. But it was a long way from there to the sex shop in Cicero–in every respect. Therefore, it didn't make much sense to sit around in hotel bars day in and day out, hoping that she might show up looking for another victim.

No, he had to think of something else.

Unpredictable, not leaving behind any traces… She reminded him of one of these mysterious jungle creatures that every now and then appeared out of nowhere, snatched some prey, but then faded into oblivion again until they struck again somewhere else.

Occasionally, poor quality pictures of such fabled animals, taken with infrared camera traps, appeared in the news. But no one ever caught one.

Like the Tasmanian Tiger, which was believed to be extinct since 1936 but still roamed the forests of Tasmania today–at least if one believed the reports of various "eyewitnesses."

Forrester McLean leaned back in his chair and closed his eyes.

How then did one catch such an animal?

146

With cunning and wits. That was something his grandfather had taught him.

He still remembered how jumpy all the farmers in the area had been when the mountain lion killed the first couple of sheep. On horses and pickup trucks they had tried to hunt down the animal.

Without success, of course.

They simply had no experience with such things–back then, in Minnesota. Even though almost all of them hunted... primarily squirrels, and sometimes even deer. But they were used to spotting their prey and maybe even stalk it, if necessary.

His grandfather had watched the whole thing until, one night, one of his lambs was killed. Then, he had put an end to it himself...

Little Forrester was just nine years old at the time, but his grandfather insisted that he join him, against his parents' will, naturally.

So, it was he who led the sheep out to the pasture on a leash while his grandpa, his rifle shouldered and his pipe in his mouth, followed him with a stake in his hand.

When they reached the collapsed barn, they had a snack: sandwiches, a piece of cheese, and an apple. His grandfather had a bottle of beer and, as usual, he was allowed to have a sip of it.

Leaning against the old stone wall, they were sitting there until the sun set and the first stars appeared in the firmament.

The sheep, which grandpa had tied to the stake about twenty yards away from them, was grazing peacefully and bleated from time to time. Its calls, however, weren't answered because grandfather had herded all other animals into the stables earlier that day.

Now, he put the remains of their supper back into his greasy canvas backpack and told Forrester to take everything to the other side of the wall. Then, he wiped the jackknife, which he had just used to slice the apple, clean on his overalls, walked over to the sheep, and stuck the blade in its side.

147

The animal shrieked briefly, and its dirty white wool turned red where grandpa had stabbed it. The wound wasn't bleeding heavily and probably wouldn't have killed the sheep. This way, it could hold out all night, bleat in agony, and emit the sweet metallic smell of fresh blood that was so irresistible to predators.

Forrester didn't know how much time had passed when his grandfather gave him a shake to wake him up.

The night sky was black now, and the moon was casting dark shadows.

Grandpa had put his index finger on his lips, telling him to be quiet.

Why? As much as he pricked up his ears, he couldn't hear anything besides the chirping of the crickets and the whimpering of the bait.

When he shrugged, his grandfather pulled him up by his shoulders and pointed in the direction of the sheep. Forrester had to stand on his toes to look over the old wall.

The wool of the animal, which now anxiously ran around the stake, had a silvery shine in the moonlight.

Even though the boy couldn't see the mountain lion yet, it had to be somewhere out there. Why else would his grandpa have brought up his rifle and assumed a shooting position?

Intently, Forrester searched the pasture for any kind of movement or a shadow–but there was nothing.

Only when one of the dark earthen mounds silently rose into the air for the briefest of moments and came down on the defenseless victim like a black angel of death, he knew what he had missed.

The mountain lion just had enough time to sink its fangs into its prey's neck and break its spine before grandfather pulled the trigger.

The blast that disturbed the otherwise peaceful silence of this balmy summer night was so loud that Forrester had a peculiar ringing in his ears as long as three days later.

148

Grandfather patiently waited for a few minutes, then he went over to the dead animals, and finally gave his grandson permission to come out from behind the wall.

The cat was much larger than Forrester had expected. Grandpa estimated it to be at least eight feet long from its head to the tip of its tail.

They gutted the animal right on the spot as it would otherwise have been impossible to carry home.

It was an excruciating grind nevertheless. For several weeks to come, bruises and abrasions reminded Forrester of how he and his grandfather had carried the dead beast dangling from a stick through the night.

He would never forget this adventure and if it was just for the fact that this was one of the last memories he had of his grandpa.

About six months after their successful big-game hunt, grandfather put a bullet in his head–with the same gun he had used to kill the mountain lion.

Forrester got to know the truth only many years later. The whole family always referred to the incident as "grandpa's accident," carefully avoiding the word "suicide."

As if one had to be ashamed when a man preferred to decide for himself when his time had come rather than slowly being eaten away by cancer. Idiots, they were all idiots!

To him, his grandfather was a hero–in life and death.

Forrester was just sorry that no one was there when grandpa left this world–no one except the mountain lion that, artfully mounted, loomed over the library from the top of a bookcase.

Grandpa himself had stuffed it and had immortalized the grace and might of this awe-inspiring creature in a diorama.

After his good-for-nothing father had wrecked the farm, the piece had been moved to the local museum where, up to this day, visitors could admire how lifelike the scene was: a full-grown cougar sinking its teeth into a sheep.

3:41 p.m.

The case was developing into a nightmare… and at a dizzying pace. Not only had the perp killed at least four people already–three of them in less than a week–but one of the victims had been a perverted serial killer himself. The videos they had found in the sex shop provided unimpeachable proof for that.

As it seemed likely that Kenneth Collins had been part of a nationwide or even international porn ring, they had agreed at their meeting to call in the FBI.

By now, the feds already had their own team in Cicero and had confiscated anything they could lay their hands on. This included recordings, customer files, and computers, which the Chicago Police had left behind–after making copies of everything, of course.

Unlike the other victims, Kenneth Collins could be identified without any problems. His grandaunt confirmed that he had a pierced tongue as well as an extensive tattoo of a dragon on his back–evidence that wasn't destroyed in the fire.

The slightly eccentric old lady, who was bound to a wheelchair since an accident four years ago, was the store's owner and had entrusted her nephew with the management of the business.

She claimed not to know anything about the videos.

The snuff movies surpassed any kind of perversion Richard had ever seen before. As they were watching parts of them during the meeting with the Chief, he remembered what Maria had said to him only a few days ago: "Why do you always let them drag you into this muck? Make babies…"

Also the others repeatedly turned away from the monitor–too horrible were the shots that showed Kenneth Collins with at least eight different victims.

Liz was especially disturbed by the unspeakable suffering the young women had to endure as they were skinned, chopped up, or strangled. After having left the conference room to throw up in the restroom twice before already, she broke down and had a crying fit.

At that point, the Chief finally stopped the screening.

Also, the political pressure on the department had quickly increased in intensity. Somehow, the press must have, as the Mayor's Office put it, gotten wind of "mysterious events" in the sex shop.

What exactly that was supposed to mean was not clear.

However, the department's official press release had, as in all other cases before, only mentioned a "structure fire with casualties."

Soon the cat would be out of the bag, and they couldn't do anything about it.

Richard's suggestion to blame the porn Mafia for Kenneth Collin's death was endorsed by everyone else at the meeting. This was supposed to distract the press and buy them more time.

Richard didn't think that, so far, any other reporter besides Forrester McLean had established a link between the different "burn victims." And he would have to deal with McLean separately.

Although the final autopsy results weren't in yet, Ron had already determined in his preliminary investigation that Kenneth Collins had been tortured quite methodically. The fingernails were missing from his severed hands, and several toes had been cut off before the feet had been amputated.

Apparently, the sadistic torturer had met his master.

Richard was sure that the postmortem would reveal more signs of physical mistreatment.

Contusions, crushings, and fractures were easily detectable. There were other torture techniques, though, that didn't leave any discernible traces, not even with surviving victims.

Not to mention the missing genitals. Penis and testicles were popular targets amongst torturers not only for their high density of nerves and, thus, sensitivity. Their psychological importance was of even greater value.

Often, merely threatening to injure or remove the sexual organs sufficed to achieve the desired result. Many a victim had betrayed his brothers in arms, revealed secrets, or made false confessions just to protect his manhood.

Richard wondered if the traditional objectives of torture, namely, to break the tormented person's will and resistance, had played any role at all in Kenneth Collins' case.

Perhaps, it was only about chastening and racking him?

And if, was it simply an act of pure self-gratification or of revenge… or both?

The ringing of the phone interrupted his thoughts.

The display showed "Unknown number," but he decided to answer anyway. "Yes?"

"Dr. Stanton, I am very disappointed in you. I thought we had an agreement! Why haven't you contacted me?"

"That was never part of our deal. If you want information, you have to come to me!"

"I'm getting the feeling that you're not taking me seriously."

"Don't worry, I won't make that mistake. So, what do you want?"

"Don't play dumb with me! I am losing my patience here. The murder in Cicero last night… that's related to the other cases you're working on, isn't it? I wanna know when the whole thing started!"

"I have no idea what you're talking about."

"Don't try to bullshit me or you can admire a picture of yourself and your braless blonde in tomorrow's paper. The bulge in your pants is quite obvious. I bet you fucked your brains out with this cutie that night…"

"Shut it, you pig! We don't know if the cases are connected."

152

"Stop prevaricating! That's just semantic hairsplitting! Of course, you don't 'know' anything–but you're AS-SUM-ING it, right?"

Richard was so angered by his arrogant, patronizing tone that he was ready to go through the line and grab the reporter by the throat. But he couldn't lose his cool with this rat. Neither his temper nor his private life should jeopardize solving the murders. And, he had to protect Stephanie.

"Sounds like you know all the answers already anyway. Yes, we're AS-SUM-ING that the cases are related, but I don't want you to report that."

"That's my decision, not yours! You are in no position to make any demands. Do you have any suspects yet?"

Richard bit his lip. "No, not yet."

Now, Forrester McLean was yelling so angrily into the phone that his voice cracked: "Do you think I'm an idiot? What about the woman? Tell me about the woman!"

Richard was baffled. How did he know about the woman? He certainly hadn't told him anything. And there had been nothing about her in the press release.

"Where did you get this information?" He tried to sound as calm and indifferent as possible.

Forrester McLean realized that he had to proceed with utmost caution. He couldn't afford for Stanton to get the idea that they were being spied upon.

"Your colleagues talked about it over lunch. They always hang out at the same places, you know. I hope you get it now that you can't fuck with me. So, tell me! Who's the woman?"

"We don't know. If we did, we would probably have arrested her already. However, so far, we don't have any cogent proof that she has killed anybody… just some sketchy clues that she might have been with one of the victims the night he died."

"What kind of clues would that be?"

153

"Videos and statements from witnesses."

"This means that you know what she looks like! I want pictures!"

"You must be out of your mind! I can't do that. We don't even know for sure that the woman has done anything illegal. It would be libel if you published her picture. And not even you would get away with it."

Stanton was probably right. It was one thing to make a fool out of the police, but it could cost him dearly to annoy a litigious private person.

Since the courts didn't shy away anymore from awarding millions as compensation payments for pain and suffering even in the most absurd cases, basically, everybody could be sued at any moment. The more money one had the greater the risk was.

There were simply too many crazy crooks that played the legal system, trying to make a killing. Like the guy–ironically enough a lawyer himself–who sued a dry cleaner for seventy million dollars because the trousers he had planned to wear on his first day of work had been lost. Or the woman that in the hustle and bustle of holiday shopping sales threw herself in front of other bargain hunters just to sue a number of department stores for failing to provide adequate safety precautions.

No, it wasn't such a good idea to print the woman's picture yet. Still, he had to find out what she looked like.

He could have kicked himself for not installing the camera in the conference room in such a way that it also pointed at the large flat-screen monitor. During today's meeting, everyone had constantly stared at the composite showing the "Beautiful Stranger."

Everyone but him.

Whatever, Stanton wouldn't give him the picture, that much was clear.

154

"Then I want to at least get all the details related to the other murders! I am particularly interested in the nature of the victims' mutilations–this kind of shit sells."

How did he know all that? Richard intended to request more discretion from everyone working on the case, himself included. He had to be more careful, too.

"Well, alright, I tell you what we know so far. But you only get hard facts from me, no AS-SUMP-TIONS."

****

Richard couldn't wait to see what would be in the paper the next day. Even Forrester McLean had to understand that they didn't have much to show for at this point.

He didn't like it, but the fact was that the lead with the woman could still turn out to be a mere flight of fancy.

And even if she had murdered Tom Maddock, did that automatically mean that she had played any part in the other killings? Maybe there were other killers, and the murders were all the result of a retaliation campaign. Perhaps, the porn Mafia was really behind it.

It didn't take much imagination to envision Maddock having connections to the sex trade. Possibly, the "Beautiful Stranger" was in fact a prostitute–something like a high-class call girl.

Again, the phone rang. This time, he recognized the number: it was Stephanie.

"Richard, darling, unfortunately I have to work until ten tonight. One of the girls called in sick. But she is going to take over for me tomorrow. Why don't you pick up Consuela at the studio and you two spend a nice evening together? I bet she'd love that."

Darling–she had really called him "darling." He looked over to the photo the two had given him as a present. How did he deserve to be so lucky?

"Do you really mean that?"

"Of course I do! Richard, I thought that we had clarified that last night. We shouldn't create any problems where there aren't any.

155

Therefore, no jealousy, but a whole lot of love and understanding instead."

Richard contemplated for a moment before he answered: "Stephanie, do you have any idea how madly in love I am with you?"

There was a brief whoop of joy at the other end of the line. "Me too!"

He had to see her again as soon as possible. "Okay, how about I pick up Consuela and we cook something at your place? By the time you come home, everything should be ready so that we can all have dinner together. And tomorrow, the three of us go shopping. You girls need a few things you can leave at my apartment so that Maria has no reason anymore to complain about you wearing my boxer shorts. And when we are at it already–maybe we can find a wider bed."

Wednesday, February 16

8:03 a.m.

SERIAL KILLER TERRORIZES CHICAGO
Enchained, dismembered, and incinerated
Killer targets men; Police have suspect

BY FORRESTER MCLEAN

CHICAGO – Blazing flames, dark clouds of smoke, scared neighbors: at first, everything looked like business as usual for the brave members of the Cicero Fire Department when they were called to the one-story commercial building on Laramie Avenue Tuesday morning. But after the fire was finally extinguished at around one o'clock, the men of Local 717 discovered a nightmare scenario in the burnt-out sex shop "Pleasure Toys" that even made experienced veterans shudder. "It was like in a horror movie," said Lieutenant Randy Watson of the C-shift, "There were charred body parts all over the place."

Amidst molten mannequin sex dolls, sooty leather whips, and seared video cassettes, the fire fighters found the mutilated remains of Kenneth Collins, the manager of the store that is especially known in the S&M scene. The twenty-four-year-old had been chained to a cage, tortured, and burned alive.

A search of the premises, however, brought to light something even more shocking: over a period of several years, Collins had himself mutilated and killed numerous young women in the building.

157

Several DVDs found in the "Pleasure Toys" store show that the man, who was described by neighbors as being friendly and helpful, made movies of his grisly acts, which he sold underhand.

According to a joint press release by the Chicago Police Department and the FBI, Collins' killer is part of an international porn ring.

So far, so good!

But is this really a truthful representation of what happened here, or is it just a red herring?

This paper has obtained evidence from a reliable source indicating that Collins is, in fact, the latest victim of a crazy serial killer who has murdered at least four Chicago men since January in a similar fashion: all were tied up, mutilated, and set on fire.

Why then does the police try to mislead the public? Is it just an attempt to distract from their own incompetence, or is it not to jeopardize their work, as Richard Stanton claims?

The well-known playboy and hobby-detective has only recently been put in charge of the investigation in a move that implies that the 13,000 regular police officers, whose salaries are paid by the citizens of Chicago, are incapable of solving the case on their own.

"We are hot on the perp's trail and are close to making an arrest," Stanton confidently said in a phone interview yesterday.

Stanton, who has an MD from UW-Madison, pointed out that the murderer was surprisingly sloppy, leaving behind lots of forensic evidence. "We even have video recordings," he confirmed. The investigator described the suspect as an unremarkable, plump middle-aged woman, who appears to take revenge on men.

"It's too early to speculate on a motive," Stanton said. "But it is possible that the woman could not cope with being turned down by men."

*Turn to **Killer, Page 5***

"What the heck…?" Richard stared incredulously at the newspaper in front of him, shaking his head. Annoyed, he flipped through the rest of the article, which was full of half-truths and made him look like a pompous jerk.

This time, McLean had gone too far. How could he dare to misquote him so blatantly? His "statements" were either completely out of context or flat-out fabricated.

Richard bit his lip, crumpled up the paper, and threw it furiously against the big picture window.

"Calm down! Don't lose your cool!" he told himself. Even though Forrester McLean was a fucking asshole, he never did anything without a reason. That much he knew about him. Why then had he written this kind of crap? No respectable reporter, not even such an unscrupulous one as McLean, would recklessly risk his reputation by publishing a poorly researched story.

Was he just trying to teach him a lesson because he had not been willing to cooperate?

Richard moved to the window and looked down at the city streets.

Streams of pedestrians wrapped up in coats or parkas hurried past the traffic jam on Michigan Avenue Bridge. As usual, there were a couple of boys sitting in front of the northeastern tender house, drumming away on plastic buckets in hope of getting a few bucks from passersby.

Richard, who knew some of them by name, always tossed a couple of bills in their hat whenever he met them on the street. He knew very well that, for them, busking was pretty much the only alternative to crime to make ends meet–and he admired their ambition.

These kids, who lived in the projects on the Southside of town, were the victims of a system that made it almost impossible for low-income families to give their offspring a decent education and, in turn, the chance of finding a respectable job.

159

Richard had become quite exasperated with the reality of the American social system and had used some of his money to establish a foundation for underprivileged children.

Since public schools and their teachers' salaries were funded primarily through property taxes, there was a direct correlation between the median income of the people living in a particular school district and the quality of its faculty. According to tests performed by the U.S. Department of Education, almost eighty percent of the 8th graders in Chicago's public schools were not proficient in reading, and the results in math were equally bothersome.

Of course, it wasn't just the teachers' fault. The system was rotten. Naturally, only students who attended class on a regular basis had a chance of actually learning something. And that's where the problem started–at an early age. It was estimated that a third of all kindergarten students from low-income African-American families missed as much as four weeks of school a year. And as the children grew older, attendance did go down even more. As a consequence, grades were often awarded based on attendance rather than academic performance.

In addition, George W. Bush's "No Child Left Behind Act of 2001," which intended to guarantee that as many children as possible acquired at least minimum skills in reading, writing and math, ironically, made it almost impossible to foster gifted students and offer intellectually stimulating programs for them. By necessity, classes were aimed toward the weakest students.

It was a catch-22 situation: the children grew up in a society in which education was not valued or remained an unattainable dream.

No wonder many youths ended up on the wrong side of the law.

There were an estimated sixty to one hundred thousand gang members in Chicago, and they were responsible for the vast majority of violent crimes. A young male growing up in the wrong neighborhood was basically forced to join one of its gangs, or he risked getting shot someday for no particular reason.

160

Richard was still bewildered by the gap that existed between the affluent and the poorer parts of Chicago.

Nobody living in the city center had to be afraid of being mugged or even being shot–the likelihood of something like this happening was not greater than in any other big city in the world. Actually, the total number of murders in all of Chicago had constantly declined since the 1960s. And yet, in some parts of town, the situation was quite different.

Especially on weekends, there was a war going on and nobody could foresee what the death toll would be by the end of the year.

Richard watched the kids for a little longer as they were slogging the white buckets and flipping and twirling their sticks. Of course, they were too far away for him to hear them, up here on the eighty-sixth floor.

He would get them a gig at his foundation's next charity event. Even though this was a mere drop in the ocean, they could use the money–and the publicity.

Goaded by some local businesses that wanted to put an end to the constant noise, the City had been trying to ban street musicians from the Magnificent Mile–so far, however, without much success. For Richard, they were an integral part of a multicultural cosmopolitan townscape.

He took a deep breath, turned around, and picked up the phone.

****

Exhausted, she dragged herself to the bathroom where, with great difficulty, she stripped the delicate straps of her silk nightgown off her shoulders.

Using a hand mirror, she examined the location on her back where she had been hit by the stun gun.

The redness was still there, but at least the pain had subsided a bit by now. A day of bedrest had certainly done her good, but it would take a while until she'd be her old self again.

161

Since she had rescheduled all of yesterday's appointments to today, she would not have much time to prepare for her next operation. Maybe it was better this way–it wasn't such a good idea to go hunting without feeling 100% fit. The last incident had made that perfectly clear.

She put on her bathrobe, fetched the mail from the mailbox, and tossed it carelessly onto the kitchen table. Although she didn't feel like eating, she got herself a yogurt from the fridge and listlessly poked at it with a spoon.

Like it or not, she had to get her strength back.

Disgusted, she gulped down the slimy white goo, grabbed the newspaper, and went to the bathroom to fill the tub. The warm water would be good for her sore body and relax her mind.

She slipped out of her white terry cloth bathrobe, pinned her hair up into a bun, and gingerly stepped into the round Jacuzzi: oh yes, this felt good!

Her eyes closed and her extremities stretched out, she lay motionless in the tub and listened to the symphony of the bath bubbles bursting. Every few seconds, a drop of water got loose from the faucet and splashed next to her left foot. The spot on her back was burning a bit, but the feeling wouldn't last very long.

After a few minutes of complete indolence, she turned on the jets and enjoyed the stream of water massaging her body. Soon, she felt reinvigorated, getting aroused by the gentle pressure of the warm water. Grabbing the tub's rim and pushing her heels against the floor, she pressed herself firmly against one of the jets and let the stream pummel her lower back. As she continued to move her body up and down slowly, the prickling sensation on her skin started to feel uncomfortable.

Nevertheless, she turned the pump to maximum power, knelt in front of one of the jets, and scooted backwards until the stream was aimed right between her cheeks. The longer the stream massaged her sphincter the farther back she crept and her moaning intensified.

162

When she was less than an inch away from the nozzle and her anus finally started to hurt, she turned around and directed the stream straight onto her clit.

The carnal scream she let out when she came echoed back from the bathroom tiles and rolled through the streets outside.

She was feeling much better now.

For a while, she just dozed in the warm water before she dried her hands with a towel and reached for the newspaper.

As soon as she saw the headline, she was wide awake.

10:45 a.m.

"Good morning, Stephanie. Hope you slept well–last night was wonderful…"

All he could hear at the other end of the line was yawning and clattering dishes before she answered: "I slept like a baby. We are about to make breakfast. Are you already at the station?"

Richard, who had scheduled a meeting with Liz and Steven for 9 a.m., had left the house in the middle of the night to give the girls a chance to sleep in undisturbed.

"Yes, but I am afraid that it will take a while. I just got out of an emergency meeting with Bob and the vice mayor. The situation is about to get out of control. Since I urgently need to talk with my team now, I have no idea when I will be done here. Why don't the two of go ahead and I'll join you as soon as I can?"

"No problem! I guess you'll just have to wait and see later what we bought in your absence. Maybe we could put together a little fashion show for you tonight–I know a nice lingerie store in Oak Street that we could visit first thing in preparation."

In the background, he could here an enthusiastic "yippee!"

Richard smiled to himself. "I'm all in! I just don't know if I can wait that long. The sacrifices we make to maintain law and order… Alright, you two have a little fun on Oak Street. There are lots of shops you can rollick through, and I'll meet you there later. And just to be clear: your little shopping trip is on me–no discussion! Just let the store clerks know where to deliver your purchases. Most of them probably know me anyway."

"Are you serious? Do you know what you're doing? You have no idea how quickly we can spend a fortune when we are in a shopping frenzy."

As a matter of fact, Richard had a pretty good idea. But he had faith in the girls and knew that they wouldn't bankrupt him. He knew it would take much more than a couple of hours of shopping to achieve that.

"Don't hold back–I want you to enjoy yourselves. But I insist on the fashion show. So, you better make sure that you buy enough stuff to show off tonight!"

****

The moment Richard stepped into the conference room, he knew that there had been a new development: Liz and Steven were standing in front of the pinboard, engaged in a lively discussion.

"Richard, there you are at last! You have to look at that!" Liz grabbed his sleeve and pulled him ungently toward the gray felt board.

Pinned up next to the Identikit drawing of the Beautiful Stranger were several photos, all of which displayed good-looking women in restaurants, bars, or coffee shops.

At first, Richard did not understand what all the excitement was about, but then he was flabbergasted: even though it was almost unnoticeable at first glance, all photos showed one and the same person.

"That's unbelievable! Where did you get these pics?"

164

Liz was beaming proudly. "I found them on various Facebook sites, thanks to our new facial recognition software. However, I wasn't able to identify the woman yet. None of the people who posted the pictures know her. Either she just walked into the shot by accident, or a jerk took a picture of her secretly because he found her hot and wanted to post it on his site. If that's not creepy..."

"Does this mean that you've already contacted these guys?"

"You bet! I could even establish a possible link to one of the victims." Liz cocked her head to the side and looked at Richard expectantly.

"Liz, don't keep me in suspense! What have you found out?"

"One of the pictures was taken Saturday night in a singles bar not too far from Lincoln Park Zoo..."

"... where the car got torched?" Richard interjected excitedly.

"Exactly!"

"That's fantastic! You absolutely must find anyone who might have seen the woman: patrons, waiters, anybody who might have been in the bar at that time. Perhaps someone even knows who she is. You get all the help you need. The mayor has made this a priority."

Richard studied the photos. "She is a real chameleon–almost unrecognizable."

"And a real knockout!" Steven blurted out.

When he noticed Liz's disapproving look, he tried to justify his comment by adding "It's true, isn't it?"

Without taking his eyes off the pinboard, Richard nodded absent-mindedly. "It's true. It's undeniable."

In addition to the surveillance videos from the hotel, they now had five photos of the woman. In three of them she was just in the background. In the other two, however, she clearly was the main subject.

Since the resolution wasn't the best, Richard assumed that the pictures had been taken in haste. They must have been taken without

165

her knowledge. There was no way that she would have agreed to having her picture taken–especially like this."

She was sitting, legs spread wide, on a barstool. Not wearing any underwear.

"She doesn't know her victims." Richard was still staring at the photos.

"What do you mean?" Steven asked bewildered.

"Just look at her! She is flaunting her body like a gift-wrapped piece of meat–in a singles bar! That doesn't look to me like a date with a friend. She is hunting… and she herself is the bait."

****

Just as Richard was about to call the girls, his phone rang. It was Ron.

"What's up, buddy? Are you calling to tell me that you can't make it tomorrow? That would be too bad if the three of us had to have dinner without you…" Richard knew exactly how to tease his friend.

"Are you out of your mind? I have organized a sub. And a sub for the sub. Just in case. And, by the way, what do you mean by 'the three of us?' Did you get me a blind date?"

"Sorry, pal, but I have to disappoint you. I am not that caring–they are both mine. But maybe, this time, you can persuade Sonya to go home with you." Every time they were dining in Ron's favorite restaurant, his friend was hitting on the attractive hostess. At least he was always behaving particularly chivalrous, never giving anyone a reason to feel embarrassed.

"Just continue trying to make fun of me, but I am not ready to give up quite yet. I am sure that one day she'll eventually realize how irresistible I am–or just feel sorry for me and I'll have to settle for some mercy sex. So what?"

"Don't you worry! She probably pities you already, but that doesn't mean that she'll go to bed with you."

"Just wait and see! But let's cut the nonsense: don't you wanna know why I'm calling?" Unexpectedly, Ron was all business.

166

"Of course! I'm sorry! Shoot!"

"I've received the results of the DNA-analysis."

"Can you be a bit more specific? Which one?"

"The one from the toothbrush you have been bugging me about, of course!"

The toothbrush... All of a sudden, Richard wasn't so eager to get the result anymore. He could see in his mind's eye how much pain the news would cause the woman that had sounded so very likable on the phone. After all, he had experienced it himself before–more than once: just one call, or perhaps a visit from the police chaplain, was enough to turn one's life upside down in a heartbeat.

"And?"

"You were right, the victim is Thomas Maddock."

****

There it was again, the red Chevy Monte Carlo. Richard didn't even try to lose the car. Why should he? He didn't care that the reporter followed him.

Richard took a left turn and slowed down. He wanted to make sure that his pursuer made it through the traffic light.

As soon as he could see the junker in his rearview mirror again, he accelerated a bit. He didn't want McLean to get suspicious.

Although the City had done a decent job plowing, and most of the streets were clear by now, Richard had taken the Supercharged today. With three people and god knows how many shopping bags, the Rover was much more comfortable than the Porsche.

Richard drove along Lake Shore Drive and tried not to think of Mrs. Maddock. For a brief moment, he had been toying with the idea of flying to Boston and delivering the bad news to her himself. But what would have been the point? He didn't even know the woman and would not have been able to console her. An experienced psychologist and her own family were certainly much more suited to do that.

And it wasn't a good time for him to leave town. Not now.

167

To his right, Soldier Field glinted in the midday sun.

The stadium, which was the home of the Chicago Bears, had been built in the Neoclassical style in the 1920s, and had a capacity of about 60,000, making it the smallest arena in the NFL. However, it wasn't just a venue for football games but also for concerts and the occasional political event. Like in 1966, when Martin Luther King Jr. led almost 40,000 followers from here to Chicago City Hall where he posted a list of fourteen policy demands of his Chicago Freedom Movement on the door.

Richard, who hadn't been to a football game in a long time, had last been in the arena to see U2.

The much-criticized renovation, completed in 2003, hadn't left much more of the old structure than a few Doric columns. Even an award from the American Institute of Architects a year later could not prevent that the stadium, which was called an "alien toilet seat" in the local papers, eventually lost its status as a National Historic Landmark. By now, things had calmed down, and people seemed to have gotten used to its unconventional blend of classic and contemporary architecture.

Leaving Museum Campus behind, Richard saw a couple of die-hard joggers and bicyclists on Lakefront Trail. In the summertime, he also greatly enjoyed running along the 18-mile path. But in the winter, it was usually too cold for jogging. The frigid and dry air could easily take a toll on one's health. Even though running on the treadmill was getting old after a while, it was better than a bad case of bronchitis.

Richard took a turn onto Chicago Avenue and a moment later at Water Tower onto Michigan Avenue. The almost 140 feet-high limestone tower was not only one of the few buildings in town that had survived the Great Fire of Chicago in 1871 but also one of the city's major landmarks. On its north side, on Pearson Street, black or white horse-drawn carriages were always ready to pick up passengers.

168

That was it! That was the answer. After their shopping trip, Richard would surprise the girls with a romantic carriage ride around the city. They would definitely like that! With the sun going down as early as half past six, they had enough time to first enjoy the city lights and still go out afterwards.

As he waited to take a left turn onto Oak Street at the Drake Hotel, he called Stephanie to find out where they were. Maybe he didn't need to find parking and could let them hop in. In this part of town, it was basically impossible to find a spot for just a few minutes.

He was lucky: the girls were currently on their way to the next boutique but didn't mind interrupting their shopping trip for a quick snack.

"Perfect timing! You're close, we are right in front of the Jil Sanders shop. Just pull over and we can get in the car."

Richard could already see them waiting for him at the curb. They were surrounded by several large shopping bags with logos of various exclusive boutiques printed on them.

As soon as they recognized him, they waved exuberantly.

Since all the parking spots along the curb were already taken, Richard decided to turn on the emergency flashers and double-park his car.

This common practice didn't usually cause any problems, but this time the honking started the moment he stopped the car.

When he got out to assist the girls with their bags, he noticed a wildly gesticulating cab driver, who, not caring the least about the oncoming traffic, angrily tried to get around his car.

Not paying any attention to the cabbie's honking and gesturing, the girls greeted Richard with particularly long, passionate kisses and were in no hurry to stow their bags and get into the car. Just as Richard was about to get in himself, the impatient driver yelled something at him. At first, Richard wanted to ignore the guy, but when he flipped him off, he had enough.

169

He politely asked Stephanie and Consuela to excuse him for a moment, then closed the door and walked over to the taxi.

"Please forgive me for obstructing traffic for a moment. But, as you know, it's almost impossible to find parking here."

"Maybe you and your broads should take a cab then–that's what they are there for, you know. Now, get your fucking fancy-pants SUV out of the way, you asshole!"

Richard couldn't have cared less about this guy calling him names, but the fact that he had called the girls "broads" wasn't acceptable. He wasn't willing to let this slide.

He took out his badge and shoved it into the guy's face.

"Well, since I already apologized to you, I only see one way to settle this without making a big scene and you losing your license: you get out of your car and very respectfully ask the ladies to forgive your uncivilized, rude behavior. What do you think? Is this proposition agreeable to you?"

"Oh, of course! I am so sorry–I had no idea!" The cabbie couldn't hide his uneasiness.

"I am afraid you are missing the point. This is not about you having insulted a police officer. You need to understand that you can't make such a ruckus and behave like this!"

"Yes, yes, I understand. Believe me!"

The driver got out of the taxi, followed Richard to the Rover, and apologized to the girls: "Ladies, I am sorry for the inconvenience. Please, forgive me! It won't happen again. Have a wonderful day!"

Richard patted him on the back and took his seat behind the steering wheel. "Now, let's get out of here before we get a ticket!"

"What did you tell this guy? He was so intimidated I thought he would start cleaning the windshield any moment." Consuela couldn't help but laugh.

"I just told him that he shouldn't behave like this in the presence of ladies."

"No one else seemed to have a problem with you picking us up there."

Indeed, nobody besides the cabbie had honked their horn.

Yet, Richard was not surprised by that. Right behind the taxi, there was an old lady and behind her a couple in a Buick. The driver probably didn't even know where the horn was located.

He also wasn't surprised that McLean, who was trying to hide behind his steering wheel, did not want to draw any unwanted attention to himself.

Like the drivers of the next two cars.

2:10 p.m.

Tailing Richard Stanton had turned out to be much more challenging than expected. He would never have thought that something trivial like finding a parking spot could thwart all his plans.

Luckily, Stanton had used the valet parking of a French bistro so that it was obvious where they were going next. But he wasn't feeling lucky at all... once again he himself was standing at a corner, freezing his butt off while their party of three was cheerfully drinking bubbly and gobbling some sort of sandwiches. The haughty playboy probably called them 'hors d'oeuvres.'

Forrester McLean didn't get it: the son of a bitch was going out with not just one but two hot chicks. And hot they were...

Even in ripped designer jeans and a wool sweater, the cute blonde looked delicious. The racy Latina, though, was in no way inferior to her. She was wearing a multicolored knitted poncho–which was just long enough to cover her butt–as well as tights and riding boots. He would have loved to be ridden by her. But he knew that this wasn't going to happen.

171

He knew exactly who her stallion would be tonight. The way the three were interacting, it was obvious that the darkhaired beauty hadn't accompanied them as a chaperone. No, Stanton was fucking both of them.

Their kissing in the street earlier had already been over the top, and now his hand was resting on her thigh.

Forrester couldn't get distracted. If everything played out the way he had planned, he too would soon parade around town with beautiful women by his side. Then he would finally get what he deserved–and Richard Stanton as well.

****

Just who was this disgusting sleazeball following them? He looked as if he had just crawled out of a trash can: soiled parka, holey pants, scuffed shoes. He had suddenly appeared out of nowhere when Stanton had left the parking garage.

Now, he was watching them through the telephoto lens of his camera, which made her believe that he was a paparazzo. He clearly wasn't the sharpest tool in the shed, or he wouldn't be standing out there in the cold but would be sitting in the bookstore. Like herself. Here, it was comfortably warm, and the coffee was surprisingly good.

She hadn't had much time to do a lot of research on Stanton this morning, but all it had taken was a couple of phone calls and a quick internet search to find out who and where he was.

In the flesh, he looked even better than in the pictures she had found: tall, brawny, striking facial features, very well-dressed... he was just her type. She would be having a lot of fun with him.

Bagging him, however, wouldn't be easy.

The two girls at his side presented serious competition. They were trim, elegant, and graceful. She had to give it to them: they were sensationally good-looking. Without a doubt, he had exquisite taste. And while she was certainly on par with them, it complicated things a bit. A sexually satisfied man, unfortunately, didn't just think with his dick but had the annoying habit of occasionally using his brain–if he had one.

And based on what she had read about Stanton in the local tabloid press, he was anything but stupid. He had an MD, had solved several "impossible" murder cases, and appeared to be something of a financial wizard. Even though he had inherited a ton of money from his uncle, he had managed to multiply his fortune by making some very smart investments.

No, this man didn't think with his dick, that much was clear.

She would have to take a different approach with him.

****

"Why didn't you have your purchases delivered to me as I had suggested? That wouldn't have been a problem, and you wouldn't have had to shlep all those bags around."

The girls looked at each other and burst into loud guffaws.

Richard had no clue what was going on.

Stephanie, who had just taken a sip of her Kir choked on it and started to cough. Regardless of how hard she tried to control her laughing fit, all her attempts were futile. The moment she looked at Consuela again, she couldn't help herself but bite into her napkin.

"Would you please tell me what's so funny? Did I say something stupid?"

Richard's question just seemed to amuse them even more. By now they had tears of laughter in their eyes.

Consuela managed to get a hold of herself first. "But…Richard…" She tried to remain serious and cleared her throat. "… we did have our purchases delivered to your place! At least, most of them."

This time, Richard joined them in their laughter. "I guess that, soon, we will not just need a bigger bed but also an addition to the walk-in closet."

Consuela looked at him with her dark, mysterious eyes. "You really would do that, wouldn't you? We've just met a couple of days

173

ago, but you wouldn't mind remodeling your apartment for us. Are you so sure that the three of us have a future together?

"I am not sure, but I hope for it. Very much so."

"This calls for a toast: to love!" Stephanie raised her glass.

"Just a moment…" Consuela leaned over to Richard and ardently kissed him on his lips. "Bueno, now we can drink. ¡Salud!"

Richard, who had insisted on being seated at a window table, tried to act as normal as he could. The last thing he wanted was the girls to notice that they were being watched.

It hadn't taken him long to discover McLean–the big camera was just too obvious.

But he still hadn't been able to spot the woman. He could only feel that she was close. It was just a feeling, an instinct. What he couldn't say, though, was whether it was the instinct of a predator or the prey–and he didn't like it.

6:01 p.m.

It couldn't go on like this. He hadn't had a decent meal all day long, and now he had to run after a fuckin' horse-carriage. He knew that he wouldn't be able to do that for much longer. Sweating and gasping for air, he desperately tried to keep the camera away from his body. The lens had just the right length to kick him in his crown jewels if he wasn't careful.

Finally, after four blocks, he realized that the carriage ride probably wouldn't just start but also end at the Water Tower. Furthermore, Stanton's car was still at the restaurant. Of course, they would pick it up there again, sooner or later. He leaned against a tree, trying to catch his breath again.

He felt like an idiot. What a shitty day this had been.

What had he been thinking? That the woman would read his article in the paper and immediately set out to kill Stanton? The more he thought about it the stupider he felt.

On the other hand, he didn't have a better idea at the moment.

Still, it couldn't go on like this. For his plan to have at least a slight chance of success, additional manpower was required. But who should he bring in? His colleagues at the paper were all useless knuckleheads. None of them were willing to get their hands dirty for a good story. He couldn't afford to hire a private eye, and the paper wouldn't give him any money for that either.

There was just one solution: he would have to recruit one of his special "buddies."

Wesley Schroder was currently in the joint again and wouldn't get out for a while. The police had found photos of little boys and girls playing doctor on his computer. Maybe this pig would never see the light of day again. How about Josiah Smith? Why not? For a few bucks this guy would sell his children's organs. Fortunately, though, he didn't have any.

He would call Josiah first thing in the morning and make him the "offer of his lifetime."

The longer he was standing in the cold the less he felt like waiting for Stanton and his chicks to return. On top of that, he still had to walk eight blocks back to his car. He had had enough for today. If he hurried, he might not even have to pay for another hour of parking.

****

The carriage ride had been quite enjoyable. She couldn't remember when the last time had been that she had done something like this... maybe as a child?

First, they had been headed southwards on Michigan Avenue. When Stanton's carriage had taken a left turn, her driver had pointed out that they were taking the long tour and that it would cost more. He probably just wanted to make sure that he would get his money.

175

She had heard stories about tourists sometimes trying to haggle over the fare at the end of a ride. Nevertheless, he had gotten on her nerves after a while.

At first, he had refused to open the convertible top because he was afraid that he would have to stop along the way and close it again should she get cold. Then, he had been chewing her ear off with the history of Chicago. Only after she had threatened to throw him off the box seat and continue the ride without him, he had shut up.

The disgusting sleazeball with the camera had been running after the others for a while but had soon given up.

When she had passed by him a moment later, he had been staring at her in bewilderment. Like someone who's not quite sure if they know the person they are looking at.

At the same time, she was used to being checked out by men.

After their carriage ride, Stanton and the two women had picked up their car at the restaurant and, after a quick stop at a deli, had driven back to his apartment.

She had found his address already this morning. Since she had brokered the sale of several apartments in the skyscraper, she knew the building quite well, which could be to her advantage.

Right now, she would settle for a bite to eat.

There was an excellent restaurant on the sixteenth floor of his building where she would be able to do some thinking. And the idea of being so close to Stanton excited her.

8:07 p.m.

As Richard opened the door to his apartment, he burst out a surprised 'Wow!'

The entrance hall was full of bags and boxes, and several garment bags were lying over the chairs.

176

"At least you took me at my word..."

Stephanie, who was standing behind him and couldn't see the amused look on his face, feared that they might have gone too far.

"Don't worry, we made sure that we can return everything!"

Richard turned around, took her face in his hands, and kissed her. "Darling, I don't worry about the money. But had I known that you've emptied out Oak Street, we could have stopped at an interior architect on our way here. And, whether you like it or not, we'll all have to sleep in my bed again tonight–the guest room will have to serve as a closet for the next couple of weeks."

Consuela took off her coat and walked over to Richard. As she kissed him on the neck, she pulled up her poncho, wrapped her leg around his hip, and started to rub her crotch against his thigh.

When her hand glided down between his legs, she could feel through his pants that he was getting hard. "I don't think you'll get much sleep tonight."

****

It looked like his article had put a bomb under the police.

Unfortunately, he hadn't placed any cameras or microphones in the superintendent's office so he couldn't know for sure what had been said during the meeting with the vice mayor. However, the summary Stanton gave his coworkers was good enough.

He was surprised how much progress they had made in such a short time. For weeks, they'd got nothing. But then, along comes wonder boy and, voilà, after just a few days they have a photo of the main suspect.

But in the age of total surveillance capabilities, everything was possible. Cell phones, GPS, electronic toll devices, traffic cameras, cameras in ATM machines and public buildings, credit cards, internet: everyone was constantly tracked, filmed, and spied on without even noticing it. No one could avoid leaving evidence–especially if it was in electronic form.

It was just a matter of time until they would find the woman.

177

What was it that Stanton had said today? "I just want to remind you that it's not enough to find her. We have to be able to link her, without a doubt, to the murders."

Forrester McLean had absolutely no interest in them solving the case anytime soon. The longer the Beautiful Stranger was at large the greater his chance became that he would be able to find her first and get an interview with her.

Even if that didn't work out, there was enough material in this story for several articles.

The investigators had left the building after their meeting and had not come back.

He would have loved to bug their cells, but he didn't see a way to do that.

Since there was nothing else for him to do at the moment, he would enjoy the evening and finally devote himself to the secretary again.

He could hardly wait to see the shots the camera under her desk had taken today.

However, when he saw the first pictures, he was utterly disappointed. "Are you kidding me? What the fuck are you wearing?"

He quickly fast-forwarded through the day's recordings–he hadn't given up hope yet. Maybe she had got bored sometime during the day and had done something naughty under her desk.

But no, all he had were eight hours of film with her scooting from left to right in her black pants.

That wasn't even enough to get him excited. And he was easy to please ever since his wife had left him and he couldn't fuck for free whenever he felt like it.

At least, he still had last day's recordings. Those were good. Especially after he had spliced together the best scenes.

Yesterday, the half-hour-long version of the highlights had turned him on so much that he had jerked off to it three times.

If he continued like this, his hemorrhoids would soon start bothering him again.

He opened the file and fast-forwarded to his favorite scene: the secretary returned from the ladies' room and sat down at her desk. Evidently, her pantyhose wasn't in the right position since she moved her pelvis up and down a couple of times, which didn't seem to solve the problem. Then, she lifted her butt a little, pulled her skirt up a bit, and spread her legs.

Forrester McLean put one hand in his baggy sweatpants and started to rub himself while the other operated the computer mouse. Zooming in on her crotch, he could clearly make out her labia under the black nylon, which stretched over her mound of Venus like a translucent veil.

For a moment, she was picking at her pantyhose, trying to smooth it out around her thighs, but that didn't seem to help either.

Jennifer Walker must have felt unobserved. Otherwise, she wouldn't have put her hand between her legs to pull the little bit of fabric that had gotten stuck down there out of her crack.

****

Richard made himself comfortable on the sofa and took another sip of the 2005 Château Margaux he was treating himself to today. Already in the afternoon, he had asked Maria to decant the Bordeaux, which critics raved about. The blend of 85% cabernet sauvignon and 15% merlot had a dark ruby-red color and was reminiscent of ripe red and black berries and dark chocolate. The perfect balance between fruit and silky tannins and its warming, persistent finish made this particularly rich wine an all-time great. Even though this vintage would only get better over the years, the wine was already a stunner. Richard had secured a couple of cases of the delicious red at the right time and was eager to see how it would develop over the years. At a price of over a grand per bottle it wasn't exactly a steal, but today that was just a drop in the bucket anyway.

179

The girls were presently in the guestroom, changing yet again. As they had promised, they were presenting all their purchases to him in a fashion show, which was as close to a professional show as could be. The way they strutted across his living room–sometimes with casual elegance, sometimes with seductive lure–they looked like experienced runway models, at home on the catwalks of the world of fashion.

Stephanie had put together a special playlist on her iPod, which was now playing over Richard's stereo. Thus, every change was accompanied by the right music.

After casual clothes and business attire, they had just shown their new evening gowns. If Richard remembered correctly, underwear should come next.

At the beginning of the show, they had told him with a cheeky wink that he shouldn't expect them to present any wedding dresses in the foreseeable future.

When they, hand in hand, entered the room to the sound of Marvin Gaye's "Let's get it on," Richard put down his glass and leaned back on the sofa.

Consuela was wearing a white lace negligee, which gently embowered her perfect body. Not only her skimpy thong but also her erect nipples showed through the sheer, diaphanous fabric. Lace hold ups and high-heeled boudoir pom-pom slippers completed her alluring outfit.

Stephanie's black push up bra and suspender belt were overlayed with delicate floral mesh lace and featured string lacing, which ended in little tassels. The smooth, extra wide plain top of her stockings was attached to the garter belt with silk straps. Richard wondered how she was able to walk so confidently on the pencil-thin heels of her black stilettos.

Moving their hips in a slinky manner to the rhythm of the music, the girls slowly danced toward him until they were right in front of him. While Consuela sat down on his right thigh and started to caress

180

her breasts through the thin fabric of her negligee with her red-painted nails, Stephanie set her right foot down on his left knee, her hands gliding from the ankle up along her stocking.

Only now Richard realized that she wasn't wearing panties under her broad waist belt.

The narrow, shortly trimmed strip of dark-blond hair literally invited him to touch her between the legs. However, when he reached out toward her, a light slap on his wrist made it unmistakably clear that, for now, he was only allowed to watch.

Stephanie's hands lasciviously brushed over her stocking a few more times before she fiddled with her strap clips for a moment and, finally, moved her hands into her lap.

Spellbound, Richard followed her fingers as they gently entered her vagina while Consuela unzipped his pants and freed his hard penis. Slowly, she glided down his leg, kneeled in front of him, and took his cock in her mouth.

He let out a loud sigh when her soft, full lips enclosed him and she gently started to suck him off.

Stephanie, who by now was ready for him to play a more active part in their game, stepped up on the sofa and spread her legs right in front of him, making it easy for him to bury his face in her pubic area.

Her crotch was hot from lust and desire, and when he started nibbling on her clit, she pressed herself harder and harder against him.

Just when Richard thought he couldn't delay his orgasm any longer, Consuela briefly let go of his manhood to take off his pants.

Out of the corner of his eye, he could see her get up from the floor and take off her thong before she placed herself backwards on top of him and started to slowly and enjoyingly move her pelvis in a circular motion to the rhythm of Quincy Jones' "Secret Garden."

When Richard noticed that Stephanie was about to climax, he grabbed Consuela's hips, pulled her closer toward him, and wildly rammed his penis into her until she also tightened and they all came at the same time.

181

Thursday, February 17

8:14 a.m.

"I wasn't the only one staring at her. Everyone else in that goddamn bar was staring at her! Am I the only one she filed a complaint against?"

"A complaint? That's not what this is about. The photo on your Facebook site…"

"Come on! You can't be serious! It's not illegal to post pictures, is it?"

"Mister Grant, if you were kind enough to let me finish, I might be able to explain why I asked you to come to the station."

Liz was close to losing her composure. From the get-go, this jerk had caused her nothing but problems. Already on the phone he had been off-putting: arrogant, obnoxious, and condescending. No wonder that he had to hang around singles bars to "pick up broads," as he called it. No woman in her right mind would hook up with such a jerk. However, he looked good.

According to his papers, he was thirty-six years old and lived in Bucktown.

"Let me start from the beginning: the photo on your Facebook site…"

"I've told you already that I've deleted that! What else do you want me to do?"

"Now shut the fuck up, or I'll arrest you for sexual harassment and invasion of privacy! We have a couple of dudes in custody… if I put you in the same cell with them, your asshole will be as wide as a barn door by tomorrow morning."

"Okay, okay. I'll be quiet."

"You better. All I'm asking is that you listen to me and answer my questions. As I said, the photo on your Facebook site…"–Liz waited a moment, making sure that he would not interrupt her again– "…which you took with your cell phone on Saturday, February 12, around 11:00 p.m. in…"

"At 11:16 p.m., to be precise. You can see that from the timestamp!"

"Alright then: at 11:16 p.m. By the way, what made you photograph that woman?"

Douglas Grant looked at her disparagingly. "What made me photograph her? Just look at her!"

Liz did not need to take a look at the picture. She knew exactly what he meant.

"What can you tell me about the woman? Did you talk with her, or did you notice anyone else having contact with her?"

"No, I didn't talk with her. She came in, sat down at the bar, ordered a drink, and checked out the men. Then, everything happened really quick: she picked one out and left with him after a couple of minutes."

"Wait a minute! What do you mean by 'she picked one out'?"

"As I said, look at the picture! She certainly didn't spread her legs for me."

Liz did glance at the photo, which made her blush. Abashed, she got a handkerchief out of her desk and pretended to wipe her nose.

Just when she thought he hadn't noticed anything, he embarrassed her: "No reason to be prudish on my account. We both know what pussy looks like, don't we?"

She decided to ignore his last comment. "What else did you notice?"

"Besides the guy slumping over in front of her, nothing."

"He slumped over? Why? Wasn't he feeling well?"

"That wasn't my impression. I have no idea… He got up again right away. Maybe he just twisted his ankle or something."

183

"What did he look like?"

"No idea. Late thirties, early forties. Around six feet. In good shape. Dark hair, suit. Loud."

"Loud?"

"You know… someone you could hear in the whole bar."

"I understand. But, if he was so loud, maybe you could hear what he was saying? Maybe his name?"

"No. I didn't pay any more attention to them. After all, there were other girls, and I didn't want to go home alone, if you know what I mean." He winked and grinned at Liz.

"Anything else unusual?"

"Hmm… I found it weird that she had a Bloody Mary."

"Why?"

He rolled his eyes and shook his head. "Because you only drink that in the morning!"

"That's nonsense! You can do whatever you want."

"You don't go out much, do you? I don't know anybody who would do that. Just ask the bartender! He seemed quite surprised, too."

"Don't worry, I'll do that. If you don't have any additional information for me, I would ask you to help my colleague create a composite of the man before you leave. You better behave, or you know what's going to happen…"

"You didn't tell me what this is all about."

"No, I didn't. You didn't ask."

11:02 a.m.

Never in his life had he earned money that easy. One hundred dollars a day just for sitting around! McLean hadn't lied–it was a piece of cake. No wonder that niggard didn't want to pay him more than eighty at first. But he had been stubborn and had cozened another twenty out of him. Actually, he would have done it for half of that.

He could always use the money. Now that he had lost his job in the supermarket a week earlier, he was as broke as ever. In a way, he had been lucky. Since they hadn't had any proof, they had not called the police. Otherwise, they would probably have put him in jail right away.

When you were out on probation, it didn't matter whether you were stealing a car or just a few groceries.

Josiah Smith was sitting in his old Pontiac Gran Am and already smoked his sixth cigarette even though he had been here for less than an hour, waiting for Richard Stanton to leave the police station again.

Yet, the dandy wasn't his real target. McLean had made it very clear to him that he should look for a woman–a beautiful woman. He hadn't been able to give him a picture but meant that he would notice her if he just kept his eyes open.

So far, he hadn't noticed anything. Only that he really needed to take a piss.

****

"As of now, we have been able to identify eight persons that were in the bar Saturday night. Most of them are useless. They remember seeing the woman but nothing else. The bouncer gave us a really good description of her, but that doesn't help us because we already know what she looks like from the photo. And he doesn't know her."

"Did you talk with the guy who took the picture?" Richard wasn't interested in hearing about inquiries that hadn't led anywhere. He wanted results.

"Yes, I did. His name is Douglas Grant… He's such a dick! Strictly speaking, I didn't get much out of him either."

"Strictly speaking–what's that supposed to mean?"

"He doesn't know her either. But two things he mentioned were quite interesting. A man she had lured with her–how should I put

185

this?–"inviting nature" suddenly collapsed in front of her although he looked fit as a fiddle. And she ordered an unusual drink."

"First things first! Why did he collapse?"

"I was wondering about that myself, of course, and that's why I contacted the barkeeper. And, Bingo! He saw how our Beautiful Stranger with a single grip prevented her chosen one from putting his hand up her skirt."

"That's indeed interesting. Did the barkeeper see what exactly she did? Did she twist one of his fingers or his wrist, or did she apply pressure somewhere?"

"If I'm not mistaken, she just touched him. He didn't mention that she twisted anything."

"She probably just pressed the Hegu."

"The what?"

"The Hegu. That's one of the energy points of Dim Mak, a form of martial arts that utilizes targeted hitting or pressing of nerve centers to incapacitate or even kill an opponent. These points are also used in acupressure, for example to alleviate pain. See for yourself!"

Richard took Liz' hand and slightly pressed the point between thumb and index finger.

"That's actually not too unpleasant."

"No, it isn't. At least, as long as you don't apply too much pressure. The Hegu point is useful for easing tooth- or headaches. It can even help with stomach pain. However, one only needs to press a little harder and the result is quite different…"

As soon as Richard applied just a little more pressure, Liz pulled her hand away.

"Hey, hey, hey! That wasn't very kind! Where did you learn that?"

"Variations of Dim Mak are found in basically all types of Asian martial arts. And I got interested in acupuncture and acupressure when I was at the university."

186

"Do you think she might do that professionally? Maybe she's a chiropractor or something like that?"

"She may just have been trained in martial arts. At least, she knows a thing or two about self-defense. What was wrong with the drink? Why was it unusual?"

"Well, Mr. Grant, the dick, said that she ordered a Bloody Mary…"

"And he found that unusual because it was almost midnight and people tend to drink this with brunch? Forget it!"

"Just hear me out! That was also my first reaction. But then I mentioned it to the barkeeper, and he told me that it wasn't a Blood Mary she ordered but a Bloody Caesar."

"Isn't that the same?"

"Nope. Instead of tomato juice you use Clamato. You know, this mixture of tomato juice and clam broth."

"Ooh, that sounds tasty! And what's so special about this rotgut?"

Liz smiled smugly at him. "That it's basically only drunk in Canada."

4:36 p.m.

She really liked the car–that was the one she would take!

Tisiphone was sitting in the hotel lobby and watched the doorman as he opened the passenger door of the silver 7 series BMW and assisted an elderly lady in a rose-colored skirt suit get out of the car.

A moment later, the driver, a gentleman of about seventy wearing a dark blue jacket and grey pants, handed the keys to the valet and received a ticket in exchange. If she had counted right, its number should end with 3387.

187

As the couple entered through the revolving door and headed for the reception, she got up and pretended to be interested in the brochures that were laid out on the desk.

"Miller, Gregory Miller. We have a reservation for three nights."

"Welcome, Mister and Misses Miller!" The young receptionist typed on her computer. "I've got a suite for you on the 26th floor with a wonderful view of the city. I also see that you have a dinner reservation with us at six o'clock. May I confirm that?"

"Yes, please."

Tisiphone put one of the brochures in her purse and left the hotel.

She would come back later to pick up the BMW. Until then, she had enough time to make all other preparations for the evening.

It had paid off to follow Stanton's girlfriends. All they had been talking about over coffee was their upcoming dinner at the fancy restaurant.

Even though they had been sitting a couple of tables away from her, she had heard everything. She had learned when they were going, who would be joining them, and even what the two would be wearing… unless they changed their mind again.

She had dined at the Michelin-starred restaurant herself before and knew that it was almost impossible to say how late it would get until one was done eating. That depended very much on the menu one chose. It would be several hours for sure.

Therefore, she had made a reservation for 9:30 p.m. at the restaurant right next door. This would give her approximately two hours until Stanton and his guests would be done.

By then, she would have paid the check, be enjoying a cup of coffee, and be ready to leave without causing any suspicion.

****

"I've talked with the barkeeper again. He didn't recall her having any distinct accent. If anything, he thought she might be from Seattle."

Richard could hear the disappointment in Liz' voice. "Or Vancouver, the difference is almost indiscernible. Have you contacted the Canadian authorities yet?" he said.

"Yes, but that hasn't yielded anything yet."

"Even if she doesn't have a criminal record, we should be able to find her in a DMV database. They should all contain driver's license photos by now."

"In principle, yes. We have already searched the systems of most U.S. states, but all we've got so far were false-positives."

"We have to extend the search to the Canadian provinces and territories. Start with our colleagues in British Columbia. Maybe we'll get lucky."

7:10 p.m.

"Consuela, Stephanie, please meet my good friend, Doctor Ron Howard."

Ron, who was wearing a black, single-breasted tux with bow tie, took a bow and kissed the girls on the hand.

"By golly, a gentleman through and through!" Consuela remarked, slightly amused.

Undeterred by the comment, Ron looked at her affably and, still holding her hand, recited a poem:

"You're an angel from the skies,
balsam for my mortal eyes.
Divine beauty, godsent sin,
tell me, how your heart I win!"

Consuela was truly impressed. "Just keep this up, my dear Doctor, and anything might happen... I am delighted to make your acquaintance!"

"Believe me, the pleasure is all mine. But, please, call me Ron!"

Richard, who until now had mirthfully watched the hanky-panky, raised his forefinger admonishingly. "Ron, remember what I told you!"

Even though Consuela felt that Richard's remark was jocular, she quickly gave him a kiss and immediately dispelled any misconceptions: "Ron, my heart already belongs to another."

"And mine, too," Stephanie quickly confirmed.

"I know, I know! Please, forgive me for being overwhelmed by such beauty. In my defense, I am just a man."

"Now, sit down and stop being so formal, or the two may think that you're always like this!" Richard indicated with a slight nod to one of the waiters that they were ready to order aperitifs.

****

"I want fifty bucks more, or you can freeze your own butt off! My car doesn't have a parking heater, and I haven't eaten anything today besides a few potato chips. Piece of cake, my ass! This job is fucking boring!"

"Calm down, you'll get the money!" Forrester McLean knew all too well how Josiah Smith was feeling. He needed to jolly him, or he would have to run after Stanton himself again–and he really didn't want to do that given the current temperatures.

"You'll get the dough tomorrow, I promise. Now, tell me: have you seen the woman?"

"Negative. I haven't spotted anything unusual all day long. But I don't give a shit as long as I get my money."

****

"By the way, what kind of doctor are you, Ron? A plastic surgeon? Maybe, one day we can use your services…"

Ron pretended to study first Stephanie and then Consuela. "No, never ever let anyone snip away at you, you're perfect! And, I really hope I'll never have to deal with you professionally." Ron's cheerfulness had suddenly given way to melancholic sadness.

190

Richard felt that he owed the girls an explanation. "Ron is a pathologist and medical examiner and often works with me on cases."

"Oh, does this mean that you perform autopsies on murder victims?" Stephanie asked surprised.

"Not only. We also examine victims of accidents, suicides, and all persons whose cause of death is suspicious. We even perform postmortems when someone is getting cremated or buried at sea. Believe me, it's a long list!"

"That sounds like a lot of work to me," Consuela remarked matter-of-factly.

"You bet. At least my job is recession-proof."

"Forgive me for asking...," Stephanie said, "... but isn't it terribly depressing to deal with death all the time?"

"That's actually a question I am often asked. To be honest, it can be pretty tough. Especially if it's young people, who had their whole life in front of them. But it helps to remind oneself that what we do is important. After all, my work might help to put away a murderer. And we shouldn't forget that we are all going to die sooner or later. Even though death and dying are touchy topics in our society, the loss of life is a natural and, from an evolutionary point of view, useful phenomenon."

"Be it as it may, I don't want to die anytime soon, evolution or not!" Consuela raised her glass: "To life!"

"I'll drink to that," Ron said, and they all clinked their glasses: "To life!"

11:24 p.m.

There they were! Tisiphone took another sip from her coffee, got up, and let the waiter help her put on her coat. It would take a couple of minutes for her BMW to arrive, but she was in no hurry.

Standing in the entrance, she watched the party saying their goodbyes to the restaurant staff. Based on her experience, it always took a while to finally go home after such an evening.

All she could do now was wait and see.

The chauffeur had gotten out of the limousine and patiently waited for his passengers, ready to open the car doors for them.

While Stanton and his girlfriends walked arm in arm toward the car, the other man was still talking with a woman that looked to be the hostess of the restaurant.

It didn't take long until the BMW came around the corner. She needed to make a decision.

****

Was it her or not? All day long, he had been waiting for something to happen. And suddenly there was this woman standing in front of the other restaurant, watching Stanton. Or was he hallucinating?

She was stunning–mink coat, high heels, leather clutch… all very stylish.

The car was a good match: classy, but not ostentatious; racy, but comfortable.

She did not look dangerous at all. Yet, that was exactly how the reporter had described her: "A wolf in sheep's clothing."

Stanton and the other women were already sitting in the car, waiting for the other man.

Maybe he should contact McLean and ask him what to do. After all, the reporter had told him that he would be available anytime, day or night.

He got out his cell and realized that it was out of battery.

"Darn it!"

The battery had been acting up for weeks, but he had not been willing to pay twenty bucks for a new one. Now he was paying the penalty.

He would have to go with his gut.

192

Josiah Smith took the binocular, which McLean had given him, out of the glove compartment, and examined the woman more closely.

When he saw her eyes, he knew she was the one.

The limousine left, but, surprisingly, the woman did not follow it.

What should he do?

He thought it over for a moment, then decided to bird-dog the woman rather than Stanton. What had he got to lose?

Friday, February 18

2:07 a.m.

The man could hardly stand anymore. The mixture of Whiskey and Rohypnol was showing now, almost two hours after she had placed the benzodiazepine in his glass, the maximum effect.

Fortunately, it was just a few more steps.

She wouldn't have been able to schlep him much farther as his feeble body, which was hanging at her shoulder like a sack of potatoes, was getting too heavy.

"Come on, don't give up now… just put one foot in front of the other!"

She didn't know if he was able to comprehend anything she was saying, but the unintelligible mumble he responded with indicated that he at least could hear her.

When they finally reached the center of the hall, she let him slide to the bare concrete floor and sat down next to him, panting for breath.

She had certainly underestimated how exhausting it would be to haul the drugged man the twenty yards from the parking lot to the shop. It would have been so much easier had she had the key to the service door. She could have simply used the car to bring him in.

At least, now, the most difficult task was accomplished. He was lying directly in front of the large steel sculpture, right under the chain hoist.

She looked at him.

In contrast to all the other guys, he had been neither tactless nor pushy. She had almost had the impression that he had accepted her invitation for a drink only out of politeness. Once, though, she had figured out what his type was, it had been easy for her to finesse him into letting his guard down.

He was into elegant, distinguished ladies that wanted to be conquered.

She had played the game with him and had pretended to fall for his charm and find his cultivated act irresistible. She had attentively listened to his discourses on music and art and courteously chuckled at his witticisms.

She could hardly wait for the drug to quiet him down.

Now he was lying motionless next to her.

She got up and walked over to the office. Earlier in the afternoon, she had deposited her stuff in there and had turned on the electricity for the infrared ceiling heaters, which had brought the temperature up to a comfortable level by now.

Except for her nylons and shoes, she took off all her clothes, folded them neatly, and put them in the big plastic bag.

Delicately, she opened the little black box, took out the ampoule with the flumazenil, and filled the syringe with five milliliters of the clear, colorless solution. That should suffice. She could always give him more later, if necessary. It was of the utmost importance that he was conscious during the punishment.

The antidote only had a half-life of about an hour, but that didn't matter. He wouldn't live that long.

She returned to him, laid the syringe on the ground, and began to undress him.

When she started to fiddle with his zipper, he became more awake and even helped her take off his pants.

But his movements were uncoordinated and feeble. In this condition, he did not pose any danger. He was defenseless.

That's why he didn't even resist when she placed the chain around his chest and pulled him up.

****

195

What on earth was she doing in there? The gap under the door was too narrow to make out anything inside. He couldn't hear anything either–except maybe some dull clanging, which reminded him of rattling chains.

He had to find out what was going on inside that hall.

Here in the front, all windows were blacked out with paint. Perhaps, he would have more luck in the back.

The tall fence, which obviously was supposed to secure the backyard, looked pretty sturdy. No holes anywhere.

At least, the owners had opted against barbed wire–all too often he had gotten bloody fingers during this type of infraction.

Josiah Smith hesitated for a moment, asking himself whether it was worth the risk; then he climbed up the chain link fence.

There were several big metal objects scattered over the property. Some were almost as tall as the single tree that looked somewhat out of place amid this industrial zone.

Here in the back, the windows weren't blacked out. They were so high up, however, that he would have to get up the tree to be able to peek inside the hall. The branches looked strong enough to support his weight… at least in the dim light shining through the windows.

Next to the tree trunk, there was a clunky steel bench, from which he could easily reach the lower branches.

Slowly, he climbed higher and higher, always careful to distribute his weight among several points. Just when he thought that he was up high enough, his right foot slipped, and he could avoid a fall only by hugging the tree firmly with both arms. This way, he only slid down a few inches, but the rough bark chafed his face and hands.

Cursing silently, he pulled himself up until he regained hold in a tree fork. He should have never agreed to this.

His hands were burning like hell, and his lips tasted of blood.

Carefully, he leaned to the side to see past the trunk and inside the hall.

What had looked like a car shop from the outside turned out to be an artist's shop. Along the walls, there were several racks, lockers, and work benches. Next to them lay piles of massive steel beams and plates of different sizes as well as pipes of varying diameters. Most of the space was taken up by machines, whose purpose he could only guess. Still, the center of the room, a circular area of at least fifty feet in diameter, was practically empty. There were only a few welding tools and a platform lift... and the enormous steel cross, of course, which was standing exactly in the middle of the hall.

Only after the chain, which was dangling from a motorized hoist above the cross, moved a little, he spotted her.

Since they were both on the other side of the cross, however, he could not make out what was happening.

With difficulty, he opened the pocket of his jacket and got out the binoculars.

The woman was standing on the lift platform at a height of about fifteen feet and seemed to be trying to affix something to the cross. Yes, that's what it was. She placed chains first on one and then on the other side of the crossbar and fastened them with spring hooks.

When she stepped to the side, he could see not only that she was almost naked but also what she was attaching to the cross.

Just for an instant, the man's left arm was hanging down in front of her bare body. It didn't take her long to chain him up at his arms and legs before she unlocked the hoist and took him off the hook.

The man was hanging on the steel structure like a crucified martyr.

Josiah Smith wasn't a religious man. The last time he had been in church had been at his mother's funeral. Thus, he did not know why he was uttering the words that were coming out of his mouth, or why he was remembering them:

> "The LORD is my shepherd; I shall not want.
> He makes me lie down in green pastures.

197

He leads me beside still waters."

The woman bent down and picked up a syringe from the lift's platform.

"He restores my soul.
He leads me in paths of righteousness
for his name's sake."

She removed the safety cap from the hypodermic needle and injected a colorless liquid into the man's arm.

"Even though I walk through the valley of the shadow of death,"
I will fear no evil..."

She lowered the lift to the ground and positioned herself a short distance away from the cross. With her hands on her hips, she looked up as if admiring the piece of art towering before her.

"...for you are with me;
your rod and your staff,
they comfort me."

When the figure on the cross started to move, her face turned into a terrifying grimace. Her piercing stare, the upward stretched chin, and her tense, erect body now unveiled pure hatred and pompous vain.

"You prepare a table before me
in the presence of my enemies;
you anoint my head with oil;
my cup overflows."

Suddenly, she yelled something toward the man on the cross. No, she screamed, and her voice echoed back from the shop's walls so that he could clearly hear each of her words:

"See how beautiful I am!
Look at me as I am Tisiphone!
Look at me as I will be the last you'll see in this world!
Look at me as I've come to end your miserable life!
Look at me as I will drink your blood and eat your flesh!
Look at me...
as I am vengeance,
and I am salvation!"

She went over to one of the racks and took something bulky out of the lowest shelf.

Only when she turned around and walked toward the lift, he could see that it was a chop saw. She started the gas engine and took the lift up again.

Josiah Smith bit into the back of his hand. What should he do? The reporter had explicitly forbidden him to get involved. He was just an observer...

"Surely goodness and mercy shall follow me
all the days of my life,
and I shall dwell in the house of the LORD
forever...
Oh my god! My god! Oh god!"

She was all the way at the top now. With a mad grin, she lifted the heavy tool and started to lash out at the man. Streams of bright red blood gushed all over her naked body.

He had to get out of here... as quickly as possible! Frantically, he hurried down the tree. While on his way up, he had made sure to distribute his weight evenly, he now wasn't so careful. That was the reason why now, halfway down, one of the rotten branches that had carried his weight earlier broke.

With a loud wham he was falling toward the ground.

When his right leg hit the metal bench and his kneecap shattered to pieces like a porcelain plate dropped on the floor, he let out a cry.

"Oh, my god! My god, my god!" He was desperately hoping that she had not heard him.

Leaning on the broken-off branch, he hobbled as fast as he could toward the car.

The fence! How should he make it over the fence?

He clenched his teeth and clawed his mangled fingers into the wire mesh. Piece by piece, he pulled himself up until he was able to slide his upper body to the other side.

Hanging headfirst over the fence, he looked at the asphalt shimmering black in the soft shine of the streetlight. Only when he was about to let himself fall down, a naked woman, covered with blood, appeared in front of him.

He couldn't see the wrecking bar–he could only feel the impact when it smashed his spine.

6:52 a.m.

Richard rested his chin on his chest and let the warm water massage his neck. Even though he had greatly enjoyed swimming a few laps in the pool today, it had been unusually exhausting. To go swimming just once a week simply wasn't enough.

Somehow, he had to make time to work out every day again.

He watched the water drops running down his ripped abs, forming little runnels and trickles, and finally flowing down his legs.

He wasn't really at risk of gaining weight quite yet–the girls were working him too hard for that. However, it was just a matter of time until his culinary indulgences would make him get love handles.

Just last night it had been no less than twenty-four courses and a good amount of alcohol. Yet he didn't have any regrets. He had cherished every bite and every sip.

Not just the food had been phenomenal–the atmosphere had been just as great.

Richard was very happy that the girls had not been bothered by Ron's awkward welcoming ceremony. They had instantly taken a shine to him. They had had lively conversations with him and had treated him like a good friend.

Richard admired how open-hearted and fair-minded they were in their interaction with other people. They were empathic and warmhearted, yet always straightforward and candid–and all the while so entrancing and charming that one couldn't help but enjoy their company.

From the very beginning, Ron, too, had been mesmerized by them.

When Stephanie and Consuela had been "powdering their noses" after the first course, he had immediately used the opportunity to let Richard know what he thought: "My dear Richard, I've got to hand it to you… you are a lucky bastard! I have no idea where you've found these divine creatures, but if there are more of them, I also want one; better even, make that two–just as you have two. But in all seriousness: Consuela and Stephanie are adorable. I can barely contain myself… how did you meet them?"

Later that evening, when they had been alone again for a moment, he had said something else that had moved Richard deeply: "They are both very special. You better not screw this up! If I were you, I would marry both of them at once–though that's probably illegal… anyway, you know what I mean."

He knew exactly what his friend had been trying to tell him. After all, Ron had accused him of suffering from philophobia more than once in the past. He had even prophesied that he would die in "emotional solitude."

Richard knew that these warnings were well-meant and not completely unfounded.

No, this time he wouldn't blow it.

Just as he was wondering if it was too early to surprise the girls with breakfast in bed, someone opened the glass door and turned on the other shower head. It was Stephanie.

"Good morning, darling!" She took his face in her hands, pushed her naked body against his, and kissed him. "Why are you up so early? Do you have to go to the station?"

"No. That means… not right away. I had a bad dream and couldn't go back to sleep. I've probably just got too much on my mind."

Compassionately, she stroked his cheek. "Oh, I am sorry. Come here, I've got an idea how to cheer you up!"

Stephanie grabbed Richard's body gel, poured a good amount of the slimy, viscous liquid in her hands, and distributed it in circular motions over his chest. Gently, she soaped his arms before she asked him to turn around.

Richard closed his eyes and rested his forearms against the slate shower wall while Stephanie massaged his shoulders. Slowly, she moved her fingers down his spine. For a moment, she kneaded his buttocks, then reached around him, and softly washed his genitals.

He immediately reacted to her tender fondling by getting hard. As she moved her slippery fingers back and forth along his stiff phallus, he responded by fervently thrusting his penis into her hands.

"Mmm, that feels good–if you continue like that, I'll come pretty soon."

"Not so fast!" Stephanie kissed his shoulder and tantalizingly and slowly let her fingers glide over his loins toward his back.

She got more of the body gel, kneeled down on the floor, and started to soap him from the bottom up: feet, legs, butt.

"Now, it's my turn!"

When Richard turned around, she already had her shower oil in her hands, proffering it to him. With an impish smile on her face, she put her head back and pushed out her boobs.

Richard could tell from her erect nipples that this kind of foreplay had not just turned him on.

She was so beautiful. Even though he could hardly wait to push himself between her legs and make love to her, he gladly satisfied her wish, opened the bottle, and squeezed the honey-colored lotion directly onto her wet skin.

He took his time to gratify her. Like a sculptor modeling a statue, he moved his hand lovingly over the contours of her flawless body, massaged her perfect, firm breasts with gentle pressure, and gingerly washed her between the legs.

At first, Stephanie responded to his tender fondling only with faint sighs, but the longer he touched her the more she got aroused. She pressed herself harder and harder against him, started to touch herself as well, caressed her breasts, and played with her clit. Her desire had now grown to the point that she did not want to delay her gratification any longer. She wanted to feel him inside her.

"Sleep with me!" Impatiently, she put her arms around his neck, clenched his stiff penis between her legs, and kissed him passionately.

Richard only needed to lift her up a bit to enter her. One hand under her butt, the other in her long, blond hair, he tempestuously pinned her against the wall and frantically rammed his dick into her until she cried out loud as she climaxed.

****

"Don't you two think that I didn't hear you!" Consuela stood in the living room door, squinting her tired eyes. The bright sunlight, which warmly wafted through the big windows, shone directly into her face. "You could have come back to bed, you know…"

It was her reproachful tone, which sounded a bit like the whining of a moody child, that gave her away–although Richard found her sulky pout quite convincing.

"We thought we'd give you a rest… after last night," he countered.

Indeed, she had fallen asleep already at around 1 a.m.–on top of him! The fabulous food, the alcohol, and at least three orgasms had finally taken a toll on her. She stuck out her tongue at him and gave him a broad grin. "At least you've made breakfast. Then we'll just have to go to bed again later, I guess."

Richard got up, gave her a kiss, and went to the kitchen to fetch her a cup of cappuccino.

When he returned, Consuela and Stephanie were standing arm in arm at the window and enjoyed the view of the city and the lake.

"Richard, I love your apartment! The view from up here is incredible! I love Chicago! Even though the winters here are a bit too chilly for my taste, it's without question a fantastic city! You just can't have it all…" Consuela took the coffee out of Richard's hand and thanked him with a peck on the cheek.

For a moment, Richard contemplated what she had just said. "Why not? Why don't we hop on a plane and fly someplace warm once I can get away from here? How does that sound?"

"Do you think you can just leave?" Stephanie asked doubtful.

"As I said: once I can get away. We could go someplace in the Caribbean. That's not too far, and we could be back in no time if needed."

"That's a great idea. How do you feel about visiting my family? If we take a direct flight, it's not even five hours to San Juan." Consuela was full of enthusiasm.

"I don't think that I will be able to go anytime soon, I am afraid. I have to report back at the Art Institute next week, and I have no idea when my boss may let me take a vacation again." Stephanie sounded disappointed.

204

"Don't worry! It doesn't have to be right away. I don't mind staying here with you. Not at all!" Richard moved between them and put his arms around them.

It was shortly before eight o'clock now, and, outside, rush hour was in full swing. Beneath them, people–looking a lot like ants–were streaming toward entrances, crossed streets, and piled into overcrowded buses.

Every so often, individual dots, as if driven by an invisible force, sheared off the line and took direction toward their respective destination. Everyone who hadn't made it to work by now was in danger of having to work late on a Friday evening rather than ring in the well-earned weekend with their family. Bankers, lawyers, clerks– day in and day out they all kept their noses to the grindstone, weren't allowed to make any mistakes, had to endure criticism and sometimes humiliation, and were still constantly at risk of getting sacked at the slightest sign of objection.

Richard had never shied away from hard work. It was true that his parents had afforded him a happy and carefree childhood and youth, for which he was very thankful. But he had not grown up in wealth. Rain or shine, he had delivered newspapers before the break of day, had shoveled snow or mowed lawns, cleaned out stables, and even felled trees to earn some money. He knew what it meant to make an honest living. College, med school, and his residency hadn't been a bowl of cherries either.

He knew very well how fortunate he was to be free of such constraints nowadays. Life was so short...

Suddenly, his cell started ringing. He did not feel like answering at all. He looked at the girls, thinking that his place was here with them. Nothing could make him jeopardize this luck.

And still, at the next ring, he answered the phone. He simply couldn't let down Bob and the department now.

9:31 a.m.

Next to several emergency vehicles, there were a couple of vans from local news channels in front of the brick hall. Press cards hanging from the rearview mirrors of a number of cars parked close by pointed toward an even larger presence of the media.

It was obvious that after McLean's article had been published in the Wednesday edition of his tabloid, also the rest of the pack had smelled blood and did not want to miss out on the chance of making the front-page of their respective outlets.

As soon as Richard got out of the Rover, several reporters with cameras and microphones surrounded him and bombarded him with questions: "Dr. Stanton, why hasn't the press been informed? What is the number of victims? Why aren't you releasing any pictures of the suspect?"

Richard just smiled nonchalantly and repeated the same answer over and over: "No comment!"

After he had finally fought his way through the crowd, an officer led him to the backyard where Steven was inspecting a couple of branches on the ground.

"Good morning, Steven. What are you doing there, crawling on the ground? Have you found something?"

"Hi, Richard. I am not sure yet, but I think that someone may have fallen from that tree. Look, the branches appear to have been broken off just recently… and I have found this!"

Steven held out a tatter of black anorak fabric, which still had some remnants of white padding attached at its back.

Richard looked up. During wintertime, it wasn't easy to tell when the dead branches had really been torn off.

"Ask someone from the fire department to get up there! They have more experience climbing trees than we do. Now, tell me what has happened here!"

Steven got up and cleared his throat. "Shortly before eight, we received a call about a fire with possible fatalities. The call came from a Jeff Thompson, a realtor who wanted to show the workshop to a potential buyer. If I am not mistaken, the shop is for sale because the owner, an artist who has used the building as a studio, wants to move to Arizona. The colleagues who arrived first at the scene immediately contacted us once they saw the victims."

"The victims?" Richard asked flabbergasted.

"Right! Two, to be specific. Come with me, you have to see this!"

Steven led Richard to the front of the building and opened the entrance door. "I wonder if you can make sense out of this…"

Stepping into the hall, Richard could not hide his surprise. "What the heck has happened here?"

"That's exactly what I've been asking myself, too!"

Right in the center of the studio, about fifteen feet above the ground, there was a badly charred body hanging from an enormous metal cross. The victim was chained to the steel construction, which reminded Richard of the cross found in the rubble of the collapsed World Trade Center. Just as the original, this replica also had a missive concrete plinth, which must have weighed a few tons itself.

Everything pointed toward the same perpetrator: the victim was male, had been tied up and then burned–and a body part was missing.

Who, however, was the second victim lying in front of the sculpture?

"What do you think, Steven? Do you have a hypothesis yet?"

"I don't think that you'll agree with me, but isn't it possible that we've made a mistake and the woman isn't involved in the murders at all? Maybe it's actually him!" Steve pointed toward the man lying on his back.

Richard gave him a doubtful look. "What do you mean?"

"Well, let's assume for a moment that he is the murderer. He brings his victim here to kill him the usual way: tie him up, mutilate

207

and burn him. Only, this time, something goes wrong. The victim temporarily gets away and attempts to climb up a tree but falls down. The perp catches the victim again, chains him to the cross, mutilates him, and just as he is about to set the victim on fire, loses his footing, falls off the platform, and breaks his neck. Who knows, maybe there was a flash of fire he tried to dodge…"

"Aren't you forgetting something?" Richard pointed toward the body on the cross.

When Steven just looked at him quizzically, he said: "The head– where is the head?"

"I see… that's a problem. We haven't found it yet. But how about that: the perp crucifies the victim, brings the head someplace else, comes back, and sets the body on fire?"

"Why would he do that?"

"Well, maybe he forgot to bring gasoline and had to get some first. Or he just changed his mind. Maybe he hadn't even planned to kill the victim this time. Only later, back home, he realizes that he's made a mistake."

Richard looked at the African American man lying on the floor. "And you really believe that he is the serial killer who's also committed the other murders?"

"We have no proof that it's not him. Even if a woman met with the other victims before they got killed–and I am not suggesting otherwise–this guy could still be the killer. Maybe he committed the crimes because he was jealous, or the two even worked together. That would also explain why the head is missing–she took it. Give me one reason why it shouldn't have happened like that!"

Richard looked around. The platform had been raised just enough to comfortably reach the body on the cross. On the floor, not far away from the other victim, lay a metal bar. At one end were the leftovers of a burnt rag. Whoever had started the fire had been smart enough to do so using a makeshift torch.

Halfway between the entrance and the cross lay a professional cut off saw. Richard was convinced that this was the tool the victim had been decapitated with. Coagulated blood and pieces of tissue on the blade hinted at the bloodbath that had taken place here. Even the gas tank and blade guard were stained red. Only the metal handles were clean–too clean. Obviously, someone had taken the time to wipe them down after the crime. The question was: who?

"Tell Ron that I need the autopsy report as soon as possible! In particular, I need to know what killed your supposed perp here. By the way, why isn't Ron here yet?" Richard was tempted to inspect the victims himself right here on the spot. But even he had to follow the rules.

"Looks like Ron's got the day off, but his sub should be here any moment. I'll make sure that whoever works this case knows how urgently we need the results... You don't believe that I'm right, do you?"

Richard got the feeling that Steve was a bit disappointed. "Steven, it doesn't matter what I believe. All that matters is that we find out what has really happened here and that we prevent more killings. Why don't we take another look outside? Maybe we could find some more clues."

As they returned to the backyard, Richard became suspicious. "Say Steven, was the gate already open when you arrived?"

"Hmm, I think so. Why?"

"Why would anybody in this neighborhood who has such a fence leave the gate wide open? That doesn't make any sense, does it?" Richard walked back to the fence and closed the gate.

"Steven, it looks like at least some parts of your theory might be correct. Someone actually was back here and may have fallen off that tree. But I bet it wasn't the man on the cross."

209

2:13 p.m.

"Shit, shit, shit! What am I going to do now?"

Forrester McLean banged his fist on the table with such force that the computer monitor flickered and turned blue for a moment. Then, the reporter buried his face in his hands.

Just what had gone wrong?

All morning long he had tried to get in touch with Josiah. When his snooper hadn't answered his phone, though, McLean had come to the conclusion that he had already had enough of earning an honest living by spying on Stanton.

And now that!

Once again, he zoomed in on the photo that was pinned to the wall, saved the picture, and opened the file in Photoshop. However, all attempts to further increase the resolution were futile. It was simply impossible to say for sure who the person on the floor really was.

One thing, however, was sure: Josiah Smith was dead.

The little slant-eyed policewoman had mentioned his name loud and clear. No less than three times he had listened to the recording already. The sound quality was impeccable. Every single time she unmistakably had said "Josiah Smith."

The cops had been able to identify him in no time from his fingerprints. No wonder, considering his rap sheet. Why they would think that he might be the killer, however, was completely beyond McLean.

When Stanton had learned that the vice mayor had called a press conference to announce that the case of the serial killings had been solved, he had gone ballistic and had put his badge and gun on Chief Miller's desk.

Not even the sexy secretary had been able to calm him down. Full of concern, she had click-clacked behind him in her high heels, using all her charm to make him change his mind, to no avail.

In front of the elevator, he had given her a kiss on the forehead before leaving without so much as a word.

Should he confess to Stanton that he had hired Josiah to find the woman?

That was probably not such a good idea. The playboy just had to put two and two together to figure out that he had been used as bait.

No, he didn't have a death wish.

Furthermore, Stanton knew all too well that Josiah had nothing to do with the murders–he had made that crystal clear to the Chief before announcing his resignation.

But what if the police figured out that he had been in contact with the ex-con? A note or a calendar entry with his name was sufficient to blow his cover. Or his phone number…

Shit!

In the last two days alone, he had called Smith at least twenty times. He had left as many as five messages on his voicemail just this morning. His number would be the first to pop up once they would find his phone–that much was certain.

But why hadn't they contacted him yet?

Forrester McLean looked at his watch. They should have contacted him by now…

Unless they didn't have the phone.

****

"Dr. Stanton, Richard, please, calm down! Have you had anything to eat today? I'll fix you something muy delicioso that will make you feel better. Just take a seat and have a glass of wine!"

Maria pushed him down onto the sofa, took off his shoes, and disappeared into the kitchen. Richard could hear her opening the door to the climate-controlled wine room and, a moment later, uncorking a bottle. Hopefully, she wasn't too concerned.

211

When she came back to the living room, he knew how she judged the situation–she had opened a 2005 Château Latour Pauillac.

"Maria…"

"¡Silencio! I don't want to hear another word! Just take a sip and relax! I'll be in the kitchen, and when I come back, you be calm! ¿Comprendido?"

The wine hadn't even had time to breathe. Richard swirled the dark red liquid in his glass. The wonderful bouquet included floral notes and aromas of black currant, plums, and graphite.

He closed his eyes, seeking to remember the vineyards in the Médoc…

It was just past noon, and he was lying on a woolen blanket under a tree somewhere at the banks of the Gironde. Next to him was a wicker basket, and one could hear the ringing of church bells in the distance. They had had baguette and pâté de foie gras with some fresh grapes, which they had picked from the vines lined up in front of them. The bottle was almost empty, and Jacqueline scooched closer and closer to him until she was suddenly lying in his arms.

Her dark blond hair smelled of honey, and her lips tasted like sweet strawberries with whipped cream.

Through the flowered fabric of her summer dress, he felt her full breasts pressing against his chest. At first, they just smooched innocently like two teenagers who want to explore the mysterious world of sexuality together. Soon, however, wet kisses alone didn't do it anymore. With fierce intensity, they began to rub their bodies against each other, fondling and groping. The initial innocence of their touches had quickly given way to primal lasciviousness, which thirsted for gratification.

Impatiently, she unzipped his pants and sat on top of him. She didn't even bother to take off her panties, but just pulled them to the side and let his hard dick glide inside her.

212

He unbuttoned her dress, pulled down her snow-white bra, and vehemently sucked her nipples while she was riding him passionately, bringing herself off.

Afterwards, they lay silently next to each other for a while until they packed up their things and drove back to Bordeaux.

When another guide picked him up from the hotel the next morning, he was told that she wasn't feeling well. The following day he didn't see her either, but this time she allegedly was on vacation.

All attempts to get in touch with her were fruitless. Her agency just kept responding to his relentless inquiries with spurious evasions and steadfastly refused to give him her address or phone number.

It was only right before his return trip back to the States a week later that he found out by accident that she was engaged and to be married to her high school sweetheart a few weeks later.

Without opening his eyes, he took the mouth-blown crystal glass to his lips, slurped some of the precious liquid, and rolled it over his tongue…

From the first moment on, sparks had been flying between them. He had been waiting in the hotel's street café for a whole hour when suddenly a beautiful young woman in a red convertible came hurtling around the corner. She parked the car on the other side of the street, swooshed her sunglasses up to the top of her head, and got out. Richard couldn't remember what she had been wearing that day. Only that her long hair and scarf were blowing in the wind when she came running toward him across the old, cobbled street. He would never have guessed that it was she he was waiting on. Otherwise, he might have been a bit more reserved. Maybe…

"Est-elle une déesse?" he asked in his rusty school French as she was about to rush past his table.

213

Bewildered, she stopped and looked at him. From her amused smile he could tell that she was flattered. "Comment?"

"The car! Isn't this a Citroën déesse–a goddess?" he tried to back out.

But she had already seen through him. "Why can't I help from getting the feeling that you speak French well enough to know the difference between 'Are you?' and 'Is this?'?"

"I don't know. Why don't you join me, have a cup of coffee, and give me a private lesson on that subject?"

Again, there was this adorable smile.

"I am sorry, but I can't. I have an appointment, and I am already running late. Thank you for the invitation, though. So long! Salut!"

Richard didn't even have time to ask her name so quickly she disappeared in the hotel.

He had already given up all hope for his tour guide to turn up when, all of a sudden, he heard a silky-smooth voice with a sweet French accent: "Dr. Stanton, as it seems, we do have an appointment after all!"

Richard turned around. "I hope you are not too disappointed."

For the fraction of a second, she pursed her lips. "Not at all. Please, forgive me for keeping you waiting, but the agency told me to pick you up at nine-thirty, not at nine."

Obviously, the fact that it was already past ten o'clock did not faze her.

"No worries. In the meantime, I have been enjoying the view. It's not every day that you get to see a goddess…"

For a week, Jacqueline had taken him through the north-western part of the Bordeaux wine-region, had shown him the most beautiful chateaus, introduced him to their wine-makers, and provided expert advice at countless private tastings.

As it had turned out, she had studied enology at the Université Bordeaux Segalen and knew everything there was to know about

214

wine. In addition, she knew the area like the back of her hand and took him to the coziest cafés and best restaurants.

And while they had always been friendly with each other during that time, they had always maintained a certain distance. Yet when they happened to touch each other by accident, it was like two magnets attracting each other, and it always took some time until they were able to let go.

"Richard?"

Her hand rested on his for a brief moment as they were both reaching for the water carafe.

"Richard, darling, are you awake?"

He opened his eyes and saw Stephanie standing in front of him. She looked worried.

"What are you doing here? I thought you were at the auto show."

"Maria called me. She told me that you are not feeling well, and so I took the next cab to get here. What's happened?" She sat down next to him on the sofa and took him in her arms.

"The vice mayor has declared that the case is closed. That's what's happened!"

"What do you mean? Have you caught the perp?"

"No. Of course, we haven't! But Steve couldn't help but take this absurd theory to the Chief, just as he was having a video conference with the vice mayor."

"What absurd theory?"

"That one of the victims we found today is the murderer."

"And you don't agree…"

"It simply doesn't make any sense! But that doesn't seem to be of any importance if one is just interested in protecting the city's reputation. God forbid, there might be fewer tourists coming to town, or some conference might get cancelled. Can you imagine what economic impact this would have? So, why not lie to the public instead? And if something goes wrong, just pin it onto some innocent policemen or send them into early retirement."

"And what did the Chief have to say about that?"

"Bob? He doesn't buy this crap any more than I do. He had no say in this. At least, he tried to persuade me to stay."

"To stay?"

"I chucked the crappy job."

Stephanie looked at him perplexed but didn't say anything. Silently, she stroked over the back of his head–as if he was a child that needed to be consoled.

It took about ten minutes until she felt that Richard had finally relaxed a bit. "Look at the bright side! If the vice mayor proclaims that the perpetrator has been caught, the real murderer might feel safe and make a mistake."

Richard gave her a kiss.

She was right. Once again, he had gotten carried away by his emotions. What else than a public press conference with the vice mayor was better suited to make her believe that she had gotten away with it?

"Come! I'll take you back to McCormick Place." Richard jumped off the sofa, lending his hand to Stephanie.

"And you? What are you going to do?"

"I need to go back to the station."

4:50 p.m.

A text message! Why hadn't he thought of that sooner? For several hours, he had been fretting about a solution to his problem. And all along, it had been right in front of him! Since she obviously didn't have any intention of answering the phone, and she probably didn't

216

have the password to Josiah's mailbox, a text message was the only way to get in touch with her.

Clumsily, he tried to type a message on his cell. Yet his fat fingers always either landed on the wrong key, or he accidentally erased what he had already written. How much easier and more personal an old-fashioned phone call would have been.

At last, he succeeded.

The message on the display read: "Would like to interview you. Anonymously, of course."

Short and succinct.

He didn't text often enough to know if there were any common acronyms for the words he had used. But that didn't matter now. What mattered was that she understood what he wanted–even if she didn't master this ridiculous text language any more than he did.

Forrester McLean stared at the phone. Should he really dare to dance with the devil, or should he just get the heck out of here and hope that she wouldn't find him?

There was no way back. It was too late for that.

He plucked up all his courage and pushed the "Send" button.

****

"Dr. Stanton, I am so happy that you changed your mind! Chief Miller is still in his office, just walk right in! I'm sure he'll also be glad to see you. Would you like some coffee? I would be happy to make some for you!"

Jenny Walker was already in her coat, ready to go home.

Nevertheless, Richard still accepted her offer–even if it was just to make her happy. "As long as it's not from the vending machine, I would love some."

Jenny beamed at him. "Of course, it isn't! It'll just take a few minutes. I'll bring you a cup."

Bob Miller had relief written all over his face. "Richard! I am so happy you changed your mind… I knew that you didn't mean it!"

"Don't be so sure, I did mean it!"

217

"Anyway, I am glad that you're back. Jenny already gave me hell. Here is your gun and your badge! Why do you always get so angry? You should know by now that I don't let any of these politicians tell me how to do my job."

Richard gave him a skeptical look. "Bob, we both know that that's not quite true."

"Well, then let's just say that I don't like it when they interfere. Better?"

"Not really, but at least it's honest. Just to be clear: I'll only carry on if you promise to watch my back–without any fuss or quibble."

"Deal! By the way, I've never bought Steven's story."

"I know."

"Still, I'm glad that the CSIs were so fast."

"I don't understand…"

"Hasn't Steven reached you?"

Richard got his cell out of his pocket. Annoyed, he had silenced it earlier this morning when he had, furious with rage, left the building. By now, he had eight new messages.

He shook his head. "No, my bad."

"Doesn't matter now. Forensics called shortly after you had left. The bloody finger marks you had found on the gate were really from this Josiah Smith. If there was someone trying to escape, it probably was him."

10:45 p.m.

The apartment building was long overdue for renovation. The wooden siding looked as if it hadn't been painted in years. Under remnants of extensively flaked-off gray-blue paint, the planks were

218

rotting away. Several windows had huge cracks, and there were lots of shingles missing on the roof.

The collection of dented and severely rusted cars parked in front of the house could have easily been mistaken for a junkyard.

It was obvious that no one living here could afford to live anywhere else.

The main entrance wasn't locked. That much was clear. Within the last hour, several people had either left or entered the building without ever using a key.

There was a lot of activity, but that was to be expected in a neighborhood like this. Especially on a Friday evening.

Nobody here would pay any attention to her. The tenants probably didn't even know their neighbors, let alone their visitors.

When she had seen where he lived, she had made the conscious decision to wear something plain and inexpensive. For a change, she didn't want to attract anyone's attention.

The windows in the entry area, which were as high as the building, granted a perfect view of everything going on in the centrally located stairwell.

She had meticulously kept track of the apartments people had left from or entered. This way, she had already been able to rule out nine of the twelve apartments.

There was no light on in one of the remaining ones, and in front of another, there was a tricycle.

This left just one apartment. Even if he didn't live there, she could always claim to have gotten the wrong address.

Since there weren't any names on the mailboxes, she simply had to take a chance.

She got out of the car, pulled her hood deeply down into her face, and walked purposefully toward the shabby house.

A door on the first floor opened, and a tastelessly bedizened, noisily guffawing couple came out. The seriously overweight woman was wearing pink leggings and a black crop top that had the word

"SEXY" written in rhinestones on the front. Her chubby feet, which she had jammed into ankle-high lace socks, were wedged into scuffed, dirty-white pumps. The short, purple-colored pleather jacket was too small to cover her huge breasts. Her face was marked by a lifetime of drug and alcohol abuse.

The man wasn't a beauty either: his face was pockmarked and blotchy. The light-blue polyester shirt stretched over his bear-belly, and when he grinningly held the door for her, she shuddered at the view of his black front teeth.

She thanked him with a nod and scuffled past them.

For the time of day, it was surprisingly noisy in the house. In some apartments, the TV was blaring while party hullabaloo or music was coming from others.

All the way up, though, on the fourth floor, it seemed to be a bit subdued.

She knocked on the door.

No response.

She knocked again.

When there was nothing to be heard from inside the apartment, she took out her cell and sent him a text message: "Open the door!"

****

"I really hope that you've made reservations. If not, we are probably not getting in, I am afraid!" Consuela anxiously pointed at the long line of people hoping to get into the popular jazz club.

"Don't worry, we'll use a different entrance!" Richard took the girls by their hands and led them past the crowd and around the building.

A van was blocking the sidewalk so that they had to squeeze between two dumpsters to get to the back entrance. Richard knocked heavily on the steel door, and a moment later an impressive, bald African American dressed in a silver tuxedo appeared.

"Richard, at last, you're here! The others are already waiting for you! Hey, who's that you brought with?"

220

"Hi, Jimmy. This is Consuela and Stephanie. Can you get them a good table?"

"Of course! It's pretty full, but I'll find something suitable for them. Just follow me, my sweethearts!"

Stephanie just looked at Richard aghast. "Excuse me, Richard! You don't seriously intend to leave us alone, do you?"

Richard gave her a kiss. "Don't worry, we'll see each other again in just a moment!"

While Jimmy was leading the girls to the auditorium, Richard went backstage, where the rest of the ensemble were already waiting for him.

But instead of Ron, Nathaniel Baxter, their backup keyboarder, was sitting behind the piano.

"Hello Nat, I thought Ron would be playing with us tonight."

"That's what I thought, too. But when Donald couldn't reach him, he gave me a call. I was planning on coming here anyway. So, it's no big deal. Hey, did you bring your girlfriends along? They're really hot!" Already during the dinner cruise, Nate hadn't been able to keep his eyes off them.

Richard ignored him and went over to Donald Silverman, their bassist and unofficial band leader. Donald had founded the combo a couple of years earlier and was the only member patient enough to run after everyone else to schedule practices or gigs.

"Hello, Donald. Nate has already told me that you weren't able to reach Ron. Any idea where he might be?"

Donald shook his head. "No. I even called his office. The secretary just said that he's on vacation."

Richard was getting worried. Last night, Ron hadn't mentioned that he wouldn't be here today. And he could always be reached–day and night–even when he was on vacation.

"He probably just took off with a beautiful girl to spend the weekend in bed, and all the banging made him forget tonight's engagement. Wouldn't be the first time!"

It was true that Ron had missed a show once before. However, he had been so overworked that time that he had slept through his alarm.

The last time Richard had seen him had been last night when he was flirting with Sonya in front of the restaurant. This time, he really must have thought that he would score as he had yelled to them that they should leave without him and that he would take a cab.

Maybe that was what had happened: they had spent the whole day in bed together, and Ron had indeed turned off his phone, not to be disturbed.

Richard glanced at his watch. With a little bit of luck, he might still reach someone at the restaurant. Maybe they could tell him more.

He took his phone out and scrolled through his contacts. Yet before he could find the restaurant, he heard Jimmy's rich baritone: "Ladies and gentlemen, dear friends and patrons of the hottest jazz club in Chicago! It is my distinct pleasure to welcome back a very special quintet that has been gaining a reputation in the scene as a hidden gem. Please, ladies and gentlemen, let's give a big round of applause for the 'Jazzy Doctors'!"

****

The only thing she could hear behind the locked door was the doorbell, nothing else.

Once again, she sent him the same text message: "Open up!"

There was a ringing, and a moment later something in the apartment fell to the floor–a glass perhaps–and someone cursed boorishly.

She had found him.

Right now, he was probably desperately trying to figure out what to do.

She could literally smell his fear.

She just hoped that he wouldn't do anything stupid now. If he called the police, the opportunity was gone. Somehow, she had to cozen him into coming out of his mousehole.

222

She decided to put all her eggs in one basket and sent him another text: "Interview, yes, or no?"

This time, the ringing was directly behind the door.

A door bar was being retracted, then another one, before she finally heard the key in the lock.

When he cracked the door open to peek out, she saw that it was also secured with a chain. The mouse wasn't out of its hole quite yet. It still had a chance of getting away–a small chance though.

"Yes? Why are you disturbing me this time of day?"

"Don't play dumb! You know exactly why I'm here! After all, it was you who called me!"

"But…"

"Do you want the interview or not? Let me in, or you'll never see me again!"

Fear was written all over his face. This wasn't how he had imagined it. He had probably hoped to meet her in a public place where he thought he would be safe: a café, a shopping mall, maybe even a museum.

He wouldn't have been safe anywhere; it would just have complicated things a bit for her.

What had he been thinking? That he could influence or even determine the conditions of the meeting?

She would beat this kind of arrogance out of him.

"Okay!" He closed the door for a moment to unlatch the chain before he let her in.

The apartment looked and smelled like a pigpen. There was trash everywhere: pizza boxes, chip bags, empty beer cans or bottles, and in between soiled clothes and piles of paper. A broken beer bottle was lying in a golden-brown puddle in front of the overflowing desk, on which there stood two computer monitors.

"What do you want from me?" His voice was a bit shaky.

"Isn't the question what YOU want from ME?"

Beads of sweat were forming on his forehead. She could literally see the thoughts running through his mind: what shall I say, what shall I say?

"Are you scared?" She looked at him with piercing eyes.

At first, he looked at her stunned, but when he couldn't withstand her look any longer, he lowered his head and just nodded twice.

What a goddamn loser he was.

"You were trying to lure me into a trap, weren't you?"

"No, no, I just wanted to interview you! I have no interest in you getting caught. You have to believe me! I am a journalist!"

"And why should I talk with you?"

"To tell the world why you are doing what you are doing? You must have a reason, don't you?"

"A reason?"

All of a sudden, there was a loud beeping sound coming from one of the computer speakers.

"What's that?"

"Oh, just an alarm. I set an alarm."

He was lying.

"Show me what it really is, or you'll die!"

Terrified, he raised his hands in front of his chest and took a step back. "It's alright, I'll show you!"

Fretfully, he kicked away trash on the floor to clear his way to the desk where he pushed a key on the computer keyboard. Immediately, the deafening beeping stopped, and one of the monitors awoke: somewhere, an elderly man in a blue coverall was mopping the floor.

"You better tell me right now what this is! And don't even think about lying to me, or you'll get punished!"

"The police station, it's the police station! I've installed cameras and bugs there to get information for my articles."

224

She was surprised that he would manage to do something like that. Maybe he wasn't as dumb as he looked.

"How about the other monitor?"

Embarrassed, he averted her eyes.

"Turn it on, at once!"

Reluctantly, the journalist turned on the second monitor.

The lap of a woman, scarcely veiled in pantyhose, appeared in front of them. It was a freeze-frame. He must have paused the video when she knocked on the door.

"Turn it on again!"

When he hesitated, she grabbed his left shoulder and pressed hard into the depression of the collarbone.

"Ouch! Oh my god, let go of me! I'll do what you want!"

It just took a mouse click for the lap to sway from side to side on a chair.

"You jerk off to that, don't you?"

There was a box of Kleenex on the desk.

He was too embarrassed to look at her and just nodded in silence.

"You're a fucking Peeping Tom! You pig!"

"I'm a man…"

"That's just the same!" She felt the urge to kill him right here and now. However, she first needed to find out how to operate his equipment.

11:52 p.m.

As the applause died down, Richard put his sax in its stand and took the microphone. "Thank you very much! We'll take a short break, and in about fifteen minutes we'll continue with an homage to

225

Michael Brecker, who sadly passed away much too soon. Thank you!"

The girls were still clapping when he joined them at their table.

"Wow, Richard, you guys are fantastic! The audience is going nuts!" Stephanie embraced him enthusiastically.

"Well, we're just amateurs, but we enjoy it, and I think it went quite well so far. But now, I need a beer!" Richard called one of the waiters and ordered a lager.

"Come on, 'The Jazzy Doctors'? Isn't that a bit corny?" Consuela grinned at him teasingly.

"Why? I think it's funny!" Stephanie countered indignantly.

"To be honest with you, it wasn't my first choice either. I would have found 'The Moody Doctors' more fitting." Richard wasn't sure if the girls knew him well enough to catch the cynicism. The more he was surprised when Consuela punched him in the arm.

"No way! Even 'Jazzy' is better than that! Now that I think about it, I may even like the name!"

Stephanie nodded resolutely. "It's much better!"

Richard got the feeling that Maria might have spilled the beans. On the other hand, the two girls had probably figured out all by themselves that he could sometimes be a bit "emotional."

"Donald first suggested 'The Jazz Doctors,' but that name was already taken. There is a band in New York that was founded by a pharmacist and two doctors."

"Does that mean that all of you are real doctors?" Consuela asked incredulously.

"No, not quite. But we all have doctorates. Donald is professor of English literature, Nate is a physicist, Lennard is a food chemist, Paul an ophthalmologist, and Ron, as you know, a pathologist."

"So, Ron also plays with you? Why isn't he here today?"

Consuela's question suddenly reminded Richard that he had wanted to call the restaurant. By now, it was too late for that. He stared at his watch.

226

"Richard? Darling, are you alright?" Stephanie looked at him with worry.

"Yeah, sorry! Consuela, what was your question again?"

"I just wanted to know why Ron isn't here today if he's a member of your band."

"I have no idea. He was supposed to play the piano. Nate just helps out from time to time when Ron is too busy. Ron confirmed for tonight's show weeks ago."

"Maybe something unexpected came up," Stephanie said encouragingly.

"Yes, maybe…"

****

"And the police can't determine where the audio and video recordings are being sent to even if they find the microphones and cameras?"

"Well, it's not impossible, but it's darn difficult. The data is sent around the globe three times, the IP-addresses change all the time, and the connection is never the same… they're not good enough to figure that out."

The revolting journalist seemed to know what he was talking about. His setup was ingenious. He could spy on the whole homicide department around the clock and obtain first-hand information without ever having to leave his run-down apartment.

Even though he was a disgusting pervert, he was smart–too smart.

She herself had almost fallen for his tricks.

Piece by piece, he had told her everything she wanted to know: that he had hoped she would follow the "playboy," as he called him; that it had been he who had hired the skinny black guy to find her; and, of course, what the police had on her.

It was time to get rid of him.

She didn't need him anymore. More or less willingly he had agreed to explain how everything worked and shown her where the recordings were saved. The idiot had even told her his password.

Even though the curtains were open, she knew that one could not look inside the apartment from the street. The house on the other side was a single-story bungalow. The key was still in the lock, and nothing indicated that he ever received any visitors.

He weighed at least 220 pounds. She did not want to drag that much weight around. That would be too strenuous–and especially too conspicuous.

She would simply cut him up into a few pieces and cart him away in a couple of trash bags. Legs, arms, torso, head–she would need maybe half an hour if she used a bone saw. A powered saw was out of the question since it would make too much noise.

It would get bloody…

The bathroom! She hoped that he had a bathtub. One with a shower curtain would be even better. This way, she could rinse everything with water afterwards and clean up with bleach.

She would also have to tidy up the place. After all, she would spend quite a bit of time here over the next couple of weeks.

Unfortunately, he refused to send the data to her own computer at home. That would have made it so much easier. But he was afraid that this would make him an accomplice, and he didn't want to go to jail for murder.

This stupid fool was worrying about his future… even though he didn't have one.

"I have to pee. Can I use your bathroom?"

"Oh, of course! Down the hallway to your left."

"Just don't do anything stupid! I'll be right back."

There were two doors in the window-less hallway. One led to a completely trashed bedroom, the other to the bathroom.

The sink was disgusting. It was full of hair and toothpaste-stains, and there was mold around the faucet. She didn't even dare to lift the toilet lid. She would definitely have to clean.

The good news was that there was a bathtub, and it even had a shower curtain. It smelled a bit musty, but she would throw it out with him.

228

She turned off the lights.

He was still sitting motionless in front of the computer, watching the janitorial staff. Most likely, he hadn't even noticed that the lights in the bathroom had been turned on briefly.

"Hey, can you come here for a moment? I can't locate the light switch."

"It's just next to the door on your right."

"But I can't find it!" she yelled determinedly.

She watched him as he struggled to get up from the worn armchair and toddled toward her through the ankle-deep trash.

"Here! Here is the switch!" He had stepped into the bath with one foot and turned on the lights.

Still, she wasn't satisfied. "The faucet doesn't work either."
"What?"

As soon as he had taken a step toward the sink and leaned a bit forward to open the faucet, she–as fast as lightening–grabbed the back of his head with one hand and the chin with the other.

Without any mercy, she jerked his head around in an abrupt rotational motion, braking his neck with a loud crack.

She didn't even give him the time to slump down but immediately pushed her body against his to shove him over the rim of the bathtub. As soon as he hit the bathtub floor with a thud, his bladder emptied.

She was content as this meant less mess to clean up from the floor.

Saturday, February 19

4:23 a.m.

"Hi, this is Ron Howard. I'm sorry, but I'm temporarily unavailable right now. Please leave your name and number after the tone, and I'll return your call as soon as possible."

Richard didn't wait for the beep but hung up right away. He had already left a message on Ron's mailbox two hours ago and had not heard back from him yet.

His gut told him that something wasn't right.

He tiptoed back to the bedroom and got his robe from the closet. The girls' breathing was deep and even. At least, they had not been bothered by his constant tossing and turning. It didn't make sense for him to go back to bed again. He wouldn't be able to fall asleep anyway–he was way too worried for that.

Quietly, he closed the door, got a glass of the Château Latour from the kitchen, and went to the living room.

At this hour of the night, there wasn't a lot of traffic on the streets of downtown Chicago. However, life never died down completely. There were always a few cabs driving around, or a police car was speeding down Michigan Avenue with sirens blaring. And, every now and then, there would be a private vehicle.

Richard suspected that the occupants of most of those cars were on their way to the next club or a party. He just hoped that they were sober and not on drugs. After all, almost half of all deadly traffic accidents were caused by drunk drivers.

Sometimes, when it became too much for Ron, and he unburdened his heart to Richard, he would tell him about the gruesomely mutilated and disfigured young bodies…

Richard wouldn't be able to do this job.

He had studied medicine primarily out of a fascination for human anatomy and since the career prospects for physicians in the U.S. were still excellent.

Medical doctors were generally held in high esteem and earned good money. Especially for someone from the lower middle class who had good grades, like himself, this was typically reason enough to want to get into med school.

Or their own family, who had no idea what the daily life of a doctor looked like but nevertheless worshipped doctors like demigods, made one believe that this was what one wanted.

That's how it had been for him.

As long as he could remember, it had been the dearest wish of his father that Richard would become a physician one day and carry the title "Doctor of Medicine." How proud he had been when his dream actually became a reality–his dream.

For a long time, it hadn't even occurred to Richard that this might not be his own dream as well. He had realized this only after the death of his parents.

Ron was different. He had become a physician and pathologist out of true passion.

Already as a child he had taken great pleasure in preparing histological samples from anything he could get his hands on and studying them under the microscope. He still possessed countless volumes of sketchbooks and boxes of masterfully prepared specimens that he greatly enjoyed showing to friends.

He had turned his hobby into a career. Could there be anything more satisfying?

Yet, Ron had many more talents: he was an extraordinary pianist and arranger, was interested in the arts, history, politics and economics, and possessed a sheer unbelievable general education.

And he was a great guy.

Richard bit his lower lip.

231

He just hoped that nothing bad had happened to his friend.

9:14 a.m.

Richard was awakened by the smell of freshly brewed coffee. Rubbing his eyes, he only slowly realized that he was lying on the sofa in the living room. Someone had covered him with a blanket.

There were two empty bottles of wine standing next to him on the table.

He vaguely remembered getting up at night and looking out the window. However, he couldn't remember for how long, or what had happened afterwards.

As he pushed himself up from the deep cushions, he felt a sudden twinge in his back. While the sofa was quite comfortable to just sit on, it was no good as a bed.

He stretched a few times before he followed the smell of coffee to the kitchen.

Consuela was standing at the stove, preparing breakfast.

"Good morning, what are you making?"

She had not heard him come in and, startled, dropped the cooking spoon into the pot. "Whoops, you made me jump! I thought you were asleep. I tried so hard to be quiet!"

"The smell of coffee woke me, and I am thirsty!"

Richard got a glass of water from the fridge and downed it in one gulp. Then he walked around the kitchen island and, standing closely behind her, kissed Consuela on the neck. "Listen, I thought you went shopping…"

She was wearing one of his T-shirts and boxers again. And the obligatory woolen socks. "Don't you like what I'm wearing?"

She thrust her butt backwards, pushing it against his groin.

"Oh, I like it. I like it a lot!"

232

As Consuela continued stirring in the pot, Richard moved his hands under the waistband and pulled the shorts down over her hips. Her skin was smooth and soft and felt incredibly good.

"I am crazy for you!"

She now rubbed her butt purposefully against the bulge in his pants, which immediately got harder and larger. "I know!"

Richard gladly accepted the invitation.

From behind, he reached between her legs and slid his middle finger into her. Feeling that she was already wet, he pulled down her shorts and undid his pants.

Willingly, Consuela spread her legs, heaving a brief sigh as he entered her.

Leaning slightly over her, Richard grabbed her breasts and lustfully pounded her until he could feel the tight embrace of her spasmodic vaginal contractions. With intense gratification and a self-indulgent sigh, he spurted his semen into her and rested his head on her shoulder.

"If that wasn't a quickie…," Consuela said.

"Did I come too soon?" Richard asked solicitously. He could have sworn that he had felt her come, too.

"Not at all–I like quickies! And the timing was perfect as our breakfast is almost done." She put down the cooking spoon, pulled up her boxers, and gave him a kiss.

"Let's eat quickly, and then we can do it again. You know… I am also crazy for you! She kissed him again, reached for his crotch, and gingerly tucked away his penis.

"I'd like that!"

While Consuela set the table in the living room, Richard made himself a quadruple espresso and peeked inside the pot on the stove. The whitish mush simmering therein did not look particularly appetizing although it smelled very good.

"Keep your hands off–it's not quite finished yet!" Consuela pushed him aside, took a few spices out of a cabinet, and started to season the pulp. She worked in the kitchen as if she were at home–and as far as Richard was concerned, she was.

"It looks like you know your way around here already. What is it in the pot if you don't mind me asking?"

"That's Avena. It's actually a rather simple oatmeal porridge with cinnamon. After all, you can't eat bacon and eggs every day. You know, oats are very healthy as they lower your cholesterol levels!"

Richard laughed. "Consuela, I actually love oatmeal. And, believe me, I really don't have bacon and eggs every day!"

He tasted a spoonful. "That's yummy! By the way, cinnamon is also healthy since it stimulates the secretion of insulin and, thus, lowers your blood glucose concentration."

She gave him a self-content smile. "Well, that's a relief! I am really glad to hear that the doctor likes the healthy type of food I've prepared for him!"

"I could get used to this." Richard put another spoonful in his mouth.

Consuela looked at him lovingly, and a happy smile passed over her face. "Me, too."

****

She really needed a break. She had been cleaning the bathroom for more than an hour and still wasn't done.

On top of that, she hadn't got much sleep last night. When she'd finally been done showering and ready for bed, it had been four o'clock in the morning already.

Everything had taken much longer than expected: first, she had to go home to get her tools; then there had been a detour on the way back here; carving up the body in the tight bathtub hadn't been easy either; and to make matters worse, some of the garbage dumpsters she had planned to dispense the contractor bags in had been locked.

As a result, it had taken her half an hour of driving around to get rid of all the bags.

She would just have to clean the rest of the apartment later. At least she could wash her hands in the sink and use the toilet even though she would continue to cover the seat with paper.

She went over to the kitchenette, pushed the dirty dishes aside, and poured a splash of bleach on the countertop. Its acrid smell was still preferable over the stench of spoiled food, sweat, and pee.

She scrubbed clean an area two feet wide and set up her coffeemaker. She'd brought everything she needed from home. She had even brought a couple of one-gallon water jugs and had toted them all the way up to the third floor. Just the thought of eating or drinking anything he had touched made her sick to her stomach. And she hated the taste of Chicago tap water.

She turned the coffee maker on and took a pod out of the box. It would take the water a few minutes to get hot–time she wanted to use to check out what was going on in the police station.

Only after she had wrapped the old armchair in two garbage bags and covered it with a bath towel she had brought from home, she sat down in front of the computer. She had muted the annoying alarm last night since she didn't want any irked neighbors to pay her an unexpected visit.

For a Saturday morning, the offices were surprisingly busy. Most desks were occupied and officers in either uniform or plainclothes were running around all over the place. Unfortunately, she did not see the Chief's secretary anywhere.

Thankfully, the reporter had told her last night who was working the case and what they had found out so far. Not without pride, he had shown her recordings of all the important persons and explained which of the many cameras and microphones were the most productive. Without this knowledge, it would have been impossible for her to know what to focus on.

This way, however, she had already obtained some very valuable pieces of information. For example, that the little Asian lady was dangerous: she was intelligent, resourceful, and hard-working.

But that wasn't all. The reporter had fast-forwarded through hours of recordings showing her at her office computer late at night, endlessly searching databases or evaluating results. She wasn't just hard-working, she was pertinacious.

Chen, Liz Chen, was her name.

Her colleague, the mustached Polack, wasn't quite as gifted although she wouldn't make the mistake of underestimating him either. Steven Kowalski.

Both of them were detectives and oversaw a whole troop of policeman doing the legwork for them.

And still, Chief Miller had appointed Richard Stanton over their heads. The more she found out about Stanton the better she understood why.

She could hardly believe how quickly he had declared her the main suspect. The police now even had pictures and video recordings of her!

For so many years she had escaped detection… and all of a sudden, the police were on her heels. The only one to blame for that was Stanton.

She had to get rid of him whatever it took.

11:32 a.m.

"Sonya? Hi, it's me, Richard Stanton. I am so glad to finally reach you!"

"Good morning, Dr. Stanton! How can I be of assistance? Would you like to make a reservation?" Sonya sounded her usual self: friendly, professional–and noncommittal.

"No, that's not why I'm calling today. I was hoping you might be able to help me with something else…" Richard wasn't quite sure how to tackle the matter. The brief pause on the other side of the line

236

made him think that Sonya was a bit surprised that the conversation was going in an unexpected direction.

"Yes? What is this about then?" Despite her effort not to betray her feelings, he could hear cautiousness in her voice.

Richard decided to put his cards on the table. "Sonya, I believe that you know me well enough to know that I would never ask you about your private life."

Again, there was a pause.

"Yes?"

"Then you'll probably understand how desperate I must be if I nevertheless ask you whether you know where my friend Ron Howard might be." Richard bit his lower lip.

"I don't understand. Why would I know that?" She sounded surprised.

All of a sudden, Richard lost the last glimmer of hope. He clenched his fist and bit his index finger so hard that he could taste his own blood.

The illusion that his friend might have been making out with the hostess for the last thirty-six hours and would be in fine fettle suddenly gave way to the realization that something terrible must have happened to Ron.

All he could do was try to find out what.

"Sonya, when we were leaving the restaurant Thursday night, Ron was talking with you. Would you mind telling me what happened after my girlfriends and I left?"

"Not at all. Dr. Howard was flirting with me and made admiring compliments–you know how he is! I even think that he had finally found the courage to ask me out when a woman, who was leaving the restaurant next door, strained her ankle on the way to her car."

"A woman? What did she look like?" Richard was starting to have misgivings.

"Very elegant: black, slicked-back shoulder-length hair; mink coat; stylish cocktail dress–all of the finest quality. She was driving a silver BMW 7 Series. The woman had class. I suppose that she twisted her ankle walking down the stairs–no wonder, considering the heels she was wearing. Anyway, she let out a cry and clutched her ankle. Ron… I mean, Dr. Howard, hesitated for a moment, but as she was sitting there, moaning with pain, he walked over to help her. It must have been pretty bad. He examined her for a moment, then, came back to me to say goodbye. All he said was that he was sorry, that the woman wasn't able to drive herself, and that she had asked him to drive her home. It's a pity–I had imagined the evening differently…"

Richard closed his eyes and took a deep breath. All of a sudden, he was feeling numb as if all his energy and life force were being sucked out of his body.

Somehow, he had to find the strength to hold it together.

"Sonya, do you think you would recognize the woman?"

"I… believe so." She sounded scared.

"If it's okay with you, I would like to send some officers over to show you some pictures. Would that be alright?"

"Of course… Dr. Stanton, do you think that something bad happened to Ron?"

Richard did not want to unsettle her but wasn't to deceive her either.

"Sonya, to be honest, I don't know. But I promise that I will keep you in the loop. Thank you very much for your help. Talk to you soon."

Richard sank into the couch.

Suddenly, he was getting dizzy. He felt as if the room was spinning, like he was drunk. He was having violent stomach spasms and was getting nauseous. With great effort, he got up and schlepped himself to the bathroom. He made it to the toilet just in time before throwing up.

12:45 p.m.

"Thank you for making it here so quickly! The reason I asked you to come is that I must tell you something I couldn't talk about on the phone." Richard paused for a moment and looked at the others.

While Liz looked at him attentively and put her notepad down, Steven just leaned back in his chair as usual and stroked his moustache. Only Bob's facial expression revealed some sort of concern, maybe even worry. Yet, it was he who tried to lift the mood.

"Come on, buddy, why don't you tell us why I had to come here on a Saturday without even finishing my lunch?"

Richard just stood there, staring at them. It had cost him so much energy to freshen up, call the others, and come here to the station. At the moment, he had no idea how he would make it through the meeting. He picked up the water bottle from the table but struggled to open the screw cap.

At once, Liz scrambled to her feet and helped him.

"Richard, why don't you take a seat–you're shivering all over!" She pulled out a chair for him and poured him a glass of water.

"Steven, there should be a box of cookies on my desk. Would you fetch it please!" Bob heaved himself out of his chair, came around the big conference table, and sat down next to Richard. "Rick, what's the matter with you? Are you sick?"

Richard shook his head. He was too weak to talk.

When Steven came back with the cookie box and set it down on the table right in front of him, Richard turned away disgusted.

"This is not up for discussion; we have to get your cycle going!" Bob took a chocolate cookie, broke it in half, and held one piece out to Richard. The other he ate himself.

Richard took a bite and soon felt some energy return to his body.

After a while he felt strong enough to continue with the meeting. He asked Liz, who was still standing behind him with her hand caringly resting on his shoulder, to be seated again.

"I am sorry, but as you can see, I am not feeling too well."

The others nodded worriedly.

Richard bit his lower lip.

Finally, he told them: "I believe that Ron has been murdered."

"What?" Liz cried out with horror. "What makes you think that?"

Neither Bob nor Steven said a word. They were just sitting there, staring at him with empty eyes.

For a moment, it was deathly silent. Then, Liz started to sob.

Bob took off his glasses and stroked over his bald head. "Richard, why do you believe that Ron has been murdered?"

"I can't reach him anywhere. Thursday night, we had dinner together–and he has been missing since."

"Missing?" Bob asked perplexed.

"He had the day off on Friday but was supposed to work the weekend shift. However, nobody in his office has any idea where he might be. I called his office again just before I came here. He hasn't shown up yet. You all know Ron–that's not like him. I have also found out that shortly after we parted, he agreed to drive a woman home that supposedly had strained an ankle."

"A woman? Maybe Ron didn't just drive her home but… you know, maybe he just forgot that he was expected to work today." Steven must have found his own theory plausible as he immediately leaned back contentedly in his chair.

Liz and Bob, on the other hand, knew Richard well enough to realize that he had considered and obviously dismissed this option already. It was gradually beginning to dawn on them what might have happened.

"I am convinced that he was lured into a trap!" Richard said firmly.

"But, why?" Liz wiped the tears from her face.

"To teach me a lesson… to intimidate us… I don't know!"

"Do you think that the woman might have been the Beautiful Stranger?" By now, Liz was white as a sheet.

"I am sure it's her. Liz, would you be so kind as to pick up a few pictures of her and show it to the witness that has last seen Ron! Her name is Sonya… I don't even know her last name, but she works as hostess in the restaurant we were at Thursday night."

"Of course!" Liz nodded solemnly.

"And what exactly do you think happened to Ron?" Steven didn't quite seem to buy the story.

Richard took a deep breath before answering the question. He looked at Liz, who had turned toward the window. Tears were running down her face again.

"Steven, I want you to get in touch with the medical examiner in charge to make sure that Ron's genetic profile is compared to the DNA-sample we got from the victim at the artist's studio ASAP!"

"Which one? The crucified?" Steven asked shocked.

"Of course, who else?"

****

There might be just enough time if she hurried. She estimated that she had at least two hours until he would be back home again. That was more than she needed.

She had to seize this opportunity.

Tisiphone grabbed her purse and was out of the door.

At the last moment, Stanton had changed his mind and had decided to accompany the little Asian girl to the restaurant. He must have thought that it would be easier for the receptionist–Sonya–to talk to him rather than to someone she didn't know. Even better!

How miserable he had been–it was almost pathetic!

She would have never thought that he would be so weak.

He was already close to breaking down.

241

With the next blow, she would knock him out and get rid of him once and for all.

2:01 p.m.

The concierge flagrantly stared at her cleavage. As expected, he did not pay any attention to the ID she was sticking in his face. He only nodded when she told him that she had an appointment to view the penthouse that was still for sale. She was sure that he wasn't paying any attention to what she was saying.

All he was interested in right now were her boobs.

In the car, she had had the foresight to take off her bra and open two more buttons of her blouse.

One should have expected security staff in houses like this to be trained well enough not to fall for these kinds of tricks. After all, the rich and famous living here paid a lot of money to be safe from any intrusion of their privacy.

But how could someone be protected from a danger that wasn't even recognized as such? No training in the world would make a man associate a beautiful woman with danger–and not with sex.

The concierge wasn't any different. He, too, was a victim of his own lust. Little did he know that his carelessness would soon cost him his job.

She gave him a friendly "Thank you," and walked resolutely toward the elevators without turning around again.

When she reached the eighty-sixth floor, she knew exactly where to go. Up here, there were only four apartments. Only last year, Stanton had bought the one with the best view and had it custom-remodeled according to his own preferences. The tabloids had extensively reported on it at the time and had even published pictures secretly taken by one of the workers.

242

She hadn't taken two steps in the hallway when she heard something that made her halt abruptly. The entrance to Stanton's condo had to be right around the corner, and exactly from there came the sound of two female voices. One sounded older and was marked by a strong Spanish accent. The other was young and full or confidence.

"Thank you so much, Maria! Just tell him that I will be waiting for him! Doesn't matter how late it gets. ¡Adiós!"

A door closed. The woman would come around the corner any moment now. Quickly, she weighed her options. She clutched her purse to her chest and determinedly walked along.

The impact was just strong enough to knock the brunette down to the floor.

"Oh, my goodness! Are you hurt? I am terribly sorry, but I didn't see you coming! Please, forgive me! Here, take my hand!" Tisiphone tried to sound as innocent and friendly as possible. The woman needed to be convinced that she was merely the victim of an unfortunate mishap.

"Don't worry, I'm fine. I didn't see you either."

Tisiphone helped her up and quickly checked her out. She was slim and buff but, nevertheless, very feminine. At close range, however, she wasn't quite as stunning as she had looked from farther away. She was young and perky, that was all.

"You must be a friend of Richard's! I was about to pay him a visit. Is he in?" Tisiphone asked.

"No. I also wanted to surprise him, but it seems that he'll be back later. How long have you known him?" The girl radiated such innocent, almost refreshing naïveté.

"Not very long. I'm a broker and found him the apartment. He immediately fell in love with the view."

"It's breathtaking, isn't it? Day or night, there's always something exciting to see."

243

"Now that I've made the trip here in vain, would you like to have coffee with me? Richard's friends are also my friends."

The girl was obviously surprised but seemed to like the idea. "Sure. I don't have any other plans anyway. Maybe all of us can go out together later. That would be fun!"

Tisiphone smiled at her. "Oh, yes, I am sure! I already have a few ideas what we could do…"

****

Richard parked his car right by the curb in front of the exclusive restaurant.

Sonya must have already waited and recognized the Rover as she opened the door even before he and Liz got out of the car.

"Dr. Stanton, I didn't expect you to come yourself. But I am very happy to see you–thank you so much!" Neither the friendly reception nor her subdued smile could disguise her nervousness.

Her uneasy gaze and tense posture gave her away.

"Sonya, thank you for taking the time to talk with us. This is Detective Chen. She has brought a couple of pictures we would like to show you."

Sonya shook hands with Liz and led them to one of the restaurant tables, already set for the evening.

"Sonya, unfortunately, I cannot share any details with you, but we are trying to find out what happened to Dr. Howard after we had dinner here Thursday night." Richard contemplated for a moment how much he could tell her before he continued: "He hasn't been seen since."

Sonya sucked her lips in and clasped the edge of the table.

Richard could see it in her eyes: Ron had been more to her than just a common restaurant patron. He saw grief. And the realization of a missed opportunity which might have changed her life.

Suddenly, oppressive silence filled the room.

One could only hear the clanging of pots in the kitchen and a male voice, giving instructions on how to serve a particular dish.

At last, Liz screwed up her courage and took an envelope out of her purse.

"As Dr. Stanton already mentioned, I have brought a couple of pictures." She put five computer printouts on the table. All showed the Beautiful Stranger–in a hotel lobby, in an elevator, and in a bar.

Sonya squinted her eyes a bit and took her time to study the pictures. One she paid particular attention to–it showed the woman on a bar stool.

Finally, she nodded. "That's her."

"Are you sure?" Liz asked." She seems to change her appearance at will as you can already see from these few shots".

"I am sure. Her hair is still black, like here in the bar. It's cut different, but I believe that this is even the same mink coat she wore Thursday night. However, that night she was much more elegant, not as trampy as in this picture, more like in the other photos where her hair is dyed red. But none of that really matters…"

Richard and Liz looked at her in suspense.

"The eyes. These eerie, piercing eyes: I'll never forget those!"

3:31 p.m.

"Wow, what a cool apartment! I could get used to this. I love lofts. Have you been living here long?" The girl was truly impressed.

Amused, Tisiphone bolted the door and took off her coat. "No, not really. Would you like something to drink?"

"A glass of water would be great. Or coffee if it isn't too much trouble."

The girl nonchalantly tossed her jacket onto the sofa and walked over to the large floor-to-ceiling windows, which provided a magnificent view of the river.

"I rather thought a glass of champagne or vodka..."

"Alcohol? At this time of day?" The girl seemed genuinely surprised but just shrugged. "Why not? Let's go whole hog: I'll have a Vodkatini!"

Tisiphone walked over to the open concept kitchen, took the bottle of vodka out of the freezer, and put a few ice cubes in two martini glasses. One she filled with vodka, the other with water.

She contemplated whether to add some Rohypnol to the vodka when the girl suddenly turned around and walked toward her.

"I don't have any olives or lemons, but I don't think we need them." She smiled at the girl and gave her one of the glasses. "Cheers!"

"Cin cin!" The young woman took a big sip and looked at Tisiphone wide-eyed. "Jeez... that's one stiff drink!" She coughed.

"Oh, is it too strong for you? Would you prefer a glass of water instead?" Tisiphone played the innocent.

"No, not at all! I like it, I like it a lot!" She took another sip.

Her glass was already half-empty. She'd soon be unconscious if she continued drinking like that–even without another type of sedative. Tisiphone didn't really want that to happen; she wanted the girl later to be aware of what was being done to her. However, another drink, or even two, should be fine.

"Alright then, have some more!" She took the glass from the young woman and filled it to the brim.

246

With every slug the girl gulped, she became more rollicking.

Tisiphone put on some music, and the girl started to dance. Although she was already a bit tipsy, she obviously knew how to move. Her eyes closed, head bent backwards, and her arms stretched out to the side, she was absentmindedly spinning in circles to Amina Annabis' "L'Inconditionnel Amour," occasionally sipping from her drink.

Tisiphone could see why Richard Stanton fancied her: her bronze skin; the long brown hair, which she had braided with a ribbon; her round breasts, which showed under the gray fabric of her short dress; the firm butt and long legs... she looked like a tanned, dark-haired Barbie doll.

Tisiphone tried to envision how she might look without clothes; what her flawless skin would feel and her pussy taste like... the longer she watched the young woman the stronger her desire became to amuse herself with her.

Originally, she had only planned to lure the girl into a trap and kill her. The death of his beloved, without any question, would deeply anguish Stanton. Watching the girl now, though, she realized that she could hurt him even more.

She had the opportunity to humiliate and emotionally destroy him.

And that was exactly what she would do.

She only had to mix business with pleasure: she would send him videos of his girlfriend having sex with another woman.

With her, her killer.

****

"Wouldn't it be better if I drove?" Liz was very concerned for Richard. She looked at him and put her hand on his before he could start the car.

"No, it's okay." He shook his head. "Thanks."

"If you don't mind me saying, I think you should rest for a while. Why don't you get away for a few days–take a step back from it all?"

Richard closed his eyes. Why would he mind her solicitude? He knew that she just meant well. He should have never taken on the case. Didn't he have everything one could dream for? The girls had even brought happiness back into his life.

However, he risked losing everything if he wasn't careful now.

Everything.

"Richard?"

The voice seemed to be coming from far away. As if coming through dense fog...

"Richard? Richard, what's the matter?"

When someone grabbed and shook his arm, he regained consciousness. "I can't rest now. Not now. We have to stop this monster!"

****

Tisiphone put her glass down and took the phone out of her purse.

If she had had more time to plan this, she would have gotten a real camera. This way, however, she would have to improvise again.

It took her a moment to find the video function on the phone. It was easy enough: all she needed to do was aim at the girl and start recording.

After about twenty seconds, she stopped and looked at the result.

She was satisfied. The quality of this first clip was much better than expected.

The young woman dancing lusciously and dreamily to seductive lounge music was clearly and easily recognizable.

248

Tisiphone put the phone in the waistband of her skirt and crept up on the girl from behind.

By now, Helena Noguerra's "Ile Amoureuse" was blasting from the speakers.

The girl was already moving quite clumsily. She wasn't really dancing anymore but just stood in one spot and moved her hips in the rhythm of the music.

The three glasses of vodka she had drunk in less than fifteen minutes apparently had taken their toll.

For a while, Tisiphone stood behind her unnoticed and just watched her. She would have loved to take her right now–even by force, if necessary.

However, this wasn't the time to lose patience. She couldn't jeopardize her plan. The young woman had to give herself to her freely. At least, it had to look like this in the video.

The girl gave a start when Tisiphone hugged her waist but relaxed as soon as she realized who was standing behind her, asking her for a dance.

Tisiphone took the glass from her and took her by the hands.

She had to take it slow. After all, she had no idea how the cutie would respond to her advances. Therefore, she danced with her for a while as if they were just two friends dancing innocently hand in hand in a club. Only then, she dared to take the next step, put her arms around her neck, and pulled her toward her.

This presumed gesture of amicable affection did not seem to bother the girl at all. On the contrary, she herself now hugged Tisiphone and continued to dance with even greater enthusiasm.

Even when Tisiphone laid her head on her shoulder, she didn't seem to mind.

Only when she was being gently kissed on the neck, the young woman backed away with surprise and looked confused at her dance partner. "What are you doing?"

"Please, forgive me…I don't know what's gotten into me. I simply couldn't resist." Tisiphone tried hard to look as embarrassed as possible. "I have to admit that I… like you and… find you attractive. I was probably just hoping you would feel the same."

The girl hadn't completely separated from her quite yet. She was obviously irritated and blinked a few times as if having trouble keeping her eyes open.

"I don't know. I… I like you, too… but…" She couldn't think straight anymore. "What about… Richard?"

"What about him? I am sure he wouldn't mind." Tisiphone pulled her closer toward her and kissed her on the neck again. Then, she conspiratorially whispered in her ear: "I've got an idea: we get to know each other a bit more and find out what we both like. And later, if you want, we surprise Richard with a threesome. I'm certain that he would like that."

The girl giggled. "If you think so… Wouldn't be… the… first time."

Tisiphone let her long fingers glide over the girl's neck, unzipped her dress, and stripped it off her shoulders.

She chuckled when she saw that the young woman was wearing a white sports bra and matching hiphugger panties.

She had secretly hoped for something more erotic–maybe a set of lace underwear. On second thought, though, the girl looked very sexy even in this sporty outfit. Her body was indeed reminiscent of a Barbie doll. And, just like the iconic plastic toy, she asked to be played with.

With ease, Tisiphone undid her bra, exposing the melon-shaped breasts. The girl didn't mind being naked. Full of self-confidence, she smiled at her playmate admiring her body.

When Tisiphone kissed her fervently on the mouth and pushed her tongue between her lips, the cutie was a bit hesitant at first. Only when Tisiphone clawed her nails into her nipples, pinched, kneaded, and pulled on them, her last resistance was broken.

Eyes closed and breathing heavily, the girl finally surrendered to her lust, responded to the kiss, and skillfully circled her tongue around the supposedly more experienced woman's. There was no doubt that she had finally made the decision to unreservedly give in on this amorous adventure of same-sex pleasure.

Still, Tisiphone was somewhat surprised when the girl took the reins, unbuttoned her blouse, and started to touch her with determination.

Her hands were soft and warm–and experienced.

She massaged Tisiphone's breasts for a while before she lowered her head and began to wildly suck on her nipples.

Tisiphone's crotch was now hot of desire. Lustfully, she grabbed the cutie by the back of her head and pulled her aggressively onto her bosom. She greatly enjoyed being touched and explored and was about to forget everything around her when the girl pushed her skirt up, gently stroked over her stockings, and put her hand down her pants.

When the phone moved out of place, though, Tisiphone suddenly recovered her wits, pulled out the cell, and documented this part of exciting foreplay in a short video.

The young woman was way too busy and befuddled by lust and alcohol to even notice.

Ecstatically, she shoved Tisiphone to the sofa, pulled her panties down over her thighs, and went down on her knees in front of her.

Willingly, Tisiphone pushed her crotch out toward her and whooped of joy as the girl's tongue expertly caressed her clit.

For a moment, she hesitated to capture this moment in a video. Not because she might have been ashamed of being filmed in such an intimate situation but because, surprisingly enough, it didn't feel right to betray the girl's trust in this way.

After all, she was giving herself to her of her own free will. Moreover, the cutie wasn't just out for her own satisfaction. No, she also wanted to give her playmate pleasure.

Tisiphone looked alternately at the phone in her hand and the head in her lap before she finally took a short video of the scene.

Then, she shoved the cell under one of the pillows, laid back, and enjoyed the girl giving her head.

She would need the camera again later when she'd introduce the girl to a different world of sexual pleasure.

4:27 p.m.

"At last!" Liz ran impatiently to her desk and looked over the fax that someone had attached to her computer screen with tape.

"You gotta be kidding me!" Her mouth wide open, she stared at the piece of paper.

"What's the matter?" A surge of adrenaline flooded Richard's body.

For a moment, Liz looked at him with an astonished gaze before she finally answered: "This is a message from one Inspector Gallagher from the Vancouver PD. He must have come across my request for help identifying the Beautiful Stranger.

With a jolt, she pulled the fax off the monitor and studied it carefully.

"And? Come on, tell me!"

"Her name is Kathryn Hamilton."

"What?" Richard asked surprised.

"Kathryn Denise Hamilton. She was reported missing twelve years ago and has been linked to the death of four men.

"What's that supposed to mean?"

"You're not going to believe this! She was a student at the University of British Columbia at the time and became the victim of a gang bang–I mean, she was raped by several men."

"I know what 'gang bang' means."

"The suspects, four men, were acquitted because of insufficient evidence. But…"

"Let me guess, following the acquittal, they were massacred and their bodies burned."

Liz raised her eyebrows: "I wonder how you came to that conclusion."

Richard took the fax and read the message himself. There it was: Kathryn Denise Hamilton.

"Do you know what this means?" Richard bit his lower lip.

"Of course! We are close to catching her!" Liz shouted with excitement. As soon as she noticed Richard's concerned look, however, her exuberance quickly faded. Don't you think this is huge?"

Richard looked at her solemnly. "In principle, yes… but it also means that she has been on the loose for more than a decade and may have killed many more men without ever having been caught."

Liz closed her eyes in disappointment and took a deep breath. "You're right. What do you suggest we do?"

"First, we have to search all data banks for Kathryn Hamilton. Just don't do it yourself but give it to one of the rookies! I bet that our Canadian colleagues have done that already, so I don't believe that this is very promising anyway. We just need to make sure." Richard read the message from Vancouver again. "I think you should call this Inspector Gallagher. I've got a feeling that he can and will tell us more about the case. Why else would he have given us his cell phone number?"

253

Liz nodded in agreement and took the fax from Richard's hand. "You know what–I'll do that right away! It's only two-thirty in Vancouver now, maybe he's still in the office."

Suddenly, Richard's phone rang. Someone had sent him a text.

"That's weird…" Richard looked at his cell with a frown.

"Something wrong?" Liz was typing Gallagher's number into her phone.

"You could say that–or have you ever been contacted by a dead person?"

"I beg your pardon?" Liz hung up and took Richard's cell from him. "Josiah Smith?" she asked incredulously. "How can that be?"

"I have no idea, but maybe we'll find out once we take a look at the attached video." When Richard tried to open the attachment, nothing happened. He became impatient when the file had not downloaded after more than a minute. "This is taking forever!"

"The file seems to be pretty large. Even if it's just a short video, it may take a while to download. If you give me a moment, I can try to transfer the file to my computer. That should be faster, and we can watch the video on the computer screen." Liz sat down at her desk and opened the website of Richard's cell phone carrier.

"Just type in your password here so that I can access your account."

Richard leaned over the desk and typed in the requested information while Liz consciously turned and looked to the side.

"You know, you could have done that as well. I don't mind you knowing my password," Richard said sheepishly.

"I appreciate your trust in me, but we better not do that for security reasons. Here, see, the file has already downloaded! Do you want me to open it, or do you wanna do that? After all, it was sent to you."

Richard gave her a reproachful look. "Just do it!"

It just took a moment until a young, good-looking woman appeared on the screen. She was holding a glass in her hand and danced gracefully amid a big, modern living room.

"Oh, my god!" Richard shouted in dismay.

"What's the matter? Do you know the woman?"

Richard was unable to utter a word. He just nodded, then he buried his face in his hands.

5:06 p.m.

The girl was still asleep. She lay naked on the sofa and panted softly while a tickle of drool trickled from the corner of her mouth onto the silk-covered pillow.

Tisiphone was surprised that the young woman hadn't thrown up after the amount of alcohol she'd had. So far at least, she had been spared that mess.

Perhaps she should take another picture of the cutie and send it to Richard Stanton. Now, that she was still unscathed.

The girl looked relaxed–and satisfied. Just like a woman that had got her brains fucked out and simply needed to rest a bit.

Tisiphone hadn't had so much fun having sex in a long time. Yes, she had occasionally slept with beautiful woman before. But none of them had ever given herself to her as licentiously as this little Jezebel. The vodka bottle had also been her idea. Tisiphone had seen a thing or two before, but even she was astonished how far the glass dildo substitute had disappeared in the cutie's body cavities.

To think that she looked so innocent!

Tisiphone wished she had taken more videos with the girl having the bottle up her ass. That alone would have driven Stanton into madness.

Unfortunately, the phone had been out of reach.

Maybe she could make up for it later. The bottle wouldn't need to be whole for that…

She would have to tie up and gag the girl anyway.

Tisiphone put on her panties and blouse and looked around the apartment. She found a big roll of packaging tape in the study and a pair of tennis socks in the bedroom.

Now, all she needed was a couple of suitable tools. Besides forks and knives, there were even poultry shears and a stick lighter in the kitchen. She would have loved to also have razor blades, but there weren't any in the bathroom. Probably, the owner of the place shaved electric.

Now that he was on vacation, he probably didn't shave at all.

It didn't matter, she could just as well use glass shards.

****

"So far, we have received three video clips. All show the same young woman. First, alone, dancing. Then having sex with another female, whose face, unfortunately, isn't seen. Anyway, we are sure that it is the Beautiful Stranger. We have not yet been able to locate the phone the videos have been sent from. It is likely that it has been turned off and the battery has been removed. We also don't know where the videos were shot. In the first clip one can see a big window in the background, but that's all. The camera didn't adjust to the different light conditions quickly enough so that this part of the picture is completely overexposed. Therefore, the surroundings are unidentifiable. The techies might be able to retrieve something useful, but that would probably take too long. We have to assume that the young woman's life is in danger and that we do not have a lot of time to save her. That means that we currently only have two leads: first, the phone; we have to make sure that we are ready to geolocate it as soon as it is turned on again. That is, if it is turned on again. Furthermore, Dr. Stanton believes that the apartment might be another loft in the West Loop. This is based on the fact that already two of the previous murders occurred in this area. In addition, one

256

can see in one of the videos that the apartment walls are made from brick and that there are steal ceiling beams. All this suggests that the woman is really somewhere there. I, therefore, need as much manpower as possible to take a closer look at every building in the area, go from door to door, and talk with the residents. Here are photos of both women. Maybe, someone has seen them."

When an officer in the front row rolled his eyes, Liz got angry. "Officer Carlisle, do you, in any way, object to our course of action?"

Embarrassed, the man just shook his head.

"Guys, I know that we are grasping for straws! But this is the only chance we've got to save the young woman. We have already divided the area into square grids. I want two teams per section, and they need to stay in contact at all times! Furthermore, everyone–and I mean everyone–needs to stay with their partners! The suspect is unpredictable and extremely dangerous. Don't you get fooled by her looks! She is a merciless killer. This being said, Detective Kowalski will divide you up into teams, and then let's go! We don't have any time to lose!

****

The girl sighed when Tisiphone pulled her off the sofa. She needed to hurry now. She turned her on her back, bent her knees, and wrapped her ankles and wrists on both sides with tape.

"Hey, what are you doing? You out of your mind?" The girl was suddenly wide awake.

"Don't get smart with me!" Tisiphone raised her hand but calmed down just in time. "It's about time that we teach your Richard a lesson…"

The girl looked at her confused. "What do you mean by 'your Richard'?"

6:59 p.m.

"To all units: suspect is likely located in section 7G. At once, drive to the parking lot at the corner of North Canal and West Kinzie Street! You'll receive further instructions there." Liz silenced the walkie-talkie and looked at the picture on her iPad again. The tech department had indeed worked their magic on the short video clip and had managed to make visible some buildings in the background–including the headquarters of the Chicago Sun Times, which were along the Chicago River.

Richard had been right.

"Have the techies shared any additional information? An address, maybe?" Richard was recklessly passing a van that simply didn't want to pull over.

"All they gave us was an approximate location. According to their calculations, there are only three blocks that qualify. Furthermore, they are sure that the apartment must be on one of the upper floors." Liz was clutching the arm rest as Richard pulled back into his lane in front of an approaching cab only at the last moment.

"Liz, would you mind getting my Glock from the glove compartment? Better safe than sorry!"

****

If the techies were right, there should be just this one last apartment left. They had already knocked down the doors to three apartments–to no avail. They might have forced their way into even more apartments hadn't the tenants been at home. Anyway, Bob wouldn't be happy about the bill or the drama.

Richard disengaged the safety of his pistol an indicated to the two policemen holding the ram to open the door to the apartment.

The two of them swung the black metal cylinder back just once and let it bang with full force against the wooden door, which immediately burst open.

258

Richard, his weapon held out in front of him, stormed into the apartment ahead of everyone else. He immediately realized that they were in the right place: the window; the brick walls; the sofa–everything was just like in the videos.

A moment later, a bunch of policemen flooded the loft to secure the rest of the apartment. From everywhere, one could hear them shout "Clear, clear, clear!"

How could it be? Richard was sure that he was right–this had to be the place!

Only when he walked over to the window to make sure that from here one had the same vista onto the Sun Times building as in the video, he saw her.

She was lying on the floor behind the big sofa, gagged with a white tennis sock. Her hands were tied to her ankles with light brown packaging tape.

11:28 p.m.

Richard put down his gun on the kitchen island and took a bottle of wine out of the wine room. As he wanted to check whether Maria had left a dinner for him in the fridge, he noticed the message that was attached to the stainless-steel door with a magnet:

Dr. Stanton,
A young lady was inquiring about you earlier today. She asked me to let you know that she will be waiting for you in room number 2040 any time after eight o'clock. Her name is Melissa.

Maria

PS: Richard, don't even think about meeting up with this young gal! Aren't the two chiquitas enough already?

Sunday, February 20

3:34 a.m.

Richard crossed his arms behind his head and stared at the ceiling. The otherwise colorless blackness above him was only intersected by a narrow, yellowish beam of light passing into the room through a gap in the curtains.

He wished the girls were here.

However, it was better this way.

Yesterday's events had tragically confirmed his worst fears.

He would have never forgiven himself had anything happened to Stephanie or Consuela.

It was terrible enough that Melissa had gotten involved in this.

But she'd been lucky. She'd gotten away alive.

Her wounds hadn't been too deep, and the plastic surgeon was hopeful that the scars could mostly be removed in subsequent surgeries.

She was a tough cookie: when the doctors wanted to stitch up her cut abdomen under general anesthesia, she insisted on getting local anesthesia. And, as soon as she was rolled out of the operating room, she wanted to give a statement to the police.

Richard doubted that she had any idea what danger she'd been in. But neither Liz nor he himself had thought it necessary to tell her.

With a perky wink, she had told them how she'd gone to Richard's apartment to ask him out and how she'd bumped into the woman on her way back to her room.

Without ever taking her eyes off Richard, she had given them a detailed account of how the two women had pleasured each other and how often she'd come.

260

It had been obvious that she'd wanted to turn him on.

Richard sat down on his bed and shook his head. No, she had no clue that she'd cheated death.

The only reason she was still alive was that, at the last moment, she'd somehow implied that she didn't really know Richard but had met him only once before by chance in the health club.

It had been a classic case of mistaken identities: both women had assumed that the other was Richard's lover.

And still, he was surprised that the Beautiful Stranger hadn't killed Melissa. But why hadn't she?

Her hatred was first and foremost directed at men, that much was clear.

However, she wanted to punish him. He'd known that for a while.

Was this really just a case of offended vanity that had made him a target, or was there another reason?

McLean's newspaper article had certainly flushed her out of hiding. But why had she, so far, only attacked people close to him but not himself?

Richard went to the bathroom, leaned over the sink, and let the cold water run over his face for several minutes.

She hadn't had an opportunity…

8:22 a.m.

As much as he tried to ignore the ringing, it simply wouldn't stop.

Finally, he answered the phone: "Yeah, Stanton!"

"Dr. Stanton, this is Daniel from the reception desk speaking. Please, forgive me for calling you this early, but I have a Mister Robertson here with me, who insists on talking with you right away." He waited for a moment before he continued: "Dr. Stanton, I have

261

tried to get rid of the gentleman, but he won't give up. Do you want me to call security?"

"No, that won't be necessary, thank you. Just send him up! Thank you very much, Daniel."

Richard put on his robe and turned on the coffee maker.

Just a moment later, the doorbell rang.

"Mr. Robertson, please come in! Would you like a cup of coffee?"

The man just looked at him and nodded silently.

"Why don't you take a seat and I'll be back in minute! How do you take it? Sugar, milk?"

"No, thanks–black."

Richard led him to the dining table and fetched two cups of espresso.

"Nice apartment. What a view!"

"Thank you. Is your wife doing better yet?"

"Yes, the tranquillizers have helped. She's slept through the night." The man took a sip from his coffee. "Mm, good!"

"Mr. Robertson, I am so sorry about what happened to your daughter; please, believe me!"

The man abruptly interrupted Richard by raising his hand: "No, Dr. Stanton. It is me who is sorry and needs to apologize! I should have never lost control of my composure this way. It was stupid of me to try to hold you accountable for what happened to my daughter. Who knows… if you hadn't been there, she might still be lying in this apartment, gagged, and tied up. Maybe, she even would have died–of asphyxiation or loss of blood. Or she may have died of shock." The man sobbed.

"Believe me when I say that I am truly happy that we've found her in time!" Richard said.

For a while, both of them just looked out the window.

"You know, Melissa is our only child. And even though she's no saint, it would break our hearts if anything bad should happen to her."

"Yeah, she's sly and precocious, isn't she?"

The man looked at him with a forced smile. "You have no idea!"

He took another sip of his coffee. "When she was eighteen, her PE teacher lost his job. At the time, I was really putting a lot of pressure on the school to sack him. But now I know that it had been my daughter who had seduced him. I'm just glad that he didn't have to go to jail."

He turned toward Richard and looked at him with sad eyes. "My daughter has told me that she tried to seduce you and that you behaved like a true gentleman."

"Um…"

"Don't say anything! I hope that you accept my apology, but I do understand if you want to press charges. I am ready to take full responsibility for my actions. I should have never slapped a police officer."

"Don't worry, Mr. Robertson! I know what you've been going through. You were in a state of shock. It wouldn't occur to me to press charges against you. I am just happy that Melissa is feeling better."

Again, the man sobbed. "Thank you. I've talked with the doctors this morning. They said that Melissa can leave the hospital as early as this afternoon. We were hoping to fly back to Florida tonight if you don't have any objections."

Richard shook his head. "As long as we can reach you by phone, it's alright."

"Of course, anytime… Dr. Stanton, have you found out what the incisions mean that this woman has cut into my daughter's belly? The doctors just called it a 'symbol'."

Richard took a deep breath. The man would see it with his own two eyes sooner or later anyway. It would be a while until the wounds would heal and scar revision surgery could be performed.

263

"It's not a symbol. It's a quote from the Bible–Dtn 32:35."

The man gave him a quizzical look. "I am afraid that I am not well-versed in the Bible."

"Deuteronomy, Chapter 32, Verse 35. It's from the Fifth Book of Moses."

"And? What exactly does it say?"

Again, Richard stared out the window and at the lake.

"To me belongeth vengeance, and recompence…"

12:51 p.m.

"Are you really sure that's the flight he was supposed to be on? Shouldn't he be here by now?" Richard anxiously changed from one leg to the other.

"Just be patient! It looks like you can't remember how it is to travel on a regular commercial flight. Everything takes a bit longer than when you fly private," Liz answered tauntingly.

"That's nonsense–and you know it! I only charter a plane when the situation requires it." Once again, Richard looked at the arrival monitor above them.

The information was still the same: the flight from Vancouver had landed already 20 minutes ago.

"You know what–I'll get another cup of coffee!" Richard turned around and was just about to head toward the coffeeshop when Liz pulled him back by his jacket sleeve.

"Too late, here they are! It's good we took the Rover!"

One of the officers she had talked to earlier was coming through the sliding door between the secure area and Arrivals Hall with a mountain of a man in tow.

The giant was at least 6' 10" tall and weighed at least 440 pounds. With his round face, chubby cheeks, and full, white beard, he reminded Richard of Santa Claus.

"Inspector Gallagher, I'm Richard Stanton. Thank you so much for coming!" When Richard shook the man's hand, it felt like his fingers were getting crushed in a vise.

"My friends call me Walt. I've heard a lot about you, Dr. Stanton. Pleased to finally meet you!"

"Please, call me Richard! May I introduce you to Liz Chen– you've already talked with her on the phone."

Liz just smiled gingerly as Gallagher's paw took her delicate hand.

"Would you like to rest for a while before we go to the station?" Richard asked. "You probably didn't get much sleep, having taken the early six-thirty flight."

"Thanks, no. I can't wait to hear what you've found out about Kathryn Hamilton. Do you have any idea how long I've waited for this moment?" There was a significant portion of enthusiasm in his deep, sonorous voice.

"Have you had lunch yet? There is a wonderful tapas bar on our way to the station. How about we talk there?"

****

"I've been trying to find this woman for more than ten years. She is like a phantom. Every now and then, I come across a murder that matches her MO. But that's it. She's never left behind any evidence that would have allowed us to identify her. How in the world were you able to get a picture of her? That's incredible!"

Gallagher took one of the photos and shook his head in amazement.

"How many murders do you think she has committed? We haven't been overly successful in finding comparable cases. Three or four show some similarities, but that's it," Liz commented skeptically.

265

"Don't feel bad about it! You can only find in a data bank what somebody has entered into it. And therein lies the problem. Probably, a lot of the murders were never identified as such, and the deaths were judged to be fatalities of building fires or traffic accidents. Consequently, the cases were prematurely closed. The victims weren't always tied up, and a missing body part could easily have been snatched by a coyote–at least in the outdoors. In addition, the cases are spread all over North America, and not every death makes the national data bank. There are many reasons why you haven't found more." Gallagher heartily bit into a shrimp.

"How many cases are we talking, Walt?" Richard feared for the worst.

"Including yours?"

Richard shrugged his shoulders.

"Including yours... I'd say, at least fifty-four. Could easily be twice as many, hard to tell."

"Fifty-four!" Liz shouted in surprise.

"Probably more…" Gallagher put another shrimp in his mouth.

"But how can that be?" Liz was stunned.

"What do you mean? That someone would kill that many people or that they wouldn't get caught doing it?" Gallagher looked at her benignly.

"Both!" Liz answered.

"I am no criminal psychologist; I am merely a simple investigator. But if you ask me… By an unlucky combination of circumstances, the good in this woman–and I still believe that there is some good in everyone–lost the battle against the bad." Gallagher paused for a moment, took a sip from his wine glass, and continued: "Kathryn grew up in the Vancouver area as the eldest child of a Roman Catholic family. Her father was a veterinarian, her mother a stay-at-home mom. Already at an early age, Kathryn often helped out in her father's practice, which explains why she possesses certain surgical skills–if you know what I mean… As far as I know, her father

266

was very strict and may even have disciplined his children by beating them with his belt. "At least that's what the youngest daughter, Allison, once mentioned. She also told me that the mother's brother, Uncle Frank, sexually abused Kathryn on several occasions. It probably started when she was about twelve years old. The parents supposedly weren't aware of it."

He took another sip. "After graduating from high school, she moved into the city to study economics. At that time, she lived in the dorms. Later, her teachers and classmates described her as a highly intelligent but introverted person. Lots of boys were hitting on her, but she rebuffed every single one of them. That's probably why she got the nickname 'The Unapproachable Blonde'... these kids had no idea what she had been through."

Richard got the feeling that Gallagher pitied the woman–or at least the child she once had been.

"So, she's a natural blonde then?" Liz asked.

Gallagher nodded.

"Did you know that the name Kathryn means 'The Pure'?" The inspector leaned back in his chair, which groaned under his weight. "I am convinced that, at that point, she still had a chance to develop into a normal, maybe even happy human being... And then, one of her classmates talked her into attending a graduation party the day after she got her degree."

"Is that where she was raped?" Liz asked aghast.

"Not right at the party. Afterwards. According to witness statements, one of the suspects, one Michael Dunham, was hitting on her at the party. At that time, most of the guests were already quite intoxicated, which explains why–later at the trial–it couldn't be established without a doubt how she responded to his advances. The classmate who had invited her to the party swore that she had turned him down in a polite but unmistakable manner. Some of his friends, however, argued that she had encouraged and even made out with him. I am sure that these were blatant lies. Fact is that she left the

267

party afterwards–alone or with Dunham; the statements regarding that were also contradictory. She claimed that she was walking home alone when she was attacked by Michael and three other young men. The bastards really did a number on her. Unfortunately, she didn't go to the police right away but only the next day. Of course, by then she had taken a shower, scrubbed her fingernails, and so on. The jury acquitted these scumbags, giving them the benefit of a doubt. Even her own parents didn't believe her side of the story. "Can you imagine that?" Gallagher, apparently agonized by the story, ran his hand over his face.

"About four weeks after the trial, the guys were dead, and Kathryn had gone AWOL. I was the lead investigator at the time. For me, the case was clear: she had taken her revenge on these bastards and had run away. However, it was impossible to link her to the murders–no DNA, no prints, nothing. And when she couldn't be found, someone came up with the brilliant idea that she probably had also become the victim of a violent crime and had been deep-sixed somewhere. Bullshit! But even her parents preferred this version over the alternative. It was obviously easier for them to believe that her child had been murdered and ditched somewhere than to accept that she was a killer on the run. A few months later, I was forced to drop the case."

"Does this mean that you are not working the case anymore?" Liz asked confused.

"No. Officially, the case was closed about ten years ago. Since then, I have been working on it after hours, on weekends, and on vacation time." When he noticed Liz's perplexed expression, Gallagher smiled at her gently. "My wife passed away fifteen years ago. Cancer. Believe me, I've got lots of time on my hands!"

"I am so sorry!" Richard said with heartfelt sympathy, for which Gallagher thanked him with a pensive smile.

268

"What I don't understand is how she was able to simply disappear without leaving a trace. Didn't she need money and papers... or, at least, a car? Did she have all that?" Liz pushed on.

"You're asking the right questions," Gallagher answered with praise. "Why, do you think, was the theory that she was dead so willingly accepted? Because nobody could envision her disappearing from the face of the earth just like that. Her ID and credit cards were found in her room, she didn't own a car, and nobody knows how much cash she may have had at the time. We even found about thirty bucks in her piggy bank. One can only speculate whether she left them there to deliberately mislead us."

"How was she able to get away with it for so long?" Liz wondered, fascinated.

"She's taking on the identity of other people. At least, for some time." It was Richard, who answered the question.

Gallagher nodded approvingly. "Exactly! Do you have any idea how many people become victims of identity theft every year in the U.S. alone? About ten million! Just imagine: ten million! Credit card information, social security numbers, birth certificates... anything can get stolen or forged. Once you've got that, it may take months or years until the fraud may be detected. Kathryn never stayed long enough in one place for that to happen. Until now."

"Walt, what do you think? How much longer will she stay in Chicago?" After all he had just heard, Richard wasn't sure at all that she was still in the city.

"Difficult to tell. As it looks, she's been here for a few months already. Based on what we know, she tends to stay in densely populated areas for a while, which makes sense! She probably was a whole two years in Los Angeles. However, she probably changed her identity at least three times while she was there. And we have no clue if she was there continuously throughout the whole period." Gallagher paused briefly and thoughtfully looked at Richard. "However, the situation is obviously different this time. Somebody's

269

got onto her–and she is aware of it. Maybe she'll just move on and disappear again, and we'll be none the wiser than before. That's what I would do If I were her. But I'm not. There is something else that's different this time. There is no indication whatsoever that in the past she knew her victims–besides Dunham and his friends of course. All men appear to have shared some common traits, but otherwise she seems to have picked them rather randomly. They were simply unfortunate enough to be in the wrong place at the wrong time. Just like your Tom Maddock. The most recent victims, however, were selected to hurt you, Richard. That means that it has become personal." Again, he paused and gave Richard a compassionate look. "We need to catch her before she can do any more harm!"

3:06 p.m.

Who the heck was this fatso? So far, Stanton and the little gook had called him only "Walt."

Like his famous namesake, Walt Disney, he looked like the archetypal grandfather. Regardless of his appearance and good-natured demeanor, though, he undoubtedly posed a risk.

He knew too much–way too much.

As soon as he had opened his mouth, she had realized that her past had caught up with her: he was Canadian.

But how did he know the name Kathryn Hamilton?

The three of them must have talked about her already earlier today someplace else. What a nuisance! This made it much more difficult for her to judge whether his arrival in Chicago really helped the local authorities.

Okay, they had a name, but it didn't matter.

Kathryn Hamilton had died a long time ago.

****

Richard was showing Gallagher the locations of the crime scenes on a map when a stony-faced Steven entered the room.

He was holding a piece of paper in his hand. "I'm sorry, I've got terrible news: the lab just sent the results of the DNA-analysis."

Richard felt his stomach contract.

Steven took a deep breath and confirmed the inevitable: "It is Ron. The crucified man really is Ron."

Liz immediately started to cry and hurried out of the room.

Richard only nodded silently.

"Is there anything I can do for you?" Walt Gallagher asked.

Richard cleared his throat. Although the news wasn't unexpected, it felt like another stab in the heart. It took him a moment to regain his composure before he responded with an icy voice: "Help me find Kathryn Hamilton!"

6:55 p.m.

"So, you found the girl right here?" Gallagher looked at the spot where the tied Melissa Robertson had lain on the floor. "And how much time had passed by then–I mean, after you received the first video?"

"A little over two hours," Richard answered solemnly.

The inspector didn't seem to approve of Richard's mood. He put his hands on his hips, placed himself right in front of Richard, and yelled at him like an angry staff sergeant: "Now, listen to me, Richard! I know that you think that it is your fault that your friend is dead, but that's not true! There was no way for you to know that something like this would happen. You are dealing with a cold-blooded killer, whose actions have always been utterly unpredictable. You should be proud of what you have already accomplished! Everyone thought that Kathryn Hamilton was dead–and yet you

271

found her! It's only because of you that Melissa Robertson is still alive!"

"Walt, I am the reason she got into this situation in the first place! Don't you understand?"

The subsequent silence was only disturbed by the faint buzzing of the fridge.

Only now, Richard realized that he had yelled at the inspector.

"It's alright, buddy, let it all out!" Rather than taking offense at Richard's outburst, Gallagher gave him an encouraging pat on the shoulder.

"I am so sorry, Walt! It's certainly not your fault."

"No worries! Everyone has their own way to grieve. After the death of my Emily, I didn't think I could go on. For three years, I numbed all feelings with booze and pills–until I was put on the Dunham case. As crazy as it may sound, but chasing Kathryn Hamilton has probably saved my life. I had a reason again to get up in the morning."

"And once you've caught her and she's behind bars? What will you do?"

Gallagher chuckled. "We aren't quite there yet, my boy! I'll think about this once she's really in jail or dead. I can still look for another case then. Because one thing is certain: as long as there are humans, there will be murder."

"That's true, I am afraid. What is your opinion now that you've seen the crime scenes? Have you noticed anything we may have missed? Should we take another course of action?"

Gallagher's eyes roamed the loft. "I believe so… maybe. I have a proposition for you: you invite me to a good steak, and I tell you how you, I mean we, can find Kathryn Hamilton–or whatever she may call herself at the moment. Detective Chen should join us, too. We'll need someone who knows how to use a computer."

****

272

"There she is!" Gallagher shouted happily when he saw Liz step into the restaurant. He was so excited that everyone else in the restaurant must have thought they were best friends.

"I hope you didn't have any plans for tonight," Richard said placatingly when she sat down at their table.

Liz looked at him ill-naturedly. "I just wanted to go to bed early for a change. And just to beat you to the draw: alone!"

Gallagher looked at her cheerfully and handed her his glass of beer. "I am glad you're here, Liz! We need your help. You know, I've got this idea…"

Liz, all ears, took the glass from his hand and took a sip out of it. "I'm listening!"

"When Richard and I visited the crime scenes this afternoon, I noticed the 'For Sale' sign in front of the artist's studio, and I was wondering how Kathryn Hamilton may have got access to the building. Same with the lofts. Richard told me that the locks hadn't been tampered with. Knowing that, I find it curious that the current owners all bought the apartments within the last nine months… without exception."

"I know what you're getting at, but all properties were managed or brokered by different realtors. The locks were from different manufacturers. We've looked into all of that before. Believe me, that's a blind alley!" Liz said.

The waitress came to their table, and Liz ordered a beer: "Same as what the gentleman's got–but a small one."

Gallagher grinned at her. "Do you know why you haven't caught Kathryn Hamilton yet?"

Liz shook her head.

"Because nothing she does is obvious and easily decipherable. That's why I've always been late a couple of months. She was always long gone by the time I'd found out that she had murdered someone and had an idea about how she'd done it… Liz, have you ever bought a house or an apartment?" Gallagher asked friendly.

273

"Are you kidding? Here in Chicago? On my salary? I'm renting!" she shouted out.

"But you, Richard. You are owning, aren't you?"

Richard nodded.

"Then, I guess, you can probably tell us everything that happens when you view an apartment."

"Okay. I just called a real estate agency, told them what I'm looking for, and they showed me a few places." Slowly, it dawned on Richard what Gallagher was getting at.

"How many places did you look at, give or take? Do you remember?"

"Maybe ten or fifteen, I don't remember the exact number."

"Doesn't matter. But were all these places owned by the same financier or investment company?"

"No. Some were privately owned, others were under construction, and one was owned by a bank–so, no."

"And do you believe that you were the only one these properties were offered to or that your realtor had an exclusive deal to show these places?"

Richard shook his head. "Of course not. You're right–we were on the right track, but we didn't think it through!"

"I wouldn't say that. After all, there were a ton of other things that kept you occupied."

"Can somebody, please, tell me what's going on here! Even though I've never purchased any real estate in my life, I'd really like to know what you guys are talking about," Liz complained.

Gallagher indicated Richard with a nod that he should answer the question.

"Liz, our department just checked which realtors were involved in the sale of these properties. What we haven't taken into account is that any old broker can arrange a viewing and get access to the keys."

"Darn it!"

274

When the waitress showed up at their table a moment later with her small beer, Liz didn't let her go before ordering her food. "I'd like the filet mignon. Medium. And fries. And wrap up everything to go– I have to get back to the office!"

11:32 p.m.

"Hello, how are you two? I hope you had a nice day!" Richard took Consuela's nightgown, a handful of satin with spaghetti straps, out under the pillow and smelled the fragrance still lingering in the shiny-smooth fabric.

"Richard, this place is amazing! I'm just sad you can't be here with us. How are you? Have you heard from Ron by now?" Stephanie sounded concerned.

Instead of answering, Richard pulled out the top of her pj's she'd worn the night before and buried his face in it.

"Richard? Richard, are you still there?"

"He's dead. The DNA-results have confirmed it."

"Oh, Richard, I am so sorry!" Stephanie was sobbing.

For a while, none of them was able to utter a word. But Richard could hear the girls crying on the other end of the line.

Eventually, Consuela was on the phone. "Richard, mi cariño, I wish I could hold you in my arms right now."

"Do you have any idea how this could happen?" Stephanie asked with a broken voice.

"The woman must have waited for him when we were leaving the restaurant Thursday night. It's not clear whether they drove directly to the atelier or someplace else first. I am just glad I got you to safety in time."

"What do you mean? Has anything else happened since we've left?" Consuela asked immediately.

Richard bit his lower lip. He shouldn't have blabbed like that. He had no intention of unsettling the girls.

They had been so calm and level-headed yesterday when he'd confronted them with the situation and told them that their lives might be in danger. Even when he had told them that they couldn't contact anybody, they hadn't protested. They had simply packed a few things and had driven to the airport.

They trusted him. He had to tell them the truth.

"A young woman, Melissa Robertson, was kidnapped in front of my apartment yesterday in the afternoon. The suspect was convinced that she was Consuela."

"Oh, my goodness! What? ¡Madre mía! Good grief!" For a moment there was pandemonium on the other end of the line.

"Is she dead?" Stephanie yelled in panic.

"No. Fortunately, she's not. Melissa could clarify the misunderstanding just in time." Richard regretted his choice of words even before he had finished the sentence. Just what was the matter with him?

"Does that mean that I'd be dead by now if she'd abducted me?" Consuela sounded surprisingly composed.

Richard took a deep breath before he answered. "To be completely honest, that could very well be the case. I am terribly sorry to have put you in this situation. Please, forgive me!"

"Richard, you didn't put us in this situation! It's only because you reacted so quickly that we are still alive. Don't you forget that!" Consuela tried hard to reassure him.

Richard was yearning for them so much. How alone he had been before he had met them.

"I am just relieved the Beautiful Stranger didn't kill the young woman!" Stephanie seemed to have calmed down a bit, too.

"Yeah. I've got news on that front as well: the 'Beautiful Stranger' isn't really a stranger anymore. We know her name and know that she's originally from Vancouver. We've even received help from the Canadians. From an Inspector Gallagher. He's flown in from Vancouver this morning just to help us with the case."

"Does this mean you're confident to catch her soon?" Stephanie asked, clearly excited.

"I don't give her much longer… after all, I want to see you again as soon as possible!"

Monday, February 21

5:07 a.m.

The little girl looked out the rear window of the dated Oldsmobile Calais with wide-open eyes. The blond brat was moving her lips continuously, but he couldn't understand what she was saying.

A red liquid, which originated from the body lying in front of her on the trunk lid, seemed to ruthlessly devour the white car paint. As if in slow motion, thick, sluggish drops fell from the bumper down onto the asphalt, forming a gradually congealing puddle.

He had to help the woman! But as much as he tried, he couldn't move. Some invisible force was holding him down, making it impossible for him to get closer to the site of the accident.

The brat was still shouting something to him.

Only now, he noticed that on the right side of her head a piece of skullcap was missing. Blood and brain matter spilled from the palm-sized wound.

What was she shouting? Was she trying to warn him?

He looked behind him but couldn't make out any other cars. Everywhere around him, bright emergency flashlights were supposed to prevent other cars from crashing into the metal obstacle behind the curve. Any attempts to secure the site of the accident with these measures, however, came too late for the young female CSI, whose lower body had been crushed to a bloody pulp. Not even her yellow safety vest had provided any sort of protection for her.

The driver of the tuned Ford Mustang had simply been driving at an excessive speed, making it impossible for him to stop the car in time.

As Richard desperately tried to free himself from the gooey mass that made it impossible for him to move, it slowly dawned on him what had caused the accident: just like her father, who–covered in blood–was slumped lifelessly over the steering wheel of the Oldsmobile, the little girl had become the victim of a senseless drive-by shooting.

Right on the expressway, the man had somehow enraged another driver. Maybe he had cut him off or had been driving too slowly. It was also possible that he and his daughter had just become the casualties of a macabre gang initiation rite… who knew?

The crime scene had been secured by the book even before the CSIs had started their work, but rules and regulations just weren't enough sometimes. At least when someone was speeding in reduced visibility.

All the jerking and pulling was futile–he couldn't get free.

Regrettably, he had to watch from a distance as the woman–jammed between the two cars–died a slow and painful death.

As the blood continued to drip, the girl's voice became clearer. And while her eyes didn't change, her face slowly turned into a skull. He could hear her words clear as a bell now–but he didn't know what they meant.

"What do you mean?" he shouted to her. "Tell me! What do you mean?"

Suddenly, he moved away from the accident and his vision of the child got blurry. Her voice became quieter, too.

He was kicking wildly and swinging his arms in circles now. He absolutely had to know what the girl was trying to tell him!

With panic, he shouted to her again: "What do you mean?"

Then he was awakened by his own yelling.

Richard was soaked in sweat. His heart was racing, and he was shaking all over.

This time, the dream had been different than the ones he'd had in the past.

Never before had he seen the girl, just Monica.

He had also never heard any voices.

Richard didn't believe in ghosts, but he knew that the child–whether she had talked to him from the beyond or was just the product of his imagination–had indeed tried to warn him. Not of approaching cars but of a different kind of danger.

"Don't do it!" she had shouted again and again. "Don't do it!"

10:33 a.m.

"As much as I'd like to help you, we do not have any records that would indicate which of our agents may have shown this particular property to a customer. I am sorry!"

The owner of the real estate agency was friendly in her choice of words, but the sound of her voice was arrogant and condescending.

Liz wasn't willing to give up so easily. "I guess I'll have to ask a judge then to issue a subpoena so that I can carefully look at all your documents and computers myself. Naturally, this will mean that I'll have to confiscate everything that isn't nailed down–and it may take quite a while until you get it back."

"Is this a threat?" The lady wasn't easily intimidated.

"What makes you think that? Not at all!" Liz answered innocently.

"Good for you! You should know that I have connections!"

Liz envisioned her sitting at her desk dolled up, feeling incredibly superior. Probably, she'd never had a real job in her life and had gotten rich by earning whopping commissions on the sale of multimillion-dollar estates. After all, her agency only brokered luxury homes. The lady didn't deal with ordinary mortals. Police officers, obviously, also fell into this category.

Liz was a bit peeved by that. "I am afraid you've misunderstood what I was saying," she said in a polite but determined tone. "I did not intend to threaten you. I wanted to… encourage you!" For a moment, she contemplated whether it wouldn't be wiser to back down; but it was not in her nature to surrender. Therefore, she was doubling down: "And, by the way, I don't give a shit about your connections! Either you volunteer the information about who was shown the apartments, or I'll clear out your office and arrest you for obstructing justice!"

****

"Guys, I think I've got something!" Without knocking, Liz came storming into Bob Miller's office where Richard and Walt were giving the Chief an update on the progress of the investigation.

"What's the matter with you?" Miller said with a stern voice. He didn't like it when someone barged in unannounced.

"I am sorry, but it's really important," she responded sheepishly.

"Okay then, what is so important, Detective Chen?"

"I spent all night at the computer and was on the phone all morning…"

"And?" Richard asked impatiently.

"I've got a name–Vanessa Kincade!" Liz shouted with excitement.

3:11 p.m.

The atmosphere was tense. In consultation with Chief Miller, Richard had decided to use just a small SWAT team.

He didn't want flashing lights and blaring sirens to draw Kathryn Hamilton's attention to them and give her enough time to escape. They had to surprise her, or she'd be gone.

Her apartment was on the fourth floor of the building. Officers working in pairs secured the back and the fire escape ladder on the west side of the complex.

An elegant elderly woman on the other side of the street was walking her dog. When the Yorkshire terrier–who was dressed in a pink puffer vest–relieved himself at a fence, the woman just gave them a nonchalant glance before moving on with ostentatious indifference. Here, in the affluent "Gold Coast" neighborhood, nobody got involved in other people's business.

They stepped into the entrance hall, and Richard sent a three-man reconnaissance team up the stairs. The rest was to wait until they were given the green light to follow.

"Walt, I want you to stay here with one officer! There is a chance that we won't catch her and she will try to get away."

"Are you serious?" Gallagher asked disappointed.

For Richard, this wasn't up for discussion so he just nodded briefly. Even though he understood that Walt didn't want to miss the moment Kathryn Hamilton was caught, he could not put his colleague in danger. No one knew what was waiting for them upstairs. Moreover, the Canadian didn't have any authority here in Chicago. Officially, he was on vacation.

If worst came to worst, they'd arrest Kathryn Hamilton but had to set her free again because of a silly formality. Stuff like that happened all the time.

The walkie-talkie clicked once short and twice long, which was the signal for them to come upstairs.

"All right. Chamber a round but leave the safety on until we're upstairs! Move!" Richard let Liz and the other members of the team get into the elevator first before he also stepped in.

Slowly, the cabin moved upwards. Nobody said a word. There was a high-pitched chime when they moved past the second and third floor.

At the third chime, the sliding door opened and Richard–followed by the others–sneaked into the hallway.

A member of the recon team, who was crouched down behind a corner, pointed at the apartment with the letters "5B" on the door.

Just like during the operation two days ago, it only took one blow with the ram to burst the door open.

Then, everything happened very quickly: the team stormed into the apartment, following the predetermined tactical plan, and secured one room after the other. The whole operation was over after a mere twenty seconds since Kathryn Hamilton was nowhere to be found.

"Walt, you can come up now!" Richard disappointedly muttered into the radio.

"Roger that!" the response came back immediately.

Richard was standing in the center of the bedroom, halfway between the bed and the big wall mirror. She'd been here only recently; he could sense it.

"Don't feel bad, my boy, we've never been that close to catching her!" a voice behind him suddenly remarked. It was Walt.

"She must have gotten wind of the operation somehow. Just look: the closet and the drawer chest are empty! She didn't even have time to pick up the clothes she dropped!" Richard remarked.

"Yes, she definitely was in a hurry!" Gallagher said triumphantly.

Richard didn't understand why the inspector was in such a good mood. "Walt, don't you want to catch Kathryn Hamilton? Forgive me, but I'm getting the feeling that you're not at all upset that she got away again."

"Richard, you're a brilliant criminologist, but you must learn to deal with setbacks! Otherwise, you'll kill yourself! You cannot force success, especially when you're dealing with such a cunning opponent. Just look at the bright side!"

"Which would be what exactly?" Richard asked.

"We've cornered her. My guess is that she was still here no more than half an hour ago–just smell!"

The scent of roses was lingering in the air. Richard nodded.

"If we're lucky, she'll make a mistake now. Maybe she hasn't had the time to create a new identity and will use her credit card again. Even if she just uses the name Vanessa Kincade to check into a hotel, we'll get her!" Walt was confidence personified.

"And if she doesn't do that? Richard asked skeptically."

"Then, we still have another ace up our sleeve…"

Richard knew what his Canadian colleague was trying to say, but he was secretly hoping that they wouldn't have to play that card.

"Oh my god, dear god!" The sorrowful cries were coming from the kitchen.

At once, Richard and Walt hurried to the other side of the apartment, where Liz–her face twisted with pain–stood in front of a big double door fridge.

"Oh my god, oh my god!" she whimpered over and over.

"Liz, what's the matter?" Richard asked warily.

"Oh my god, oh my god!" She did not hear him.

"Liz, calm down!" Slowly, Richard approached her from the side. He couldn't see yet what it was that disturbed her so much.

"Oh my god, oh my god!" She just stood there, tears running down her face and her fingers spasmodically writhing in pain.

Richard took another step toward her, then he put his arms around her to pull her away from the refrigerator.

When he suddenly saw Ron's severed head before him, he joined in her wailing: "Oh my god!"

5:48 p.m.

She would have to stay here for a while. At least until she could find a more adequate accommodation.

She hadn't decided yet whether it would be in Chicago or somewhere else.

One thing, however, was clear: she wouldn't leave town before settling accounts with Richard Stanton.

She'd had it so nice here. She could have stayed for at least another year.

The possibilities had seemed endless–at least, until he'd shown up.

Tisiphone looked around the small apartment and started to get angry.

This place was a shithole! Even after she'd tidied up and cleaned it, Forrester McLeans' apartment repulsed her.

It was poky and stuffy. Not even the air freshener spray had helped to subdue the musty, frowsy smell.

She was mad with rage.

She would make Stanton pay for this.

****

"Steven, I've sent Liz to Dr. Redcliff. It's possible that she'll declare her unfit for service for a while. Could you please come here to take over! I've seen enough." Richard stood in the kitchen of the apartment on East Bellevue Place and stared out the window.

Behind him, two CSIs transferred the last body parts, which were floating in glass chars, from the fridge to Styrofoam boxes.

"I'll come right away! How is Liz doing? Is it bad?" Steven asked.

"She's devastated and seems to be in shock. Hard to tell how long it may take her to recover. I think that Forensics will take another two or three hours here to collect evidence. Officer Rudy will bring you up to speed once you're here. Do you have any news?"

Steven had staid back in the police station to search the internet and data banks for the name Vanessa Kincade with the tech team.

"We haven't found much yet. Some credit card activities look promising. However, I find it surprising that, with few exceptions, we couldn't find any charges from restaurants or bars."

"I don't think that's a surprise at all. Usually, someone else pays the bill," Richard interjected. "What were the exceptions?"

"Hmm, on Thursday she dined in the restaurant right next to yours. She was really lying in wait for you, just as you thought."

Richard bit his lower lip. It was true that he had assumed that Kathryn Hamilton had been waiting for them. However, he hadn't thought her to be impudent enough to dine in a Michelin-starred restaurant while doing so. However, something else worried him even more: the operation had been carefully planned. Just like at their restaurant, one couldn't get a table without a reservation there either. This, though, meant that she had known ahead of time where they would be Thursday evening. How?

"Anything else?" Richard asked tiredly.

"Well, there is a suspicious activity on Wednesday evening," Steven was beating around the bush.

"What is it?" Richard asked impatiently.

Steven cleared his throat before he continued. "Richard, she had dinner in your building's restaurant already on Wednesday evening. Wasn't that the day McLean's article came out? Do you think that's a coincidence?"

Richard stared at the building across the street, in which more and more lights were being turned on. Behind a window on the fourth floor, a woman was setting the table for supper.

No, he didn't believe in coincidences.

9:04 p.m.

"Richard, have you really thought this through? I can prepare the papers for you to sign tomorrow if you insist. However, for the record, I am doing this under protest. As your legal counsel, I must advise against taking such a hasty step. You met these girls only a couple of days ago!" Jonathan Rosenbaum was sitting at the large dining table, shaking his head, and nervously spinning his fountain pen.

"I've made the decision. I'll stop by at your office tomorrow afternoon to sign everything." Richard got up, walked over to the window, and took another sip from his wine glass.

"Do what you want! But if I may express my opinion as your friend and not your lawyer: you must be mad!"

Richard watched the cars on Michigan Avenue Bridge. Without turning around, he said: "Just do it!"

"As you wish! Then, let me summarize the most important facts: all payouts to various friends and relatives add up to about ten percent of your total assets. A third of the rest is going to your foundation; and two thirds, that means about sixty percent of what you own, will be divided among the two girls... Do you have even the slightest idea how much we are talking here?"

"I guess about five hundred million, give or take, depending on current property values," Richard answered emotionlessly.

"As a matter of fact, you are crazy!"

Richard turned around, looked at his lawyer, and repeated: "Just do it!"

Tuesday, February 22

12:16 a.m.

How focused he had always been when playing piano. He was sitting hunched over his keyboard… eyes closed. He'd tilted his head a bit, paying close attention to every note the other band members were playing.

The photo had been taken a few years ago at the Chicago Jazz Festival in Grant Park. The Jazzy Doctors had been invited to play as second-day opening act in the Petrillo Music Shell. What an honor it had been to share the stage with some of the greatest Jazz-musicians on the planet.

Miles Davis, Ellis Fitzgerald, Lionel Hampton, Stan Getz, Count Basie, and even Benny Goodman–they all had performed here at some point.

Richard turned to the next page of the photo album. It showed the band arm in arm at the end of the concert, enjoying the audience's applause–exhausted but thrilled. Ron was grinning from ear to ear. Rightly so as he had played the best performance of his life… his short life.

Richard closed his eyes tightly and threw his head back.

Maybe he should open another bottle of wine, just to help him fall asleep.

He was so tired. So tired…

Just as he was dozing off, his phone rang.

Annoyed, he felt around the sofa cushions until he finally found it. "Stanton!"

"Richard, please forgive me for calling you at this hour, but I urgently need to talk with you. Can we meet somewhere?"

It was Walt Gallagher. And he sounded anxious.

"What is this about? Can't we discuss it on the phone?"

"We'd better not."

"Walt, to be honest, I probably shouldn't leave the house again tonight. You know, I've been drinking… How about I send someone over to pick you up at your hotel and we talk here at my place?"

"If you don't mind…"

"Not at all. It will probably take the driver about fifteen minutes. Is that enough time?"

"Absolutely! I'll go down to the lobby right away and wait there. See you soon."

What was it that the inspector wanted to talk with him about that couldn't wait till the morning?

Richard called the chauffeur service, then went to the bathroom to freshen up a bit.

His face was marked by the efforts of the last week. He had dark shadows under his red eyes, and his skin was dry and pale.

For a while, he looked at his mirror image, which clearly had been impacted by lack of sleep and grief. Then, he went to the kitchen and made himself an expresso.

Fatigued, he took a seat at the kitchen island and waited until he heard someone knock on the door.

"Hi, Walt, please, come in! Would you like something to drink, a coffee maybe or a glass of wine?"

"I wouldn't say no to a glass of wine."

"Just go straight to the living room, I'll get a glass."

When Richard returned, Gallagher stood in front of the coffee table and studied the label of the almost-empty wine bottle.

"Must be good," Walt finally said and gave the other man a pitiful look.

Only now, Richard realized that the other bottle he had emptied over the course of the evening was still on the table.

"It's been a long day…"

"Buddy, no need to apologize. Just open another bottle! I could really use a drink myself."

Richard fetched another bottle and uncorked it.

"You know, on days like this, it's okay to have one too many. It shouldn't become a habit, though." The inspector took a sip and nodded approvingly. "Very nice!"

"Glad you like it. Now, please, take a seat and tell me why you needed to talk to me right away!"

"Of course." The big man grabbed the armrest of the sofa and awkwardly lowered himself onto the cushion. "Richard, when I was lying in bed before in the hotel, I simply couldn't sleep…"

"I can relate to that," Richard interrupted him.

"No, don't get me wrong. Usually, I sleep like a baby! Sometimes, however, when I have the feeling that I missed something, or something doesn't make sense to me, I'll lie in bed wide awake all night."

"So, what kept bothering you tonight?"

"The fact that Kathryn Hamilton escaped."

"I don't understand…"

"Just think about it! It was obvious from what the apartment looked like that she'd packed her stuff in a hurry and got out of there as fast as she could. She didn't even bother to take her trophies with her. The question is: why? Why was she in such a hurry? What reason did she have to leave this comfortable hiding place right now?"

"Haven't you yourself told me that she never stays in the same place for very long?"

"That's certainly right. But so far, all her 'relocations' were carefully planned and prepared."

"And the fact that we got–how did you put it?–on her heels? Wouldn't that be reason enough for her to run?"

"Maybe. But how did she know that? Richard, do you remember the first thing you told me today–I mean yesterday afternoon–when I arrived at the apartment?"

290

Richard looked at the inspector confusedly. "No, not exactly. Wasn't it something about the clothes she had dropped?"

"The first thing you said was that she somehow had gotten wind of the operation. I couldn't stop thinking about that. How in the world did she get wind of the operation?"

"You're right. We tried very hard to keep the mission a secret. That's also the reason why I worked with a small team. She couldn't have known that we were coming. Unless…"

"Unless there is a leak."

Richard took a moment to think this over. "There's something else…"

"Yes?"

"She knew where we'd be Thursday night. However, I don't see how these two things are connected."

"They don't necessarily need to be. Did you tell anyone in the office that you'd eat at this restaurant?"

"No. Only Ron knew about it. And the girls… That could be it: she somehow got the information from the girls!"

"Are you implying that your girlfriends–if I may use that term– had contact with Kathryn Hamilton?"

"No, I don't think so. But she may have followed them and overheard a conversation they may have had about it. I am quite sure that she was following us as early as on Wednesday."

"That would make sense. However, this brings us back to our original question: how did she know about the apartment raid?"

The inspector looked at Richard in silence for a while. Although his expression revealed his thinking, he didn't say it.

"Forget it, there aren't any snitches on my team!" Richard blurted out.

"Okay, okay!" The inspector raised his hand conciliatorily. "I didn't say anything… but, somehow, she must have gotten the information. Do you have another explanation?"

Richard poured himself another glass of wine and walked over to the windows. Below, the white terracotta tiles of the Wrigley Building were glistening in the bright lights of the countless spots illuminating it at night. The big clock faces of the tower clock showed almost one o'clock.

All of a sudden, something occurred to him. "Darn it!"

He turned around to Gallagher. "Walt, we better switch to coffee after all. I am afraid we have a long night ahead of us."

5:08 a.m.

Judge Kuebler hadn't been particularly thrilled to be roused out of bed in the middle of the night just to put his signature to a search warrant. It had taken quite a bit of arm twisting to dispel his concerns. Again and again, he'd pointed out that it wouldn't be a good idea to mess with the press. Only after Richard had told him that it would be even stupider to let a serial killer run around free during an election year, he'd caved in.

However, finding someone who knew how to detect listening devices at this time of day had turned out to be an even bigger challenge. They'd been calling around for an hour just to get the right man with the right equipment on the line. Later, when the guy had finally been done searching the station, everyone had been shocked by what he'd found.

Presently, Richard was standing again in front of a door about to be breached by a SWAT team.

To his surprise, Bob had insisted on sending a full team to McLean's apartment although they weren't even sure that the reporter had actually shared information with Kathryn Hamilton. Obviously, Bob wanted to play it safe… or at least teach the "skunk" a lesson.

Richard gave a nod, and the door was burst open.

The white beams emerging from the weapon lights mounted on the unit's M4 carbines raced nervously through the grayish black darkness in front of them.

Right away, they saw that there was nobody in the open-concept living room.

A flashlight in one hand and his gun in the other, Richard was the first to push past the kitchenette and into the small hallway behind it.

The bathroom to his left was empty.

The door to his right was ajar.

Without hesitation, he kicked it open and entered the room.

Nothing.

"Clear!" he shouted to the others–sullenly, disappointedly.

He reached behind his back and switched the lights on. This was apparently McLean's bedroom, but the reporter wasn't in his bed.

Nor was anybody else.

Richard had not expected the apartment to be empty.

What surprised him even more, however, was the fact that there was no blanket, pillows, or sheets on the bed–just a blank mattress, wrapped in plastic foil.

He pushed aside the two officers standing in the hallway and scurried back to the living room. "Lights! Somebody turn on the lights!"

When the lights came on, he could see that the chairs here were also covered with plastic foil. There were also two desktop computers, one laptop, and two monitors in the room.

Otherwise, the apartment was practically austere. Nothing was lying around, cabinets and closets were empty, and it smelled of household cleaners and air freshener.

"Walt, Steven, come in! Everyone else out, out! I can hardly turn around in here…"

It took a moment before the three of them were finally alone in the apartment.

"So, what do you think?" Richard asked as he conspicuously looked around the room.

"I know that some people put plastic covers over their furniture to protect it, but this junk here is beyond saving," Steven said.

"That's certainly true!" Walt agreed. "To me, it doesn't look like somebody wanted to protect the furniture. Rather, someone didn't want to sit on it directly. Who knows what you might catch?"

Richard nodded. "Steven, you've met Forrester McLean, haven't you?"

"Sure, he's at every press conference."

"Do you think that he would wrap his own furniture in plastic?"

"Nope."

"That's what I think." Richard thoughtfully stroked his chin. "I have the feeling that he won't get on our nerves anymore... ever. Kathryn Hamilton has probably taken care of this problem for us. Let's check the computers! Steven, that's your territory!"

Steven sat down at the desk and turned on one of the monitors. At once, a screensaver appeared: naked women sitting on rockets, flying from one side of the screen to the other.

"How tasteful...," Walt remarked bemusedly.

As soon as Steven moved the computer mouse, the women disappeared, giving way to a bird's eye view of the conference room in the police station.

Even though the fact that the department had really been spied on was painful, Richard felt some sort of relief that indeed McLean had been behind it. Otherwise, the disaster would have been even bigger. "All right. Steven, get everything packed up and brought to the station! Get in touch with Bob and HR and find out who can take a look at the computer files! We have to make sure that nobody unauthorized gets access to these videos."

The camera under Jenny's desk had been among the first they had found. Richard hoped she would never find out that she had been the victim of such a despicable act of voyeurism. The more he thought about it the angrier he got, and the more he wished that McLean was dead.

"Shall we seal the apartment?" Steven asked.

Richard looked at Walt, who just shrugged his shoulders.

At this moment, Richard regretted that he'd given the order to break open the door. But hindsight was 20/20.

"No. Get the door and the frame fixed as soon as possible and have three officers guard the apartment! If she comes back, we'll arrest her."

8:00 a.m.

There were three knocks on the door.

"Room service!" someone called through the door.

Another knock.

She slipped into the white terry bathrobe and opened the door.

A young, blond man in a waiter vest was standing before her.

"Your breakfast, ma'am! May I put the tray on the table?"

"Yes, please."

Of course, he couldn't help it but peek at her when he entered the room.

She wondered how old he might be. Nineteen? Twenty?

He put the tray down and adjusted a little vase with a yellow rose in it.

"Is there anything else I can do for you, ma'am?"

She looked him up and down. What a handsome boy he was. And he was in her room. Alone.

Her heart started to beat faster, and her breathing sped up.

What would he do if, by accident, her robe belt fell to the floor, allowing him an even better look at her naked body?

"Ma'am?" he said again–a little uneasily this time.

She ran the thick strip of terry cloth through her hands and deliberated whether to untie the knot. How much time would she have until he'd be missed? It was likely that he had more trays to deliver. And in a hotel such as this, the guests didn't like to be kept waiting for their breakfast.

"Ma'am?"

No, it was too risky. And she liked it here. She didn't want to move yet again. Moreover, she wasn't left with too many options right now. Going back to the stinky dump of an apartment was out of the question. She had not been able to stay there for more than two hours even after she'd cleaned up.

She got a ten-dollar bill from her purse and gave it to the boy. "Thank you, that'll be all."

"Thank you very much! Now, if you could just sign here, please."

"Of course." She took the clipboard from him and, with great panache, put her signature under the guest check.

The boy looked at the form. "Have a nice day, Miss Edward."

"Edwards," she corrected him. "Cynthia Edwards."

11:21 a.m.

Richard wasn't even five steps out of the elevator when Jenny came running toward him already.

"Dr. Stanton, have you heard the news yet?" She was visibly shaken.

"Good morning, Jenny. What news are you referring to?"

"That we may have been spied on! Can you believe it? Nobody seems to know any details but, presumably, bugs have been found in our department... and even cameras!"

Richard didn't feel that this was the right time to say anything.

"Bob has called a meeting for everyone in ten minutes. He wants to make an announcement. I am so glad you're here."

Pensively, she walked along next to him, shaking her head. "I cannot believe it! Wouldn't we have noticed something? Where would these cameras have been?"

Again, when Richard did not respond, she abruptly stopped. "Wait a minute… you know something, don't you?"

Richard tried to look as guileless as possible. "Jenny, I am really sorry, but I can't tell you anything right now. You need to understand!"

"So, it's true…"

"Jenny, please, let's wait for what Chief Miller has to say!"

For a moment, she seemed to contemplate whether she could wait that long. Finally, she gave in. "Fine. I am just wondering where these cameras may have been. Just the thought of somebody watching us without our knowledge makes me uncomfortable."

Richard took her hands, pulled her toward him, and gently kissed her on the forehead. "Don't worry!"

****

"Okay guys! Can you all quiet down, please!"

Bob Miller raised his hand, but the anxious murmuring around him would not die down. All the police officers, secretaries, and janitorial staff of the department that were cooped up in the cube farm, waiting to finally learn what had happened, were simply too incensed.

"Quiet, for god's sake!" one of the lieutenants suddenly yelled, and the Chief gave him a thankful nod.

Eventually, the crowd calmed down a bit.

"As you've probably heard through the grapevine already, earlier this morning, several electronic devices were discovered in the department that may have been used for surveillance purposes."

An indignant murmur went through the crowd.

"What kind of devices? For how long? Who was it?" were the most frequently asked questions one could make out in the general tohubohu.

"Just shut up and let the Chief talk!" the lieutenant now screamed, and it became quieter again.

"All I can say at this time is that several microphones and cameras have been seized and that it's probably just one perp. I don't have any more information myself right now."

The crowd became more agitated again but quieted down when the Chief raised his hand again. "I can assure you that we will do everything in our power to solve this case. We are working very closely with the Law Department, Human Resources, and the various unions to make sure that everybody's privacy rights are being protected. I can't tell you anything else at the moment, but I promise that I will keep you posted. Thank you for your understanding."

The Chief stepped off the stool he had been standing on while giving his speech and was bombarded immediately with more questions.

"Sorry, but I simply don't know," he hollered with a shake of his head as he fought his way back to his office, closing the door behind him.

Throughout Bob's announcement, Richard had been standing ready to answer questions if needed. Fortunately, however, it hadn't come to that.

He understood why everyone was frustrated with the situation. The people were discomforted. And for a good reason.

The whole thing was a debacle–in every sense.

"Dr. Stanton?"

Only now, he noticed Jenny who must have been standing directly behind him the whole time.

"I know that you can't say much, but… may I still ask you something?" Her tone was diffident, insecure.

"Of course."

298

"What did Bob mean by saying that everybody's privacy rights will be protected?" She looked at him sorrowfully.

How was he supposed to respond? Pull the wool over her eyes? Tell her the truth?

"Jenny, how do you feel about having lunch with me? We could talk in private then. When can you take a break?"

Jenny gave him a bewildered look, glanced at her watch, and courageously said "Now!"

****

It was a pity that she couldn't hear what they were talking about, but she was sitting too far away from them. She had not been able to convince the waiter to give her a better positioned table. Clearly, the staff had been given orders not to seat anybody in their vicinity. The tables next to Stanton's remained empty even after all others in the restaurant were occupied and new potential patrons had to be sent away.

It didn't matter–she couldn't take the risk of him recognizing her anyway. Thus, she sat in the opposite corner of the restaurant and pretended to be immersed in a women's magazine.

What were they talking about? Their behavior, body language, and facial expressions all cried relationship crisis. But that would mean that they were romantically involved…

The longer she watched them the more plausible it seemed. All the time, the secretary was throwing him amorous glances and seeking physical contact. Already on the way to the restaurant, she had been walking very closely next to him, occasionally brushing up against him. Then, when they had reached the bottom of the stairway leading to the restaurant, she had reached out for his hand to be guided up the stairs.

Although he did not seem to mind her tender advances, his behavior was much more reserved. He was cordial and polite but looked a little sad, just like someone having a heavy heart.

They were seated on the dais at the very back of the restaurant. Facing each other with their lower arms resting on the table, they were absorbed in an animated conversation.

As for the secretary, she seemed to be on an emotional rollercoaster. At first, she had been optimistically beaming at him. But then, in the course of the conversation, her facial expression had changed to one of bewilderment and, finally, outrage.

Right now, she was looking very angry.

Stanton took her hands and talked to her softly, but she obviously did not want to calm down. She was seriously pissed.

What the heck had he told her? Had he admitted that he had been cheating on her with two other women?

She seemed to have a lot of questions for him, and it was clear that she demanded answers.

Willingly, even remorsefully, he complied and gave the requested information.

She now looked disappointed, hurt.

Stanton gallantly raised from his seat when she suddenly got up and hurried toward the ladies' room.

Her stride alone revealed how upset she was. With her purse firmly clutched under her arm, she almost lost her balance in her high heels as she was running down the hall.

Tisiphone put the magazine on the table and followed her. When she entered the luxurious, marble-covered bathroom, the secretary had already disappeared into one of the stalls.

She was crying.

Tisiphone felt the urge to comfort her, but that was out of the question. Why else then had she followed her?

Tisiphone wasn't sure.

Only when she saw what the secretary had left behind on the vanity, she knew that it had been the right decision to follow her.

Right next to the carefully stacked, lily-white guest towels, there was a purse.

When Jenny returned to the table, she looked much more composed. Richard pulled out her chair for her and sat down next to her.

She smiled bravely, took a tissue out of her purse, and wiped away a tear. "I have to admit that I had imagined our first date to be a bit different."

Again, she attempted a smile but, instead, started to cry.

"Jenny, you know very well what I feel for you. You are a wonderful, gorgeous woman, but…"

"Don't say a word!" She pulled him toward her and kissed him on the lips.

4:49 p.m.

Tisiphone laid the aluminum case on the bed and opened it. She really hadn't had much time to pack her stuff before leaving the apartment at East Bellevue Place. Fortunately, however, she'd been able to grab these tools, her clothes, and her stack of drugs. While she had only taken the bare essentials with her to the hotel, she had stored the rest of her belongings in a self-storage unit for now.

The lunatic from the sex shop had certainly spent a small fortune on these surgical instruments. Each piece had its designated place in the customized foam interior of the sturdy hard case. If everything went according to plan, the cold surgical steel would soon slice through Stanton's flesh.

Tisiphone took one of the Volkmann Retractors out of the case and held the cool handle of the eight-and-a-half-inch-long wound hook to her cheek. She had already tried out the instrument, which was reminiscent of a fork but whose three prongs were tapered and deeply curved, on the pervert.

Nevertheless, she was certain that she'd come up with some new uses once she'd be working on Stanton.

She walked over to the window and looked out at the city.

Lost in thought, she let the metal instrument glide over her body. Gently, she ran the flat side of the retractor over her neck and chest, down to her nipples. At first, she just pressed the back of the long, cold tines against her teats, but then, she turned the instrument around and started to scratch her stiff paps with the trenchant points. The more she thought of Stanton the harder she drove the steel claws into her flesh.

It was a cloudy, gloomy day. Even from the twenty-fifth floor of the hotel she could only see a few miles. Again and again, wisps of fog passed by her window and obscured the view onto the surrounding buildings.

When she felt a warm drop of blood running down her left breast, she let go of her bosoms and moved the sharp hook downwards over her belly and thighs, and then a bit higher again. Pushing her lower body forward, she spread her labia apart and bared her clit.

The fantasy of Stanton lying at her feet–naked and tied up–aroused her even more than the sharp pain in her genital area. She imagined how it would feel to ride him and being fucked by his stiff dick.

As she twitched wildly and climaxed, her gaze fell upon the clockface of the Wrigley Building right across from her. It was four o'clock exactly now.

****

"And you really think this is gonna work?" Steven scratched his head. It was apparent that he didn't think the plan would be successful.

"Do you have a better idea?" Richard tried to stay calm.

"If I may say something: in my opinion, it's at least worth a try. Furthermore, I don't see any alternatives," Walt said conciliatorily.

"But how do we know that Kathryn Hamilton is still in town? And do you really believe she is crazy enough to go after you?" Steven asked provocatively.

Richard and Walt exchanged conspiratorial looks before the inspector answered: "You bet!"

"If you think so… you don't need my permission anyway. And how exactly do you want to approach this? You can't just walk around town and wait for her to emerge, can you?" Steven gibed.

"Basically, that's exactly what I'm gonna do. However, we agreed that I'd have two plainclothes officers guarding me while I'm doing it," Richard answered cooly.

"Are you talking around-the-clock surveillance?" Steven asked surprisedly.

"No, I don't need that. I'll briefly stop by the office in the morning and afterwards go shopping in the city. I'm gonna buy a couple new shirts, have lunch someplace, and so on. Nothing about this will be unusual or give her any reason for getting suspicious. And as soon as she gets close to me, we strike." Richard had discussed the plan with Walt before. It was simple, albeit a bit risky. Yet it was feasible.

And they really didn't have any idea how else they could possibly catch Kathryn Hamilton.

8:33 p.m.

"We spent most of the day at the beach. Consuela's cousins got a boat and took us to a secluded bay. The water was crystal-clear, and we found a nice spot in the shade of Cocos palms. I still may have gotten a little sunburnt, I'm afraid, but it was wonderful nevertheless! For lunch, we visited a little seafood restaurant right by the sea. We relaxed on the veranda, had a glass of wine, and shared a red snapper, which the waitress let us pick out ourselves. She came to the table with a tray with three or four freshly caught fish on it and asked us which one we'd like. I left it up to Consuela to choose one. To me, they all looked great, but she really took her time to check them all out. As a side, we had vegetable-mofongo–you know, this smashed plantain-dish. Oh, and as a starter we had grilled octopus in garlicky olive oil. That was super yummy as well! When we got back to the beach, we all napped for about an hour." Stephanie giggled happily, warming Richard's heart. He was truly glad that she was in such a good mood.

"Yes, and you turned really red," Consuela butted in.

"It's not that bad," Stephanie tried to soft-pedal the issue.

"Have you got something for sunburn?" Richard asked with concern. "Otherwise, you should go to a pharmacy!"

"I have already greased her whole back. She'll survive," Consuela teased.

"I certainly will! By the time you arrive, you won't see a thing. Do you have an idea yet when you're coming? We miss you terribly." All of a sudden, Stephanie didn't sound happy anymore.

"I miss you, too. But I am convinced that my work here will come to an end soon–one way or the other," Richard said exhaustedly.

"What do you mean?" Consuela inquired immediately.

Richard bit his lower lip. Once again, a lapse in concentration had caused a slip of the tongue. It must be due to the lack of sleep. "Well, it's quite possible that the woman has left town and gone into hiding already. If that's the case, there's nothing left to do for me here. If she surfaces somewhere else again, it's up to the FBI to deal with it."

"And if she's still in Chicago?" Stephanie asked anxiously.

"Then, we'll catch her. I'm sure."

"How can you be so certain? Do you have a plan?" Consuela seemed suspicious. "Richard?" she prompted him to answer.

304

"Don't worry, I've got everything under control."

"You can't be serious! Have you already forgotten that this woman has killed your friend Ron... and god knows how many other people?" Consuela exclaimed furiously.

She certainly didn't mince her words–but that was one of the things he loved about her. "Of course, I haven't forgotten. How could I? I'll be careful, I promise."

****

Toward the end of their conversation, Richard had tried hard to dispel the girls' worries and be his usual self. Still, it had been very hard to say goodbye to them.

Neither Consuela nor Stephanie had bought his feigned confidence, and the phone call had ended in tears.

He was wondering whether he'd be in this situation now if he'd met them sooner. A few months or weeks sooner–or just a few days– and Bob wouldn't have been able to persuade him to give the Sherlock Holmes again... or would he?

The truth was that during the two years he'd been sailing around the globe he'd missed something. He'd missed doing something meaningful. Yes, he wanted to do something important, something that made a difference. It wasn't about killing time. His life wasn't that boring. And he certainly wasn't out for the thrill. It was about locking away pitiless killers and making the world a safer place.

Richard opened the wine cooler and contemplated which bottle to drink tonight. Should he uncork one of his real treasures?

No, this would be a sin.

He took a 1999 La Mouline from the shelf but changed his mind and put it back.

Maybe he shouldn't drink any alcohol tonight. After all, he had to be fit tomorrow. And he was so tired that he probably didn't need a nightcap to fall asleep.

Just as he was about to get some water from the fridge, his cell rang.

Richard put the glass down, ran to the living room, and finally found his phone behind one of the couch pillows.

The display showed "Jenny."

He closed his eyes, wishing that he had had been successful in persuading her to take a few days off and visit her mother. Instead, she had insisted on going back to the station and work–as if nothing had happened.

When he had told her about the cameras under her desk, she had been consternated at first. However, the first shock had soon given way to anger, followed by sadness. She had talked about feeling violated and abused. Richard had had to promise her that nobody in the department would ever see the recordings. He had assured her that the files would only be made available to an external psychologist and be kept sealed until it was decided whether they could be deleted.

This had calmed her down a tiny bit, if nothing else.

Then, suddenly, she had kissed him and confessed her love to him.

She had been so vulnerable and doleful.

Bravely, she had listened to him tell her about Stephanie and Consuela. She had even managed a smile when he'd told her how happy he was.

At that point, Richard had really thought that she'd be over the worst.

But now, she was on the phone.

Richard took a deep breath and waited for another ring before he picked up.

"Jenny?"

No answer.

"Jenny? Please, say something!"

He could only hear calm, steady breathing on the other end.

All of a sudden, Richard realized that it wasn't Jenny on the phone.

"Who is this?" he shouted angrily.

306

"Don't you know?"

"Kathryn Hamilton, isn't it?"

"No, she died a long time ago."

"Who are you then?"

"Tisiphone."

Richard recognized the name: Tisiphone was one of the three Furies in Greek mythology.

"The goddess of vengeance? But Tisiphone only avenged murders. You, in contrast, are just an unscrupulous killer of innocents. Who, for heaven's sake, do you think you are avenging?" he yelled contemptuously.

"Kathryn Hamilton," she answered tersely.

Richard buried his face in his hands.

"What have you done to Jenny? Where is she?"

"Jenny is fine, don't worry! And if you do as I say, this won't change. I do not intend to harm her. However, if you don't follow my instructions, I will vent my anger on her–and you know what that means…"

"What do you want from me?"

"I want you to save Jenny! I want you to rush to her apartment like a knight in shining armor and prevent me from hacking her to little pieces! You've got exactly fifteen minutes. After that, I will begin pulling out her fingernails. Come alone, or she dies!"

"But…"

"Ticktock, ticktock," was the last thing Richard heard before she hung up.

For a brief moment, he contemplated calling Steven and Walt but decided that it was too dangerous. They'd certainly call in a SWAT team. Maybe not Walt, but Steven for sure. He couldn't risk putting Jenny in danger just because some inexperienced officer might feel like racing through town with flashing lights.

Or, because he himself wasn't man enough to hold his own against the killer.

307

Tisiphone… she was even more disturbed than he'd thought.

Resolutely, he fetched his Glock from the bedroom and hurried out the front door. If he made haste, he might be able to get to Jenny's apartment before the fifteen minutes were over. Fortunately, he remembered where she lived. A year ago, he had dropped her off at home after work once. She'd invited him to come up for "a cup of coffee," but he'd politely declined and had merely escorted her to the front door.

When he finally reached the garage, he purposefully ran toward his Porsche. Last night's dusting of snow had all melted during the day so there was no reason to take the Rover.

Moreover, he knew that he'd need to extract every last horsepower from the sports car to make it in time.

He was almost at the car. He pressed the unlock button on his key fob and pulled the driver's door open. He was in such a hurry that he didn't pay much attention to the van parked right next to the Porsche.

Only when he felt something poking him in the neck, he wondered who might have put it there.

Then, he got dizzy.

****

Tisiphone grabbed the slumping body and dragged it into the van.

The dose she had given him probably would have sufficed to knock out a grizzly bear. She had tried to estimate his body weight, but the amount of opioid she had injected had certainly been on the generous side, just to make sure that she'd get enough of it into him.

She drew some of the antidote into a fresh syringe, felt his pulse, and checked his breathing. So far, there didn't seem to be any complications.

While it was unlikely that he would regain consciousness anytime soon, she still restrained his hands and legs with zip ties.

As she was taking her seat behind the wheel of the Ford Transit, she was overcome by a feeling of pride. She had outsmarted the brilliant Richard Stanton!

She had conceived the idea for this trap when she had seen the cell phone in the handbag.

Had Stanton really thought that she'd be stupid enough to wait for him in Jenny's apartment, naively hoping he'd come alone?

She was actually a bit disappointed in him for being so easily fooled.

On the other hand, though, he was just a man and, predictably, had acted like one. Even a few hundred thousand years of evolution hadn't been enough for the male Homo sapiens to lose his most primitive protective instincts. Riding on waves of adrenaline and testosterone, the "stronger sex" had always been rushing headlong into disaster whenever a damsel in distress needed to be rescued from hordes of barbarians or a fire-breathing dragon.

Men were impulsive and careless, yet high-handed and overly confident of victory... she simply couldn't stand this do-or-die attitude.

She was wondering if he had notified any of his colleagues.

The idea of some hypermotivated police officers standing, right now, in complete bewilderment in Jenny's apartment amused her. She envisioned them looking in surprise at Jenny, while she was innocently sitting on her sofa, watching a movie, and eating a bag of chips or even a big cup of vanilla ice cream with chocolate sauce. And the idiots wouldn't have a clue what had gone wrong again this time.

It didn't matter. All that mattered now was that she had caught Stanton.

It took her twenty minutes to arrive at the warehouse. The company that once had stored Italian wall and floor tiles here had gone bankrupt years ago. They, too, had become a victim of the housing market collapse. Nobody needed tiles, especially not marble tiles from Italy, when no new homes were being built.

Tisiphone quickly glanced at Stanton, who lay lifelessly on the floor of the cargo space. Then, she got out of the van and opened the big service door leading to the hall.

Countless rows of massive metal racks lined the approximately fifty thousand square foot space. About a third of them were filled with pallets of stacked cardboard boxes. The bankruptcy liquidation had still not been completed since nobody was interested in buying the luxury tiles.

Tisiphone drove the van into the hall and closed the door. She parked the van, used a flashlight to find her way to the fuse box, and flipped over a switch. Earlier in the afternoon, she had affixed metal chains to four rack posts facing each other in one of the aisles. Now, with a loud bang, the ceiling lights in this very aisle came on.

It took a while until she could first make out the white van and, just a moment later, the gray storage shelves flanking it.

The aisle was reminiscent of a secluded alley, which–framed by skyscrapers reaching to the night sky–drove a wedge of cold light into the darkness of the surrounding unlit city.

Tisiphone struggled to haul the motionless body out of the van. Inch by inch, she dragged him by his feet through the backdoor until he was out far enough for her to let him slide down over the bumper and onto the warehouse floor.

With a scalpel from her instrument case, she cut the zip ties and replaced them with leather cuffs; then, she tethered him to the metal chains.

She fetched the rest of her stuff from the van and then parked it outside the service door again. After all, she was planning on getting away from this place as quickly as possible once she'd set it on fire.

As she was returning to Stanton, he briefly moved his head a bit. However, he was still far from waking up by himself without medication.

Since there was no heating in the warehouse, it was cold–cold enough for her breath to condensate and form white clouds.

Nonetheless, she stripped naked, folded her clothes, and put them in a plastic bag, which she placed on a shelf a few yards to the side.

She was glad that she'd brought her fur coat. It was warm and had served her well over the years. Gently, she stroked over the soft hair with the back of her hand. Despite her attachment to it, though, the coat would also burn to ashes tonight. The mink was simply too conspicuous for her to be seen with it in public. After all, the police had pictures of her wearing this coat.

Whereas her upper body was getting warmer, her feet were still freezing. Quickly, she put on the garter belt and the black back-seam stockings and slipped into her high heels.

This helped against the cold.

Maybe it would have been wiser to bring him to an apartment. It definitely would have been warmer there… but also more dangerous.

Somehow, the police must have figured out that she had been working for the real estate agency. How else would they have found Vanessa Kincade? Thus, it was very possible that all properties she had ever been the listing agent of were under surveillance right now.

It was for that very reason that she had brought Richard Stanton here. Only once she had been at this place before, filling in for a colleague, who had been attending a family member's funeral on the West Coast. At the time, she had met a prospective buyer in the warehouse and shown him around for about ten minutes. Afterwards, she had copies of the keys made at a hardware store.

Nobody would be able to see a connection between her and this place.

For a moment, she contemplated waking him up but decided against it as the idea of just watching him for a while intrigued her too much.

With scissors, she cut up his clothes and pulled the tatters off his body until he was bare naked.

He had a beautiful body. It was obvious that he worked out on a regular basis and lifted weights. However, his muscles weren't abnormally bulky like some wannabe bodybuilder's but aesthetically toned and natural-looking.

Every part of his body was athletic and well-proportioned.

Every part…

She knelt down next to him and let her hand run over his bare skin. First, from his neck to his chest, then, over his ribbed abs down to his loins.

She tenderly caressed his penis and his balls for a while, but he did not show any reaction. He was clearly too deeply sedated to get an erection.

It was time to wake him up.

Expertly, she inserted the needle into an arm vein and injected the antidote.

Moments later, he regained consciousness.

"Where am I?" he asked groggily and coughed.

"You're with me!"

Again, he coughed. "Where am I?"

"Where your desire led you. You've arrived at your destination."

He abruptly opened his eyes and looked at her in disbelief.

"You wanted to come to me, didn't you?" she asked him seductively and opened her coat.

"What do you want from me?" He tried to sound commanding, but to no avail.

She threw him a smug smile and started to fondle her breasts.

Richard felt the sedative wearing off, and his thinking became clearer again.

Tisiphone must have ambushed him in the parking deck.

How could he have fallen into her trap so blindly?

He tried to move his arms and legs, but they were attached to sturdy posts with chains. He couldn't wiggle an inch.

Her black-lacquered nails clawed into her nipples, which looked red and sore.

When he turned away, she got angry.

"Look at me, will you!" she yelled, and her voice cracked.

Richard weighed his options and decided to obey. It wasn't prudent to enrage her. If he did, she'd just start mutilating him sooner.

And he needed time.

"Do you see how beautiful I am?" She pulled the coat farther back so that it was scarcely resting on her shoulders now.

He nodded.

Full of haughtiness, she strutted around like a peacock, showing off her naked body. While her left hand caressed her right nipple, the other moved slowly toward her groin. When she placed herself directly above him, he had a direct view of her vulva.

"Do you fancy me?" She spread her legs even more and parted her labia.

"Do you fancy me?" she yelled when he did not respond immediately.

He nodded again.

"Really...," she said without conviction and glanced over her shoulder.

"I can't help it, but I don't think you're being truthful. If you were, wouldn't I be able to see that you fancy me?"

Somehow, he had to buy time.

"It must be the sedative," he tried to make excuses. "You are very beautiful."

She seemed to accept that.

"Do you want me?" she asked lasciviously.

He needed to buy time.

"Yes, I want you," he replied.

She squatted down next to him and started to massage his penis.

Richard closed his eyes and imagined Consuela and Stephanie being with him.

"Look at me!" she called.

He opened his eyes and tried to forget what atrocities this woman had committed.

She was beautiful–very beautiful.

He needed to buy time.

When she leaned down and took his penis in her mouth, he immediately felt it fill with blood.

Skillfully, she moved her tongue over his glans and sucked his dick until he was completely hard.

Then, she sat down on top of him.

At first, she moved her lower body slowly and tenderly up and down, passionately caressing his manhood as if they were two lovers who had sworn eternal fidelity to each other and were making love for the first time.

The longer she was riding him and the more ecstatic she became, though, the wilder and more violent she got–and the harder she sunk her sharp nails into his chest.

However, he didn't feel any pain as he was completely focused on the one thing that could keep him alive and bring him back to Stephanie and Consuela: he had to pleasure her for as long as possible.

For no other reason he let her have her way with him and lifted and lowered his loins as much as his manacles permitted.

When she got too wild, he tried to slow down the rhythm, and when her enthusiasm seemed to drop, he rammed his cock into her as hard as he could.

Yet, regardless of how rambunctiously they copulated, he never got the feeling that she would ever lose her self-control. On the contrary, she was always alert, constantly watching him. Never did she close her cold eyes, not even for a moment.

He didn't know how long he had been inside her when he realized that he wouldn't be able to delay his orgasm for much longer.

Desperately, he tried to slow her down again and hold his ejaculation. But, this time, she refused to reduce the pace.

Instead, she rode him even harder and looked at him with an expression of superiority on her face. "Come! Show me how much you desire me and come inside me!"

Richard could feel that she was about to climax as well.

He didn't want to come inside her. Not only because he didn't want to give her the satisfaction but also because he felt that the moment he released his semen into Kathryn Hamilton he'd finally be unfaithful to Stephanie and Consuela.

Yet faster and faster the warm, tight cavity worked his penis, sucking on it with slippery-moist lips.

And as much as he tried to think of something else, he couldn't.

He was too aroused–and the automatisms that momentarily would lead to a contraction of his genital ducts, his pelvic floor muscles, his prostate, and various other parts of his reproductive system too far advanced–to further resist the urge to shoot his semen into this gorgeous female body.

When her vagina firmly clasped him in pulsating rhythmic muscle spasms, he finally surrendered and spurted his slimy-white juice into her.

Tisiphone let out an earsplitting scream. Then, she sank down on top of him.

For a while, she did not move. Just when he thought that she might have fallen asleep, however, she whispered something into his ear: "If it's a boy, I'll call him Richard. What do you think?"

Richard was trembling with anger and raised himself as much as he could underneath her. But he couldn't shake her off.

Rather, she, still sitting on his lap, straightened up and laughed at him.

315

"What's your problem? Didn't you like it? You asked me what I wanted from you, didn't you? Now you know!"

"Why? Why me?"

For a moment, she looked at him perplexedly, and he thought to see something vulnerable, human behind her cold eyes.

"Because you're my type," she whispered.

"And the other men?"

Suddenly, her face looked callous and remorseless again.

"Losers, weaklings, pigs!" With every word, her voice got louder.

She jumped up and stood above him.

"You're all pigs!" she yelled like a madwoman.

"But…"

"Shut your trap!" She brutally kicked him with her pointed shoes, went over to the rack to his left, and took a metal case from the bottom shelf.

When Richard saw the surgical instruments, he realized that he didn't have much time left.

"How many people have you killed?"

She looked at him distrustfully.

"Just tell me: how many?"

He needed to buy time. Somehow, he needed to buy more time.

But she wasn't to get involved in a conversation.

Silently, she took some suture thread and a needle holder out of the case and knelt down next to him.

Tisiphone was surprised that he didn't seem to be afraid.

Didn't he know what she was about to do?

She wondered if he'd battle her or simply succumb to his fate. She didn't expect him to plead for his life, like so many others before him had done.

When she approached his face with the needle, it became clear that he would put up a fight. Frantically, he clenched his teeth and shook his head side to side.

316

Quickly, she grabbed him behind the ear and pressed her middle finger into the hollow under his ear.

He let out a brief sigh and immediately stopped contorting.

"Be a good boy, this struggling won't help you anyway!"

Cruelly, she stuck the curved suture needle, slightly above his upper lip, into the right corner of his mouth just to quickly change the orientation of the tip and pass, with a swift motion of her hand, the needle through the tissue below his lower lip.

Without mercy, she drove the hooky metal thorn through the tender flesh until she reached the left corner of his mouth and tied a knot.

More than once, Richard thought he might faint. But he couldn't give up. He had to hold out for as long as possible and somehow buy more time.

How much had he left?

The man they had found in the sex shop had probably been tormented for several hours before she had burned him alive.

He just had to hold out.

She picked up the case and held it in front of his face for him to see her torture tools.

"An impressive collection, isn't it? What do you think I should try first? This scalpel perhaps? Or maybe one of these beautiful, long needles? Or rather some pliers? Do you have any preferences? No? Then, I would say we start with these pincers here."

Richard tried to stay calm. If he panicked now, his blood pressure and heart rate would rise, and his risk of dying from an injury would increase. Going into shock was just as dangerous. The more stable his circulation was the better his chance of survival was.

And he wanted to survive.

He needed to control himself and try to ignore the pain.

But how? Just how?

He closed his eyes and imagined Stephanie and Consuela being here. At once, he calmed down.

317

"Look at me!" she yelled and punched him in the stomach.

Again, he obeyed but, when he opened his eyes, he was in Stephanie's apartment. The girls were dancing samba and teased him to join them. How vivacious and cheerful they both were.

And how happy he himself was.

When she amputated his little toe, he noticed his neural pathways desperately sending distress signals to his spine and brain, but his mind was somewhere else.

He was smooching with Consuela–and Stephanie, who was standing naked behind her, was pulling down her friend's panties.

When she cut off the next toe, he remembered how gentle Stephanie had been as she had guided his penis into Consuela's vagina.

All of a sudden, Tisiphone dropped the pincers, jumped up like a bat out of hell, and rushed to the same rack she had taken the case from before.

At first, Richard didn't understand what had just happened, but only a moment later he heard a familiar voice: "Hands up or I'll shoot!"

Desperately, Richard pulled on his chains, but to no avail. He could not free himself. He could not even warn his friend. Regardless how hard he tried, he could not open his mouth.

Helpless, he had to watch how Tisiphone cocked his Glock and assumed a two-handed shooting position.

"Drop your weapon!"

He couldn't tell where the voice was coming from, but Tisiphone fired two shots into the darkness.

Suddenly, there was another shot–Richard immediately recognized the sound of the Ruger LCR–and Tisiphone collapsed beside him. She must have been hit.

Again, he heard the blast of his Glock right next to him. Then, he blacked out.

318

Wednesday, February 23

9:32 a.m.

"Stephanie, my name is Jonathan Rosenbaum. I am a friend of Richard's–and his lawyer."

"Yes?" Stephanie opened the patio door and frantically waved at Consuela, urging her to come back into the house.

Richard's lawyer calling them in Puerto Rico probably didn't portend well.

Stephanie set down on the bed and took a deep breath.

"Yes?" was all she could utter.

"Stephanie, Richard recently asked me to inform you in case something should happen to him…"

"Oh my god!" Stephanie screamed and dropped the phone.

"What is it?" Consuela asked worriedly when she came running into the room.

Stephanie bit her hand and merely shook her head.

Consuela picked up the phone. "Who is this?"

"Am I talking to Consuela Rodríguez Morales?"

"Yes, this is she. But who the hell are you? What did you say to my friend? She is completely freaked out and shaking all over her body."

"Consuela, I am Jonathan Rosenbaum. I am very sorry to have upset your friend–that was certainly not my intention. But I am afraid I've got bad news…"

319

5:08 p.m.

"I hope you had a pleasant flight!"

The young police officer, who was watching them in the rearview mirror and was awkwardly trying to involve them in small talk, was probably just being friendly.

However, the girls weren't in the mood.

After receiving the phone call from the lawyer, they had hastily gathered their stuff and had hurried to San Juan Airport, where a jet was already waiting for them.

Throughout the five-hour flight back to Chicago, they had consoled, held, and comforted each other.

And now, the young man, who had introduced himself as "Officer Clark," wanted to know if they had had a pleasant flight.

"Can you tell us what happened?" Consuela asked.

"I am sorry, ma'am! All I was told is that I should pick you up at the airport and bring you to the hospital. That's it."

When they arrived at Northwestern Memorial Hospital, they were greeted by another officer, who led them past patients and doctors to the right ward.

There, another policeman opened a glass door for them and pointed at a big, white-bearded man, who was sitting in front of a room at the end of the corridor.

The girls thanked the two officers and walked hand in hand down the hallway.

When the man saw them, he arduously arose from his chair and walked toward them.

"You must be Stephanie and Consuela! I am Inspector Gallagher, but, please, call me Walt! I am pleased to make your acquaintance. I am a friend of Richard's."

"Where is Richard? How is he doing?" Consuela inquired while she was shaking the inspector's hand.

320

"Given the circumstances, he is doing well. He is asleep right now. I thought we'd talk first before you see him. How do you feel about going to the cafeteria? The coffee there isn't all that bad."

"I would rather like to see him right away," Stephanie said piteously.

Consuela put her arm around her. "Let's talk with the inspector first…"

****

"The woman incapacitated him with anesthetics in the parking garage and then brought him to a warehouse. There, she tortured him."

"Tell us how he's doing, will you! Is his condition life-threatening?" Consuela asked impatiently.

"No, it is not. Hasn't anybody talked with you yet?" Walt wondered.

The girls hugged each other and wept tears of relief.

"No, nobody told us anything besides that Richard is injured and in the hospital," Stephanie whimpered.

"Oh, I didn't know that," Walt said sympathetically.

"What has the woman done to him? How serious are his injuries?" Consuela wanted to find out how Richard was really doing.

"He was lucky. It looks like she had just started to torture him when his friend Andrew Kendrick came to his rescue."

"Andrew? Did you say Andrew Kendrick?" Stephanie looked at him confusedly.

Walt nodded.

"But that's the captain of his motor yacht we were on last week. What's he got to do with all this?" Consuela said surprisedly.

"Richard had Andrew secretly surveil him."

"Surveil him? What's that supposed to mean?" Stephanie asked bewilderedly.

"Richard told me that he hired Andrew as kind of a bodyguard last week, right after the newspaper article had come out. He must have foreseen that he'd become the target of an attack even then.

321

Andrew followed him everywhere whenever Richard left his apartment."

"But how, then, was the woman able to ambush and harm Richard? Why wasn't Andrew there to protect him?" Consuela inquired critically.

"Andrew was at home. After all, Richard had returned to his apartment and had dismissed him for the night. Thankfully, they were using a GPS tracker that allowed Andrew to monitor Richard's whereabouts. As soon as Richard was more than a hundred yards away from his apartment building, an alarm was sent to Andrew's phone. Unfortunately, Andrew was in the shower at that time. Otherwise, he would have arrived at the warehouse sooner. However, it is only thanks to him that Richard survived."

"Walt, you still haven't told us what this woman has done to him," Stephanie remarked.

"She amputated two of his toes…"

The girls flinched in horror.

"… and sewed his mouth shut."

"What?" Stephanie screamed in consternation, and Consuela grabbed her hand.

"Furthermore, his body temperature was a bit low. It was quite cold in the warehouse, and he was lying on the floor there for a while. For that reason, however, he didn't lose too much blood. At least, that's what the doctors said. They called it a 'mild hypothermia,' which causes vasoconstriction–that means a narrowing of the blood vessels–in the extremities. The severed toes have been reattached by now, and the surgeon is hopeful. All in all, he was pretty lucky."

The girls heaved a sigh of relief.

"And Andrew? How about him?" Consuela wanted to know.

"Andrew… Well, he wasn't quite as fortunate."

The girls looked at Walt anxiously.

"Don't worry, he's alive! But shots were fired, and he was hit in the chest. He is currently in the ICU here in the hospital. The

322

doctors think that he'll be up on his feet again in a few weeks. If it wasn't for a security guard, who was making his rounds in a nearby warehouse, heard the shots, and called the police, it might have ended differently. This way, however, it wasn't long before they both received emergency care."

"Thank god! But what happened to the woman? Is she dead?" Consuela's tone left no doubt as to what answer she was hoping for.

"To be honest, we don't know. Andrew must have hit her, and she lost a lot of blood. But she managed to escape."

****

When Richard woke up, Stephanie and Consuela sat by his bed and smiled at him encouragingly.

"Hi!" was all he was able to mutter, but even that made him cringe in pain.

"Don't talk! The doctors said that it will take a while until the swelling around your mouth goes down enough for you to speak normally and without pain again." Stephanie stroked his hand and gave him a kiss on the forehead.

"So happy...," Richard grunted and squeezed his eyes shut.

"Hush now! We are also happy," Stephanie said and started to cry.

"Walt has told us what happened. He thinks that you were very lucky." Consuela looked thoughtfully at Richard. "He's also convinced that the woman has left town by now. That is, if she's still alive. Have you thought about what's coming next?"

Richard knew exactly what she meant: she wanted to know whether this was the kind of life she had to expect if she stayed; whether every time he worked on a case, she'd have to be afraid that he might die. She wanted to know if he was able to let Kathryn Hamilton get away.

He nodded.

"Bueto Eco," he whispered indistinctly.

323

"Puerto Rico? You want to go to Puerto Rico with us?" Consuela shouted enthusiastically.

Richard nodded again, and the girls bear-hugged him.

Monday, March 14

10:57 a.m.

"Let's just take the darn wheelchair! I don't understand why you're so embarrassed." Consuela knit her eyebrows in an attempt to look stern.

Without success–Richard saw right through her and playfully brandished his cane at her. "How dare you make fun of me in my condition, I'll show you!"

"Catch me if you can!" she teased him, laughingly hopping around him.

"Richard, Consuela, just stop monkeying around or you'll hurt yourselves! Maybe it would be better to take the wheelchair," Stephanie said in a motherly tone.

The two just grinned at her, snorting with laughter.

"Seriously, if the wounds reopen, it's over! Then, we'll be stuck here for another three weeks," Stephanie tried to reason with them.

Richard leaned on her shoulder and kissed her on the cheek. "Forgive me, darling, but a lot will have to happen before I'll use the wheelchair!"

They all linked arms and continued their walk toward the departure hall.

"I am really looking forward to finally getting to see your boat," Consuela suddenly said. "By the way, what's it called?"

The question took Richard by surprise, and, for a moment, he didn't know what to say. Eventually, he plucked up his courage. "Monica... my boat's name is Monica," he responded wistfully. "Does this bother you?"

325

"Not at all!" Consuela said.

"I couldn't think of a better name," Stephanie consented.

****

"What a cool plane! I wish I could afford to travel so luxuriously. But the likes of us... Maintenance alone must cost a fortune."

"That's certainly true. However, this is not a privately owned jet, it belongs to an aircraft charter company–it's for rent!"

"Oh, and I thought this guy's a millionaire."

"But he is! Don't you recognize him? That's Richard Stanton, the playboy. He's got a ton of money! And he's famous for only going out with the most beautiful women... just look at these two! I surely wouldn't say no to them."

"I bet they're flying to Paris to go on a shopping spree."

"Bad bet!" the security guard exclaimed jovially. "They are departing for San Juan, Puerto Rico, in twenty minutes."

"How wrong was I!" Tisiphone said in a friendly tone and made her way to the ticket counters.

326

WHEN LUST HAS CONCEIVED

Raimund Auerbach was born and raised in Germany. He moved to the United States more than twenty years ago and currently lives in the Midwest with his wife and daughter. *When Lust Has Conceived*, originally published in German under the title *Mord in Seidenstrümpfen*, is his first novel.

Printed in Great Britain
by Amazon